The Forgotten Diaries of Trudy Mansfield

Dedicated to the memory of my brother Allan, whose stories about the war years inspired this work. This book is also dedicated to the Trudys I have known as a clinical psychologist and as an adjunct professor at California State Polytechnic University, Pomona.

The Forgotten Diaries
of Trudy Mansfield

B. R. Johnson

Published by Claremont Behavioral Studies Institute
250 West First St., Suite 352
Claremont, CA 91711, USA

Library of Congress Control Number: 2017901611

The principal characters and events in this book are fictitious. Any
similarity to real persons, living or dead, is coincidental and not intended
by the author. Historical figures may or may not have actually
participated in the events described.

Visit Web site www.TrudyMansfield.com

Cover photo: Sunset view of UCLA, Security Pacific National Bank
Collection, Los Angeles Public Library

Cover Egyptian Hieroglyph for woman: E.A. Wallis Budge, *An Egyptian
Hieroglyphic Dictionary*, Vol I., 1920, London, John Murray, Albemarle
Street.

Back cover photo: Ansel Adams, Ansel Adams Fortune Magazine
Collection, Los Angeles Public Library

ISBN 978-1-884425-09-7

190625

ACKNOWLEDGMENTS

This story was originally conceptualized as an alternate history in which the Axis powers won the Second World War and the United States stood alone as the only power strong enough to resist the dominance of the fascist states. I was interested in the impact this scenario would have on ordinary citizens living in Los Angeles. The work was much longer than this book and had a storyline more complicated than *War And Peace*. Fortunately, my writing coach Jason Buchholz, and editor, Hayley Orecehio, gave me feedback that guided me to redirect my ambition to creating something more focused and grounded in actual history. I cannot thank them enough for the efforts and patience they committed to this project and the numerous corrections and pointers that they gave me.

I wish also to thank my wife, Betty, and our children, Phi-Yen, Denton, Eric, and Colette, who each provided feedback and support, despite their busy schedules and commitments.

A special thank you is owed to Gloria Jolly, who provided valuable feedback and assisted in the promotion and marketing of this book.

In the beginning, I had one research assistant, Kayla Winn, who found valuable original source material, some of which was used in passages that have survived over eighteen major changes and are in the final version.

There are many other people who read drafts reflective of various stages of development. I hesitate to cite any because I am sure to will forget to mention someone who provided encouragement and suggestions. You all know who you are, and I thank you most sincerely.

2009

Prologue

The Girl with Her Back to the Camera

Nell paused at the open doorway. She stood flanked by her 17 and 22-year-old daughters. Kat was a lanky high school student and pint hair Brittany a college senior.

For years, the downstairs bedroom had served as her mother's study. The glow of the Southern California sun, filtering through the golden curtains, revealed that the space had become a jumble, in contrast to the tidy order, which had characterized her mother's house when she was alive.

Nell crossed the room and parted the drapes. Through the north-facing window, gray-domed Mount Baldy and its brother peaks of the east San Gabriel Mountains regarded her like silent sentinels.

Along the opposite wall, half in shade, were bookcases, vacant cavities now. They looked like thin old men who had been unburdened of the volumes that Nell's mother had been accumulating since the beginning of time. Fortunately, a former colleague accepted all the books and hauled them away.

Nell's girls fanned out from the doorway and moved around the room, silently surveying the piles of boxes and grocery bags of household items that had been gathered and sorted by their mother and aunt. The computer, printer/scanner and giant monitor that had dominated the old woman's desk had been removed. A few crumpled post-its lie around where the screen had sat.

"Over there in the corner—that's all trash," Nell pointed out. "This little pile here we will take home. The rest goes to Goodwill."

"Okay, what do you want me to do?" Brittany groused. Nell's oldest may be close to graduating from college but at times had the sullen attitude of an adolescent middle child.

"Well, first," her mother answered, "there are picture frames all over the house. Gather them up and take the photos out. Put the frames in a box for Goodwill and the pictures. . . . over there, with that stuff we'll sort out later."

Kat wandered over to the trash heap and looked down at the assorted jumble.

"What are these?" she asked, bending over and picking up two old paperback composition tablets. The paper had yellowed and looked as dry as fall leaves. The girl opened one and flipped through a few pages. She smiled.

"What'd you find, Indiana Jones?" Brittany asked. Kat handed her one of the workbooks.

"These must be Grand Mom's diaries," Kat said. "When she was a teenager, I guess. Mom, why are you throwing these out?"

"You want to read the pouting of a teenage girl?"

"When she's Grand Mom, yes I do. And I don't think she was a pouter. Even when she was a kid."

Nell should have known better than make the comment. Kat had a special bound with her grandmother.

"You can have her diaries," Nell said, resigning to the inevitable, even if the girl didn't need more stuff to add to the clutter in her bedroom. "Put them down for now. We have things to do."

The girl grinned and instead of putting the composition book aside, stooped and pulled others out of the trash.

Brittany had opened the one she held and started to flip through the pages as she walked back to her grandmother's desk.

"God. Most of these are written in hieroglyphs. Can you believe? Even when she was a kid she knew that stuff. Hah, look! Mickey Mouse." She showed the page to her mother, who really didn't want to look, but she had to admit the figure formed of three circles looked like the Disney icon. In the middle of the page three words in English stood out—*College Why Not*.

"This one's in English." The younger sister handed the tablet up to Brittany, who looked at the spin.

"1941. Isn't that the year Pearl Harbor was bombed?"

Nell glared at her daughters.

"Come on girls. Let's get to work."

"Okay," Brittany mumbled and dropped the diary on the stack her sister had begun building.

"Kat, you can get those later. Help me in Grand Mom's bedroom."

*   *   *   *   *

In contrast to books, Nell's mom had routinely disposed of clothes she no longer wore. The garments left were nice and relatively new—articles that would be considered upscale in a thrift shop.

"Grand Mom's bedroom has such a fresh scent," Kat said, carefully folding a cashmere sweater. "She didn't smell like an old woman."

Brittany trudged into the bedroom with a stack of photos in her hand.

"Okay, I took all the pictures out of all the frames I could find. Who's Rebekah Wolff?"

Brittany handed her mother a sepia tone photo of a woman. The picture looked like it had been taken in the forties. The woman had kind but wise old eyes.

Nell shook her head.

"And who's this man?" She held up a photo of a white-haired man in a robe. "Was Grand Mom once in a cult or something?"

"That's a headshot of an old-time actor. Your grandmother was a big movie fan. Is it autographed?"

"No," Brittany said and flipped the picture over. "*Lost Horizon* is stamped on the back. I guess that's a movie."

"Can I have it?" Kat asked, reaching up for the photo.

"I don't want to see you selling it on eBay."

"Gee, like you think I would."

Brittany joined her mother and sister going through drawers, placing clothing on the bed, folding and sorting.

"Mom," Kat said. She had been pulling items out of the night stand. "This book looks like you defaced it when you were a kid."

Nell had no memory of marking up any of her mother's books. Heaven forbid.

On the title page, the name Heinrich had been crossed out and above the name was clearly printed, in her mother's hand, "Nelly." A book in German, *Ein Ernstes Leben* by Heinrich Mann.

"I didn't start going by my middle name until college. Your grand mom did that. I have no idea why."

Kat created a potpourri of pastel notes and cards when she dumped the contents of the bottom drawer of the night stand onto the corner of the bed, dismantling whatever order the salutations may have been in. Amongst the paper jumble Nelly noticed a cameo brooch.

"This looks old," she said, pulling the adornment out of the clutter. A purplish black ribbon that had, no doubt, once been a shimmering jet, threaded through the tarnished mounting.

"Is that an Egyptian artifact?" Brittany asked.

"It looks Italian," Nell said.

Her daughter eyed the peach-colored piece, considering its possibilities as some kind of fashion bauble. It matched the hue of her

5

pink hair.

"Can I have it? I think it looks cool."

*   *   *   *   *

When the three finished for the day, Nell drove them home. Brittany sat next to her, thumbing the iPhone she held a few inches from her nose. The brooch hung around her neck. Kat slumped on the back seat between piles of her grandmother's diaries. As she flipped through one of the composition books, Nell watched her in the rearview mirror, noting her wispy smile and somber eyes.

"Did you know that Grand Mom had a boyfriend when she was in high school?" Kat said in a bright tone.

"She always said she wasn't into boys when she was a teenager," Nell replied. Her mother had been a self-proclaimed wall-flower as a kid.

"Well, she had a boyfriend named Karl. And he took her to the junior prom."

"I never heard about that."

"She wrote all about making her dress. Wow, they really made their own gowns in those days?"

"Yes. Some people still do."

Nell heard her daughter put down one diary and pick up another.

"Ooh," Kat purred. "She just saw the movie *Of Mice and Men*. I read that book in the tenth grade. February 24, 1940. Grand Mom thought the story of George and Lenny sad. She didn't mention anything else that day except she saw the movie at the Bruin with *Brother Rat and Baby*. That's a strange title. Would that be an old Disney animated film?"

"I don't think so," her mother said. She then remembered something that made her feel wistful, like she had touched something forgotten but precious found in the back of an old cabinet drawer.

"Kat, did you know when your Grand Mom was about your age, she met Charlie Chaplin?"

Brittany put the phone in her lap and turned to look at her mother.

"Wasn't Charlie Chaplin, you know, into teenage girls?"

Nell had never made that connection. She knew the meeting was special to her mother, but maybe for reason she had never revealed.

6

"She always spoke fondly of Charlie Chaplin," she admitted.

"Gee. My grandmother had a fling with a famous movie star."

"That doesn't sound like her," Kat said. There was a defiant tone in the girl's voice. Glancing at the rearview mirror, Nell saw the girl's glaring eyes fixed on her sister.

"Well, maybe she did," Brittany replied.

Like boiling water in a pot taken off the stove, the bubbly chatter ceased. Nell drove on, thinking about her mother, not sure what to make of Brittany's interpretation.

"Mom," Kat said. "Did you see this? Grand Mom printed this from the Internet and stuck it in one of these hieroglyph diaries."

"I can't see. I'm driving."

"It shows a couple of African American businessmen walking through a parachute plant. The caption of the picture reads 'Eddie Rochester Anderson and Howard Skippy Smith touring their company, Pacific Parachute.' In the picture one woman has her back to the camera. Grand Mom drew an arrow and wrote, 'Me.' She must have worked there."

Nell had no idea. She thought her mother worked in a flashlight factory during the war. She may have told her about a parachute job, but that would have been so long ago, when Nell herself was a kid. Her mother had told her lots of things about growing up, but Nell tended to tune her out. When she was a kid, she had no interest in stories about the "Dark Ages" as her mother called her childhood and adolescence. Nell would rather listen to music and play sports.

"Here's a Christmas card from Helga Schneider. How did this get in the 1945 diary? It's from 1972."

"Who's Helga Schneider?" Brittany asked.

"She was your Grand Mom's neighbor," Nell said. "In West Los Angeles, during the war. Grand Mom always called World War Two 'the war.' When I was a kid, we used to visit Helga. She had a thick German accent. She loved to bake and made delicious bread. Is there a note in the card?"

"The note. . . . It's in German. I guess it's German."

"Probably just a Christmas greeting. I guess we'll never know."

"I'll use Google to translate."

"She and her husband were so lucky," Nell observed. "Imagine! They left Germany before the war. They got away from Hitler and the Nazis. Coming to California must have been like going to heaven, living on the border of Santa Monica, so close to Hollywood. Girls, can you imagine back then? All those movie stars."

Brittany and Kat did not respond. They sat absorbed in their own worlds, one preoccupied with her phone, the other with the catch of brittle composition books.

1941

Chapter 1

Metropolitan Tahiti

Max, I must say again, we have come to live on the very edge of the earth."

Helga and Max Schneider stood in the small front yard of their new home, a stucco bungalow on Wellesley Avenue. The street was on the western border of Los Angeles and only a short distance from the gray Pacific Ocean. Their children, Jonathon and Marlene, played on the grass with a partially deflated sun-bleached ball the boy had found in the street gutter.

Helga held herself against the late spring coolness. A hint of mist crept through the air in advance of the evening fog—nothing as cold as she had known in Germany but a chill that somehow felt more penetrating.

She watched their landlord, Fred Nakamizo, tend his plot of lima beans on the lot across the street. The short Asian waddled down the furrows between the thick stringy plants growing over the dark earth, stooping, at times, to inspect a spot of the knotted harvest on the lookout for evidence of gophers and other pests.

"Palm trees. Orange groves. Movie studios," Max said.

"I'm not Greta Garbo and you're not Peter Lorre. You don't even enjoy the cinema or citrus fruit."

"I have a full professorship at a young university," he replied. "There are also many of our countrymen in this city, people who speak our language."

The other Germans were émigrés who had been forced to flee to the United States. They referred to Los Angeles as *Metropolitan Tahiti*. The city was at the same time bright and dull, exotic and ordinary, rich and vacant, a sprawling metropolitan unlike any they had known in Europe.

"Radical philosophers, communist writers, actors, composers. These people are not part of our circle," Helga said, wearily shaking her head.

"Yes, but most are not so bad. Can't some of them be part of our circle, as you say?"

Helga looked down at the ground. Her fair complexion appeared pale. Her once straw blonde hair had gradually turned to lightly burnt butter, dull and somber in the gray afternoon. Still, at twenty-seven, thirteen years younger than Max, she could pass for nineteen.

"I don't fit here," she finally said. She wanted to pose that as a question instead of making a statement. She was beginning to sound like her mother—a harpy.

"Helga, you will adapt."

"I don't agree!" Her tone surprised her as much as it did Max. She sounded like her mother berating her father.

"Well then, think of our lives this way," he replied, his eyes drifting off in the detached, airy look he often assumed when formulating a response to a question concerning an academic subject. "We are part of the great movement of European Intelligentsia who have found a home here. You should embrace our new status."

In the 1930s and early 1940s the world experienced a migration unlike any witnessed before. Many important minds and some of the greatest authorities in physics, medicine, philosophy, literature, cinema, theater, history, music, and all the other sciences and arts left their homes in central Europe. They fled their countries in fear for their lives. Most were Jews, but some were political thorns to the Nazis like the Noble laureate Thomas Mann. Others, like the famous actress Marlene Dietrich, were simply unwilling to live under Hitler's "New Order."

While this flood of intellects found many places to settle, the young city of Los Angeles ultimately became home to the largest number. Having an outlook and manner defined by the old world, these immigrants now found themselves stranded in a modern place with, at most, a superficial link to any tradition.

The Schneiders were not part of this exodus and, contrary to what Max said, did not share the same "status" with the intellectual refugees. Unlike the émigrés, who were stripped of their citizenship and forced to leave their homelands with little more than the clothing on their backs, Max and Helga still had German passports and their possessions. They could return to Germany, if they wished—and if the British blockade of ships bound to the European continent did not prevent the journey.

Helga frowned.

"Many are as anti-establishment as the Nazis. Their excesses and decadence during the Weimar Republic made that man Hitler seem like a savior of German virtue. God only knows what their indulgences will bring down on all of us in *this* place."

The two had had versions of this conversation before. Normally

12

a sociable person, Helga felt uncomfortable with the avant-garde tastes and Marxist views of many of the émigré. Because of this, she had avoided making friends and found herself alone.

"At least they don't burn books or crack skulls," Max replied, oblivious to the real issue. "And as far as what will happen here, some will, I am sure, find themselves unwelcomed and be forced to leave. The rest, including you and me, will go on with what we do."

Helga watched Nakamizo move deliberately through his field pausing from time to time to inspect something that only a person of the soil would recognize. He wore knee-high rubber boots caked with mud from the furrows.

"I never understood why we left Germany in the first place." She had said this many times, but never received a satisfactory explanation.

"I had an opportunity in Paris," he replied, giving his usual answer.

In 1934 Max, rather abruptly and without discussing their moving, had secured an academic position at the French Université de Paris et de la Sorbonne. His teaching at the school had been a dismal experience, although he never admitted it. Max, like so many German men, kept the troubles of his professional life to himself.

"I wish we had returned to Germany before the war instead of coming here. The Nazis never would have noticed you."

Max's mouth twitched. He looked down at their children.

"Forget that I would have had to swear an oath to Hitler in order to teach. Think of Jonathon and Marlene."

The two-year-old girl glanced up and smiled at her father.

Helga wearily shook her head.

"It would have been an empty oath. And as for our children, they will now be Americans and in time speak only English." This inevitable consequence of living in America had troubled her for months.

"They would be forced to be Nazis," her husband answered dryly. "Members of the *Hitler Youth,* saluting their teachers and elders with the *sieg heil.*"

Helga continued to shake her head.

"When we return to Germany, we will be with family. I hate the wind and the loneliness of this place. I have no one to talk to. My English is so poor. The neighbors—what neighbors there are around these empty streets—must think I'm an idiot, smiling and nodding at everything they say."

Max had picked this house for her. Inconvenient for him in relation to the university, the empty yard in the back allowed her to plant a vegetable garden, something she once enjoyed tending in Germany. The soil was rich, the weather fair, but she had still not determined what would grow—other than the landlord's cash crops. Max hoped for asparagus.

"And if the United States goes to war," she added, revealing a worry she hadn't spoken.

"We can expect to experience the same trouble we faced in France," Max said dryly.

"I cannot go through that again," she answered.

"That will not come to pass. Hitler's ambitions are in Europe, and the American people do not want to see their men sent off to war. Just read the newspapers."

The two silently watched Nakamizo cross his field and return home.

Helga pointed up to the sky and smiled.

"Black birds. There are so many black birds here."

"They are common birds."

"They leave droppings on the laundry," Helga replied, smirking.

"I'll make you a scarecrow."

"Don't! I like the black birds. They chase off the feral cats. I'd rather have the birds than the cats."

The teenage girl who lived in the house at the other end of their block came down the street on her bike, returning home from school, Helga assumed. The woman had seen her from time to time but had never talked to her.

The girl whisked by, pushing the pedals down with strong legs, steering the bike around the pits in the gray spider-webbed pavement. She had thick, brown curly hair that flew in different directions and flapped down her neck. She glanced in their direction, smiled and waved.

14

Chapter 2

Shangri-La

As Helga Schneider had guessed, Trudy Mansfield was riding her bike home from school.

Halfway to Wellesley, Trudy had begun daydreaming about *Lost Horizon*, a movie she admitted to seeing twice but had actually seen four times. Most of the story took place in hidden Shangri-La. This secret garden valley remained untouched by war and misery. The rising forces of the fascist powers threatening the modern world could not penetrate the massive barrier of the giant snowy mountains which kept Shangri-La a veiled refuge, about which elderly Hindu priests reverently and guardedly whispered.

Daydreams often lifted Trudy out of self-conscious discomfort, and this afternoon, she needed daydreams. The residue of an unsettling experience earlier that day throbbed in her like a festering bee sting.

If there was one truth Trudy wholly believed about herself, it was that she was blatantly unattractive, and today, this unpleasant self-appraisal was set off, once again, by her friend Susan French. This time she chatted about the boy she was taking to the "Sadie Hawkins" dance. After going on and on about her dress and how perfect she expected the evening to be, Susan then looked inquisitively at Trudy and asked whom she would invite. Trudy felt the heat fill her face as she fibbed about a promise she had made to her mother to go to Claremont on a family visit that weekend.

At the moment, Trudy felt like Sadie, the character from the Lil' Abner comic strip, the "homeliest gal" in the world. There was, of course, a critical difference. Fast, devious, and determined, Sadie Hawkins chased boys. Trudy shied away.

Trudy brooded about how unfair puberty had been. She *was* ugly. About that she had no doubt. She could not see what others recognized—that the course from childhood to becoming an adult had begun to reveal attractive features. All she saw were the migrating red blotches and white-tipped pimples spattering her cheeks, forehead and chin. She dismally concluded that her eyes were not a pretty sapphire blue, like Susan's, nor a pleasant brown. No, her irises looked something like tiny pots of stewed-vegetables, a dull green with floating stalks of over cooked meat edging around the pits of her pupils. She also fretted over her hair. The mop remained a thick frizzy mess of boring brown tangled tresses, a jumbled mass no matter how much she brushed or how she tied it back. She did not see her strong cheek bones and finely shaped nose nor understand that she had simply not learned how to master her rich curly hair. Neither had she come to appreciate that she had beautiful hazel eyes which already dominated her face. She could not see ahead to the time when her complexion, giving her such despair, would clear and the aftermath of adolescent acne would be covered with a whisk of makeup. Her crooked lower teeth were the only real imperfection, but in time she could learn to hide them when speaking or smiling by barely parting her lips, like many women not blessed with pretty teeth.

At fifteen, she was not opened to any positive assessment about her appearance and mentally discounted compliments given by her mother and other adults. Every day, the evil magic mirror on her bedroom wall showed her what she took as truth.

As she rode her bike, she pushed into the chilly breeze which blew off the ocean in the afternoon, the cool air numbing her cheeks and picking at her sweater. Feeling this, she imagined the icy cold wind blowing down snow banks in the Himalayas and pretended to be searching for the tunnel in the mountain, the passage to the hidden valley. The Shangri-La of *Lost Horizon* was *her* refuge where the peaceful residents not only enjoyed contentment and health but had great knowledge and a deep understanding of life's mysteries. The high Lama, who had guided the people of Shangri-La for hundreds of years, revealed to the British hero, Robert Conway, the deep but simple truth to this happy life, a formula for eventual world peace summarized by the maxim, "Be Kind." Trudy had been so touched by his words that she begged her friend Joan Fulbright, whose father worked at Columbia Studios, to secure a picture of the wise old man. The photograph now hung framed on Trudy's bedroom wall.

As far back as she could remember, Trudy had been enchanted by the idea of discovering the remains of some forgotten people and bringing their stories to light. While Susan and other girls daydreamed about boys and romance, Trudy had a secret fascination for ancient ruins and lost civilizations. Her parent's meager book collection contained a copy of *The Dawn of Civilization*, and she loved to look at the pictures to see what discoveries had been unearthed by archeologists and the upper crust of ancient culture excavators, the Egyptologists. She read the text and studied and restudied the book's smoky photographs of broken statues and ruins of ancient temples so many times that the book's binding had become floppy. She told no one of her obsession, sure her friends and family would laugh. People were fascinated with modern advances, not mysteries of old, buried cultures. They wanted to know what wonderful new invention would appear tomorrow, not who invented the wheel.

Still floating through the Tibetan Himalayas, Trudy saw the German couple when she turned onto Wellesley. She smiled at the two as she passed and waved. The woman smiled and waved back. The man seemed to nod.

She had been curious about the German family since they had moved into the house. The man looked like a professional, maybe a lawyer or an accountant. In the morning, he walked to work, down the weeded curb to the bus stop, always in a dark suit, wearing a somber fedora and carrying a scuffed leather briefcase. He appeared so European and formal, completely out of character for the neighborhood.

Trudy glided her bicycle up her driveway and passed under the carport. She parked her bike in the garage in the tight space behind her brother's Schwinn and next to their mother's Ford. The vigorous ride and sojourn to Shangri-La had lifted her somewhat out of her glum mood.

In the house, the living room radio was turned to the local station broadcasting *Superman*. The house reeked of her father's stale cigarette smoke.

"Mom."

No answer.

Walking through the hall and into her bedroom, she glanced through the open doorways of the bathroom and her parents' bedroom looking for her mother. Her brother's door stood open enough that she could see him slouched in his chair reading a comic book, his feet up, resting on the windowsill. Their mother would kill him if she saw this. Barely fourteen, he looked like a scrawny circus roustabout in his red striped knit shirt, grass stained blue jeans and scuffed shoes.

"Where's mom?" she asked, walking into her room.

No answer.

"Andy," she said louder, "Where's mom?"

"I don't know."

She sat her book bag on the floor next to her bed and noted the high Lama serenely looking down at her. He reigned as the contradiction to her mother's view that old people were grumpy and impatient. Certainly, Trudy's grandpa, her dad's unpleasant father, was as opposite to the high Lama as an elderly person could be.

She returned to the living room and changed the radio station.

"I was listening to that!" her brother hollered. Trudy ignored him, switching the stations randomly. The pointer never lined up correctly with the stations' broadcast frequencies.

Like she had rubbed a genie's magic lantern, the Andrew Sisters jumped out of the speaker and grabbed her, swinging her around with *Boogie Woogie Bugle Boy of Company B.*

"Hey!" her brother yelled.

"Read your funnies," she snapped back and danced around the room. She clapped her hands in rhythm to the bouncy song, swung her hips and shrugged her shoulders to the beat the way she remembered Patty Andrew boogied in Abbott and Costello's *Buck Private.*

The tune was barely over when her mother came in the house. She had on her long, decade old, out-of-style blue white polka dot dress with a white collar she sometimes wore when not doing heavy housework.

"The radio's too loud," she complained.

"Sorry."

Trudy's mother walked into the kitchen. After adjusting the volume, Trudy followed her.

"I saw our new neighbors," she said.

"Oh?" her mother said, setting a bowl down and opening the utensil drawer.

"They were standing in front of the Nakamizo rental."

"I can't think why a German family would want to live way out here."

"We moved *way out here*," Trudy said.

"We moved to be closer to your father's work." He designed airplane parts at Douglas Aircraft, a few blocks from the house.

"Well, maybe they like the peace and quiet," Trudy said, "out here in the sticks."

"Trudy, we're not in the sticks. Look out your bedroom window. They're building a new movie theater right over on Pico. Soon we'll be able to walk to the show."

Her mother pulled dinner ingredients out of the refrigerator and a can of corn from the pantry cabinet. Trudy tried to help but found herself in the way. Without being asked, she gathered up the plates, glasses and flatware to set the table, and then went to her room. Pulling

18

out her latest diary notebook, she made an entry referencing her exchange with Susan and waving at the German neighbors. She also recounted that she was the only student in her history class who enjoyed listening to Mr. Greene talk about the unification of upper and lower Egypt and the thousands of years that followed, a time during which the people of the Nile built pyramids and temples, worshiped a family of strange gods, and created a written language of exotic picture graphs.

Chapter 3

"Ich Bin In Der Schule Lernen"

The following Saturday, the Mansfield's neighbor Martha Lewis phoned to ask Trudy if she could babysit that evening. Martha apologized for the short notice, but Trudy had become accustomed to these last-minute requests and regrets. Martha probably had come to assume that Trudy did not go out on dates and didn't need to be called in advance.

Fred Nakamizo's daughter Mary was at Trudy's house when the call came. The two had been doing their math homework at the dining room table. Mary whistled along with the radio broadcast of Sammy Kaye and his orchestra performing *Daddy*.

"Mary, please. I can't concentrate," Trudy said.

"Oh, sorry." Mary stopped whistling and erased something she had just written, careful not to whisk the rubber flakes across the table or onto the floor. The two worked on a geometry assignment, talking through the problems, working up the proofs and always checking to make sure they came up with the same answers.

Like Trudy, Mary didn't have a boyfriend. At least she didn't talk about boys. She was pretty in an exotic, oriental kind of way, like Charlie Chan's daughter, and she seemed to study even harder than Trudy. She had told Trudy she planned to go away to college after high school. Maybe Stanford or Berkeley. She wanted to be a doctor.

"Why not be a nurse?" Trudy asked. She guessed there were women doctors, although she had never actually heard of one, except in the movies.

Mary crinkled her little nose. "All that training just to change bedpans. Sorry. I want to diagnose and treat diseases. Maybe be a surgeon."

What a strange ambition for a girl.

After Mary left, Trudy went to her room and wrote in her diary. She really didn't have anything to write about but had gotten into the habit of jotting down something every day about her "boring" life. In the four years that she had been journaling, she had already filled five notebooks, which lay hidden under an extra blanket in her closet.

When the time came to babysit, she walked across the street to the Lewis house. Martha stood on her porch talking to the German woman. Trudy slowed her pace. She wished she had welcomed the woman after the family moved in.

"Hello," Martha said. Trudy smiled at Martha and looked at the other woman. Her light complexion, drawn eyes and fair hair underscored her tired appearance. She was encased in a stretched out charcoal sweater that appeared as worn as she herself.

"I don't think you know . . . " Martha hesitated with the name and glanced at the German. "Elga . . ."

"Helga," the woman corrected.

"Sorry. Helga Schneider. She is our new neighbor." Turning to the woman she said, "This is Trudy Mansfield, my babysitter."

"Hello," said Trudy. "I've seen you in front of your house but I've never introduced myself. I guess I haven't been very neighborly."

"Hallo," Helga Schneider said, pleasantly.

Trudy realized the German lady may not have understood her.

"Excuse me, Helga," Martha said. "I have to get ready. I'm going out. It was nice to talk with you. I'm glad to have a new neighbor."

"I've seen you . . . on the avenue," Mrs. Schneider said after Martha went in the house. Her accent was heavy. "On your . . . *fahrrad*. Excuse me, please. I do not know the English word."

"Bicycle."

"Bicycle," the woman repeated, mentally filing the word away.

"I live over there," Trudy said, motioning in the direction of her house. "On the other side of Nakamizo's lima bean field."

"*Naa kaa me so*, please?" Mrs. Schneider asked. She listened carefully, clearly needing to attend to each English word as much as Trudy did while struggling in her German class.

"Oh, sorry," she replied, a little slower. "Nakamizo is the farmer who lives on the corner. He is your landlord." She then took the risk and said, "*Nakamizo ist das viertel landwirt.*"

"Ah, yes," the woman said with a joyful smile. "The farmer! The *Japanisch* person. You speak German, yes?"

Her reply suggested to Trudy some urgency.

"*Ich bin in der Schule lernen*," Trudy answered. A simple sentence with simple words, telling the woman she was learning the language in her school. She didn't want to overstate her mastery, but she had taken the language for two years, always earning A's and the praise of her instructor.

"You are learning *gut*. Good," Mrs. Schneider answered.

Trudy smiled, feeling awkward and not sure what to say other than, "*Danke.*"

"I can help with your studies of the German," the woman said. "If you wish."

Trudy did not expect Helga Schneider to be so friendly. German people were rather private—or at least that was what Trudy thought.

"I would wish," she answered and added in German, "It would be helpful to have a tutor."

"I must go home," Helga said and added in German, "*Wir werden mehr bald bitte sprechen.*"

The girl easily translated this: *We will talk more, soon, please.*

Trudy nodded. Mrs. Schneider seemed so nice.

Chapter 4

After meeting Helga Schneider, Trudy began stopping by her house whenever she saw the woman in her front yard. She was often outside during her children's nap time, spending a few peaceful moments outdoors.

Initially, the two spoke in a disorganized mixture of English and German. During this verbal collage, Trudy volunteered to help Helga with housework. Helga smiled and shook her head as if Trudy had said something amusing.

"How are your German lessons?" she asked in English.

"We mostly read and translate passages," Trudy answered in German. "Less speaking."

"It is good to learn to read and write German in the classroom," the woman replied in English, "just like you learned to read and write English. Yes? It is much better to learn to talk the language by conversation."

"*Gespräch?*" Trudy said, not sure if this was the correct word.

"Yes. Speaking to another person. Making the talk."

"I'd like to learn at least one German word a day."

"One word? You will not learn a lot."

"I guess you're right."

"When you come home from school, stop here. We will have conversation only in German and you will learn many new words and the correct way to put them together."

Trudy liked the proposal, but didn't think it fair since Helga struggled with her own language barrier. She had told Trudy that she read detective stories to learn English, believing the clues hidden in the stories would encourage her to search out the meaning of words she did not know.

"Wouldn't you like to learn to speak more English?" Trudy asked.

"Yes, of course."

Trudy had an idea.

"We can alternate."

"Alternate, please?"

"Tomorrow we *Sprechen Sie nur Deutsch*. The day after, we will speak only in English. We will go back and forth. *Hin und her.*"

"Ah, yes, yes! That would be splendid!"

Helga Schneider had a sweet smile, neither condescending nor trite. Her good-fairy blue eyes were warm, sincere, and safe.

On the *Deutsche Tage* afternoons, Trudy greeted Mrs. Schneider in German, and they chatted about the Trudy's day at school. Helga corrected her pronunciation, supplied a missing word here and there, and answered Trudy's "Was ist das?" as she pointed to things like buttons, rose bushes, the driveway, the foggy mist in the air, and the low hills below the far away mountains. Trudy amazed herself with her retention and one night found herself in a dream not only talking but thinking in German.

Trudy began calling Helga Schneider by her first name. In Los Angeles, even young children addressed adults by their first names, something different from what she saw in movies like *Andy Hardy* where children, teens, and adults addressed their elders as Mr., Miss, or Mrs. Some days Helga's two children, Jonathon and Marlene, were up from their naps and stood by their mother as she and Trudy conversed. They silently watched the teen, the boy with a suspicious frown and his sister with a bashful smile.

During the "English" days, Trudy learned that Helga's husband was a professor and that the Schneiders came to Los Angeles in 1940 for him to teach at UCLA. While Helga did not say that they had left Germany for political reasons, Trudy assumed that Professor Schneider gave up a prestigious position at a German university to get away from the Nazis.

Trudy had caught a glimpse of a small rose gold crucifix below the hollow of the woman's throat, suggesting the Schneiders were not Jewish. She wondered if they were Communists, but Trudy knew that Reds were atheists so that didn't fit.

When Trudy had told her mother that was friends with Helga Schneider, her mother became silent.

"She's an older woman," she finally said.

"Not that old. She's younger than you—only in her mid, maybe early twenties."

"A woman," her mother replied. "Not a girl."

"Well, I like her. She's nice."

"You hardly know her."

"I think I know her." Trudy frowned. "You should meet her. She is our neighbor."

"You haven't been dusting your room," her mother said

changing the subject. "I sneeze when I walk in there."

*   *   *   *   *

In late April, on a dreary Thursday afternoon, with haze and low clouds hinting at the possibility of showers, Trudy managed to nudge her mother out of the house to meet Helga.

They walked together toward Helga's house along the curb of the rough road. There was no sidewalk on this side of Wellesley. Nakamizo's cabbage grew as big as straw hats along the edge of the gritty asphalt border.

Helga was trimming the bushes in front of her house.

"Helga," Trudy said in English as they approached. "You've never met my mother."

The German woman turned and smiled at her neighbors as they walked up the driveway.

"Hello," she said, placing her cutters in the burlap bag lying on the ground.

"My mother has wanted to meet you," Trudy cheerfully lied, hoping her mom would get the hint to be neighborly. "I told her you have been helping me with German."

"Yes. And you are teaching me good English."

"Teaching you English?" Trudy's mother repeated, clearly suspicious that more was going on than her daughter had suggested. "You're learning to speak English from Trudy?"

"Ah, yes. My English is improving nicely, thank you. We can have a gathering for speaking English now. Yes?"

Trudy noticed her mother glance over at the Schneider's house.

They began to casually chat about children. Helga's two were still down for their naps. Trudy began to relax.

"Aren't girls so much easier to rise than boys?" her mother said at one point. "Trudy is so helpful and usually home when she's supposed to be."

That comment had a subtle edge that put the girl on guard. Helga appeared confused. Trudy translated what her mother said.

"Ah, yes," she said with a smile.

Trudy's mother silently studied the woman.

"We live close to the ocean. Yes?" Helga said. "This. . .land is new for me. The sea. I never saw until I was much older, Trudy's age possibly. The Ostsee. . ."

25

"The Ostsee?" Trudy mother asked.

"Yes, such a cold *ozean*. . . ocean."

"I think that's the Baltic Sea. *Ja?*" Trudy asked

"Yes, yes. The Baltic *See.*"

"I have a brother in the U.S. Navy," Trudy's mother said, Trudy guessed, maybe to make conversation. "He is on a battleship in the Pacific."

"A battleship?"

"A large war ship," Trudy clarified. She had no idea why her mother mentioned him.

"Ah, *ein kriegsschiff.*"

"A battleship," Trudy's mother said, obviously making the point that an American battleship was a *battleship* not a *kriesgsschiff.* "Billy is on the Arizona, one of the biggest ships in the U.S. Navy. He is a petty officer."

"An officer is an important person," said Helga.

"He has important duties and is trained to be outside on the deck in bad storms. They have typhoons in the Pacific."

"Typhoons?"

"Terrible storms at sea. They can rip the steel plates right off the hull."

Helga looked confused and lost.

"It is dangerous," Trudy said and repeated that in German, "*Das ist sehr gefährlich.*"

"Oh, I see," Helga replied, nodding her head and appearing rather awed.

Trudy knew *of* her Uncle Billy but had met him only once, a long time ago. She remembered that he wore a white sailor suit and gobbled food like he had not eaten in days. And he belched which caused the other men to laugh and embarrassed her mother and aunt.

"Do you have any family in the German army?" her mother asked Helga. The question came out like she was asking if the woman ever had a toothache.

"My sister's son," Helga said carefully.

"What do you think of Hitler?"

Shocked, Trudy back stepped but forced herself not to turn around.

"He is very bad," Helga said without hesitation.

*   *   *   *   *

"I don't know much about my Uncle Billy," Trudy mentioned as she and her mother walked home. She was relieved when Helga's daughter woke from her nap and put the visit to and end.

"My brother has made a career of the Navy. For him hitching up was a godsend."

"What do you mean?"

Her mother did not respond at first.

"Your uncle had a wild side," she finally said. She shook her head. "The Navy's been a good home, and he has been able to make something of himself. Thank goodness the Arizona's in the Pacific. With the fighting in the Atlantic, he could be in danger."

"Don't you worry about the Japanese? They've got a navy."

Her mother almost laughed. "They might be able to invade China, but they don't have what it takes to pick a fight with America."

*   *   *   *   *

Two weeks later, just before sunset, Trudy walked the short distance between her house and the Schneider's. The open air reminded her how much she preferred being out of the constant reek of cigarette-smoke from her father's chain smoking indoors. Even in the crisp breeze, with low clouds smudging the darkened gray of the early May sky, she felt better being outside. She could breathe.

Usually on Friday, after an early dinner, the Mansfields went to the show. This evening, only Trudy and her mother were going. They planned to see Charlie Chaplin's *The Great Dictator* and Peggy Moran in *Double Date* which had just come to the Tivoli. Trudy's father and brother groaned when they heard the selection and said they would stay home. But then, that afternoon, Helga asked Trudy if she could babysit. Trudy would have declined, but Helga said she and her husband had been invited at the last minute to attend an event honoring an important German exile who had won a Nobel prize. How could Trudy say no?

Her mother took the news like she had discovered someone had stolen the garden hose. She didn't say anything, preferring to sulk and snap at Trudy when she did not move fast enough peeling potatoes.

After dinner, Trudy's mother sat at home darning socks while her husband and son sat in front of the radio, listening to the broadcast of an inconsequential Hollywood Stars baseball game. Being a proper lady, her mother would never drive to the show alone at night.

Trudy skipped onto the Schneider's porch. After ringing the

doorbell, she heard the quick thumping of a child's feet racing around the other side of the door.

"*Verlangsamen Sie sich!*" she heard a man order.

The door opened, and a rather handsome man, about her father's age, with neatly trimmed blonde hair, stood in the doorway. He wore black dinner dress with a white bow necktie the likes of which Trudy had only seen in the movies and in *Life* magazine. Behind him, the children peeked at her, miniature towhead versions of their parents. They ran across the room into the hall after she made eye contact.

"Good afternoon, Professor Schneider," she said in German. "My name is Trudy Mansfield. I'm the babysitter." She actually said *das kindermädchen*, the nanny. She could not find a translation for babysitter in her English/German dictionary.

"Please come in," he said in excellent English. "You speak German."

"A little," she answered in German.

"Your pronunciation is quite good."

"Thank you. Mrs. Schneider has been helping me."

The two children raced back into the room and hid behind their father.

"Hallo. Jonathon and Marlene. Yes?" Trudy asked, continuing to speak German.

The little girl ran behind her brother to look at Trudy over his shoulder.

"Don't be rude," her father said to his daughter. "Tell her your name."

"Marlene," the child said shyly.

"Jonathon is my name," her brother said.

Helga walked into the living room. She wore a long blue-grey formal dress with full length sleeves and a modest neckline. Her blonde hair was carefully arranged and held in place with mother-of-pearl combs. She looked beautiful.

"Hello, Trudy," she said in English.

"Good afternoon, Mrs. Schneider" the teenage girl replied in German. She didn't say "Helga" fearing the professor would not approve of the informality. When she came near, the scent of her rose perfume laced the air.

Helga smiled, as if suddenly amused by something.

"Please," her husband said. "Speak English. We want the children to learn the language."

Trudy noticed Helga become somber as she looked down at her children.

"I have put food on the stove for dinner," she said. Looking up at the girl she added, "I considered that you had not eaten. There will be enough for you too. After we eat, we allow the children to play. I then read stories before . . . *schlafenszeit*. I do not know the English word."

"Bed time," Dr. Schneider said.

"Bed time," Helga repeated. "They normally go to sleep at nine o'clock."

That was later than Martha Lewis allowed her children to stay up, but then Jonathon and Marlene took long naps during the day.

Helga walked Trudy through the house, showing her the children's bedroom and the kitchen where dinner warmed in covered pans on the stove. She told Trudy that she had placed fresh homemade bread in the basket on the kitchen table. Her husband remained in the living room with the children. Trudy could hear him telling them to behave and mind their manners.

"Do not allow Jonathon to run outside or make too much noise," Helga said returning to the living room. She looked down at her son and repeated in German what she'd said. He smiled.

"We will practice English," Trudy said, and looking at the children added in German, "We will play a game of the speaking of English. Talk like the neighbors. Like Stevie and Johnny across the street."

"*Gut!*" the boy remarked, brightly.

As Trudy sat on the living room floor planning the night with the children, an older man arrived wearing a tuxedo with a black tie. She watched as Professor Schnieder helped Helga with her coat. They all said their goodbyes and then Trudy was left alone with the children.

The evening passed quickly as Trudy spoke in English to Jonathon and Marlene, enjoying their eagerness to learn the English words for objects around the house. She was also learning new German words as the two pointed to things in their language. As the sun set, they went into the backyard where Trudy discovered the Schneiders had a vegetable garden, neatly laid out, weeded, and in spring foliage. The children pointed out what grew there, and Trudy did her best to figure out what the plants' names were in English.

Helga had placed three plates on the table. The food she prepared was different from the meals Trudy's mother put together, and also unlike Martha's cooking, which was seasoned with fresh Italian herbs from her own garden.

Trudy dished out fried cutlets of meat, solid potatoes, and white asparagus. The food emitted a strong but pleasant fragrance that tickled her nose. She poured milk in the large glasses.

After they ate and while Trudy cleaned the dishes and pans, Jonathon brought out a derelict deck of Bicycle Playing Cards. Its members were badly bowed, scratched, and dog-eared. No doubt the deck had cards missing.

The three played something like war, but the boy kept changing the rules to assure he would beat Trudy and his sister. Marlene enjoyed just handling the playing cards and did not understand the point of the game. Trudy doubted Jonathon got away with this mischief with his parents.

At bedtime, Trudy helped Marlene change into her night-wear, while Jonathon took his time getting into his blue striped pajamas. He went into the bathroom and took more time behind the closed door. Trudy heard funny kid sounds. He was obviously playing around and delaying going to bed. Trudy finally called him out.

After the children were in bed, Trudy decided to make up her own bedtime story, borrowing characters and plot twists from some of the tales she remembered as a child and from stories she read to the Lewis children. Martha's husband, Chuck, worked at the Disney Studio and brought home books Trudy assumed were being considered for future animated features.

"I will tell you about a magical nanny," she began her story, choosing this subject because she knew the German words for nanny and magic. "Her name is . . . "

"Trudy!" the boy guessed.

"Don't do that, Jonathon," said Marlene, with a cranky glance.

"Her name is Mary Poppins. One day a strong wind blew her to the home of . . . Jonathon and Marlene! They lived in a little house with a nice garden. . . . "

In the middle of nowhere, she almost added, but censored herself. She went on to improvise a story that included bears, honey, tea cups, gold coins, and a wayward sea-serpent. The tale may have made no

30

sense and recalled a Mary Poppins sillier than the stern nanny Trudy read about to the Lewis kids, but Jonathon and Marlene seemed satisfied. They were particularly interested in the scaly monster she conjured out of the cold waters of the Santa Monica Bay.

After she turned out the light in the children's room and closed the door, Trudy wandered around the house, curious and a little nosy. She wondered what sorts of things Germans would have in their homes. Much of the furnishing and knickknacks were different from that found in a typical American residence. Trudy concluded that the Schneiders had attempted to make their home a German *haus*. While most of the big pieces of furniture were of an American style and rather new, a few chairs, one table, an old chest of drawers and the knickknacks came from Europe.

Trudy almost expected to find a wooden bucket and a European broom with a round head of bristles in the laundry closet, but to her disappointment discovered that Helga had the same modern broom, wet mop, and galvanized pail the Mansfields had.

Trudy had brought the textbook for her reading class but did not want to do homework. It was Friday night. Instead, she nosed around the Schneider's reading material.

Neatly stacked on the side table next to the sofa were magazines. The top few were a German language periodical, *Freies Deutschland*. "*Free Germany*." Intrigued, she decided to attempt to read an article or two and looked around the living room for an English/German dictionary. She couldn't imagine how Helga Schneider could survive in this country without the dictionary. She went to the bookcase which had more books than she had ever seen in a house.

Looking at the titles, she saw the word *Ägyptologie* appeared on many of the volumes. Although she had never seen the German word, she knew immediately the English translation was *Egyptology*.

She stared at the books awed, excited, and intrigued. She knew that Professor Schneider taught at UCLA but until that moment she had no idea in what field.

"Oh, my God!" she said, reaching up and sliding out one of the volumes. She thumbed through the book, written using many words beyond her mastery of German. She noticed notes neatly written in blue ink on the margins of the pages. She returned the book to its place and withdrew one of the five thick, dark-green leather-bound volumes titled

Wörterbuch der ägyptischen Sprache—Dictionary of the Egyptian Language. On the pages were columns of German words alphabetically arranged, paired with hieroglyphs. The book appeared well used. Professor Schneider must be a master of ancient Egyptian. There were many notations on the pages.

Carefully turning the book's pages, Trudy backed into the stuffed chair next to the bookcase and sat, engulfing herself in the soft upholstery which smelled of Helga's rose perfume.

She noticed that Egyptian symbols were usually combined to make words. She knew some of the German words, which allowed her to translate a few of the Egyptian symbols. She committed to memory some of the hieroglyphs so she could write them down when she got home. She was especially captivated by the symbol for woman 𓁐 which she traced with her finger until the figure could be reproduced as spontaneously as the letter *a*.

How fascinating, she thought, turning the pages of a particularly richly illustrated book. There were no civilizations older than ancient Egypt, the land of the pyramids, sphinx, mummies, buried tombs, and gold treasures. Her mind began to spin imagining what secrets the tomes in the bookcase contained. If only she knew more German.

Trudy lost track of time. It was almost eleven o'clock when she heard a car pulling up in front of the house. She restored the book to its space on the shelf and picked up her school text. She was afraid that Professor Schneider would not approve of her browsing through his library.

The professor gave her the fifty cents she asked for. Although he appeared tired, he still had a commanding presence. Dressed formally with his handsome blonde features making a striking presence in the lamp lights, he reminded her for an unpleasant second of a Nazi leader she had seen in a magazine or news-reel. Then he looked over to Helga and smiled, and the look he gave her broke the unbidden illusion.

Trudy thanked them and wished them a good night.

Her house was dark and cold when she walked through the front door. Before going to her room, she retrieved *The Dawn of Civilization*. She closed her bedroom door and took out her journal to draw the hieroglyph for woman and the other marks she had memorized earlier in the evening. She then quickly changed into her nightgown and slipped between the chilly sheets of her bed, propping herself up against the pillow and laying her drawings on the edge of the blanket. After she got comfortable, she opened the book. Thumbing through the chapters on ancient Egyptian, she could hear the refrigerator in the kitchen hum. Under the watchful eyes of the high Lama, she examined the illustrations to see if she could find the signs for woman and the other words she had learned.

Chapter 5

A Girl With A Brain

Monday, at lunch, Trudy sat with Susan French, Joan Fulbright, Alice Long, and Nancy Pierce. Susan told the others about her date Saturday night with Robby Thompson. Trudy listened attentively, but not with the other girls' enthusiasm.

"Robby has an almost new Packard convertible," Susan said. "He is such a gentleman and so full of surprises. Can you believe it? He took me all the way to Hollywood to see the new Mickey Rooney, Spencer Tracy film, *Men of Boy's Town*, at Grauman's Chinese Theater."

"He took you to the Chinese Theater?" Joan swooned. Going to the Chinese was a rare treat for any girl their age.

"After we saw the movie we walked around the forecourt and inspected the footprints. I wear the same size shoe as Judy Garland! Then we strolled down Hollywood Boulevard. The street is so romantic at night. Robby bought ice cream cones at Schwab's drug store where that movie director discovered Lana Turner. . . ."

The girls were momentarily distracted by a commotion at the next table. Some of the Jewish boys were laughing and roughing up an unfortunate Karl Black who had tried to sit down. One of the taunters, Leonard Horowitz, plucked off the boy's glasses. His buddies laughed as he threw the frames in the air. The spectacles landed on the asphalt. Karl turned around and bent over to pick them up. Leonard then pushed him with his foot causing him to dive forward, dropping his lunch, and almost landing on his face. Red clumps of Jell-O bounced over the ground.

"Get lost!" Leonard ordered. To his friends he added, "What a schmuck."

Trudy felt sorry for Karl. He only wanted to sit down to eat lunch.

Joan sneered an ethnic slur and said, "He better think twice next time before he tries to sit with them. Anyway. Where were you?"

Trudy didn't feel comfortable with the name calling and Joan said it loud enough for the boys to hear. Susan ignored Joan and continued telling the story about her date.

"Did you kiss Robby?" Alice asked, her dreamy eyes drawn to Susan.

"On a first date?" Susan gasped, mimicking shock.

"You gave him a good night kiss, didn't you?" Nancy pried.

"I shook his hand," Susan said with a smile that revealed the truth.

The other girls laughed, including Trudy.

Trudy thought that Susan was so pretty. She had smooth skin, eyes the color of a summer sky, even white teeth and nicely shaped blondish hair. Studying her and the other girls, Trudy felt like the ugly duckling but not one that would turn into a swan. Maybe a pelican.

Trudy walked with Nancy to their next class.

"I have a new boyfriend," Nancy announced. Her eyes crinkled in a smile. "I'm telling only you. Not Susan, Alice, or Joan or anyone else. You're good at keeping secrets, and I've just been dying to tell someone."

At least she was good for something.

"Why is it a secret?" she asked.

"Well," Nancy replied, beginning to hesitate, "his family is Mexican. He's not a cholo or a zoot suitor or anything like that. If his last name wasn't Pico you'd think his family came over on the Mayflower. He doesn't look Mexican. He even has blue eyes."

"Pío Pico was the last Mexican governor of California," Trudy said. She learned that a long time ago in elementary school.

"He's related."

"Does he go to school here?"

"He graduated last year. His name is Gary and he works at a printing plant, and—this is so embarrassing—he is training to be a stripper."

"A stripper!" Trudy squealed. She couldn't imagine a man doing such a thing. It was bad enough that women took off their clothes on the stage.

" He's not becoming *that* type of stripper," Nancy said, laughing and punching Trudy's shoulder. "In printing, a stripper prepares plates for the offset presses"

*   *   *   *   *

Trudy moped through the day's last three class periods. In geometry, she sat behind Karl Back who slumped in his chair like he had been dipped in tar. She couldn't help but feel bad for him.

"I saw what happened at lunch," she said leaning forward.

He turned around and looked at her. He didn't look beaten or offended, merely washed out. Trudy thought his eyes reflected more on what he pondered in his mind than what he saw around him.

"You had every right to sit there. They're just . . . creeps."

Carl's mouth twisted into something not quite a smile. "Thanks."

*　　　*　　　*　　　*　　　*

After her last class, Trudy went to the school library where she looked up some things for world history. She didn't want to take too long, but she couldn't resist retrieving the recent issue of *Time* Magazine. Thumbing through the pages she could not ignore all the stories related to the war. A person would think that the U.S. was already fighting. She came across a large photograph of the Douglas B-19, a "flying battleship" built just blocks away from her house. Her father said the plane was as slow as a fat cow jumping over the moon. It nonetheless caused her to feel pride knowing that her father worked on this modern marvel.

She flipped to the movie reviews.

> *In Model Wife Joan Blondell is not a mother. She is a stenographer who spends most of her time avoiding the advances of her boss's son and keeping her marriage to boyish Dick Powell secret. . . .*

Trudy's mother would probably like this. She ate up light-romances like they were candies. Trudy tended to be more picky, enjoying just a few of the comedies, like she only cared for some of the assorted chocolates found in a box of Sees candy. *His Girl Friday*, starring Cary Grant and a self-assured Rosalind Russell, had been as delightful as a piece of dark butter cream. Others cinematic confections left a bad taste in her mouth. The heroines in most of the movies were easily flustered, interested in little more than getting a husband, overly

36

scheming in that pursuit, and not necessarily very bright—although they had certain charms, style, and glamour which meant they always got their man in the end.

"Trudy, a man doesn't want a girl who is smarter than him," her mother said after they saw *Philadelphia Story*. In one scene a tipsy Katharine Hepburn seems to melt when James Stewart tells her she is "a golden girl, full of light, warmth, and delight."

"You spend too much time studying for school," her mother added.

"I like school," Trudy protested, meekly.

"You want to be an old maid?"

"No."

"All right. Men like women who are pretty, have a nice, warm personality, are joyful . . ." her mother said, probably unaware that she repeated in her own words what Stewart told Hepburn. The description made Trudy think of golden haired Susan French. "They're afraid a smart woman will want to wear the pants. And being a dreamer makes a woman seem dizzy. You have a nice personality and are friendly. We just need to do something with your hair. . . ."

Trudy wondered what happened to her mother's nice personality. She seemed to be cross most of the time and sometimes yelled at Trudy's father.

Trudy returned the magazine and went back to studying. She was a girl with a brain. So what? She wasn't pretty no matter what she did with her hair. No harm done if she got all As this semester. Who would notice? And her daydreaming—it made the world seem so much more . . . interesting.

Chapter 6

Nelly

Helga Schneider was taking more time than usual to finish her baking. She still wasn't used to the American oven. Looking through the kitchen window, she wondered why Trudy hadn't come by. She usually rode up about this time. Today they would chat in English and they could talk while Helga made bread.

Instead of the girl on her bike, Helga saw a flashy American car drive up the street. The maroon sedan bumped over the pitted pavement, pulled up, and, nearly jumped onto the lawn before coming to a stop in front of the house. She could not see the driver. Curious, she watched and then became alarmed when she saw Nelly Mann get out of the car.

Nelly was the wife of the writer Heinrich Mann, the brother of Nobel laureate Thomas Mann. The two men had been the guests of honor at the party Helga and Max had attended the previous Saturday. During the gathering, the blonde Nelly had followed Helga around like she was her long lost younger sister. Most of the other women at the party did not want to have anything to do with Nelly. A former barmaid, she was considered vulgar and beneath them. Helga overheard one of the women say that Heinrich was struck down with Nelly as with an infectious disease.

Before the end of dessert, Marta, the wife of the novelist Leon Feuchtwanger, had the decency to propose a toast to Nelly for saving her husband's life crossing the Pyrenees. "She supported Heinrich with her loving strength and gave courage to us all." Marta looked down at Nelly.

As if attending a play, Helga watched Nelly cover her face with her hands as the others toasted her. She began laughing uncontrollably when she realized that her red dress had become unbuttoned revealing her breasts barely contained by her frilly brassiere.

Helga had no idea how Nelly learned her address. The tall German beauty wore a tiny flowered turban with a sheer veil that flowed over her head. She had on a navy-blue skirt and short sleeve jacket over a white blouse. She held a piece of paper and glanced at it and up at the street address on the house. Satisfied, she walked up the driveway.

Helga flicked the flour off her apron and quickly washed her hands. She stooped over to pick up a few toys off the floor as the doorbell rang. Marlene and Jonathon were down for naps.

"Helga, I'm so glad to find you home," said Nelly. She spoke German with a hint of low intonations revealing she originally came from Saxony. Smiling, she appeared excited to see Helga.

"This is unexpected," Helga said. And inconvenient.

"I would have called, but I could not find your phone number," the woman said strolling into the house. Although she had at least fifteen years on Helga, she didn't look much older. She glanced around the house like she was looking for spider webs.

"Your house is comfortable." Noting the bookcase in the living room she added, "You have many books. Like Heinrich, but at least your husband's books are not all over the house. We live in a tiny little apartment and there are books and manuscripts everywhere."

Helga had no desire to discuss books.

"You'll have to excuse me, Nelly," she said. "You caught me in the middle of baking."

"You're baking?" the woman said sitting down. "Mmm! I can smell bread in the oven."

Helga continued to stand, hoping Nelly would get the message.

"Bread is so inexpensive here," Nelly added. "And convenient to purchase."

"The bread is so plain," Helga said. "So dry, with no texture."

"But the time baking takes! How do you do it? Women in Germany spend all day making bread." Nelly's mouth opened erupting a piercing laugh. Her eyes then settled on the startled Helga. "I love good German bread, but I'll eat the American bread. I will not spend time in the kitchen like you."

Nelly became more serious and began to talk about the long hours of drudgery typing Heinrich's manuscripts, works for which he had not found a publisher. As she talked, Helga determined that she was neither shallow nor stupid, just rather crude, unsophisticated, and clueless about social graces.

Helga smelled something burning.

"Oh! Excuse me. I need to check the bread."

She rushed in the kitchen and saw a ribbon of smoke sneaking out of the oven vent. She grabbed a hot pad and opened the door. The loaves in the back had blackened.

"Oh, my word," Nelly said standing in the kitchen doorway. She watched Helga pull the loaves out of the oven. "I'm so sorry. I distracted you."

"I must stay in the kitchen," Helga admitted as she opened the window to let in air and began to remove the bread from the pans. The burnt loaves were ruined. As she struggled with the bread pans, she noticed Marlene standing next to Nelly. The two-year-old had the sullen look of a child still half asleep. Nelly turned to Marlene and gently touched her hair.

"Your daughter is so pretty. She looks like you."

Marlene looked nothing like Helga and had the eyes and mouth of her father.

"Hello, little girl. What is your name?"

Marlene looked up and said nothing.

Nelly began to laugh, shaking her head.

"I should leave. This is not a good time to visit. I am sorry I caused this accident."

As she turned around and nearly tripped, Helga realized something she should have noticed when Nelly first walked in. She was tipsy.

After dumping the burnt loaves into the trash bin and setting the pans to soak, Helga followed Nelly outside and stood on the porch, holding Marlene's hand. Nelly leisurely strolled by the flowerbed, pausing to admire the pretty blooms before going to her car.

Helga noticed Trudy coming down Wellesley and waved to her. The girl turned onto the driveway.

"Hello, young lady," Nelly said in German.

"Good afternoon, madam," Trudy replied. "You have a pretty car."

Nelly didn't seem to be surprised that an American girl spoke to her perfectly in her native language as casually as a young person in the Fatherland. She stepped onto the street and walked around the rear of the vehicle, smiling at Trudy. Opening the door, she said to the girl, "Soon you will have your own fine car. This is America."

Trudy walked her bike toward the porch looking back at the

automobile. It took Nelly a moment to get settled in her car before she started the engine and pulled away. Crossing the asphalt field of pot holes and giant cracks, her car swayed and rolled like a boat in choppy waves.

"I would invite you into the house," Helga said in English, "but I have a mess in the kitchen."

"Please, I can help you," Trudy replied in German and then, remembering the day, added in English, "I'm very experienced in cleaning."

Back in the house Helga was confronted by the pungent odor of the burnt bread and a smoky haze that had drifted into the living room. She moved to the side of the room to open the windows.

"I had a baking accident. I am making bread and a few loaves became, ah . . ."

"Burnt?"

"Yes, burnt."

They walked into the kitchen, with Marlene racing them through the door. Over the sink the breeze rippled and picked up the window curtains chilling the room.

Helga showed Trudy the bread trays soaking in the sink and asked for their English name. Trudy volunteered to "scrub" them. The girl's rough hands indicated that she had cleaned many pots and pans. Undertaking the chore, she worked with energetic effort and removed the specks of burnt-on crust that stuck like black vitreous enamel to the trays. This was a girl not afraid of hard work.

Chapter 7

Boredom

Two weeks after the Fourth of July, Trudy was already become bored with summer vacation. Since the end of school last month, each day of the week had become a Saturday in which she had to help her mother do chores around the house and yard. She barely had time to visit Helga, play with Jonathon and Marlene, and eye the *Ägyptologie* volumes. She hardly strayed off Wellesley Avenue except to go shopping with her mother or to the movies.

Movies were her refuge. Once in the theater, Trudy would quickly forget about her boring life.

When she was a child, Trudy thought of movie theaters as magicians' palaces. The conjuror's assistants were the usherettes, candy counter venders, and ticket sellers. Now sixteen, she pretended she still believed this.

What magic! When the lights went down and the curtains parted, the world expanded before her eyes, sometimes in wonderful Technicolor. She stared at the screen transfixed, cheering the triumph of heroes, melting warmly at the tenderness of new love, worrying over the fate of a protagonist facing potential defeat, swaying to the music as Fred Astaire danced, laughing at Bob Hope's wisecracks, gasping in amazement when the great Charlie Chaplin slipped between the gears of a giant machine, and jumping in shock at the aberrations that appeared out of the shadows of the horror films. And every now and then she discovered strangely wonderful places like Shangri-La.

At home there was not much to do, except chores and laying around listening to the radio as she wrote in her diary. To distract herself when she was doing housework, she would think about Professor Schneider's books. Given the excitement she felt for what she had discovered on his bookshelf, someone would have thought she had stumbled across an old map to *Cíbola*, the legendary Seven Cities of Gold. The hieroglyph dictionary was like such a map to her.

Trudy fretted. The ancient Egyptian words she had already committed to memory were like seeds, magic seeds which were planted in her mind but needed to be tended. What could she do?

One day, she told her mother that Professor Schneider was an Egyptologist. Her mother seemed impressed but concerned. There were risks, she said.

"Risks?" Trudy asked.

"You know of the discovery of King Tut's tomb?"

"Sort of."

"It was a big news story. There were front page headlines in the newspapers every day. Soon it came out there was the curse."

"The curse?" Trudy had never heard of "the curse."

"The pharaoh's priests placed a curse on the tomb. Anyone who disturbed King Tut would die an early and horrible death. And you know what? All those connected with the expedition died mysteriously."

That was spooky.

Trudy told her mother of her fascination with hieroglyphs. Her mother somberly looked at her.

"You're not thinking of getting into any kind of hocus-pocus and black magic, are you?"

"No, I just think hieroglyphs are interesting. It's the way the Egyptians in the time of the pharaohs wrote. I'd love to learn more."

Her mother frowned and said, "Isn't it enough you're taking German?" She then turned and walked away. From the dining room she said, "You're so impractical at times."

Stunned, Trudy took the comment as an undeserved slap. She didn't think of herself as impractical. She did tons of practical things around the house every day.

Rather than being discouraged, Trudy became increasingly determined to learn about the ancient form of writing. She needed something stimulating to forget about her mundane life after she dusted, waxed the floors, canned fruit, pulled weeds, and did all the other house and yard work.

Trudy wished she had the nerve to talk to Professor Schneider. He was an Egyptologist and probably knew everything there was to know about the subject. But he was a Professor! And . . . formidable and scary. Why would he take the time to explain this stuff to a high school girl? Maybe she could mention her interest to Helga, but the woman might laugh and say that her husband did serious research.

Trudy then had an idea, an idea she dared not tell anyone. It would only make her mother more upset, no doubt amuse her father,

43

and probably cause her friends to laugh. Her idea—actually a scheme—would have to remain a secret. During the remainder of her summer vacation she would learn to read hieroglyphs.

What an exciting plan! To learn a language that had been dead for thousands of years. Of course, the question was, "How?" There were no classes and no one to teach her—except Professor Schneider. This would require her to learn not just the symbols but syntax and other grammatical rules. Those details didn't overwhelm her. Her increasing mastery of German gave her the confidence to learn another language—even a dead language. Once she learned enough of the old script, she could risk demonstrating to Professor Schneider her budding grasp of hieroglyphs, and hopefully he wouldn't brush her off. He might even help her, just as Helga guided her with German.

She retrieved the volume *The Dawn of Civilization* from the bookcase in the living room. Under the watchful eyes of the high Lama, she sat at her desk and poured over the pictures of statues and ruins, memorizing the scant details regarding the Egyptian alphabet. She learned that twenty-five symbols composed the alphabet, but the book didn't show them. This was a tantalizing start, but it did not give her any idea how to proceed.

She visited Helga. She wanted to look again at the Professor's bookcase. As they chatted, she kept glancing at the private library behind Helga. The large green volumes of the *Dictionary of the Egyptian Language* stood out on the shelf and drew her attention like cherry tarts setting unattended on a pasty tray. She suddenly felt an urge to mention the books.

Before she could say anything, someone knocked at the door. The pretty German lady Trudy had met a few months before stood at the door, dressed fashionably in a blue and white dress and a broad summery hat.

"Hello, Nelly. I was not expecting you," said Helga

Nodding, the smiling woman crossed the threshold and looked around the room. There was nothing snooty in her manner. She looked down at the children and smiled.

"Hello, little professor," Nelly said with a pleasant smile. "And there's my sweetheart, Marlene. Nelly has something for you. . . ."

Opening her purse, she pulled out two small lollipops and, crouching down, held them out to the children.

"Lutschers! One for each of you. But maybe your mother will want you to eat lunch before you have these." Nelly glanced up to their mother who shook her head.

"You may eat them after lunch," Helga said. "Thank you, Nelly."

Helga took the lollipops and put them in her apron pocket.

Marlene and Jonathon watched their mother but kept looking at Nelly. Remembering that Trudy was in the room, Helga smiled at the girl and looked to her friend.

"Nelly, this is my neighbor, Trudy Mansfield. Miss Mansfield, allow me to introduce you to Mrs. Nelly Mann."

"*Wie geht es dir?*" Nelly asked, inquiring how Trudy was doing, using the informal manner of address, normally limited to close friends and family.

Trudy responded by saying she was fine and thanked her for asking,.

"I had to get out of the house," Nelly said to Trudy. Turning to Helga, she added, "For days I have been typing Heinrich's manuscript. He hopes he can finally get something published here in America."

"Your husband is a writer?" Trudy asked, awed that she was conversing with the wife of an author.

"Yes, and highly acclaimed, but he has not been able to find a publisher in America, although his work is famous here. . ."

Trudy's expression must have revealed that she had no idea who he was.

"You are probably familiar with *Professor Unrat?*"

Trudy shook her head. She did not want to admit her ignorance but wouldn't lie.

"You must know of the Lola character. No? Then you must know the movie based on his book. *The Blue Angel.*"

Trudy nearly gasped. The movie was notorious, more known of than actually seen. Several scandalous scenes had been censored out before the film could be shown in the United States. Trudy would never tell her mother she had met the wife of the man who wrote the smut, although Nelly seemed perfectly nice.

As Helga and Nelly continued to talk, Trudy's attention returned to the bookcase. She almost said something but caught herself after Helga mentioned that her husband was working hard to prepare a new course he would be teaching in the fall. If she babysat again, she could come equipped with paper and her English/German dictionary.

*   *   *   *   *

The next day Trudy rode her bicycle to the Sawtelle branch of the Los Angeles public library. She looked for books on hieroglyphs but could only find one volume on ancient civilizations, and it had hardly any information about Egyptian writing. The *Encyclopædia Britannica* had an article on hieroglyphs that described word-signs, phonograms, and determinatives but didn't go into much detail. Frustrated she considered being brave and just asking Professor Schneider if she could look at his books. That seemed so simple, but she quickly got cold feet.

Trudy talked to the Sawtelle librarian who treated her like a silly child, tersely telling her to look in the encyclopedia before turning away to more important matters. But, then, at the Santa Monica Public Library a stern looking old librarian actually listened to her.

"You want to learn to read and write Egyptian hieroglyphs, is that what you are saying?" she asked, holding the girl's attention with gray eyes that were magnified through thick bifocals.

"Yes," Trudy admitted, sure the woman would shake her head.

"I'm sorry, honey, but there is nothing in our library that will help you. But there is a place not too far where you will find what you need."

"Where's that?" Trudy asked.

"UCLA. The library is open to the public. You can't check out the books, but don't let that discourage you. Scholars who study old manuscripts can't check out those materials either. They do their work in reading rooms. Bring lots of paper and plan to spend hours, maybe days there, and you'll find what our looking for."

Situated on a hill north of Westwood Village, UCLA was not far from University High School.

Trudy thanked the woman who said, "Good luck. It's nice talking to a girl who is not asking about the latest romance novel."

Chapter 8

Sir Alan Gardiner's Egyptian Grammar

As summer wore on, the long, lazy days became noticeably shorter. The dull weather already felt like early fall. The morning sky overshadowed the neighborhood with a gloomy gray overcast dominating the landscape more often than the sun. The month of August was all but over.

After finishing her chores, Trudy headed again to UCLA library. She ate a fast, early lunch, told her mom she would be home in time to help with dinner, ran out of the house, and biked up to the university.

The first time she went to the library, she had dressed in a way she thought a college co-ed would—in a pigeon gray tuck-in blouse and a blue fan-pleated skirt, an outfit too nice to wear to high school. She had her thick hair pulled back. She even wore makeup—something that would have been her death mask if her father or mother saw her face. She thought her puffy lips, crooked teeth, and Katherine Hepburn cheek bones made her look like a marionette puppet. She had hoped makeup would improve her appearance or at least make her look older.

She had asked Susan for assistance. Her friend already wore lipstick, eyebrow liner and facial foundations.

"I want to go up to UCLA and use their library," she told Susan on the telephone.

"Trudy, it is the middle of the summer! Let's go to the beach. School work can wait till September."

"I'd like to go to the beach, but I still have to go up to UCLA."

"What on earth for?"

Trudy didn't know what to say, so she just admitted the truth. Susan was silent.

"I'm trying to impress someone." That was actually not a lie. She wanted to impressed Professor Schneider.

"He better be as handsome as Errol Flynn," said Susan. "So, how can I help? And don't tell me you want me to look through the card catalog."

Trudy told her she wanted to try and use makeup to look older. She didn't want to stand out when she went on the campus.

The next day in her friend's bedroom Trudy learned to pluck her eyebrows and accent them with a dark brown pencil. She then applied muted eye shadow. But that wasn't enough for Susan. She went to work on Trudy's face, applying some of the different cosmetics that sat on her vanity. She rubbed on an oily foundation and highlighted each cheek with smears of rouge. This even out her complexion and covered the acne, but it also gave her skin a varnished sheen. Susan frowned. To Trudy's horror, Susan then darken her eyes even more with black mascara, a deeper color eye shadow and heavy eyeliner which caused Trudy's eyes to appear sunken. Then Susan smudged on deep red lipstick, making Trudy's lips look crocked and even puffier.

"You look older and I see no zits," Susan said, putting down the lipstick.

With blushed cheeks, accented eyebrows, and reddened twisted lips, Trudy looked older but now appeared even more like a marionette. She felt Susan was only using her as a plaything.

Without being asked, Susan took a Kleenex, dipped it in cold cream and cleaned Trudy's face.

"Let's try again," she said.

*   *   *   *   *

That first time Trudy went to UCLA, she applied a conservative amount of makeup that may not have done much for her skin but at least made her pass for a girl in her late teens.

Nothing had prepared her for the experience of walking around the center of the campus. To Trudy, the UCLA buildings were old—classic halls of higher learning like Oxford. She did not realize they were built two years after she was born. She felt like she was walking in a dream, like she had been transplanted to Europe. But then, she rounded a corner and saw mosaic sun bursts, sporting sunglasses, which were inlayed between the arched windows of one of the brick halls and the fantasy dissipated. She was definitely still in California.

As she didn't know the location of the school's library, Trudy walked down the paths between the buildings, peeking into doorways, maintaining a casual stride and crossing her tracks several times before she finally found the entrance. Passing through an ornate stone doorway, Trudy found herself in a foyer unlike any she had seen or even smelled. To her, the musty odor represented the olfactory signature of centuries of knowledge!

That was over a month ago. Excited, confident and feeling a little rebellious, today she took the library steps two at a time, and then slowed her pace once she got to the doors. After all, this was a great depository of knowledge, its hundreds of thousands of volumes were the work of many, many scholars dating back to the time when the Greeks wore sheets and everyone else hardly wore anything, except maybe the Hebrews.

On this visit, she wore no makeup, and she dressed in her everyday clothes, indifferent to what the university people might think. Actually, she didn't dress that differently from the older girls around the campus.

She scampered down the tile steps admiring again the stone banisters with carved owl totems leaning back against the end columns. Amongst the crowded rows of shelves on the ground floor she knew exactly where to go to tap the vein of the most promising volumes on ancient Egypt.

She was looking for Sir Alan Gardiner's *Egyptian Grammar*, the title of which she had come across in the library's card catalog. But once again, the book was not on the shelf. Disappointed, she retrieved two frayed old books by E. A. Wallis Budge and took these to the table in the corner, which had become her hostel amongst the stacks. Sitting down, she closed her eyes and reminded herself what she wanted to accomplish. She would not allow herself to be distracted again, reading about these ancient people whom she learned had high ideals and strived to be decent, even to the lowly. Women were also respected and had rights that females achieved in this country only two decades ago!

Trudy skimmed the Budge texts. After turning many pages, she came upon a table which illustrated the twenty-five symbols of the hieroglyphic alphabet. She had learned about the letters weeks before when she read *The Dawn of Civilization*. The table listed the object each symbol stood for and the sounds the characters represented. Finally, she found the key for understanding the writings of the ancient Egyptians!

She carefully copied the table into her notebook. She would later memorize the characters which would allow her to read the old words. That thought popped like a soap bubble when she realized she would still not know what the words meant.

After transcribing the table, she read the chapter on the Egyptian alphabet. To her consternation she discovered that, in addition to the twenty-five symbols, many other hieroglyphs were used alone or in combination with the letters to represent specific words.

By the middle of the afternoon, the time had come for Trudy to pack away her things and head home. She looked over to the bookcases and noticed a librarian returning books in the aisle where the Egyptian volumes were stacked. On a whim, she stood up and walked down the aisle to see if anything of interest had been returned to the shelves.

Trudy didn't know what else to look for besides the Gardner book, and she doubted she would find it back on the self. But there the volume was—a thick, large, gray-blue tome, dominating the other books.

She reached up and slid the book out, impressed by its weight and thrilled that she actually held it in her hands. Hugging the book, she returned to her seat.

Carefully, she opened it up and read the full name of the work on the title page: *Egyptian Grammar: Being An Introduction To the Study of Hieroglyphs.*

"This is it!" she silently screamed.

She read the preface, which described the text as "a book for beginners, an elaborate treatise on Egyptian syntax."

If Trudy had devious scruples, she would have found some way to camouflage the book and sneak her plunder out of the building. But just having the thought embarrassed her. She avoided looking at anybody, afraid someone had read her mind.

The time to head home had long passed. She returned the volume to its place in the stack, said goodbye to Gardener's work, and exited the library, hoping that she could come back soon.

Chapter 9

Sunday

Mid-morning, on the first Sunday of December, Trudy and Andy's mother called them into their parents' bedroom.

"And what do you want for Christmas?" she asked after she sat on the bed.

Until three years ago, Trudy had never been asked. She and her brother were excited to receive whatever little gifts Santa placed under the scrawny Christmas trees. But times had changed. The country had pulled itself out of the Great Depression, and their father had a steady job and she suspected a comfortable income.

Andy bleated out an answer: He wanted a model plane kit. Trudy thought for a second before speaking. Not that she didn't know what she wanted. She just doubted her mother would actually get her the gift.

"I want a book," she finally said.

"A book?" Her mother's tone said more than her words.

"*Egyptian Grammar,* by Sir Alan Gardiner."

"What?" her brother said. "That is the dumbest thing I've ever heard. I thought girls wanted clothes or a purse."

"I want to learn to translate hieroglyphs," Trudy said glancing at him and looking back at her mother who didn't seem to know what to say.

"Gee, I thought you got over that ages ago," the boy groaned.

"Trudy," her mother said, "stop being silly."

"You asked me what I want for Christmas, and that's what I want."

Her mother's piercing eyes glared at the girl.

"Give me your second choice, something I'd be willing to get you."

"My driver's license. That will only cost you a dollar."

"Another woman driver," Andy groaned. "The Wellesley sidewalk will not be. . . ."

"Andy, be quiet. Please," his mother said. "Trudy, you're too young . . ."

"I'm sixteen."

". . .to own a car and I cannot let you drive mine. I need it during the day, and your father and I will not allow you to drive at night."

Trudy glanced away, refusing to look at her mother. Andy would probably get his license when he turned sixteen.

"Tell me something else you want that I will actually get you."

"A radio. But I'd rather have the book." She paused and added, "Or my driver's license."

Through the open bedroom window, Trudy heard the distinctive sound of leather soles grating on concrete. She figured her father had been standing just outside the room, enjoying the warm sunshine while he smoked a stinky cigarette. She noticed the hint of fresh tobacco mingling with the stale smell of old cigarettes that hung in the bedroom. He was probably eavesdropping. She guessed he smiled when he heard her say she wanted the Gardiner book.

*　　*　　*　　*　　*

After the "talk" with her mother, Trudy went to her room and made up new words using the Egyptian alphabet. While other students doodled or pencil sketched cars or dresses, Trudy now exclusively wrote hieroglyphs. She had memorized the twenty-five letters. She knew what she created did not correspond with actual Egyptian words but the exercise gave her mastery writing the symbols and associating them with their sound values. She had also learned more than two hundred Egyptian words she copied from Professor Schneider's hieroglyph dictionary when she babysat.

She had begun to write from right to left. She had learned that the ancient Egyptians did not have a formal rule for how the lines ran, left, right, up or down. It seemed to be more a matter of the writer's taste. Being left-handed, Trudy settled on this orientation. She could rest her hand on the paper and not smudge the ink.

She thought about riding her bike to visit one of her friends, but hesitated. They seemed to be keeping their distance—all but Nancy—like she had stepped in stinky dog poop. No one had told her there was a problem—maybe it was just her imagination playing tricks.

She decided to go in the backyard, sit on the patio chair, and read her mother's *Photoplay* and the new *Life*.

The latest edition of the fan magazine had the usual jumble of ads for movies and articles about movie stars, many supposedly "told to" a journalist by an actor or actress.

Glamour Girls Are Suckers, written by Carole Landis. "They let men hurt them because they don't know how to handle men," the subtitle read. The dreary little account only added to Trudy's negative opinion of romance.

> *I think I have always been a sucker. By a sucker, I mean someone who is very vulnerable, who wears her heart on her sleeve, who is easily hurt, who, in fact, almost asks to be hurt. . .*
>
> .

Trudy refused to finish the article. If big, gorgeous movie stars like Carole Landis were so stupid when it came to men, what chance did ordinary girls have? Trudy thought this knowledge should make her happy that she didn't have a boyfriend. But it didn't.

She turned to the *Life* magazine which had a stiff, arrogantly posed General Douglas MacArthur on the cover. She flipped through the first few pages, ads and letters to the editors. She came to a three-page spread of New York's Time Square at night with photos of servicemen and blazing signs and marquees. Even without the title, she instantly recognized the location. Nothing else in the world looked like New York City.

She skipped through a few more pages of ads. The first big article covered the growing industrial and military power of Japan. She skimmed the text, which restated the growing tension between the United States and Japan, a "stage set for war."

Almost all the other articles concerned the war and the U.S. military. The magazine did nothing to cheer her up.

Finding herself falling in a grumpy mood, she decided to see what her father was doing in his workshop. The door was open, but she had not heard any of the thumps, raspings, or clanking sounds that usually emitted from the little shop when he fiddled away at his workbench.

Her father sat with his back to the door leaning over the drafting table that he had recently set up in the back of the room. Even with the door opened, the room stunk of cigarette smoke. It hung in the air like drying window sheers on a clothesline.

"Hi, Dad. What are you doing? Hiding from mom?"

"How'd you guess?" he answered, picking up his cigarette, taking a draw, and retrieving his pencil to add lines to the paper.

Trudy watched him draw.

"I hear a rumor that you want to learn Egyptian hieroglyphs," he said not looking up from his drawing.

"Yeah," she confessed. Why pretend she didn't?

"You're smart. How about learning mechanical engineering instead? You're good at math."

"Girls don't do that."

"Be the first!"

That idea turned her off. She watched her father use a plastic French curve.

"Doing homework?" In the fall, her father had started a night school drafting class at Santa Monica City College. He probably had to practice what he was learning.

"Just like you and your brother. Well, just like you."

She looked closer over his shoulder. She didn't know much about what he did for work. "What's that?"

"A mechanical drawing," he said picking up a straight edge to add another line. He moved his hand precisely.

"Oh, I see," Trudy said noticing the funny looking metal part that sat on the side of the drafting board. "You're making a drawing of that thingamajig."

"It's a three-dimensional perspective of the servo unit."

Trudy tried to decipher the lines and realized that her father had drawn two sides and a top view of the servo.

"Damn it!" he snapped, slapping down his pencil and grabbing an eraser. "At least this is supposed to be a three-dimensional perspective," he said, removing the line he had just drawn. "Trudy, God bless your heart and all your other vital organs, but could you please go out and help your mother or do something else so I can get this blasted thing done? I'll show you when I get it right."

Trudy went into the house and headed straight for the hall to telephone Alice Long. Her friend picked up on the third ring.

"Hi, Alice. It's Trudy. Hey, how are you doing?"

There was silence on the phone.

"I'm really busy right now," Alice finally said.

"Maybe I can call this evening."

"I got to go, Trudy," Alice replied.

"I'll call you tonight."

The phone had clicked as Trudy spoke. She couldn't be sure her friend heard her. The uneasy feeling she had that something was wrong grew stronger. Usually, Alice had a minute to talk, no matter how busy she was.

Trudy felt suddenly alone.

She wandered into the living room. Her mother had the radio tuned to a classical music program. Her mother liked to listen to the longhair music broadcasted live from New York on Sundays.

"What'cha doing?" Trudy asked, walking in the kitchen. Actually, she could see that her mother was making a Jell-O fruit salad. In the background, a man's voice could be heard during a pause in the radio music.

"What's he saying?" her mother said turning around and looking into the living room, her face suddenly showing concern.

"I wasn't listening."

"Ssssh!"

"... details are not available," the radio voice droned somberly. "They will be in a few minutes. The White House is now giving out a statement. The attack apparently was made on all navel and military activities on the principal island of Oahu. . . ."

"Oh my God," her mother gasped, backing up to sit down on the kitchen stool.

Trudy's heart began to pound. Where was Oahu? Who had been attacked?

Her mother sat frozen, leaning back against the wall. Trudy was petrified and didn't know what to say.

"Mom, what's wrong?" she finally asked

"Oahu is where my brother's ship is stationed. Honolulu."

"Oh."

Her mother remained paralyzed.

"It must have been the Japanese," Trudy speculated, remembering the statement in *Life* that the U.S. and Japan were on the verge of war.

Her mother didn't respond, her eyes focused on nothing in particular.

"You want me to get Dad?"

Her mother nodded.

Trudy ran through the house. The station had resumed its regular broadcast like nothing of any consequence had happened. She jumped down the back steps and bounded to the open workshop doorway.

"Dad!"

"What?" he snapped, his shoulder's pinched together.

"Something bad has happened. The Japanese bombed the American naval base in Oahu."

Her father dropped his pencil and turned around in his chair. His face seemed to go through several transmogrifies, as if he were attempting to grasp the implication of what she had said. He finally looked blank.

"It's on the radio. They interrupted the program to make the announcement." She added, "I guess this means we're at war."

"I can't say I didn't think this would happen," he muttered walking out of the workshop. "Damn it. We've been pushing the Japanese for months, daring them to do something."

The phone rang, and Trudy ran into the house to pick it up. She figured one of her friends had learn the news and wanted to talk.

"Laura?" an older voice said after she answered. It sounded like her aunt, but she lived way out in Claremont. This was an expensive long distance call.

"Aunt Myrna, it's Trudy. I guess you've heard the news about the Japanese attack."

"Yes. Is your mother there?"

"I'll get her."

Her mother and her aunt talked on the phone for what seemed like an hour. Trudy could not imagine how much her aunt's telephone bill would be. When she hung up, her mother came back into the living room still in a daze. Trudy volunteered to make dinner, but her mother said she would be all right.

The radio remained on in the living room. The stations soon stopped interrupting their regular programing for news flashes and devoted their air time to the attack with commentators who kept repeated themselves. Not much was known so not much was said. Someone made an ominous statement about the possibility of sabotage in Los Angeles, especially in the harbor, with all the "Japs" in the area. Trudy reacted to this statement with a queasy feeling. There were many Japanese families who lived in Los Angeles, like the Nakamizos, who had kids with first names like Mary and Daniel. They were not spies.

Finally, at around two in the afternoon, CBS switched to its Washington bureau.

A newsman said, "The President's brief statement was read to reporters by Stephen Early, the President's secretary. A Japanese attack upon Pearl Harbor would naturally mean war. Such an attack would naturally bring a counter attack and hostilities of this kind would naturally mean that the President would ask Congress for a declaration of war. There is no doubt from the temper of Congress that such a declaration would be granted."

There was a pause of a few seconds.

"Just now came word from the President's office that a second air attack has been reported on army and navy bases in Manila."

*   *   *   *   *

After what Trudy considered the worse dinner she ever ate, she had to get out of the house. The tension and cigarette smoke were suffocating.

The afternoon was a beautiful, lazy type of day, unusually sunny and warm for December. The imposing range of mountains, way off beyond Claremont on the east end of Los Angeles County, could clearly be seen. The traffic two blocks away on Bundy Drive moved along as it always did, separating Nakamizos bean fields from the blocks of houses across the street. The breeze curled the branches of the trees and the shrubs. Everything remained the same and unchanged from what Trudy looked at each day. But bombs had fallen on American military installations out in the Pacific and the country was now at war with Japan. How could the world around her be so calm and unaffected?

On impulse, Trudy walked over to the Schneider house, uninvited, something she had never done on a Sunday afternoon. Professor Schneider answered the door and looked at her inquisitively. Trudy heard the same somber voice on the radio that her family had been listening to.

"Professor, I hope I'm not bothering you," she said in German, avoiding eye contact and not admitting she needed to talk and had no one but Helga with whom to converse.

"Come in," the man said, opening the door wider.

"*Danke.*"

"*Bitte.*"

Jonathon and Marlene were playing in the living room close to the shelves of books on Egyptology. Glancing at the collection, Trudy felt no attraction nor interest, although just a few hours ago she had been practicing writing hieroglyphs. The children greeted her and were delighted by the unexpected visit. On the radio, the announcer said something about smoke choking the skies above Honolulu.

Helga stood in the kitchen, finishing her after-dinner cleaning. She glanced into the living room. Her face appeared drawn, maybe even upset, her hair dull and limp, but she did attempt to smile when she saw Trudy. The effort made her look more unsettled. She looked like a tired, overworked woman, not the girlish lady Trudy normally saw.

"Hello, Trudy," she said pleasantly.

"I hope I'm not disturbing you," Trudy said. She sensed that coming over had been a mistake. Helga did not need a confused, worried girl to bother with at this moment.

Helga shook her head and said, "That is fine."

Drying her hands with a dish towel Helga said, "It is not a good day, yes?"

"Yes. The Japanese attack on Hawaii is bad."

"This changes things for America."

Trudy stepped into the kitchen.

"I don't know what's going to happen."

Helga silently watched her.

"My uncle's ship may have been attacked. He's in the Navy. My mother is worried for him. I am too."

"I will pray that he is safe."

"Thank you. With the attack on Honolulu there is fighting now everywhere in the world. I just worry."

"I worry too."

"I guess by coming to America and Los Angeles you thought you could get away from the war."

Helga looked at Trudy for a moment. Trudy wondered what she was thinking and realized that she may have said something she shouldn't have. She felt uncomfortable.

"I never felt we got away from the war," Helga finally said. "We are German citizens. My family still lives in Germany. I just hope . . ."

Helga didn't finish the thought and after a pause silently shook her head.

"I just hope," she started again, "that there will be no complication."

Trudy had no idea what she meant.

"That America and Germany will go to war," the woman clarified.

"That would be bad," the girl replied.

"Trudy, *es gibt Dinge, die geschehen, über den wir keine Kontrolle haben.* I don't know how to say that well in English."

"*There are things which happen over which we have no control,*" Trudy translated, surprised that Helga could not say that in English. "I think that's what you said."

Helga nodded and put the dish towel down.

"We will watch events happen. That's what women do."

The statement hit Trudy like she had been splashed with the hose. She had never thought of herself or other women as nothing more than silent witnesses, but . . . as uncomfortable and as unhappy as the statement made her feel, she realized that what Helga said was exactly the way things were. She would be an observer, watching things unfold as her brother and maybe even her father went off to war.

Chapter 10

The Day After
A Date Which Will Live In Infamy

Back home, Trudy went to her room and spent over an hour writing in her diary. By the time she went to bed, the news about the attack on Pearl Harbor still remained fuzzy. That evening, an NBC reporter had noted that "viewed from a hill, columns of black smoke went skyward from Pearl Harbor."

Before she turned off the light, the high Lama looked down at her, his presence reminding her that only Shangri-La remained protected from modern war.

Trudy woke early the next morning, surprised she had slept so soundly.

She wrapped herself in her fuzzy pink robe and went to the kitchen. Early morning sunlight burned through the living room sheers giving the room an airy glow. She smelled fresh coffee. The radio was turned on and a deep-voiced newsman repeated for the umpteenth time the same information they had been broadcasting since yesterday afternoon.

In the kitchen her mother sat in her robe leaning against Trudy's father who, with a cigarette clumped between his fingers, sat holding open the newspaper as both of them read. Above the banner the Los Angeles Examiner declared in bold letters "War Extra." Below it the even bigger headline screamed, "JAPS, U.S. AT WAR!" The sub-headline read "Bombers Attack Honolulu, Manilla; 2 U.S. Ships Sunk in Pearl Harbor." The girl's heart started beating. Was one of the two ships the Arizona? Stepping closer she read that the two ships were the Oklahoma and the West Virginia. She felt uncomfortable relief knowing that her uncle's ship had not been sunk, while so many sailors had probably been killed on the other vessels.

Trudy heard the slapping of bare feet crossing the living room floor. The sound stopped, followed by the volume on the radio being turned up.

". . . all military personnel on active duty are to return immediately to their post and be in uniform. We repeat. All leaves have been cancelled." There was a pause. "Today the Congress of the United States convenes in a solemn joint session, a session that will hear the President of the United States deliver his message that will ask for a declaration of war with Japan. The galleries started filling early this morning and are now packed. . . ."

Trudy went into the living room and stood next to her brother who looked like a scrawny scarecrow in pajamas. Ignoring his morning snuffling grunts to clear his sinuses, she listened to the newsman and, in her mind, envisioned the members of the House gathering and House Speaker Rayburn calling the chamber to order.

The newsman went on speculating about what the president would say in a few hours.

Her brother plucked sand out of his eye, turned, and walked back into his bedroom. Trudy returned to the kitchen. She noticed a second paper, the Los Angeles Times, spread out on the kitchen table's yellow oil cloth. Her father must have gone up to the corner to buy it. The headline read, "Japs Open War On U.S. With Bombing Of Hawaii. Fleet Speeds Out To Battle Invader." Hopefully her uncle's ship was safely out at sea and would remain safe as the fleet chased the Japanese.

"Let me make you breakfast, dear" her mother said sliding out from behind the table. "You want your eggs sunny side up or scrambled?"

"Scrambled with chopped bacon," he answered not looking up from the news story that had his attention.

"Anything about the Arizona?" Trudy asked.

"No news and that is probably good," her mother said. She looked tired. Trudy doubted that she slept much.

Trudy walked over to the table and sat. She picked up the Times. She carefully read the main article.

Before she finished, her mother told her to get up and start making toast. Standing up she read an alarming paragraph:

"This is the war that Adolf Hitler started in September 1939, exploded at last into a real World War, with the great navies of the United States and Japan seemingly destined to play the major role in what probably will be largely a sea campaign."

That meant that even if the Arizona was safe, great perils lie ahead for the ship and its crew. The paper made it clear the United States *and* Japan had large navies, and the battle between the fleets would be fierce, unlike anything that had been seen in the Atlantic. Japan would not be flattened like a paper doll.

*   *   *   *   *

Riding off to school, Trudy noticed two big sedans parked in front of the Nakamizo house. She wondered who would be visiting so early in the morning.

When she reached the corner of Exposition and Bundy, she glanced south and saw a large army truck crossing the intersection at Pico, then a second and then another. She realized they were part of a convoy.

Instead of turning north to school, she pushed her bike off to the south. Halfway to Pico she had to veer onto a driveway and continue down the sidewalk. Bundy had become blocked with stopped autos as the long line of army vehicles rumbled toward Santa Monica. Several people had gotten out of their cars and were waving.

She watched these heavy, ugly drab green trucks slowly pass, some towing big guns. They billowed nauseating stink from their exhaust pipes. War had not only come to the nation but had rolled into her neighborhood. For as long as she lived, Trudy knew she would remember this unsettling moment. She also began to fear that her family would be forced to move inland.

*   *   *   *   *

At school, somber students clustered into circles, sharing what news and rumors they had heard. The Japanese students kept to themselves and were met with hostile glares. With the exception of Bob Tanaka, one of the school's three yell leaders, and Helen Matsui, an energetic member of Tri-Y, the girl's service club, most did not socialize much outside their circle.

Some students were in a panic state, fearful that the Japanese would invade the coast at any moment or bomb L.A. in the same way London was blitzed by the Germans. Someone spoke of seeing what looked like a plane with Japanese markings flying in from the sea. Another kid said he had heard that Japanese submarines would land troops in Santa Monica during the next new moon.

62

Trudy began to feel-light headed as she listened to the hysteria, but then began to calm as the cooler heads pointed out that it was one thing to bomb an island in the middle of the Pacific and quite another to mount an invasion thousands of miles further east, even with submarines.

"Come on," Karl Black pipped in from outside of the knot of students. "The Germans have far more subs than the *Japs* and have never used them to invade England. They only sink ships in the Atlantic."

Except for Trudy, the others seemed to ignore him. Trudy mentioned the army convoy going west on Pico. Her report reassured some.

"Our coast line and the aircraft factories will be protected," said a boy named Tommy, Joan Fulbright's boyfriend. Joan silently glowered and avoided eye contact with Trudy. Tommy wore his ill-fitting ROTC uniform that day and proudly set an oversize garrison cap on his head. His uniform seemed to give him the authority Karl lacked.

In her first period class, a somber, black-haired Miss Snow silenced the class and stood with her arms crossed, looking over the room with her dark eyes. Nothing about her had the wintry appearance suggested by her name. She told the students she understood that their minds were on yesterday's "awful attack," but they had a responsibility to focus their full attention on their studies.

"We will win this," she said. "Our citizens are the best educated people on the planet. Today you are all students, but most of you boys will become soldiers. sailors, and Marines. Many of you girls will become nurses, secretaries in the airplane factories and take on other jobs supporting our men. What does English have to do with this, you might be thinking? The answer is simple. All of you must know how to write and read in order to do what your country asks of you. 'Sailor, read these orders!' 'Soldier. Here are your instructions!" 'Ladies, write to your sweethearts overseas every day. Their morale needs your support.'"

In second period P.E., all the girls changed into their athletic wear. Stretching, running around the girls' grassy field and playing their sports would not be disrupted by enemy planes.

After ten minutes of calisthenics, the girls were told to form their squads and assemble for their assigned venues. Trudy's group played field hockey. The girls had to strap on shin guards. Most were not good at hitting the ball down the field, and the missed swings of the hockey sticks frequently connected with opponents' legs.

Under the watchful eye of Mrs. Reed, the two teams of seven players caroused around the field. They chased and yelled after the ball that got knocked across the grass. One of Trudy's teammates, the pint size Mary Nakamizo, seemed to get more attention than the ball. Trudy watched two of their own team members deliberately swing their sticks like bats at Mary's legs. Shocked, Trudy wondered why Mrs. Reed did not blow her whistle. She was acting as referee and saw it all.

Trudy ran to Mary's defense and was ready to swing her stick to deflect the blows, but before she could engage, the gym teacher tweeted her whistle. The woman glared at Trudy.

As the girls drifted apart, either ignoring Mary or giving her dirty looks, Trudy stepped up to her and whispered, "I don't hold you or your family responsible for what happened yesterday."

"We are Americans too," the girl said. "The Japanese attacked all of us."

"I know that."

"If I had blonde hair or my last name was Schmidt or Toscanini would anyone question my loyalty?"

Trudy realized that was true.

Mary's sad, angry eyes locked on Trudy's. She was close to tears.

"I'm proud you're my neighbor and my friend," Trudy said.

*   *   *   *   *

It was during third period that Roosevelt addressed the joint session of the Congress. Her trigonometry class marched into a tenth-grade classroom across the hall where there was a radio. Trudy and the other "visitors" stood along the wall.

In somber words, the radio newsman called off the names of the various officials of the government who had assembled in the chamber, filling time until Roosevelt came into the room. Finally, he said, "We take you now to the speaker's platform as the President is arriving." There followed a pause, and then a man with a deep voice declared, "Senators and representatives. I have the distinguished honor of presenting the President of the United States."

Cheers and enthusiastic applause lasted for what seemed like minutes. The choppy noise emitting from the radio sounded like the jumbled racket of a thumping machine.

"Mr. Vice President. Mr. Speaker. Members of the Senate and the House of Representatives," declared the firm, golden baritone that the average American probably recognized more confidently than any movie star. "Yesterday, December seventh, nineteen forty-one, a date which will live in infamy, the United States of America was suddenly and deliberately attacked by naval and air forces of the empire of Japan.. . . ."

Trudy straightened her spine to stand at attention in response to the vocal presence of the President. She carefully listened to his words.

". . . The attack yesterday on the Hawaiian Islands has caused severe damage to American naval and military forces. Very many American lives have been lost. In addition, American ships have been reported torpedoed on the high seas between San Francisco and Honolulu. . . ."

Trudy gasped. She had no idea that ships had been sunk between Hawaii and California. The fear of Japanese submarines off the coast may not have been a mere speculative rumor. What if, in the middle of the night, they landed saboteurs to plant high explosives at Douglas? What if a Japanese commando squad lost direction and ended up in her backyard?

Trudy realized her imagination was getting the better of her. She forced herself to calm down and stay focused on the President's message.

"Yesterday," the President continued, "the Japanese government also launched an attack against Malaya.

"Last night, Japanese forces attacked Hong Kong.

"Last night, Japanese forces attacked Guam.

"Last night, Japanese forces attacked the Philippine Islands.

"Last night, the Japanese attacked Wake Island.

"This morning, the Japanese attacked Midway Island.

"Japan has, therefore, undertaken a surprise offensive extending throughout the Pacific area. . . .

"I ask that the Congress declare that since the unprovoked and dastardly attack by Japan on Sunday, Dec. 7, a state of war has existed between the United States and the Japanese empire."

Returning to their classroom, several of the pumped up male students made confident predictions that "the Japs" would be whipped before they knew what hit them.

"We'll blast those little yellow men with our battleships," someone proclaimed, punching his companion on the shoulder. Trudy remembered her Uncle Billy and hoped that the Arizona was swiftly moving across the broad Pacific Ocean, the ship's racks of giant guns loaded and ready to fire their massive projectiles against the Japanese. This thought caused her to pause. For the first time she realized she had no hesitation about her country aggressively fighting the enemy. Her enemy. Japan.

*   *   *   *   *

After lunch, an unusually somber and no nonsense Miss Ramsey stood by her desk, silently watching the students enter the room and take their seats. Even the more boisterous of Trudy's classmates, upon making eye contact with her, dropped their chatter and quickly moved to their places.

Some weeks ago, Susan French had started calling the teacher "Annie, Queen of the Amazons." Anne Ramsey certainly appeared strong as a stallion. Trudy knew *mare* would be the correct simile, but the word just didn't seem to capture the tawny strength the teacher exuded. Maybe Annie the Amazon was a good nickname. In her early twenties, her face had a freshness without circles under the eyes or permanent frown lines that made most of the teachers appear to be in a continuous state of dreary dissatisfaction.

Watching the teacher before the bell rang, Trudy noted the stiff cast of Miss Ramsey's face and her quick eye movement. She may have been standing in the room, but Trudy had the impression her thoughts were racing around someplace else. Hardly a surprise.

After Miss Ramsey checked the roll, she moved to stand inches away from the front centered desk. The boy seated there seemed to push back in his chair. In a mechanical voice she said, "We were going to discuss article three of the Constitution and the powers of the Supreme Court. You did homework which you do not have to take out. I will ask for it tomorrow. Today's events are a living lesson of a process defined by the Constitution, for the declaration of war. . . ."

Miss Ramsey became visibly frustrated when the students she called upon could not explain the process by which the country went to war. Trudy found this hard to believe, especially after hearing Roosevelt's powerful speech. They assumed the President of the United States had already declared war! Mary Nakamizo, in her stilly voice which she attempted to raise without being shrill, correctly identified that Clause 11 of Section 8, Article 1 of the Constitution gave Congress the power to declare war. For a moment Miss Ramsey's expression softened as she thanked the girl for her answer. Mary then said something that must have shocked some of the students.

"My family came to this country from Japan in 1887. We are citizens. My father and mother vote. My brother is a sergeant in the United State army and stationed at Fort Knox, Kentucky. I am utterly angry at Japan and its fascist government which have brought total disgrace to its people and those like me who are Americans of Japanese descent."

Silence. Someone coughed. Miss Ramsey seemed like she was about to cry and said, "Mary, I can only imagine how hard this is for you. Thank you for speaking up."

The remainder of the class hour was spent comparing the current situation to 1917 when the United States declared war on Germany.

Watching Miss Ramsey, Trudy noticed her eyes become troubled and vacant and her movement go from still and calm to nervous, darting, and restless like the stomping of a caged stallion. Although Miss Ramsey did not wear a wedding band or an engagement ring, Trudy wondered if she had a sweetheart, maybe a Marine or naval officer stationed in Hawaii, or the Philippines, or another outpost in the Pacific at risk of being attacked by the Japanese.

"We are a brave people," the teacher said before the class ended, "and we must rise to the occasion as one nation to defend our land and to defend democracy. Remember, all of us in this room, all of us, are descendants of immigrants who came to these shores to have a better life. Believe me when I say we are more alike than different and stronger because we are united."

After class, Trudy vented to Susan about how difficult the last twenty-four hours had been. Scowling, Susan just nodded.

"Is there something wrong?" Trudy asked.

Susan looked down for a moment and then said.

"You know," she answered looking up, "I think this is the first time you have not mentioned Egypt or hieroglyphs in months. It's gotten old, Trudy."

She didn't know what to say. She suddenly felt small.

Chapter 11

War

With the terrible turn of events that began with the Pearl Harbor attack over shadowing everything, an incident happened during those early days in December that, while trivial in the scheme of things, was most troubling to Trudy. Two days after December 7, she found herself confronted with the unpleasant reality that the distance she sensed between her and her friends was not imagined.

With Alice Long standing on her right, Joan Fulbright snipped, "Look, missy, we have really grown tired of your Queen of the Nile chatter. None of us want to hear any more about mummy land, or the sphinx, or that secret code you scribble in your notebook and draw on the blackboards."

Trudy thought it was cute to put a hieroglyph or two on the chalk board when the teacher wasn't looking. Her signature fixture was the first glyph she had learned, the one that stood for woman.

"Stop acting like you're a cult priestess—it's weird!"

She didn't think of herself as dabbling into anything magical or superstitious. Her interest was "scholarly," a word she had come to use when thinking about her pursuit. But after being confronted by Joan, she realized others didn't think of her interest as scholastic. A lot of kids had started calling her "Nefertiti," which she now realized was not said endearingly. She guessed everyone at the school thought of her as some kind of freak. As if the country going to war with Japan wasn't enough of a burden, she now had to contend with the hostility her passion had brought down on her.

With tears, she meekly apologized and silently pledged to herself that she would never mention Egyptology or hieroglyphs to anyone again.

That afternoon, after the scene with Joan and Alice, Trudy came home to find her street invaded by the army. Ugly military trucks rolled over the curbs and drove over Nakamizo's field, their giant tires flattening the freshly plowed furrows and stitching a crisscrossing pattern of tracks on the lots. Soldiers pulled out equipment and crates from the back of the trucks while other doughboys dug trenches and holes and put up tents. One would have thought that the circus had come to town, if their gear wasn't so drab and the fear of a Japanese attack so real.

She learned from her mother that the army was positioning anti-aircraft guns and search lights in the neighborhood. The Nakamizo family had been ordered to move. Trudy immediately went over to their house. Mary told her that Wellesley fell within a designated military zone, and all people of Japanese descent had to vacate, regardless of their citizenship. Trudy would have been hysterical if her family had been told this. The Nakamizos were moving to Japantown, south of University High, where they would stay with friends.

When Trudy's father came home that afternoon from Douglas, he helped load the Nakamizo truck and allowed the farmer to park his tractor on the dirt patch behind the garage. He also stored their farm tools in the garage. Trudy helped Mary and her mother pack up the kitchen. She realized that in the all the years she had known the Nakamizos, she had never been in their kitchen.

"What are we going to do with all of this?" Mary's mother said in her soft voice looking at all the food in the pantry. There were boxes of food stuff, including many that had Japanese characters printed on the label.

"When this is all over," Trudy overhead her father tell Harry, "I'll come over and drank that damn warm sake you keep pushing on me."

The old man smiled and said, in his gravelly voice, "Good."

Before the Nakamizos drove away, the two men shook hands. Some of the soldiers in the fields watched, a few sneered. Her father seemed indifferent to their reaction. Walking home with Trudy he said, "The oldest Nakamizo boy is a staff sergeant. He outranks all those gawking green draftees."

She did not think of her father as a paladin, but that day he made her proud. His standing up for the Nakamizos was the only good thing that had happened that week. And things were about to get worse.

*   *   *   *   *

The following morning, riding her bike to school, Trudy was

shocked that windows in the Nakamizo house had been broken, no doubt by the soldiers. With all the racket from their camp, the sound of the glass breaking had gone unnoticed. The sight made her sick. She was tempted to find the officer in charge and complain but feared that making a stink would only cause trouble. Feeling powerless and angry, she remembered, bitterly, what Helga said about females. They only watched. Maybe her father would raise hell with the troops. After all, they were stationed on those empty lots to defend US citizens, not antagonize them.

At school, Susan talked with her, but her other "friends," except Nancy and Mary, continued to give her the cold shoulder. In P.E. she paired with Mary causing the other girls and the gym teacher to glare at her like she had decided to side with the enemy. Trudy did not tell Mary that the windows of her house had been broken. Things had to be hard enough for her without learning that her home had been vandalized. The wasting of the fields of crops that Mary's father spent weeks plowing, planting and tending was bad enough.

At lunch Trudy sat by herself at the end of the table occupied by some younger girls about her brother's age. It was a bench that was as far away as she could get from where she and her friends normally ate. She couldn't help but think that in one week her whole world had been turned upside down. She felt locked inside a snow globe that had been violently shaken.

Trudy had been picking at her tuna fish sandwich when Nancy came over with her lunch bag and sat down across from her.

"What are you doing over here?" Nancy asked.

Trudy shrugged.

"I don't want to eat with them either. I heard what Joan said to you. I know you're a little goofy, but I think your Egyptian stuff's cute. I'm impressed that you can read those hieroglyphs. If I call you Nefertiti it's because I like you."

"You can call me Nefertiti," Trudy said, not looking up, afraid she would start to cry.

"Okay, Nefertiti." Nancy opened her lunch bag. She pulled out a green apple, a Helm's Bakery cupcake and a sandwich wrapped in wax paper.

"Gary's not waiting until he's twenty-one to be drafted," Nancy said somberly. "He's going to enlist in the army."

Trudy looked up. Nancy daintily pulled the wax paper off her sandwich.

"Do you want him to do that?"

"No," Nancy answered, "But a lot of guys are signing up. We're at war. Millie Ward's dad enlisted in the Marine Corp. Can you believe it? A man our fathers' age joining the military?"

Trudy wondered if her father would, but then he had an important job designing military aircraft. He could do more for the country by staying put.

"Just a few days ago nobody would have thought our men and boys would be falling over each other to get a chance to fight in the war," Nancy added. "Pearl Harbor changed everything."

Chapter 12

Knox's Admission

F riday morning, a report in the Los Angeles Examiner reignited Trudy's mother's worry. A page one story gave credence to a rumor that had been whispered the last couple of days.

> *Japanese naval claims have included the sinking of the U.S.S. Arizona and the sinking of two other American capital ships, in addition to destruction of an aircraft carrier, a cruiser and several destroyers. Washington, on the other hand, has announced the loss of but one battleship, described as an old man-of-war, during the attack on Pearl Harbor. In view of the extravagance of previous Tokyo claims, officials heavily discounted the Japanese broadcast.*

"But Washington is not denying the sinking of the Arizona," Trudy's mother said, her voice somber and stern.

"I wouldn't take any stock in that claim from Tokyo," Trudy's father said, setting down his coffee cup and picking up his cigarette from the ashtray. "Washington reports only an old man-of-war got sunk. Probably some relic from before the First World War."

Trudy could tell this did not reassure her mother.

"I won't feel sure that Billy is safe until I get a letter written in his own hand," her mother said.

Worry made Trudy's stomach churn. She feared the worst. Other stories in the paper reported that Japan had widened its offensive. Washington minimized the seriousness of the situation but it was clear from the stories that the fighting in the Pacific had boiled over and American forces were being pressed on all fronts. The fate of the Arizona remained uncertain, despite the denials, and Trudy understood her mother's insistence on hard proof before she believed that her brother was safe.

*   *   *   *   *

The next day, Trudy stood in the living room, between her mother and Andy, looking at the Christmas tree. They had just decorated the evergreen with twinkling colored lights, glass balls, strings of popcorn, and tinsel icicles. The fragrant fir radiated Christmas joy but failed to touch her with the spirit of the season.

The Mansfield and Schneider houses were now nestled within the iron arms of a military outpost. The battery's big guns, ugly tents, and army vehicles parked on the fields of trampled lima bean and cabbage were daily reminders of the war. The neighborhood was totally changed. Piles of wooden crates were stacked on the lots. Smoke whiffed out of a stove pipe poking from the roof of what had to be the soldiers' mess tent. Guards with rifles slung over their shoulders paced around the perimeter, looking bored as if they longing to be stationed some place other than on that dreary edge of the world.

Trudy watched the soldiers practice loading the guns. Each anti-aircraft piece had a designated crew, and each member of the crew had a specific task. There was a lot of yelling as they fumbled targeting the barrow, loaded the breech and jumped back as the squad leader screamed "bang!" They performed this dance over and over again.

*   *   *   *   *

On Monday morning, as Trudy biked off to school, a couple of soldiers whistled at her. This was so unexpected she didn't know how to react and quickened her pace. Returning to the neighborhood that afternoon, she briskly rode her bike with dread, anticipating that she would be accosted again. She stopped at the Schneider's house and raced to the front door.

Helga looked tired and uneasy. Trudy deliberately spoke German although this visit was probably an English-speaking day. A few days before, Hitler had declared war on the United States, and Friday Congress responded, voting unanimously to go to war with Germany and Italy. Trudy didn't want Helga to feel that this made any difference in their friendship.

"How was your day at school?" Helga asked.

"Routine," she answered, intentionally being vague. Only Mary, Susan, and Nancy were talking to her.

Helga looked out of sorts. Hitler declaring war on the U.S.

certainly would not have lifted her spirits. Trudy kept the visit brief and dashed off to her house.

The really bad news came within minutes after she walked into the living room. A radio news-flash announced Secretary of the Navy, Franklin Knox, admitted that the Japanese attack on Pear Harbor had been far worse than the government had earlier reported. Almost three thousand service men were killed and six warships sunk, including Billy's ship, the Arizona.

Hearing this, her mother sat down and stared at the radio. Trudy did not know what to do or say, numbed herself by the news and the possibility that her uncle had been killed. After a moment, her mother stood up, a tear on her cheek, and went to telephone her sister.

After her mother got off the phone, she walked into the kitchen and carried out the motions of preparing dinner.

*   *   *   *   *

For the next few days, Trudy sensed her mother thought only about Uncle Billy.

"How are you doing today, Laura?" asked the butcher at the Food Palace. Holding the grocery bag, Trudy stood next to her mother, attentive to what she would say.

"Not good, Sam. My brother was on the Arizona."

"Oh, my gosh!"

"I'll take four lamb chops. Not too fatty."

"I'm so sorry about your brother. Is he all right?"

"We don't know. Most of the men on the ship were killed. I fear the worse."

"Let's hope he survived. Tell me when you find out."

"I'll let you know."

"He's a hero, you know."

Her mother silently nodded.

"Damn Japs," the butcher muttered, selecting four chops.

The attack on Pearl Harbor made the Japanese seem a much greater enemy than the Nazi Germans or Fascist Italians. People may have hated Hitler and thought Mussolini a pompous brute, but they held a special contempt for Japanese Prime Minister Tojo, who instantly became the buck-toothed, bespectacled face of evil drawn in editorial cartoons.

Trudy wondered when her family would finally get some word about her Uncle Billy, a man who had become one of America's first heroes of the war, a gallant sailor of the doomed battleship Arizona.

Chapter 13

Blackouts

The whole nation may have been at war, but the Mansfields actually lived in a war zone. Whenever Trudy walked out the front door, the guns and troops, poised to go into action, reminded her that they were on the edge of the battle and at any moment could be caught in the middle of the fighting.

What frightened Trudy more than the guns were the blackouts. The first outage occurred two days after the bombing of Pearl Harbor, unceremoniously placing the city in total darkness. With the distant wailing sirens, streetlights going off and news flashes instructing people to stay inside their darkened houses, Trudy anticipated that at any moment the guns in the fields would begin to fire. Huddling in the darkness under her bedcovers she watched the radium dial of her alarm clock and felt her pulse race as she thought of the newsreels of the London Blitz. The Germans may have lost the Battle of Britain, but their planes inflicted terrible destruction. What if the same thing happened to her city?

Each blackout was an unnerving false alarm. The U.S. fleet had been smashed at Pearl Harbor—Secretary Knox denied this, but the Navy's initial disclaimer of the real losses weakened his credibility. The big question remained: Where was the Japanese fleet and its aircraft carriers? Those floating islands were lost in the vastness of the Pacific Ocean. For all anyone knew, the enemy's armada of planes could have been positioned off the coast of California, just waiting for the right moment to attack. Everyone feared that one night a blackout would be the precursor to an actual attack.

A few days before Christmas, Trudy went to Nancy's house after school. She intended to come home before dark, but she got caught up in a deep conversation with her friend. Nancy had at one point asked Trudy what her ideas were about love.

Trudy hesitated, not because she had not given the subject any thought but because she had never told anyone her opinion. She studied Nancy, wondering if she would laugh.

"Did you ever see *Modern Times*?" she finally said. "The Charlie

Chaplin movie?"

"A long time ago."

"Do you remember the last scene in which the Tramp and his girl had to run away and are sitting on the side of the roadway, way out in the country?"

Nancy nodded.

"She's discouraged and says it's hopeless. Charlie gets this concerned look and tells her to 'buck up and never say die. We'll get along.' He's so convincing, she starts to perk up."

Nancy looked confused.

"That's my idea of being in love," she added, feeling exposed. "Two people struggling and supporting each other when life gets hard. Remember how the movie ends? They walk away, down an empty road, arm in arm, united to face whatever new trial or lucky chance awaits them."

Nancy did not laugh. Instead she grimaced and looked down.

"I don't think that's possible, with the war and the way things are today," she finally said.

Once again, the reality of America at war challenged something she believed deeply.

Nancy worried about Gary. He had signed his enlistment papers and could be ordered to report for duty at any moment.

"The newspaper says that every day there are crowds at the train stations and bus depots with all the mothers, fathers and sweethearts wishing the soldiers and sailors luck."

Tears appeared in the corners of Nancy's eyes.

"When the time come to wish Gary off," she sputtered, "I know I'll make a scene. That might be the last time I'll ever see him. Trudy, he may not come back from the war!"

Trudy thought about her Uncle Billy but kept her personal concern to herself. She took her friend's hand and squeezed her fingers.

*   *   *   *   *

Mrs. Pierce invited Trudy to stay for dinner, and Trudy's father said he would pick her up at 7:00. That was early enough to avoid a blackout, if one got called that night.

The Pierce Christmas tree glowed in the corner of the otherwise

78

dark living room as they ate in the kitchen. Dispirited, Nancy listened to the others chat, saying nothing. No one mentioned Gary.

Promptly at seven, Trudy's father honked his horn.

Walking outside, Trudy became enveloped in the darkness of the night. The day was almost the shortest of the year. There was no moon, and a mist hid the stars. Lights from the houses and her father's car provided the only illumination.

Trudy opened the car door and was instantly assaulted by a cloud of cigarette smoke. Glenn Miller issued pale and tinny from the radio.

She slid onto the upholstered bench and turned her hips to find a tolerable position. The passenger's seat was lumpy and not as comfortable as the seat in her mother's car. She put her school stuff on the floor. "Thanks for picking me up. I'm glad you didn't have class tonight."

"Classes have taken a backseat for now. I'm working late most nights. In the future I won't be able pick you up."

The car had been moving along Olympic, still a few blocks east of Bundy, when an announcer interrupted the music. The siren began to wail. The sound was much loader than heard at the Mansfield's house.

"By order of the Federal Communication Commission and the Fourth Interceptor Command, there will be a complete blackout immediately from Bakersfield to San Diego and as far east as Boulder City and Las Vegas."

"Damn it," her father snapped. As if he chanted an incantation, the street lamps and signal lights went off. He slowed to a crawl and turned off the headlights. The other autos on the street dropped their lights. Most pulled over to the curb. All that could be seen in the blackness were occasional brake lights.

The Ford was soon surrounded by a blackened void with the only source of light in the car coming from the tip of her father's cigarette. Trudy could see the vague hint of his frown. Down the street, a car with its lights still on continued to move toward them. Didn't the driver get the message about the blackout?

"Shouldn't you pull over?" she asked. Her father did not have Superman vision and couldn't see any better than she. There had been car crashes and people killed in the earlier blackouts.

"My eyes will adjust."

"Dad, there is no light! Pull over, please!"

She could feel the car slowing.

"I can't even see the damn curb," he finally muttered.

The lights of the car ignoring the blackout gave the only reference to where they were on the street. Trudy thought she saw the hint of another car, no more than a blacker form against the night.

"Dad, I think there's a car in front of you. Stop!"

He hit the brake and leaned over the steering wheel, his action traced by the cigarette tip. It was impossible to see anything outside.

"Trudy open the car door and tell me what you see."

She didn't understand, but then realized the dome light would go on, breaking the blackout rule but allowing her to see what was around them. Her father had rolled down his window and stuck his head out, waiting for her to open the door.

She twisted the handle and pushed the door open. The light went on. She immediately saw that the car was headed at an angle toward the curb and pointed at a car maybe fifteen feet ahead. She could make out the hint of an eerie face looking out the rear window.

"You're maybe five feet from the curb, but there's a car parked in front of you. Dad, turn the wheel to the left to straighten out. Then back up."

Just like he was parallel parking, he backed up and at Trudy's direction turned the wheel to avoid hitting the curb. He turned off the engine.

Trudy got back in the car.

"We're a good team," he said, lighting another cigarette.

"What are we going to do? The blackout may last all night."

"We're going to walk home," he said, opening his door and causing the dome light to go on again. "We just have to cross this street and Bundy. We'll hear when cars are coming, so we'll know when it's safe to run across."

Trudy would have preferred to stay in the car, even though she was getting cold, but she chose to go along with her father's.

Trudy had no way of keeping track of time, but for what seemed like an hour, they walked in the dark. The whole time she kept fearing one of them would fall down and break a bone. At her father's instruction, she walked by sliding her feet on the ground so that her toe would bump into something before she tripped over it. The sound of their shoes shuffling was as unpleasant as chalk screeching on a blackboard.

Crossing Olympic was unnerving, a broad boulevard, which, that night, seemed as wide as a football field. She feared a car would come racing in the dark, its driver even more stubborn than her father. But no cars crossed their path. Her father used his lighter like a flashlight. With his free hand holding hers, he led her briskly across the asphalt. They continued to hold hands as they walked down the sidewalk. There was just enough light from the sky to allow them to keep their bearings. At one point her father started to laugh.

"We never made the father-daughter dance," he said, "but I guess I'm making up for that."

"Thanks, Dad," she said. She didn't think his wise crack funny.

When they finally crossed Bundy and reached Exposition, Trudy felt like she was on her home grounds. She could almost count the steps it would take to get to Wellesley and to her house. Then she remembered her schoolbooks and papers were still in her father's car. Before she could say something, a voice barked, "Who's there?"

"What the?" her father said, stopping.

Two flashlights interrupted the darkness, their beams pointed at Trudy and her father. The light was bright and caused Trudy to turn her head and squint. When the light was momentarily pointed to the ground, she could make out two soldiers, blocking the sidewalk, each with a rifle strapped over his shoulder.

"This is a restricted area," one said in a twang, a vocal tone from some place over the Rocky Mountains. With the flashlights pointed back at her face, she couldn't tell which one spoke.

"We live over there on Wellesley," her father said.

"You always take strolls at night?"

"Of course not. We got caught in the blackout. I parked the car on Olympic."

"Well, we can't let you pass."

"What do you mean? We live next to your guns, for Christ's sake. My wife and son are home. You can escort us to our front door, if you wish."

"We can't leave our post."

Trudy noticed her father fishing out his wallet from his hip pocket. One of the soldiers slipped his rifle off his soldier and pointed it toward him. Trudy's heart began to beat harder.

"Don't move."

"I want you to see my driver's license. It shows my address."

"Drivers' licenses only have thumb prints. How do I know it's yours?"

Trudy could not believe this. She and her father looked as American as apple pies and didn't carry anything that could be a bomb or a gun. Her father asked if he could take out his wallet. After being given permission, he did it in a deliberate manner, so the two armed soldiers could see he was not up to any tricks. Flipping open the billfold, he pulled out a card and held it out to the sentry pointing the gun.

"That's a photo ID. I work at Douglas Aircraft. This red badge means I have top secret clearance." He added in an angry voice, "You want to see my driver's license to prove that I live where I say I live?"

"We have our orders, sir," said the man, not much older than a boy. "We'll let you go on. But do not leave your house after dark again."

"And if I have to work late? We are at war, and my job is critical at this moment."

"You'll have to take that up with our captain." The soldier obviously had no intent of being helpful.

"Thank you," her father replied, his tone anything but thankful. Trudy knew from the strain in his voice that her dad was steaming.

When they got home, the house was dark. Trudy's mother had not been able to find the blackout cloth needed to make drapes to cover the windows, so all the lights were out. The only illumination came from the radio dial, giving the room a faint yellow cast.

"What took you so long?" her mother asked.

It didn't reassure her, when her father told what happened after they crossed Bundy.

Trudy felt her way to her room and closed the door. She lay on the bed and knew that on the darkened wall, the high Lama was looking down at her. "Be kind," she chanted, telling herself that the soldiers were only doing what they had been ordered to do. Then she had an ugly thought. Maybe the sentries had seen her and her father help the Nakamizos and intentionally hassled them, considering them "Jap lovers." The thought made her mad. If she was braver, she would look up those two soldiers after school, demand to see their commanding officer and file a formal harassment complaint against them.

Sucking in a breath, she whispered again, "Be kind."

1942

Chapter 14

Enemy Aliens

This is an expensive camera. I can't take it."
Trudy tried to hand the Leica back to Helga who just shook her head.

"I'm only asking you to keep it for us."

"I understand. But if I drop it!"

"I don't think you will drop it, but if you do, it won't break."

Trudy looked down at the sleek, heavy device with its shinny steel dials and metal lens barrel. She shook her head.

"Use it, please." Helga picked up the leather case with a shoulder strap and handed it to Trudy. "There is a close-up lens, film canisters and instructions in German, but nothing you cannot read."

Helga watched Trudy walk to her house, carrying the camera case as if she were balancing a tray of delicate stemmed glasses.

Helga trusted Trudy with the camera, but giving it to her reflected an ugly reality she had hoped she would never face again. For the second time in little more than two years, Helga found her family declared enemy aliens.

Hours after the attack on Pearl Harbor, all Japanese, Italian, and German nationals living in the United States had been categorized as enemies by President Roosevelt. At the end of December, the enemy aliens residing in the Pacific Coast states were ordered to turn over to the police their short-wave radios and cameras. Helga chose to give the camera to Trudy. That way, the device might be put to good use.

The day after the Japanese attacked Pearl Harbor, Max read in the morning paper the news of their new enemy status. With somber eyes and a voice void of emotion, he told Helga there was a possibility that there could be trouble. They were not émigrés stripped of their citizenship, but German nationals with German passports branded with the Nazi swastika. Helga worried that an order would soon be put out demanding all enemy nationals to report to a public stadium or a fair ground converted to house aliens. That was what the French had done in 1939.

Later that morning, Helga watched from the children's bedroom

87

as government agents searched the Nakamizo's house. As the old man and his son escorted the investigators around the property, she could see that they were trying to cooperate. When the agents left, they took a table radio and the small caliber rifle Mr. Nakamizo used to shoot gophers and ground squirrels. Helga ran to the bathroom and threw up.

All day, she waited for the agents to come knocking on her door, but no one came except Trudy, who spoke in German about her day at school. She also told Helga that she worried for the Nakamizos. Many people had bad feelings toward the local Japanese, despite the fact that most were born here and were American citizens. The bad feelings did not surprise Helga. Germany wouldn't even grant citizenship to Asians.

Trudy did not seem concerned about the Schneider's safety nor did she make any mention of their status as enemy aliens. Maybe she was unaware.

Through the rest of December, Helga woke up each morning, nauseated.

*   *   *   *   *

Bitterly, Helga remembered their predicament in France, and the difficulty they had leaving the country to come to the United States. As the outbreak of war got closer, Helga was certain they would return to Germany, but then Max shocked her with the news that he had accepted a new academic appointment at an obscure school in California. He packed up their books, his cases of potsherd hieroglyphic notes, and the family's larger personal possessions and arranged for their shipment to the United States.

But then on Tuesday, September 5, two days after France declared war on Germany, and weeks ahead of their embarkation date, the Schneiders found themselves classified as hostile foreigners by the French government. For years, Germans had lived in France as refugees from the Nazis with no issue. Now, they were identified as a threat to the nation's security. Max realized he had to get the family out of the country immediately. This proved impossible.

Overnight, posters were put up throughout Paris stating all male "enemy aliens" needed to report to the Stade de Colombes, a sports stadium which had been the main arena for the 1924 Olympic game, but now served as a prison camp.

Max took his documents to the local prefect of police hoping he would be issued an exit permit but instead received stern instructions to go to Colombes. Before following the policeman's order, he returned to the apartment and told Helga there was a good chance that he would be detained at the Colombes. Maybe for days.

"You are no enemy to France," Helga said in protest.

"These are strange times. The French have to sort things out. I'll be all right. Have faith."

What followed was a nightmare. At the stadium, Max found himself one of the thousands of refugees and resident German nationals. Helga had hoped he would quickly be granted an exit permit and allowed to leave the country. Instead, he became a prisoner.

For more than three weeks he remained in the Stade de Colombes, much of the time sitting in the stadium seats with a group of other academics who had somehow found each other. The camp had inadequate shelters, no hygienic facilities, and no one with any authority to whom Max could argue his case. There was no way to get word to Helga, who sat at home with the children, terrified that Max was in danger. She stretched the little money he had left her, purchasing only the bare essential, subsisting primarily on bread she made each day and a bit or two of meat or vegetables she purchased for the children.

And then one evening, as Helga read to Marlene and Jonathon from her battered copy of *Der Struwwelpter*, Max finally walked into the apartment, smelling horrid and looking more disheveled than he had ever been during his wildest days in Egypt. But he had their exit permit. Helga embraced him tightly and cried. Max cleaned up, drank strong coffee, and the first thing the next morning went to the steamship line's office where he arranged passage on an ocean liner sailing the following day.

The Schneiders took a train to Bordeaux where they boarded the S.S. Roosevelt. Once in their stateroom, Helga dropped to her knees, made the sign of the cross, and thanked God for their deliverance.

*   *   *   *   *

A week into the Wellesley military occupation, Nelly made

another surprise visit. This time, she did not come into the house smiling or chatting about insignificant pleasantries. Panicked, she said instead, "I am worried sick."

Nelly looked through the window at the soldiers and guns and shook her head. Helga asked her to sit down, but she paced to the other window instead like one of the American soldiers had stalked her. She finally turned.

"Did you hear that government agents arrested Doctor Kaufmann?" she asked, her eyes unusually somber. "For no apparent cause. And he's Jewish!"

Helga shook her head and hid her distress. She did not want to get caught up in Nelly's anxiety, an anxiety which surprised Helga. This was the woman who saved her husband's life by half carrying him across the Pyrenees.

"Why would they arrest Doctor Kaufmann?" Nelly asked.

"Maybe Doctor Kaufmann is not who he passes himself off to be. Maybe he is an *Abwehr* agent[*]." Or maybe he was the first of many who would be rounded up because they were German nationals. Helga could not allow herself to think this.

Fortunately, Nelly's visits tended to be brief. She barely sat on the sofa before she stood up and moved toward the door, saying that she had to chauffeur Heinrich to the studio in the San Fernando Valley where he was contracted but had yet to be given any writing assignment.

*   *   *   *   *

A month after the United States entered the war, a few German and Italian nationals had been arrested, but most, at that point, had been left alone. They were restricted, without approval of the U.S. Attorney's office, to travel beyond the limits of their home communities. Otherwise, they could carry on their normal lives.

*   *   *   *   *

Two ugly guns had been planted between the Schneider and Mansfield houses and more across the street on both sides of the

[*]German military intelligence spy

Lewis's home. The big guns and giant searchlights were pointed vigilantly at the sky.

Helga had never been in a war zone and despaired that, after traveling across a great ocean and a mighty continent, she had not escaped the horrors of cold, modern warfare.

At least her distress did not affect the children. Jonathon leaned on the window sill, fascinated with the soldiers and their guns and equipment. He would salute at any soldier that happened to look in his direction. Marlene only seemed curious that the soldiers lived in tents.

Chapter 15

Opportunity and Shame

Lunch period was almost over. Trudy pulled a notebook out of her locker. Slamming the door shut and twisting the lock, she slumped off to the business arts building where she had typing class. She had reluctantly agreed to take the course, something her advisor told her would help her get a job after she graduated high school. Trudy protested, saying she wanted to go to college. Actually, Trudy hadn't given college any serious thought. She just knew she didn't want to be some girl working in an office.

As if the advisor possessed extrasensory perception and saw through Trudy, she said, "You got to think about your future. A girl cannot have enough practical work skills while she waits for the day to come when she starts a family."

Trudy noticed the advisor didn't wear a wedding band.

"You'll thank me a year after you graduate," she said, putting Trudy's name on the typing class roll sheet.

The new school term hadn't started off any better than the old one had ended. Most of the girls acted distant, although they no longer looked through her like was she invisible. They would respond curtly, if she said something at lunch, but only Susan, Mary, and Nancy would actually engage her in conversation.

In the privacy of her bedroom, Trudy continued to practice writing hieroglyphs, a passion she could only feed a little bit at a time, given her limited access to Professor Schneider's books and the inability to go to UCLA. The hieroglyphs distracted her from the ugly news about the war, including an upsetting report of a proposal to draft single American women for wartime work. There had also been a chilling story of a plane-submarine battle south of Santa Monica verifying that the Japanese were, indeed, patrolling the California coast. Where was the Japanese aircraft carrier strike force? The frequent blackouts meant the army still considered Los Angeles in danger.

She wished she could babysit the Schneider children and have another look at Professor Schneider's books. She had exhausted her notes and could do no more than make up play words with the

Egyptian alphabet.

The typing lab was in one of the portable classrooms that bordered the teachers' parking lot. The wood slat buildings were either miserably cold or unbearably hot, depending on the season.

A few of the students had already sat down at their L.C. Smith typewriters and begun to practice, clattering away on the keys, clicking much faster than Trudy was able. These were the girls she knew wanted to be secretaries.

Trudy took her place behind the typewriter assigned to her. Karl Black sat at the machine next to hers.

She opened the typing instructional book to an exercise page and began to slowly peck away, resisting the urge to glance down at the keys.

"Trudy, could I borrow a couple sheets of paper?"

Trudy stopped typing. Karl gave her a lopsided, weird smile and looked like he had just asked for five dollars.

"Sure," she said, pulling some paper out of her notebook. She turned back to her typewriter.

"Thanks," he said. "This is the first time I've forgotten paper. I'll give you some tomorrow."

"You don't need to."

Trudy started typing again. She hardly finished a line before Karl said to her, "I don't know about you, but typing is harder than I thought it would be."

His words broke her concentration. She pulled out the paper and decided to wait for the teacher to begin class. She glanced at Karl.

"Why are you taking this class?" He was one of the few boys in the room. Trudy couldn't imagine a boy becoming a secretary.

"I want to be a playwright," he said.

"You mean, write plays?"

She remembered seeing him hanging around the back of the theater building and guessed he had become one of the miscreants who worked on the school plays.

"You can't write longhand anymore." He looked into her eyes, his face suddenly uncomfortably close. "You have to type. I understand most writers hunt and peck. . ." He demonstrated this with his forefingers dancing over the keys. "They can type away really fast, like Ben Hecht, the big Hollywood screenwriter, but I figured I could type even faster if I use all my fingers and thumbs. Ideas come to me so quickly."

Karl smiled and seemed embarrassed. He pulled back.

"You want to be a writer? That's interesting," she said.

This conversation would have ended if Trudy hadn't glanced down to the books stacked next to his typewriter. She noticed the letters stamped on the fore-edge of one of the books: "Southern Branch of the University of California." She reached across the table and slid the book from the pile. The binding was old and the pages soft, like they had been thumbed many times by many hands.

"This is not a book you normally find around here," she said, reading the title on the spine and flipping through the pages. It was a history of the Tudors.

"I'm doing a history paper on Henry the Eighth."

"This didn't come from the school library."

"It came from UCLA. My dad checked it out. He teaches there. Chemistry."

How lucky, Trudy thought.

"He's been getting me books since I was at Emerson Junior High."

"Your dad can get you any book you want?" Trudy asked beginning to think that there may be an advantage knowing Karl.

"Any book in the UCLA Library."

Trudy handed the Tudor text back to Karl and smiled. He was a thin boy with rusty hair and uneven facial features. Until that moment, he probably hadn't caught the attention of any girl at school. To Trudy, he suddenly looked like the Frog Prince.

*   *   *   *   *

Returning home after school, Trudy paid no attention to the soldiers, their big guns or the searchlights that looked like giant base drums, although she remained aware of the possibility that some *dogface* would whistle—it now happened all the time.

The neighborhood appeared especially grim under the dull overcast sky. The ground was muddy from recent rain and the air was cold and biting.

After stopping to talk briefly with Helga, Trudy went home. The mailman had just dropped letters into the letterbox. She retrieved the mail and, thumbing through the correspondences and bills, squealed when she saw a Navy envelope addressed to her mother. Her uncle's name was scribbled in the left-hand corner. He was alive! She ran into the house.

"Mom, Mom," she yelled. "There's a letter from Uncle Billy!" Her mother ran out of the kitchen and grabbed the envelope.

She ripped the seal and pulled out a postcard and letter. Glancing at the picture she handed the card to Trudy and slapped open the folded paper. She silently read the note.

The postcard was of an old fashion sailor boy cozying up to a Hawaii girl in a grass skirt. They reclined on the beach while in the harbor, his ship sank. Given what happened at Pearl Harbor, Trudy thought the postcard in bad taste.

"That son of a bitch," her mother growled. Had Uncle Billy lost the family farm in a crap game? Her mother rarely swore, so he must have done something really bad. She threw the letter on the dining room table and stormed off to the kitchen. Trudy retrieved the correspondent.

> *Dear Sis,*
>
> *First off, I'm okay. You probably know the Arizona got sunk by the Japs and I lost most of my buddies. Only Joe Jackson didn't get killed. He got burned pretty badly and is in a hospital. You remember him, don't you? The last time I was in L.A. we squired a couple of ladies around town. Most of the crew died when the magazine blew and tore the ship apart. Our grandfather's watch and all my stuff are gone. It was really bad for everyone. I'm truly sick. A fine crew of men was lost, gallant sailors who were not given a fighting chance to defend themselves.*
>
> *Don't start to cry your eyes out about me. Yours truly was deprived of being in the thick of all this. The night before I got into it with two bully Marines who danced into a strictly Navy bar in Honolulu. They wanted to pound on some swabbies. I was pretty drunk and I guess I crowned one of the jarheads with a beer bottle and tattooed the other's face with the bottle's broken neck. That's what the report states although that is not my style and I can't remember anything. The rum over here has to be distilled in*

Davy Jones' locker.

The shore petrol threw me into the brig. I didn't wake up until after the last Jap planes high-tailed it back to wherever they came from. I came out of it with my eyes burning from the smoke that blew inland from Pearl Harbor. I didn't know until hours later what had happened.

We are censored so I cannot tell you what's going on, other than we are going after those Japs to sink their God damn navy and burn Tokyo to the ground.

My new commander did not take kindly to my run in with those Marines. He slapped me with a summary court martial and broke me down four notches to second class seaman, which is just above green recruit. After all these years in the Navy and I'm demoted to below half my pay grade. I tell you it's just not right. It's a tradition for sailors and jarheads to brawl. It's part of the esprit de corps, *as we say.*

Anyhow, I'll be put on another ship, maybe a carrier. I'll keep you informed of my postings.

Keep the home fires burning and buy war bonds. We're at war.

Your Big Brother, Billy

Trudy felt her stomach twist. She didn't know whether to laugh and curse. She didn't know if she should feel relieved or upset that her uncle avoided death by being a drunken carouser.

She felt it best to leave her mother alone and went to her room to do her homework. Looking up at the high Lama, she wondered what wise words he could whisper concerning Uncle Billy.

*   *   *   *   *

"I got a letter from Billy," her mother told Trudy's father and Andy after they had sat down for dinner.

"He's okay?" her father asked looking up. His voice expressed genuine concern.

"Oh, he's fine." Her voice had enough ice to make a snowball. "He was sleeping it off in the brig during the attack."

"Well, that's your brother," he said, returning his attention to his

96

Swiss steak. "He's not dead. That should be a relief."

Trudy tuned out the conversation and thought of Karl and his access to UCLA Library books. He could check Gardiner's *Egyptian Grammar* for her. But, then again, why would he? They weren't friends.

The conversation between her parents dropped, and for a moment they ate in silence.

"Trudy," her father said. "You've been quiet all evening. Got something on your mind?"

"Just school."

"Well, this summer you can get a job. There will be a lot of work with all the boys going into the service."

"Did you see what's showing at the Bundy?" her mother asked, obviously changing the subject. The Bundy was the new theater, a couple of blocks away, which had opened a few weeks after the Japanese attacked Pearl Harbor.

"What's showing, Mom?" Andy asked.

"*Wild Geese Calling* and *Hold That Ghost.*"

"Is that with Abbott and Costello?" Trudy asked. "The ghost movie?"

"It came out late last year," her mother answered. "Looks like it might be fun. The other's a western with Henry Fonda. Phil, you want to go to the movies? We can walk."

Gas was now in tight supply, and Trudy's parents had to cut back their driving.

"Cowboys and a comedy? Sure. I'm ready for some fun and some popcorn."

"Then let's go Friday night," the woman said firmly. "That way we won't have to worry about a blackout."

They hadn't been caught outside during a blackout since the one incident before Christmas, but if they did have to walk home in the pitch black again, there likely wouldn't be a problem. Trudy's father had spoken with the officer in charge, Captain Newman, and most of the soldiers now knew the Mansfields on sight.

Trudy's mother looked over to her. "You want to join us?"

"My twenty cents," her father said.

"Sure," Trudy said barely looking up from her plate. She glanced from her mother to her father, who smiled back.

Chapter 16

The Wall Flowers

T rudy sat across from Karl Black on a table bench in the shade of the redolent fir trees. The location was a few yards from the natural Indian spring that flowed in the middle of University High just above the girls' sports field. Two weeks before, they had begun eating lunch together.

Karl didn't have many friends, and most of Trudy's continued to be cool, having diagnosed her with "King Tut Lunacy." Sometimes Susan and Nancy joined them, but they usually moved on after a while to allow the two their privacy.

The first time they sat down together, Trudy had been walking in the lunch yard when she saw Karl coming out of the cafeteria carrying his tray. She said hello as he passed. He paused, looking around for a place to sit.

"There's a bench by the flag pole no one uses," Trudy said, remembering the incident the previous spring when he got roughhoused. She then added, with her heart jumping up into her throat, "I was just going over there. Care to join me?" She sometimes sat there by herself, under the trees, doodling hieroglyphs.

"Kind of far from typing."

"It's not that far—come on."

She couldn't believe she had been so bold.

This afternoon, Karl asked, "Have you read Steinbeck's *The Grapes of Wrath*?"

Strange question, but Karl often talked about books and topics that weren't on the minds of most kids.

Trudy shook her head.

"I haven't, but I know Steinbeck's an important writer."

"You should read him. Start with *Of Mice and Men*. The book's not long and you can do a book report that will impress your teacher."

"I saw the movie with Lon Chaney. It was sad. I felt so bad for poor Lenny. He just didn't know his own strength."

"The Milestone movie was good, but the book is superior," Karl replied. He then went on to talk about *The Grapes of Wrath* and how the

98

movie starring Henry Fonda failed to reveal the depths to which humans can fall and how far they will go to survive. "They changed the ending. There was no way they could put *that* on the screen."

Trudy wasn't sure what Karl meant by his last remark, as she hadn't read the book, but his tone made her hesitant to ask. She changed the subject to *Sullivan's Travels*, a movie she liked, which also dealt with the downtrodden.

"Preston Sturges is good," Karl said, rather somberly with creases in his forehead.

"Preston Sturges?"

"*Sullivan's Travels'* writer director. He's witty, not superficial, not trite. Sturges took a serious subject and made the audience laugh while they also felt for the poor and their struggle for justice."

Karl then went on to list his other favorite authors and complained that the school library had a limited selection of good, contemporary reading.

Although she did not share Karl's enthusiasm for the literature, she would rather listen to him talk about books than talk about the war, which seemed to come up in almost every other conversation. Things had gotten worse and people were nervous. Hong Kong and Singapore had fallen. Japanese forces continued to race unchecked across the ocean, occupying islands in the South Pacific and threatening Australia. Their fleet of aircraft carriers remained elusive and just waiting to strike again. And at home, the country had sunk into the reality of being at war. Every day, more boys were signing up for the service or being drafted. And the government just announced that ration-coupons would be issued for purchasing gasoline and sugar. New tires, bicycles, typewriters, and cars had already become impossible to find. Canned foods and meat were in short supply or not available at all. Even ordinary things like hair ribbons and toothpaste were not always on the shelf. Even if the big guns were not situated on the lot next to her house, Trudy could not avoid experiencing the impact of the war.

At one point Trudy mentioned to Karl her interest in the ancient Egyptians. That got his attention. He enjoyed history even more than Steinbeck.

"Everyone knows about Tutankhamen," she said, "King Tut to most people, but the real story of the New Kingdom is about the heretic King Akhenaten, whose name means *he who worships the sun god*,

99

Aten."

Trudy couldn't believe someone was actually listening.

"As pharaoh, he was the absolute ruler of Egypt. He forced the Egyptians to abandon their devotion to the other gods, especially Amon, who had been the most important deity. . ."

For someone to seem interested was new. Even Nancy would only listen to Trudy talk for so long before she began to fidget.

". . . What I really want is to learn how to read hieroglyphs."

"Hieroglyphs?"

"The writing of the ancient Egyptians. I believe that to understand a people you must learn their language—to know how they thought."

These words just came out. She liked the explanation. It sounded deep.

"My neighbor is an Egyptologist," she added.

"No kidding?"

"No kidding."

"You're lucky."

"I haven't told him my interest. He's important—a very busy scholar. A professor at UCLA. He comes home late." At least Trudy thought he did. "I talk to his wife. She's helping me with my German."

"My father's the same way. He comes home late, and then spends the evening in his study working on papers for publication."

*   *   *   *   *

An hour later, in sixth period government, Miss Ramsey paced around the front of the room, her hands clasped behind her back.

To Trudy's right, Susan French drew circles instead of taking notes.

Several students had raised their hands while others talked out of turn. Miss Ramsey motioned for them to put their hands down and stop talking.

"Most of you haven't heard," she said, "the Army has been given the power to relocate people of Japanese descent"

100

Trudy hadn't, but this didn't come as a surprise. For weeks, local officials had been demanding Federal authorities oust the Japanese Americans from the Pacific Coast.

"I heard the news at lunch," the teacher said.

"Isn't that good?" someone asked.

The teacher shook her head.

"Many loyal citizens are affected because their facial features are the same as the enemy's. Look around you. Mary, Kenji, Tom and Ida will be forced to move. They are no different from you, except their parents or grandparents came to this country from Japan. Some of you have German and Italian heritage, but there is no intent to relocate *you* hundreds of miles away from your home."

"You can say that, Miss Ramsey," Bobby Boyle said in a sardonic voice. He had been a vocal Isolationist before December 7. "But I cannot for the life of me see any similarity. The students you named are Japs."

If Miss Ramsey's skin had not been burnished with a deep tan, Trudy believed her face would have blanched. As it was, her features froze into a mask, like a photo snapped before an impatient setter had made a pose. The teacher used formidable self-discipline not to ram Bobby's words down his throat as Trudy wanted to.

Miss Ramsey glanced around the room, maybe looking for someone to speak up. Trudy wanted to but was tongue-tied and her heart was racing. She helplessly looked at Mary, who had turned in her chair and looked daggers at Bobbie.

"Isn't it enough that some of us have already been forced to move," Mary said, "because our homes were close to Douglas?" Her words were sharp and biting. "We are American citizens, not the enemy. My neighbors are German nationals, but they remain in their home. I don't see the justice in this. The Schneiders moved to get away from Hitler. My family came here to have a better life."

Trudy assumed what Mary said about the professor and Helga was true.

"Don't you go to Japanese school?" Johnny Lopez asked from the back of the room.

101

"Yes," Mary said without hesitation. "I am proud of my cultural heritage like you must be of yours. We are taught the Japanese language, arts and traditions. But that does not make us Japanese. We salute the American flag like in regular school."

"Japs of any citizenship are enemies," Bobby snorted, ignoring Mary. "As far as I'm concerned there is going to be a real disaster unless they're moved. There are vital defense areas here and the potential for sabotage. Something should have been done weeks ago."

"Citizens have constitutional rights," Miss Ramsey said calmly but with eyes that stared down at the obnoxious boy.

"As far as I'm concerned," the boy replied, "civil liberties must be put aside in the interest of safety and national defense."

"You have the right of free speech to express that," the teacher replied, "which is only one of the rights granted by the constitution. The fifth amendment of the Bill of Rights guarantees due process before the law. Do you know what that means, Bobby?"

The boy glared through his prim, wire-framed glasses at the teacher, but said nothing.

Chapter 17

The Air Raid

By the end of the third week of February, Californians had developed a case of the jitters. This time the populous had not been shaken by an earthquake, but rather, were rocked by the news that the Japanese had actually shelled an oil refinery in Santa Barbara. Admiral Knox announced that the Navy was protecting the west coast "as well as possible" which did not sound reassuring.

From December 7 on, the Pacific Ocean had become a combat zone. Tojo's forces appeared to be attacking everywhere. With rumors flying about and the Japanese navy and its aircraft carriers remaining elusive, deadly, and ready to strike again, people living along the edge of the Pacific felt vulnerable. Many believed that the West Coast was now in Japan's cross-hairs.

With her house surrounded by anti-aircraft guns and the neighborhood crawling with soldiers, Trudy's cozy impression of Los Angeles had vanished. Never as isolated as Shangri-La, the region had still seemed a great distance from the rest of the world. The war had literally come to her home, with blackout curtains hung on the windows, buckets of sand placed in the attic in case incandescent bombs were dropped on her house, and her brother's white civil defense helmet and gas mask kit hanging by the front door. Her world had become another newsreel film clip spliced amongst scenes of the occupation of Paris, the firebombing of London, the ravishing of China, and tanks rolling back and forth across North Africa.

At lunch Trudy continued to sit with Karl in the shade of the fir trees that carpeted the ground with brittle needles and scented the area with a dry, green odor. The location provided a haven from the war, but the reality of the fighting occasionally blew in between the branches.

"Are you concerned that you'll be drafted when you turn twenty-one?" she asked, unable to contain her concern.

"No."

"Are you enlisting?"

Karl shook his head and said, "None of the services will take me."

"How come?"

"Asthma."

She didn't know if he felt lucky. While she didn't know if any boy would admit it, she was sure some had no desire to fight and risk being killed.

"How are the hieroglyphs going?" he asked, obviously changing the subject.

"Slow," she said, her voice purposefully lacking enthusiasm. In her mind, she had practiced this exchange for days. She avoided eye contact, uncomfortable. She was being a bit devious.

"What's the problem?"

"Well, it's like you said," she went on with a shrug, "the school library doesn't have much of anything including good books on Egypt and hieroglyphs. Neither does the city library."

"You'll only find books like that at UCLA," Karl said. She was going to say that next.

"I went there last summer. They have the books I need, but I can't check them out."

"Oh, my dad can get the books," Karl said.

Trudy could not believe how easily that idea was breached, and she didn't even have to suggest it.

"You mean your father can check out any book? On any subject?" Of course, she already knew he could.

"Just tell me what you want."

"You'll have him check out a book for me?" she asked to make sure she had really heard Karl.

"Sure."

"That would be great!" Her eyes sparkled. "You're sure it won't be a problem or anything?"

"My dad doesn't even go to the library. He sends a grad student to get whatever he wants and whatever I want."

"Gee," Trudy gasped. "Thank you."

104

Karl smiled.

"Don't mention it. He's a professor, so you can keep the books for as long as you need them."

Trudy didn't want to seem pushy but she couldn't contain herself.

"There is only one book I really, really need. I've got the call number at home. I'll bring it tomorrow."

"You got a telephone?"

Trudy nodded.

"Call me this afternoon. I'll have the book by Friday."

Trudy understood that boys were supposed to call girls. But she guessed that since they were not boyfriend-girlfriend, really, her calling would be okay.

After school, Trudy raced home, still barely believing that in two days she would have the Gardiner book all to herself.

She wondered if the ancient people of the Nile had invented the period or the question mark. Did they have quotation marks? In no time at all she would find out. Two long, long days before she would find out.

At that moment, riding her bike down Bundy Drive, she felt incredibly alive. The chilly air stroked her face and tangled her hair. Even in the hazy afternoon sun, the places she passed seemed vividly real, like she was looking at the world through a window, finally cleaned of years of accumulated dirt. The old barn she rode by almost every day appeared even more weathered, derelict and spooky.

Passing the Olympic Trailer Court and crossing the Pacific Electric track, she turned onto Exposition Boulevard and pedaled harder as she approached Wellesley. How amazing it now seemed that in this unassuming neighborhood, mostly open fields, just a few miles from the Pacific Ocean, she would become one of the few people in the whole world who could translate and read the exotic script of the ancient Egyptian civilization—a land most people associated with a camel on a cigarette pack and gruesome, walking mummies from spooky movies.

She whizzed by Nelly Mann's nice car and turned into the

105

Schneider driveway. She didn't think Helga would mind her dropping by while Nelly visited. Trudy enjoyed talking casual German with the two.

"How are you?" she asked Nelly as she caught her breath. Helga stood across the room and actually seemed relieved that Trudy had come by. She smiled wearily at Trudy.

"Going crazy," Nelly answered putting her hands to her head. "Heinrich is writing a new book, and he's frustrated that he cannot find a publisher who won't demand changes to his story. He's grumpy."

"I'm sorry to hear that."

"Oh, he gets in one of his moods from time to time. If it's not this, it's something else. His teeth."

Nelly looked over to Helga before Trudy could ask what she meant.

"Have you told Trudy the good news?" Nelly said, her eyes beaming.

The girl looked over at Helga.

"I'm going to have a baby," she said with an embarrassed smile.

*   *   *   *   *

Trudy didn't stay long, sensing the two women wanted to have a conversation she did not want to be part of.

She walked her bike the short distance to her house. As frequently happened, one of the soldiers whistled. Another yelled, "Hi, honey!" At least they were keeping their distance. A month ago, a soldier had approached her. She told him she had a boyfriend in the Marines. She couldn't believe that he accepted the lie and backed off. No one had walked up to her since.

After she got home, she waited a few minutes before calling Karl.

The telephone sat on a shelf her father had built in the hall. With nothing to sit on, she stood facing the wall, looking down on the black device. The phone rested on the thick local directory and an L.A. Yellow Pages.

After Karl's number rang a few times, a woman picked up. She had an older voice, and Trudy guessed the lady was his mother.

"What is this regarding?"

Trudy didn't expect the question and stammered something about their being in a typing class together. She wanted to kick herself for mentioned typing. It wasn't the kind of course for which students would have a reason to share notes.

The woman didn't speak at first and then said in a tone that suggested she had been given a heavy burden, "Wait a minute. I'll get him."

"Trudy?" Karl asked when he finally came on the phone.

"Hi."

"I'm sorry. I was at the other end of the house. I didn't hear the phone ring. My Aunt Rose wasn't rude, was she?"

"No." Trudy wondered how big a house he lived in that he couldn't hear the telephone.

"Sometimes she's a little nosy," the boy went on. "Just ignore her. Everyone else does."

There was a brief pause, as if neither knew what say next.

"You got much homework?" Karl finally asked.

"Nothing I can't get done before I have to help my mother with dinner."

"Lucky you. I have this advanced math class that my father insisted I take. Chemists are big about math, you know. I'm expected to learn more than I will ever need—especially if I become a dramatist someday."

"You mean like William Shakespeare?"

For the first time, Trudy heard Karl laugh.

"I would so wish," he said. "I'd be happy to be Eugene O'Neil—or the German, Bertolt Brecht. Most Americans don't know him, but he is an important playwright."

"Gee," Trudy said on reflex. She had never heard of Bertolt Brecht but guessed he was important. Karl said he was.

"Did you know that the most important German intellectuals live here in L.A., including Brecht? Thomas Mann, Fritz Lang, Bruno

Frank, Franz Werfel . . ."

She didn't. Then again, giant sound stages and backlot mazes were all over Los Angeles, and she had never seen a movie star. The idea that there were so many important European intellectuals living in Los Angeles suddenly made the city seem cosmopolitan.

"I know Heinrich Mann's wife," Trudy said, suddenly remembering Nelly and trying to sound like she had her own connections to this elite circle. "Her husband wrote *The Blue Angel*."

"Have you met her husband?"

"No, just Nelly. She told me he's writing a new book and looking for a publisher."

"Do you know what it's about? I wonder if he will tie in his experiences in America."

"I'll ask Nelly the next time I see her. She's typing his manuscripts."

Saying that made her feel important.

"Did you tell her about your interest to hieroglyphs?"

"No. You're about the only person I tell." She failed to add, *Everyone else thinks I'm nuts.*

"Don't be so shy."

Trudy's mother walked into the hall from the kitchen. The scent of freshly cut raw onions accompanied her. "Trudy, you've been on the phone a long time."

Her mother was scowling. Was there some chore she had forgotten to do?

"I have to go."

"Wait! You didn't give me the call number."

"Oh, yeah." She had absent-mindedly pushed the index card between the pages of the phone books. She pulled the slip out, smiled at her mother, and quickly read the call number.

"I didn't get that. Say that again a little slower."

Trudy repeated the number.

"What's the name of the book? Who's the author?"

"Gardiner is the author," Trudy said. She didn't want to say the title with her mother standing next to her, so she said, "The title's

Grammar."

"Just Grammar? Not Egyptian Grammar?"

"Yeah, that's right. That's the name. I really appreciate you getting it for me. I'm sorry. I have to go. I'll see you at school tomorrow. Bye."

Her mother moved her head with a barely discernable shake. She probably had another headache. Most of the time she never said anything, but Trudy could tell.

"I want you to walk over to the market. I'm out of dish soap, of all things."

"Okay," Trudy said. She felt relief that she was not in trouble. "If you want me to help with dinner when I get back. . ."

"I have everything together. Just put it on the stove when you get home. I'm going to lie down."

The woman turned and walked into her bedroom and closed the door. She must be really hurting, Trudy realized. She hadn't given her the money for the market.

*   *   *   *   *

That night Trudy went to bed early. In the dark hours after midnight, she was pulled out of a deep slumber by blinding white light, followed by a loud sound that nearly threw her out of the bed. She opened her eyes seeing the pictures of the high Lama awash in bright red flashes streaming through the window. Another loud blast shook her room and another, rattling the lamp and clock on her nightstand. Distant roaring sounds echoed the loud explosions. It took her a moment to make sense of what was going on. The anti-aircraft guns in the fields were firing.

She crawled over to her window, too afraid to stand and saw the search lights were scoping the sky, crisscrossing other lines of light, emitted from distant locations. Like on a tapestry, Nakamizo's field was illuminated with reddish flashes as the guns fired streaking projectiles into the sky, each ear-throbbing blast silhouetting and freezing in the split-second burst of light the soldiers manning the guns.

She heard her parents' and Andy's bedroom doors open. She put on her robe and ran into the hall and stopped, afraid she would collide into someone or trip in the dark.

"Oh, my God!" she cried to herself. "It's happening. The Japanese are attacking!"

In the living room, she saw the forms of her father standing next to her mother and Andy looking out the big window. The blackout drapes were pulled apart. She ran over to her father, bumping into the coffee table. He put his arm around her. Through the window, she saw the black sky illuminated by search lights and shells that streaked golden ribbons and exploded over the Los Angeles basin like a hundred Fourth-of-July fireworks going off at once.

Still holding Trudy, her father leaned over and switched on the radio, the amber glow of the dial slowly brightening.

"I got to go to my post." Andy said, running back to his room.

"What?" her mother gasped.

"I'm a civil defense messenger," he said. "I'm supposed to report to the center in an emergency."

"You're not going !"

"I have to go," he said. "It's my duty. You signed the form."

Andy ran toward his room. Even in the dark, Trudy saw her mother, like a dark specter, springing down the hall after him.

The voice on the radio reported that at 2:25, the 4th Interceptor Command had ordered a complete blackout of all Southern California. The announcer attempted to remain somber and steady, but Trudy detected a nervous edge to his voice. "Civilians have reported to this station that they have seen unidentified planes and balloons coming in from the ocean and signals flashed along the shore. These are unconfirmed reports. If these prove true, one can only suspect enemy aliens and American born Japanese have guided this attack. . ."

"What bunk," her father muttered.

"Are they just attacking, like they did at Pearl Harbor or could this be an invasion?" her mother asked, coming back in the living room. Andy remained in his room.

"I don't think we're under attack."

"How can you be sure?"

"Do you see any explosions on the ground?"

"I don't think so."

"That's because the only things you see are anti-aircraft shells being fired in the air. I think we're witnessing buck fever."

"What's that?"

"Something I saw when I was a kid—beginner hunters who were so excited they'd shoot at boulders in the bushes."

Trudy jumped each time a nearby gun fired. Still, she respected her father's knowledge of military aircraft and aerial combat.

*　　*　　*　　*　　*

The soldiers continued to fire their guns throughout the night, and the shells' yellow tracers interlaced with the searchlight beams until dawn.

That morning Trudy rode her bike to school. She was exhausted from the stress of the night before. The dewy morning air had a strange burnt metallic scent that stung her nostrils and stuck in her throat. Passing the guns, she noticed spent shell casings strewn over the ground. The soldiers, still wearing their soup bowl helmets, milled about, no doubt fatigued. Some were moving crates from the guarded "ammo dump" in the far corner of Nakamizo's lot. None paid her any attention. Dark smoke bellowed out of the stove pipes of the mess tent. No doubt many pots of coffee were being brewed.

Trudy rode through Japantown hoping to see Mary walking to school. She noticed a store front with a big sign reading, "America - We Are Ready - Anti-Axis Committee - Headquarters. Join Now In Defeating Axis Japan." She wished she had the Schneider's camera to take a picture.

School buzzed like a beehive, the students exhausted but bursting with their stories of what they saw and "knew" about what happened over Los Angeles. Some brought in the shell fragments that littered whole neighborhoods, damaged cars and wrecked roofs. A few believed the chunks were the remains of Japanese bombs. Other

111

students reported seeing planes in the sky, even dogfights between Douglas A-20 Havocs and Japanese Zeros. Someone said Havocs, just off the assembling line, were launched from the Santa Monica plant to engage the enemy. Another person said the Japanese had torpedoed the Ocean Park pier and its roller-coaster was now under water.

In Miss Ramsey's class, the consensus was "the Japs" had to go, echoing what the morning newspapers had been demanding. Bobby was the most vocal: "There is convincing proof that there were shore signals flashed to the enemy."

Miss Ramsey didn't challenge the cocky boy but stood glumly in front of her desk, arms folded below her bosomy chest, glaring down at Boyle. Trudy wondered why she did not call him out. She was equally confused with Mary, who although visibly upset, did not speak up.

After class, Trudy approached Mary.

"Why didn't you say something?" she asked.

"Why didn't you?" Mary replied. The comment cut Trudy like a dull knife.

"I'm sorry. I don't like to debate."

"Well, I do, but my parents are displeased that I have been so outspoken. They tell me that accepting relocation is the only way we can show our loyalty as Americans."

"That makes no sense! Your brother is in the army."

"Tell me about it."

Trudy hated herself for not speaking in class. She tried to think of something she could have said but the words in her head were a jumble. She just knew it was not right to punish a whole people for the actions of a few individuals or maybe one or two—if there had actually been any enemy agents with flares.

Chapter 18

The Bread King

In early March, General John L. De Witt issued a proclamation declaring that all Japanese, both American and foreign-born, would be moved from the Pacific coast. A definite date for the relocation had not been set, but there was no question the eviction would happen soon.

That evening, Harry Nakamizo called Trudy's father. Working in her bedroom, on a hieroglyphic exercise, she could hear her father on the phone in the hall just outside her door. "I can get that stuff together and take it to your church," she overheard him say. His tone was reassuring. After he hung up, there was a long silence. Peeking around her bedroom door, Trudy saw him standing with his forehead against the wall.

She had resigned herself to the inevitability of her friend's relocation. Whenever she looked at Mary and the other Japanese American students, she felt shame. The fact was most people were scared and acting out of fear. The prevailing attitude was that the "Japs" were the enemy and a "menace." It was as though everyone else had forgotten the years of being neighbors, classmates, and even friends. They were blind to the shared history, and all they could see now were the differences.

Trudy distracted herself from the war with schoolwork, her interest in hieroglyphs, and Karl, whom she hesitated to call a boyfriend, although he was a boy and a friend.

Karl surprised Trudy by not only getting her the Gardiner book, but also a two volume work she didn't even knew existed, E. A. Wallis Budge's *Egyptian Hieroglyphic Dictionary*. How had she missed that title in UCLA's card catalog?

Susan kidded Trudy by calling her and Karl Queen Nefertiti and young Moses, but not in a mean way. The references were obvious.

In February, Trudy gave Karl a Valentine's card. It was nothing romantic, just a cute card asking him to be her Valentine. With a lopsided smile and a confused look, he opened the note and said, "Thanks." He didn't have anything for her, but she was okay with this. She knew he was as new with this as she was.

Neither Trudy nor Karl was accustomed to boy-girl talk. At first, they chatted about their literary and historical interests. After a couple of weeks, they began talking about their families.

Karl's dad wanted his son to be a research chemist or, at the very least, a physician. His father tolerated Karl work with the stage crew, saying a boy needed a hobby, but he also insisted his son study biology and chemistry

"That's my dad's life, test tubes and reagents. Have you taken chemistry?"

"I had it in the fall."

"So, you know chemistry stinks. Literally stinks. My father comes home from the lab, and his clothes reek."

"How does your mother put up with that?

"My mother lost her sense of smell ages ago."

"Are you the only writer in your family?" Trudy asked.

"No. I have an uncle in New York. I've never met him, but I've read his stories in Harpers. He's good. My father reminds me he also drives a cab. That's his way of saying he's a failure."

"I guess there are worse things than driving a taxi in New York."

"In my family, if you're male and not called doctor or professor, there's nothing worse."

"My parents didn't even finish high school," she confided, "but my father takes night classes at Santa Monica City College. He gets As."

*   *   *   *   *

The afternoon that Trudy brought *Egyptian Grammar* home, she went through Gardiner's first lesson, and then took a quiz on the Egyptian alphabet. She had to write out from memory several words in hieroglyphs, having only the English sound equivalence. She was

114

pleased to find that she missed just one—and only partially. The practicing she had done the last few months had not been a waste.

Trudy began spending an hour, sometimes two, occasionally three, each day doing the hieroglyph exercises. She gave her parents the impression she was spending extra time doing schoolwork. Her mother was not happy but she would have been more upset if she realized Trudy was indulging in writing Egyptian "magic symbols."

*   *   *   *   *

In the middle of March, Karl met her at lunch excited like he had just found a five-dollar bill someone left in a library book.

"Guess what? Bertolt Brecht will be speaking this Saturday at UCLA."

Trudy vaguely remembered Karl mentioning the name but couldn't place it.

"Trudy, Brecht is one of the most famous playwrights in the world! He has written great plays, like *The Threepenny Opera* and *Saint Joan of the Stockyards*. He's also written important essays on drama. Most are not published in English. But his ideas are mentioned all the time in articles and books. I will finally hear him speak. His talk is open to the public. Anyone can come."

"That's great."

"Would you like to go with me?" Karl asked.

"To UCLA?"

"He's speaking at Royce Hall. It's across the court from the library."

"I know where that is."

"Would you meet me there?" he asked, increasingly eager for her to say *yes*. "The talk will start at one."

"Sure," she answered. She had nothing planned Saturday and, truth be told, she felt obligated after he had been so nice in getting her the books.

*   *   *   *   *

Saturday proved to be a pleasant spring day. The Mansfield garden was green and flowering, an island of beauty surrounded by the brown, drab of dangerous army gear and gun placements. The sky had a few cloud streaks that did nothing to diffuse the sun.

At dinner the night before, she told her parents about the lecture. Her mother said nothing.

"Who is this Brecht fellow?" her father asked.

"He's a famous playwright. We're studying theater in English," she exaggerated.

"You still have your chores," her mother reminded her.

"I know. I'll get them done."

"UCLA's a big campus. Don't get lost," her dad cautioned.

"I won't. I'm going to meet a friend."

"Who?" her mother asked. "Susan?"

"No." Trudy felt an urge to say Nancy but decided to tell the truth, although she didn't feel ready to announce to her parents that she had a boyfriend.

"Karl." It was strange to hear his name come out of her month. Her mother looked up, her eyes crinkling with a grin.

"You have a boyfriend?"

"Well, we're friends. We eat lunch together. Sometimes."

"Trudy. You never told me," her mother said in a voice too pleased to be scolding.

"I didn't think it was a big deal," she said.

"Does Karl have a last name?" her mother asked. She also looked pleased.

"Black. Like the color."

Her father smiled, although he avoided eye contact.

She finished her Saturday chores, then, feeling grubby from all the dusting, took a quick shower and washed her hair. She didn't have time to brush it, so she quickly combed the knots out and tried to do something with the fake pearl hair combs she found in her mother's vanity drawer. She eyed herself in the mirror. The thick mess looked a little better, she supposed. She also sneaked on some of her mother's makeup. Not too much—that would get her in trouble. Susan had given

116

her good advice of what to use. Fortunately, her skin was fairly clear at the moment, and the makeup did a passable job covering over the acne scars. She sprayed herself with the nice perfume her mother never used, something her father gave her for Christmas.

She put on her pink rayon blouse and the one skirt she had with a matching short sleeve spring jacket. She finished the ensemble with her mother's little white pillbox hat that had a light pink bow across the front. Looking at herself in the mirror, Trudy decided she rarely looked this nice.

Instead of riding her bike like she usually did, Trudy opted to take the bus. That way, she wouldn't ruin her outfit and get sweaty. She would also be able to walk through the Village and window shop after the event.

She had arranged to meet Karl outside the entrance of the UCLA library. She rode the Santa Monica Blue Bus to The Village. Inside the conveyance, the advertisements above the windows encouraged the riders to give blood and do service on the home front. One poster featured the face of a beautiful woman before a rippling American flag. The header asked, "Are you a girl with a star-spangled heart?" If so, "Join the WAC now!"

When the bus turned onto Westwood Boulevard, looking east, she could see Twentieth Century Fox's huge sound stages, backlot, and the sky against the sky—the studio's always changing giant cyclorama. The maze of structures was one of the region's fabulous magical workshops.

She walked briskly, for what seemed like a mile across the school grounds. Fortunately, there was a pleasant, cool breeze.

Climbing the brick steps that lead to the court between Royce Hall and the library, she saw Karl. He had on the same boring clothes he normally wore at school. Maybe she had overdressed.

He smiled when he saw her walking up to him.

"Hi, Trudy. You're just in time."

"I'm not late?"

"No. I just got here. Come on. Let's get our seats."

She had hoped he would have noticed her effort to look nice

117

and maybe even compliment her on her appearance, but he didn't.

Crossing the court, he began telling her more about Bertolt Brecht. He had apparently been reading up on the man since they last spoke.

Trudy and Karl approached the beige brick and creamy stone of Royce Hall's triple archway front. They merged with a scattering of people who walked to the building from other directions, most too old and nicely dressed to be college students.

Once they passed under the archway and entered the veranda, Karl led Trudy to a stairwell. He knew exactly where he was going.

He continued to talk about Brecht, but Trudy barely heard him. She was distracted by the size of the staircase and the architecture's *stately elegance*—the only words she could think of to define the intricate detail and clever use of tile and brick.

Even before reaching the third floor, they could hear a milling of voices and the scuffling of feet. Reaching the top of the stairs, Trudy saw a large group of men and women exiting one door and crossing the hall to another.

"Looks like they need a bigger room," Karl said.

The pair blended in with the crowd and moved with them into a large conference room flooded with warm California sunlight coming from two pairs of tall, arched windows. At the front of the room, three men were engaged in an animated conversation. One had an outgrown army crewcut. He wore a drab suit that fit like a potato bag and had a dour expression. His gestures suggested displeasure with the room.

Karl and Trudy took seats toward the back. The chair on her right remained unoccupied.

Trudy assumed the man with the strange looking haircut was the German playwright. The two men standing with him appeared to acquiesce to whatever he demanded and walked away, one to the front corner of the room and the other to the right side, where he grabbed the heavy maroon drapes and pulled them across the windows. As he crossed the room, the overhead lights were turned on.

After a few minutes, a distinguished looking man in a finely tailored doubled-breasted suit and smoothly combed gray hair moved

118

over to the podium and welcomed the attendees. He restated many of the things that Karl had said, but with a warmer elocution.

After being introduced, Brecht came up to the podium. He casually leaned on the platform, his eyes wandering around the room and up to the glass saucer light fixtures hanging from the barrel ceiling. With black discs in the center, the fixtures looked like giant eyes staring down, examining the assembly.

"Shortly after arriving in this city," Brecht began, "Fritz Kortner told me the endless sunshine here desiccates the brain so severely that people end up only being able to write Hollywood films."

A pleasant chuckle came from the assemblage.

"I choose to live in the shadows. In the soft glow of the electric lights." Brecht smiled and glanced around the room, his mouth turned down, though his eyes remained amused and sardonic, dancing behind what looked like dime-store black-framed glasses.

"Nowhere is speaking about theater more difficult than here, where all you have is theatrical naturalism. I will begin my talk by clearing up the difference between realism and naturalism because so many do not know the difference between these approaches of creating a story. . ."

The playwright's command of English was excellent. Trudy had to focus carefully, though, to understand him. His statements went way over her head like, "Realism exposes all the veils and deceptions that obscure reality," whatever that meant. She glanced over to Karl, who leaned forward and sucked in the words Brecht spoke as if the playwright were passing on the recipe for making gold out of flour and swamp water.

As Brecht spoke, a man quietly slipped into the empty seat next to her. Trudy noticed he was rather small and had graying hair. Making eye contact with Trudy he nodded and smiled pleasantly. She smiled back and returned her attention to the stage. The man looked almost familiar, like a teacher at school—but too nicely dressed.

After his lengthy lecture on realism, Brecht began making disparaging comments about life in America and the American people. He complained that bread in this country had no taste, being massed produced with the goal to make money.

"The Americans are nomads," he said with a shrug. "They don't know anything about eating. They have no use for real bread, because real bread isn't sold sliced. In America, bread has to be pre-sliced so it can be eaten on the move or wherever they happen to be standing."

Some in the room laughed softly.

"Fleischhacker and I have developed this as a subject for a film. *The Bread-King Learns To Bake Bread* is the title. The story is an indictment of the American habit of making things with no substance or character. The hero is a poor baker who prides himself on the breads that come out of his oven. The bakery has loyal patrons who pay the little extra bit for his fine, fresh loaves. One day the bread king happens in his shop and, curious, samples the poor baker's bread. He is amazed and troubled because he cannot allow this bakery to exist. The poor baker's bread reveals how terrible his own bread is. He must find a way to shut down the little bakery. This is an example of the function of realism to structure a story."

The man next to Trudy stirred and leaned closer to her.

"I suspect," he whispered in her ear, "that Mr. Brecht envisions The Little Tramp coming out of retirement to be the struggling baker, ruined by the Bread-King." It took Trudy a moment to realize that he referred to Charlie Chaplin's Tramp.

"I loved the little guy in *Modern Times*," she whispered. "I wish he would return."

"I miss him too."

"He could also play," Trudy replied, also speaking low, "the part of the Bread King like he played Hitler in *The Great Dictator*."

She looked over and saw the man nod and smile. Although older than her father, she found him handsome, almost boyish. She smiled back, being careful, as she had practiced, not to reveal her crooked teeth.

"The Bread King needs to be a bigger man, physically imposing, domineering," he said.

"What about Sidney Greenstreet? If he made a silent film, it wouldn't matter that he's British."

"Now that would be interesting casting."

"I've been asked if I wish to write a Hollywood film," Brecht continued. "'Yes,' I reply. There are good actors and good directors here. The trouble is how does a Marxist go about submitting a script to the studios? Here, all they are concerned about is *selling* an evening's entertainment. . ."

As Brecht went on about this and making other critical observations of things American, Trudy's mind began to drift, thinking of Charlie Chaplin as the poor baker. She tried to refocus, but she was not as attuned to the speaker as Karl. Fortunately, the German playwright soon ended his lecture. When he finished, the people clapped. All appeared to be suitably enlightened and entertained, not offended by his negative remarks about the United States and the movie business, although Trudy suspected there were movie people in the room.

Karl looked energized, ready to go home, sit at his typewriter, and pound out a story.

"I will take your suggestion about Sidney Greenstreet," the man next to her said.

"It's just a silly idea," she replied, shrugging, self-conscious, and feeling rather foolish for having made the comment.

The man looked at her, concerned.

"Don't deprecate yourself, dear." He put his arm over her shoulder, reassuringly. The gesture shocked her. Holding her, he leaned his head close to hers and in a conspiratorial whisper said in her ear, "We think too much and feel too little. Be a dreamer! Listen to your heart."

Trudy turned to look at the man. He smiled, his eyes close and expressive, warm and familiar. Nodding, he squeezed her arm, stood up and walked away.

Rather uneasy, she looked over to Karl who appeared to have just seen a ghost.

"What's wrong?" she asked. Maybe he wasn't supposed to be here. Did someone his parents know see him? His father taught at the school.

121

"That's Charlie Chaplin," he answered, watching the man exit the hall.

"Huh?"

"You were talking to Charlie Chaplin."

"Are you sure?" Trudy turned and saw the man walk out the door.

"He's right," the woman behind her confirmed. "That was Charlie Chaplin sitting next to you."

"And he talked to me!" Trudy suddenly felt dizzy like she may need to sit down. She noticed a tingly sensation where he had touched her arm and sensed a residue of the warmth of his body. Her mind went blank. For a moment she didn't know what to say.

"No one will ever believe me when I tell them," she finally told Karl.

"I saw him too," he replied.

"No one will believe you either."

*   *   *   *   *

As soon as she got home, racing to her bedroom, Trudy told her mother that she talked with Charlie Chaplin and that he was "as nice as nice could be." Her mother never had a chance to react as her daughter vanished into the hallway.

Trudy threw her purse on the bed and phoned Nancy. Her friend picked up but didn't sound like herself. She sounded like she had been crying.

"What's wrong?" Trudy asked, her excitement choked by her sudden concern.

"Gary has to report to duty," she said. "After he signed up, his papers got lost or something. They found them. He has a week to settle his affairs."

Trudy remembered Nancy's fear of seeing Gary off, and her premonition that he would not come home from the war. For weeks, she had been telling Trudy that she had been having nightmares.

"You have to be brave," Trudy said. As she spoke the words,

they sounded insensitive and trite. She added, "Brave enough to let him see your tears." That didn't even make sense.

"He's seen my tears."

Trudy had no idea what to say to lessen her pain and fears.

"I'm so sorry, Nancy. These are scary times," she finally said. "Just try to enjoy the moments you have with him before he leaves."

"He teases me because I cry."

"Guys don't like tears, I guess." Trudy had never seen her father cry, and the only time she could remember a man crying in a movie was when Clark Gable's daughter died in *Gone With The Wind*.

They talked a little longer. After hanging up, Trudy realized she never told Nancy about Charlie Chaplin.

Chapter 19

The Book Of The Dead

T rudy stood on the edge of the Schneider's concrete driveway, hesitant to walk onto their front porch and knock on the door. The sky had grown gray and somber. Cold April air briskly raced onto Wellesley from the ocean. The leaves on the trees and bushes quivered with each breath of the breeze. Trudy's sweater hardly kept her arms warm.

Professor Max would probably not be home—at least Trudy hoped he wouldn't. She wanted to talk to Helga, alone. Although she normally felt at ease around her, at that moment she was nervous.

This had been a bad day. The mass relocation of Japanese Americans had begun. For the last few days, the newspapers reported the news as if it were a story of the city being purged of some infectious disease. The Nakamizos were already gone. A few days before Trudy and Mary had talked. Both understood that Mary would soon be forced to board a bus and be taken to the Santa Anita Racetrack where the army had set up a center to process all Japanese Americans. The military stressed the beautiful facility where Seabiscuit had raced was not a concentration camp but a temporary "Assembly Center" where evacuees would be housed until final locations could be sorted out.

"Write me and let me know you're okay." Trudy told Mary.

Mary nodded. She kept her head down and avoided eye contact. She had conformed to her family's demand that she demonstrate her American patriotism not by protesting but by blindly obeying the government. Trudy could feel her bottled-up resentment and indignation.

"Please write me," Trudy repeated. "I want to know that you're okay."

Mary nodded.

"This isn't going to last forever" Trudy said. "Things will go back to normal. You'll get to medical school. I just know it! Someday you'll even be my doctor."

"I want to be a pediatrician," Mary replied.

"A pediatrician?"

"A baby doctor."

"Well, maybe someday you will be my children's doctor, then." She could not imagine being married or having children. The mental picture made her frown.

They shook hands, and that was the last time Trudy saw Mary. The next day in Miss Ramsey's class the only Japanese American was Tom, who sat in the back of the room but caught the glares of a number of the students. One boy kicked his desk as he passed. Most had forgotten that just weeks ago they had cheered Tom and the other Japanese Americans who were the core of the school's strong gym team.

*   *   *   *   *

"All Germans are Nazis," was a common opinion expressed in class. "They all love Hitler. Don't you watch the newsreels?" The last person to say this to Trudy was Andy after school before she left to visit Helga. He said that she was "giving aid and comfort to the enemy" by hanging around the Schneider house. Trudy's cheeks flushed with anger. She walked out of the kitchen while he was still talking. If she heard one more stupid comment, she was going to blurt out something regrettable. The last thing she wanted was get in a big fight. Her mother would take Andy's side, like always, and order her to stop visiting Helga and babysitting Jonathon and Marlene.

Trudy knew that the Schneiders were not Nazis or Jewish. A gold crucifix hung from Helga's neck. She believed they had left Germany to get away from Hitler, an assumption supported by the anti-Nazi German language magazines in their living room that Trudy leafed through every time she babysat. Also, Helga would never speak Hitler's name. She would instead say, "that man," whenever the topic of the situation in Germany came up.

As she walked to Helga's, she went over and over the question she planned to ask, trying to word it, in her head, in a way that couldn't be misconstrued.

She rang the doorbell. After a moment, she could hear Jonathon racing around the room announcing that someone was at the door. Through the door, she could her his mother, in a stern voice, tell him to return to his room.

Trudy forced a smile when the door opened.

"I thought I would stop by and say hello," she said in German. She glanced behind Helga to Marlene. "I haven't seen you in a while, little girl."

Marlene smiled shyly then hid her face behind entwined fingers.

Helga looked tired. Her sunny eyes had dull rings under them. Even her buttery hair appeared lifeless. Her tummy and breasts had noticeably expanded. She asked Trudy to follow her into the kitchen so she could continue making dinner. Trudy replied that she would be happy to help.

The way Helga looked her, she must have sensed something was on Trudy's mind. As they walked through the living room, Trudy noticed a glass top curio table standing in the corner by the entrance to the hall. It hadn't been there before. There appeared to be a colorful piece of Egyptian papyrus unrolled under the glass. She would have to look at the artifact before she left.

"Where is Jonathon?" she asked, speaking in German. She had become fluent in conversational German and the words came out easy and casual.

"Oh, he did something naughty and is in his room."

Trudy smiled.

Trudy sat down at the table and helped Helga by snapping string beans. This morning's *Los Angeles Times* lay beside the bowl. One of the headlines read, "Palm Springs Hotel Taken Over by Army." The article went on to say that the luxurious El Mirador would be turned into a military hospital for the duration of the war.

"Can I ask a question?" Trudy said looking up from the paper.

"About?" Helga asked, without looking away from her cutting board.

"I read and hear all sorts of things about the German people.

126

I'm not sure what to believe anymore. You and the professor left Germany, but you're not Jewish, so why did you have to? To get away from Hitler? Everyone I know thinks all Germans are Nazis. But I know you're not."

Trudy looked down at the string beans. She didn't want to catch Helga's eyes if the woman turned. Her heart began thumping in her chest. She could hear Helga put down the knife and rub her hands with the dish cloth.

"We left Germany because my husband secured a professorship in Paris, and then we came to the United States. Don't misunderstand me. What happened in Germany at the time was disturbing but that is not the reason we are here."

"Are most Germans really Nazis?" Trudy asked. She couldn't believe she asked that.

"Most German people are not Nazis," Helga replied. "Yes, many sympathize, but others deplore the National Socialists and remain silent. They make themselves invisible by going about their daily lives and attempting to get by."

"Why is that?"

"It is treason to speaks out against the man and the Nazis."

"How can that be? Germany was a democracy. If most of the people are not Nazis, why didn't they rise up? Rebel when Hitler abused his powers?"

"Through violence and legal trickery, the National Socialists took control. The other political parties were banned. People who spoke against this were put in concentration camps. There are no anti-Nazi demonstrations in Germany. The army, businesses, the workers, the newspapers are today all part of *Die Neue Bestellung.*"

"The New Order," Trudy translated, injecting a few words of English.

Helga stepped over to the stove and lit the burner under a black frying pan. She dropped a spoonful of lard into the pan, then watched with somber eyes as the fat began to sizzle.

Marlene had moved over to Trudy. Trudy picked her up and sat her on her lap. The girl reached for a scrawny string bean which she

127

tried to break.

"Do you miss Germany?" Trudy asked, recognizing the silliness of the question as soon as the words came out of her mouth.

"Yes," Helga answered. "Every day. I wish I was home. We would survive somehow."

Trudy wanted to ask how Helga imagined survival under Nazi tyranny but before she could the front door open and Professor Max entered the house. He paused in the living room, to look through the mail sitting on the table by the door. When he finally walked into the kitchen, Marlene slipped off Trudy's lap and jumped into his arms.

"Good afternoon, professor," Trudy said in English.

Jonathon came running out of his bedroom. He wearily looked at his mother. She gave him a dirty look but told him he could stay.

"Hello, Trudy," the professor said, also speaking English. She sensed that he wanted her to leave. He kissed Marlene on the forehead.

"I better be going," Trudy said in German. She stood up. "Thanks for talking to me," she said to Helga.

As she walked out of the kitchen, she looked at Schneider. She felt an impulse to say something light.

"Do you have a mummy?" Trudy asked in English and instantly felt dumb. Of course, he did not! Even though she asked just to make a joke, her question just sounded stupid. Stupid!

"No," Max Schneider replied rather gruffly.

She wanted to undo the bad impression and walked over to the new display case.

For several seconds she stood transfixed, looking down at the ancient papyrus. She had never seen the real thing and was knocked over by its beauty. The drawings and black and white photographs in the books didn't even come close to revealing the colorful artistry of Egyptian illustrations and hieroglyphs.

"Wow." She took a step closer. "This is new. You've got some really neat stuff, Professor Max."

"That is an Egyptian artifact."

She leaned over the glass case, her arms stretched out and her palms resting on each side of the wooden frame. She suddenly felt hesitant, aware that Professor Schneider stood just behind her, possibly about to say, "Don't touch." She put her hands behind her back.

She studied the lines of glyphs, inspecting the figures that ran up and down the page next to the beautiful illustration of a handsome man and woman. The ancient Egyptians were gracefully portrayed, serene and even noble in their posture and face.

Trudy turned her attention to the hieroglyphs. These were not the simple renderings about which she had been learning, but, rather, an exceptionally elaborate form of script.

"I can't read this," she said. She concentrated, sure she could make out some of the hieroglyphs. After all, she had memorized the most common words.

"This is ancient writing," Professor Max answered. She heard the impatience in his voice.

Some of the glyphs began to become clear.

"I know," Trudy said, "this says something here about the temple of Osiris lifting up. What's this word there? Earth, I think? I know some of these other words, but not enough to make any sense. Enough to figure out a phrase here and there."

The professor repeated, "Phrase?" He called his wife and asked her in German, "Did you shown Trudy the papyrus?"

Helga walked into the living room.

Trudy returned her attention to the scroll. Pointing down to different glyphs and looking up at the professor and Helga she read, "'Underworld, gods, day.' Those are easy words to pick out. This is from *The Book of the Dead*, isn't it? Here it reads, 'I have fought,' something, something. 'Osiris over his enemies on the day of judgment.' No, no. 'Of weighing,' yeah, weighing of something, something. I don't know that word, but this is 'mighty.' Can you read it?"

"'I am Thoth, making victorious Osiris over his enemies on the day of weighing of words in the dwelling of the Old Man mighty in Heliopolis.'"

Trudy expected the professor to quote the text, but it was Helga who read the line in German.

Beaming, Trudy turned around and looked up at the Schneiders.

"Have you been teaching Trudy to read this?" the man asked his wife. She shook her head. Looking back at Trudy, Professor Max said, "That is good. You can pick out words and are attempting to read sentences. How in the world did you learn that?"

"I only read a little."

"Only a few can read what you just read."

Trudy saw the professor was impressed. She felt her heart begin to flutter.

"I have a friend at school," she said, "whose father also teaches at UCLA. He got his dad to check out Sir Alan Gardiner's *Egyptian Grammar* for me. Have you heard of the book?"

The professor nodded.

"It's been hard learning to read hieroglyphs, and I don't know a whole lot. I'm still learning how to put words together to make sentences. Even with the lessons, it has been hard."

"Even with instructors, I had to read many books to learn the language," Schneider said.

"I figured that out," the girl said. "I've noticed your books over there."

The professor looked at his wife.

"Trudy," Helga said in English. "The books. They are mine."

It took a moment for this to sink in.

"This is amazing, Trudy," Professor Max said with a funny smile. "Latin is a dead language, but the language of the ancient Egyptians is not only dead but had been lost until the last century and then only to a few. This is not an easy language to learn."

"Yeah, I'm finding that out."

"Especially without a teacher."

"I thought you would think I was stupid, trying to learn to read Egyptian hieroglyphs." She looked at Helga. "I had no idea you read hieroglyphs."

"At the university, I was what you would call an assistant of the research to my husband. Before we married."

"You explore temples and pyramids for artifacts?" she asked, feeling freer.

130

"No," the professor said. "I study old texts like these and the inscriptions on walls of temples and tombs. Mostly I study the writing on broken pottery and bits of stone."

"Broken pottery?"

"The Egyptians used potsherds and limestone flakes like we use note paper. These bits and pieces are my primary source of information. I have boxes in the garage. Young lady, you read glyphs!"

"To tell you the truth, I got excited when I saw your books the first time I babysat." She looked at Helga. "I hope you don't mind, but I looked through the hieroglyph dictionary."

"To learn to read the old Egyptian, you must be . . . dedicated and have access to a great deal of books and . . . *Fachzeitschrift.*"

"Professional journals," Max translated.

"If I can look at your books from time to time and if you have any journals you think would help, that would be great."

Helga shook her head.

"You need a teacher to learn the hieroglyphs," she said.

Trudy stared at the woman, sensing for the first time the magnitude of the task she had set for herself. She felt like a heavy weight had just been put on her shoulders.

"I will be your teacher," Helga said.
Trudy felt the load lighten.

"And this would be good. For me. There is much I have forgotten. This will help me get back into translations. You must be dedicated. This cannot be merely a . . . a . . . *fantasie.*"

"I want to learn," Trudy replied.

*   *   *   *   *

Trudy left the Schneider's in a daze, walking on air. The professor's reaction was nothing she had expected. And to find out that Helga too had mastered the language—what a wonderful discovery! And she would be her teacher!

Passing the ugly gun emplacements and the tents, their drab canvas rumbling in the wind, she had another thought. No one had ever been amazed by her before, and this afternoon she had actually astonished a university professor and his wife. And Professor Max was a *real* Egyptologist and Helga a university research assistant!

She picked up her pace. Feeling so light, she felt her steps bounce. She didn't care if the soldiers directed wolf calls at her. She felt incredibly alive.

Chapter 20

The Junior Prom

At lunch, a week later, Karl sat down next to Trudy at their favorite table, Immediately she could tell that something was wrong. He avoided eye contact with her, he barely ate his meal, and he could barely hold up his end of the conversation. She asked him what kind of sandwich he was eating, and he sputtered off something about F. Scott Fitzgerald and his recently published unfinished tale about a Hollywood tycoon. Finally, Trudy couldn't take it any longer.

"What in the world is the matter with you?"

Karl stopped and took a deep breath.

He looked at his sandwich.

"I would be honored to escort you to the Junior Prom," he said, looking up at last, anticipation shining in his big eyes that almost popped through his glasses.

"Karl, that's so sweet! Yes. Yes, you may."

The junior prom may not have the grandeur of the senior prom, but the event nonetheless allowed the eleventh-grade girls to announce that they had blossomed into women.

The event was just two weeks away, which meant that Trudy didn't have much time to prepare.

Because of the war, the prom would be subdued. Getting ready would be simpler than in years past. Girls could demonstrate their patriotism by keeping their dresses simple. The boys, if they were in the ROTC, would wear their dress uniforms, sporting the ribbon bars and badges they had earned. The War Production Board had already instructed women to be conservative and use what they had in their closets rather than buying a new garment. The Board further requested that if they absolutely had to go out and buy a new skirt or dress that the item be tighter and the hemline shorter. The government panel hoped to save a hundred million yards of cloth a year.

Trudy had never imagined going to the prom. When Susan,

133

Alice, and Joan talked about their preparations and the dinners their dates would take them to, she slid into the background, attempting to be inconspicuous. Nancy was the only girl not thinking about the prom this spring.

Poor Nancy. Gary had finally been inducted. She carried his most recent letters in her purse, notes that he illustrated with cartoons. In his last, he drew a soldier with a puffed lip and throbbing shoulder, elbow, and knees. The caption read, "We fired the caliber 30 Winchester for the first time today. This rifle really has a KICK. Everyone around here has a swollen upper lip."

Within minutes of the invitation, Trudy began to have second thoughts. Karl was a Jew, and good girls weren't supposed to go out with Jews. She had had qualms about having lunch with him but always rationalized their eating together as something they were doing as fellow classmates. They mostly talked about things they were learning. Even going to see Brecht was not a date. It was an educational outing where she met Karl.

Her gnawing doubts finally chewed a hole when Susan reacted to the news with eyes that grew like she had discovered a cockroach in her cold cream.

"Is that wise?" she asked.

"What do you mean?" Of course, Trudy knew what she meant.

"He's Jewish. Trudy, you can get in trouble."

"I know."

"Well. Be careful. Make it sound like his father is a Presbyterian minister. You know how our moms are."

*   *   *   *   *

When Trudy returned home that afternoon, the Helms Bakery coach was parked in front of the Lewis house. Trudy skipped across the street to indulge her sweet tooth. Martha Lewis was just stepping away from the mustard-yellow gypsy van with her purchases.

"Hi Martha."

"Oh, hello Trudy." Martha's eyes were tired, and her posture was limp like she had been carrying a heavy bundle all day.

"Guess what? I'm going to the Junior Prom."

"Sounds exciting," Her tone did not mirror any excitement.

Trudy retrieved a nickel from her coin purse and stepped onto the bakery coach. The sweet smells of desserts and bread engulfed her. Despite what the strange playwright Brecht said about American sliced bread, Trudy had a taste for the mass-produced loafs Helms delivered fresh daily to people's front doors, all over Southern California.

She bought a white cupcake with a slice of strawberry on the top.

By the time she walked through the front door, she had licked the sticky crumbs off her fingers and there was no trace of the cupcake. Her mother lay on the sofa, reading a copy of Photoplay. She sometimes took a break in the afternoon, after her day's chores and before she went in the kitchen to prepare dinner.

With hardly a glance up from the fan magazine, her mother greeted Trudy.

"I got some really, really exciting news," Trudy said, setting her school stuff on a chair and approaching her mother.

"I hope you haven't brought home a kitten."

"No," Trudy replied, too excited to be detoured or have her spirits dampen. "Mom, I just got asked to the Junior Prom!"

Her mother put down the magazine and gave Trudy a big smile.

"That boy asked you to the prom." That sounded more like a statement than a question.

"Karl."

"Trudy's going on a date," her mother purred.

Trudy nodded her head.

"Well, then we're going to have to make you a nice dress."

"Nothing fancy. You know, with the war."

Experiencing something that could only be described as enhanced confidence, Trudy quickly did her chores, rushed through that day's homework, and settled in her room with the Gardiner book opened to lesson twelve, "Sentences with Adjectival Predicate." With a little patience and without giving into her initial temptation to scream, she managed to grasp the first part of the lesson. She felt pleased.

$$* \quad * \quad * \quad * \quad *$$

For the next week, Trudy's mind bounced between hieroglyphs and the creation of a prom dress. She had found a pattern for an evening gown that looked like the one Judy Garland wore in *Love Finds Andy Hardy*, one that did not require excessive amounts of yardage. The design had a simple layer of taffeta and a modest neckline that would just come off her shoulders. Her mother helped her pick the light-blue rayon cloth at Sears. Trudy was surprised that the store still had a full inventory of yard goods. Her mother guided her as she cut the pattern and pinned together the pieces of fabric. This was difficult. Scissors were made for right-handed people, and Trudy was a lefty. On Saturday afternoon she sewed together the parts.

She had never had high heels and was excited to buy her first pair. Like most everything else, shoes were in tight supply. Her mother would have lent Trudy her heels, but the girl's feet were too big. She had one pair of silk stockings, which she treated like angel wings. Silk and nylon finery had completely disappeared from the stores.

She went to sleep each night thinking of heels and dressing up for the prom.

Chapter 21

A Cameo Broach

In the days before the prom, Trudy was in a dither, panicking one moment and feeling overwhelmed with anticipation the next.

She regularly put on makeup now, using the pancake cream, face powder, eyebrow pencil and accents that Susan had found for her. She bought the makeup at Woolworth and secretly put it on before running out the door (and then removed it before her mother saw her).

Unaware of Trudy's routine, her mother spent time trying to find ways to improve her daughter's appearance. Trudy sat at the dressing table in her parents' bedroom facing the mirror as her mother applied different combinations of creams and colors as if she were a cosmetologist working on a Hollywood starlet at the Max Factor make-up studio. Her mother also fiddled with her hair, but left her locks in combs that kept the unmanageable curls out of the girl's face.

As she worked, she asked questions about Karl to which Trudy would give vague replies, not saying anything that might cause her to be suspicious. She just made it sound like Karl was a nice boy who was serious about school. For all her mother knew, Karl's father could have been a Presbyterian minister.

Trudy arranged for her friend Alice and her boyfriend to pick her up on prom night. That way, her parents wouldn't actually have to meet Karl. Due to the gas rationing, it was believable enough that Karl did not have gas to drive to Wellesley. With the war, nothing seemed unusual anymore.

On the afternoon before the big night, Trudy was giddy. Her worries had slipped away, like water leaking out of a rusty five gallon pail. By that evening ,she felt confident that everything would go well.

She put on her dress and was carefully slipping up her stockings when the phone ring. Her mother answered. Trudy could not hear the words with her radio on but caught a change to a somber tone of her mother's voice. Trudy tensed. She came out of her room just as her mother hung up. She glared at Trudy. The girl tried to act innocent. There was nothing to be afraid of—she hoped.

"What's wrong?" she asked. "Something happened to Uncle Billy?"

Her mother leaned forward, like she was about to pounce.

"That was Linda French on the phone, and don't act like you don't know what's wrong." She stared at Trudy, her silence demanding that the girl 'fess up. Her heart racing, Trudy silently looked back, her mind blank. She feared her silence was answer enough. Before either spoke, her father came into the house. On his way to the bathroom, he stopped in the hall when he saw them.

"Well, don't you look nice, Trudy."

Her mother glared at him. Trudy looked at him with desperation on her face. He suddenly appeared concerned and confused.

"What's wrong?"

Her mother turned back at the girl, with fire now in her eyes, and said, "Trudy's date is a Jew boy."

Trudy's dad did not say anything but appeared to want to back out of the hall. Trudy suspected he wished he had urinated in the bushes.

"Trudy," her mother said, "you are not going to the prom."

"But mother,' Trudy sputtered.

"But mother nothing! You are not going to the prom with a Jew. What were you thinking?"

"Karl's a nice boy," she answered.

Her mother looked at the girl's father.

"Tell your daughter she can't go to the prom."

Trudy looked at her father, her eyes pleading.

"He's really not my boyfriend," she blurted out, not giving her father a chance to speak. "Just a friend at school. Really. We talk about school work and stuff. We just wanted to go to the prom to see . . . to see what it's like."

"Trudy, you heard me! Phil! Tell her she can't go!"

"What can I say?" he replied. He looked like he was facing a firing squad. "You already told her she can't go."

138

"I don't know what the big deal is," Trudy cried.

Her mother rolled her eyes.

"He's a Jew," she said. "Respectable girls don't go out with Jews. You know that, so don't act like you're dumb."

Desperate, Trudy looked to her father. He glanced away, as if rays from her eyes burned his face.

"Trudy," he said to the ground, "you heard your mother." His voice was not harsh like the woman's. He walked into the bathroom and closed the door. Trudy wondered why he didn't stand up for her. He had been so brave supporting the Nakamizos in front of the soldiers who hated the Japanese!

Her mother turned and walked out of the hall. Under her breath, she muttered an ugly anti-Semitic slur.

Dread whirling around her head like a cold wind, Trudy called the Black house, hoping to catch Karl before he left. She just missed him. Reluctantly she spoke to his mother.

"I'm sick to my stomach," she said. She didn't have to fake sounding ill. She felt like she was going to throw up.

"Oh, you poor dear," Karl's mother said. "Have you taken Pepto Bismo?"

The woman's concern made Trudy feel even worse.

"I can't stop throwing up," she lied. "I feel better for a little bit and then I get sick again. I just want to lie down."

"Go lay down," the woman said. "Oh, I'm so sorry for you. To miss your prom."

"Tell Karl I'm so sorry I couldn't go." Hearing the words slip out of her mouth, Trudy realized how that sounded. She quickly added, "I should be at school Monday."

Hanging up, Trudy went to her room. She looked at her reflection in the mirror. She had felt pretty just a moment before and now she saw an ugly, hopeless girl, her acne pushing through the skin cream and her tears making a mess of her mascara.

Still in her pretty dress and high heel shoes she plopped down on the bed and cried. The peaceful high Lama watched over her. His presence did not sooth her. She wanted to scream and muffled her yell in the pillow.

Later, exhausted and spent, she called Nancy.

"What's wrong?"

"I can't go to the prom."

"What!"

"My mother found out about Karl."

"What do you mean?"

Trudy stiffened. She noticed her brother sitting at the dining room table, like he was a scrawny owl in a tree, watching her in the hall. He had been fiddling with parts to a model plane.

"It's a big thing to my mom that he's Jewish."

"Oh," Nancy, said as the answer sunk in, like she got this for the first time.

*   *   *   *   *

Trudy remained in her room Saturday night and Sunday morning, exhausted from crying. Her mother avoided her, and her father hid in his workshop. Thank goodness, she had agreed to babysit the Lewis children Sunday afternoon. Her grandparents were coming over, and she could just imagine her grandpa making some uncouth snip about Jews and her grandmother asking her what she had been thinking. Both were like her mother.

Late that afternoon, when Chuck and Martha returned, she hung around and chatted with Martha. She didn't want to go home. When Martha invited her to stay for diner, she accepted.

But finally, she couldn't avoid returning home any longer. She went directly to her room, ignoring her father who attempted to get her to pause in the living room to listen to the news broadcast on the radio. Passing through the room, she heard enough to learn that the U.S. Army had conducted a major bombing raid on Tokyo and great fires were raging in the Japanese city.

She closed her door. After she kicked off her shoes, she noticed a peach colored oval object, circled with a black ribbon, glowing under the lamp on her vanity. Stepping closer, she discovered the object was

140

a pretty cameo brooch. Under the piece was a note scribbled by her father, "Grandma thought the prom was next week. She wanted you to have this. I told her the dance was last night, but you got ill. She still wants you to have this."

Trudy assumed her mother was too ashamed to contradict him and tell the truth.

Her father's lie did not sooth her anger. She thought him a coward. At the very moment that she needed him to stand up for her, he ran into the bathroom.

She dropped the trinket in the back of her dresser drawer.

Chapter 22

Apologies

Trudy went to school on Monday prepared to maintain her lie with Karl that she had been sick all Saturday night. She didn't have to exaggerate too much. The whole experience had left her nauseated. When she met Karl at lunch, he expressed his concern with such sympathy for the unfortunate timing of her illness she couldn't look at him. She feared he would become upset if he learned the truth, but she told him anyway. He seemed to take the news well.

"My mother had told me she didn't think you'd be able to go out with me. I just hoped she would be wrong."

"If I had known what your mother thought, I'd believe she was mistaken. I just didn't know." She did know, but pretended that she didn't. She was troubled that she was putting another knot in her string of deceptions.

"It's nothing new," he said.

"It's new to me, and it's wrong!" That was true.

"My family's not religious, which is an understatement. I haven't even been bar mitzvahed."

Trudy had no idea what he was talking about. She knew nothing about his faith.

"But even if I wasn't Jewish," he went on, "it hasn't been easy being me. I don't have any friends. The other Jewish kids don't like me. They've been teasing me for years. You're really the only friend I've got."

Starting to tear, Trudy leaned forward and gave him a kiss on the cheek.

"No one can stop us from being friends," she said.

He smiled at her and, for the first time, didn't seem to know what to say.

Trudy cared deeply for Karl and strongly believed what she said. She had no idea at that moment how wrong she was about the fate of their friendship.

*   *   *   *   *

When Trudy saw Susan in the hall, she felt her face contort into a glare. Susan grimaced like a rifleman had pointed a gun at her, but instead of backing away or smirking, she came up to Trudy. Her eyes weren't bright and sparkly. She took Trudy's arm and pulled her to the wall.

"I'm so sorry," she gasped. "I didn't tell my mom Karl was Jewish. Honestly! I just told her you were going to the prom. I felt so good for you. Your first date! I thought you two were cute and I wanted you to have a good time. My mom asked me who was taking you and I told her 'Karl.' She asked me 'Karl who' and I told her. I didn't think there was a problem to say Karl Black. Black's a really common name. I didn't know my mom knows Karl's mom from PTA. Honestly! I felt so bad when I found out what happened! I'm so sorry."

Susan started to cry—it was the first time Trudy had ever seen her cry. She sensed that Susan had been as miserable that weekend as she had.

*   *   *   *   *

The next day, Karl didn't eat lunch with Trudy nor the next. He became visibly uncomfortable when she approached him between classes and when she tried to talk to him in the typing lab. She believed he was angry at her. She didn't blame him if he was.

Finally, on Friday in typing she asked Karl why he'd stop talking to her and hadn't met for lunch.

Visibly nervous, he whispered that her brother and his friends had threatened him, and they meant business. Hearing this, she became furious. She said her brother had no right to do this.

"He may have no right, but he and his friends didn't seem to care about that technicality."

Between typing and government, she cornered her brother,

143

dressed for ROTC and walking to his next class with his friend Jerry.

"WHAT GIVES YOU THE RIGHT TO STICK YOUR NOSE IN MY BUSINESS?" she screamed, indifferent to the crowd of kids who were walking by.

Andy might have grown bigger, but she could still pound him into the ground. And she would do it right there on the school grounds even if hitting him meant she would be suspended.

"It is my business!" he said, stepping back as she advanced on him. Jerry had moved away, so Andy stood there, facing her by himself. "You're my sister. If you don't care what other people think, I do. I'm tired of my friends laughing at me about you."

"So what! They're really laughing about me, and I don't care if they do."

"You're still my sister. And I won't let you embarrass our family."

"Did Mom put you up to this?"

"No," her brother said unconvincingly. "Mom didn't have to tell me to do anything."

She shoved her brother and walked away.

She was so upset that in government class she could barely pay attention to the discussion of the Fifth Amendment. Miss Ramsey talked about due process of law which didn't mean anything anymore to Trudy. The way those of Japanese descent had been hauled away, their lives destroyed, went against everything she had been taught about American democracy. The way Jewish people were treated like second class citizens, and the way her mother and brother had interfered with her friendship with Karl turned her stomach. The teacher gave the students a written assignment which she failed miserably, mostly because she no longer believed in due process. Miss Ramsey must have sensed something was wrong. She gave her a C-, which was more than she deserved, and scribbled in the corner of the paper, "Trudy, don't lose faith."

144

Chapter 23

The Ghost Audience

Before the Junior Prom, Trudy had been careful and only told Susan, Nancy, and Alice that Karl Black was taking her to the dance—she knew others would see her and Karl at the gala, but she would deal with that then.

Nancy backed Susan's claim of innocence, telling Trudy that she heard from Mary West how miserable Susan appeared at the prom, confirming Trudy's belief that her friend had been deeply upset. She felt a deeper bond with Susan, realizing that their mothers had ruined the event for both girls.

Alice Long, who with her boyfriend Trudy had planned to go to the prom, was a gossip and probably told the other girls that Karl was her date but, at the last minute, Trudy's mother wouldn't allow her to go.

Nancy seemed to be the only person in the world who did not know it was forbidden for a gentile to go out with a Jew. Joan Fulbright alluded to this rule when she said, "Birds of a feather stick together." Trudy didn't have to ask what she meant, and from that moment hated her.

Sitting next to Karl in typing became more and more difficult. Both were uncomfortable but tried to act normal which had become impossible: Trudy because of her shame and Karl because he was afraid someone would report him to her brother. He began coming into the room just as the bell rang.

She wished she had the courage to revolt. She wanted to tell Karl that she would like him to take her to the movies. Forget what her mother would say. They would find some way to arrange an assignation. Of course, she knew this was only a romantic fantasy. If she and Karl showed up at a show, their presence would likely be noticed and gossiped about for days. Her brother would know of it in no time and their mother within hours after that.

In the middle of May, Trudy decided she had to cut the one tie she still had with Karl. This would be hard for more than one reason.

During lunch period, Trudy walked into the backstage of the school auditorium where she figured she would find Karl. He was there, working by himself, off to the side, in a paint stained shop-coat, fiddling with a metal can that looked like a theater light. She didn't see the teacher which confirmed her suspicion that the boys had the run of the place during breaks. The stage crew was a strange bunch. They didn't associate with kids like her brother. She figured this was a safe place to meet Karl.

"Karl," she said softly.

He looked up. Seeing her, he appeared surprised but not nervous.

"Hi, Trudy," he said, casually enough and returning his attention to the fixture.

"I want to return the Gardiner book and the hieroglyphic dictionary," she said, holding up the massive volumes. "They have been so helpful. More than you can ever realize. Thank you for getting them."

"You can keep them longer," he said, not looking up as he slipped a round, green tinted glass plate through a frame at the bottom of the light.

"I wouldn't be able to use them," she replied, being less than truthful. "We have finals coming up, and I have a lot of studying."

Karl took the light and walked across the workshop toward the dark drapes that served as baffles, separating the work area from the stage.

"Well, put them over by my notebook, there on the table."

Trudy sat the treasured volumes next to his stuff. She looked at the books, experiencing the same sensation she felt when her father took her dog to the pound during the worse days of the Great Depression.

"What are you doing?" she asked, shaking the mood and turning her attention to Karl. She followed him through the gap between the drapes and onto the stage.

146

"Replacing a burned-out lamp."

Trudy had never been on *the boards* as she heard the stage called. The curtains were parted, and she glanced over to the vacant, dimly lit auditorium. The open space was rather creepy with the rolls of empty seats. She could almost see a ghost audience sitting in the shadows watching her.

Four feet over the floor hung three long assemblies of light fixtures, each strip the length of the stage. Trudy assumed these were normally overhead. Karl placed the fixture he carried into a gap between other lights and uncurled a short cable. He plugged this into an outlet.

"Why green?" she asked.

"You mean the roundel?"

"If that's what it's called," she said, pointing to the bottom of the light.

"Let me show you."

He walked to the wing of the stage where he tugged on a rope that pulled the front strip of lights up about ten feet.

"Stand under the lights," he said. "Don't worry. I won't drop the rigging on you."

She moved as requested and looked up at the lights. Every fourth canister was missing a colored glass disc. She thought that curious.

"Hold out your arm," Karl said from some place off the stage.

Trudy did as he requested and was suddenly blinded when the strip of lights went on, blue, red, green, and natural light beaming out of the open fixtures.

"Look at your arm."

Her skin and the sleeve of her blouse looked normal. Trudy wondered what the big deal was until Karl switched off all the lights but the unfiltered lamps. Under only the white light her arm lacked the richness and color that it had from the blend of the colored lighting.

"If there were no green, blue, and red, just white, the effect would be dull, which sometimes you want for certain illusions." He switched back on the colored lights. "We can also dim or rise each of the colors to change the blending to make different hues and tones."

147

Raising her hand to shade her eyes, Trudy looked around trying to figure out where Karl was. She spotted him in a space that looked like a cage high up, off the stage. She could see some of the electrical panels with large levers she guessed controlled the lights in the theater.

"Karl, can you come down here?" she asked, suspecting that he was about to do another demonstration. "I want to talk."

"Uni has a really good theater. Don't you want to see . . ."

"No. I want to talk."

Waiting for him, she glanced at the empty seats and rehearsed again what she wanted to tell him.

Karl walked out onto the stage. He appeared a little uneasy, like he was concerned about what she would say. Not that he needed to be.

"I just wanted to tell you . . ." She hesitated. "I'm sorry we don't eat lunch together or talk before typing. You're avoiding me which I can understand after what happened. But . . . it was nice the last couple of months. I felt I could be myself around you. I liked hearing you go on about writers and other serious stuff." She smiled. "You listened to me talk about hieroglyphs without acting bored. And only you know I talked with Charlie Chaplin and that he put his arm around me."

"Maybe in another world things could have come out differently," Karl said stiffly.

She wanted to say that maybe they could start to make this a different world but kept that thought to herself.

"That doesn't mean we can't act normal," she replied. "Like we did before. When we sit next to each other in fifth period, we can still talk, can't we?" She smiled. "After the Brecht lecture you got so excited. I'd love to hear about what you're writing."

"Things are not like they were before," he said.

What could she say to that?

"The bell will ring any minute," he said, ending an awkward silence. "We should probably go."

"I'll leave first," she said, resigned, although she wanted to say more. "Give me a few seconds, and no one will know we met."

Even in the rich theater lighting, his expression remained empty and emotionless.

148

"Goodbye, Karl," she said and walked off the stage.
She turned away before she started to cry.

Chapter 24

Hieroglyphs and Summer Jobs

Before dinner, Trudy sat at her vanity, reading *Egyptian Grammar* and practicing translating sample sentences into hieroglyphs.

Shortly before school ended, Professor Max brought home the Gardiner book. This was the same copy Karl had procured, marked with her thinly erased penciled notes. She was surprised and grateful. A few days before, Trudy had confided to Helga that she had broken up with Karl and returned *Egyptian Grammar*. She said nothing about not going to the prom nor that Karl was a Jew. That could be like poking a hornet's nest. After all, Helga was German and would no doubt take her mother's side. Then Trudy experienced a sinking feeling. She had mentioned the boy's last name once, and Professor Max said he knew Karl's father. He had to know he was Jewish! What did he think of her? Did he mention this to Helga?

Helga spent every afternoon with Trudy teaching her hieroglyphs. She explained that "sound" symbols revealed the precise meaning of the stylized pictures of objects. Otherwise, one glyph could represent a number of different words.

Setting aside the book, she decided to try again to figure out how the ancients would have composed the word *jerk*. Maybe she could use the symbol for an ass or donkey coupled with the sign for woman to represent her so-called friend Joan Fulbright.

Trudy had already been upset with Joan for her comment about birds of a feather. Joan was clever. She had a way of making digs that she could deny meant anything unkind. A few days before the end of school, Joan showed her the photo taken at the junior prom of her and her boyfriend. She gloated about what a wonderful evening she had and told her things about the dance blatantly designed to make Trudy jealous.

"It's too bad you couldn't go," Joan cooed. "I'm sure some *nice* boy will ask you to the senior prom."

Trudy tried to smile, said nothing, and at the first chance excused herself to study for a test.

Trudy had tended to think Susan was the tease, playing with her by giving phony compliments. Trudy had come to realize Susan actually meant the things she said, although she could not understand why her friend thought she was pretty. Maybe she didn't believe Susan because she had been jealous of her friend's soft beauty.

Trudy toyed with creating the *jerk* glyph for a bit and then went back to the writing exercise she had started. *Egyptian Grammar* was like a regular school textbook with lessons followed by assignments. Trudy wanted to learn enough to begin writing her diary in hieroglyphs. This way nobody could read what she wrote. She knew her mother snooped.

Trudy wished she had more time to study, but she worked all day. Like so many of the kids at school, she took a defense plant job for the summer.

The last weeks of school had been a time of joy, angst and tears. Trudy thought she was watching the end of an era, not the completion of the academic year. These were days for saying goodbyes, often with a finality that Trudy had never witnessed before. The farewells were somber with the knowledge that some of the teachers who had been called up or enlisted and the graduating boys who had signed up for the service would not return from the war.

One more thing troubled Trudy. Over a month had passed since Mary and the other students of Japanese descent had been placed in camps far on the other side of the mountains. It was like there was a silent understanding at school that no one was to speak of them. Their photos in the annual, *The Chieftain*, provided the only evidence that they had been an integrated part of the school community.

* * * * *

Soon after General MacArthur abandoned Corregidor, the last American stronghold in the Philippines, the island rock was conquered by the Japanese. The Dutch East Indies had also fallen. Burma and a string of islands in the Pacific were taken by the Japanese. So were

151

islands in Alaska. Each day the news reported naval battles, stories of the American Navy sinking "Jap" ships and savagely pounding the enemy. Still, the Japanese appeared to be advancing. Trudy could not stop worrying about her Uncle Billy. The family hadn't received a letter since he jotted a note in late March saying he had been assigned to a supply ship. She suspected that he was in the thick of things and in constant danger. After all, supply ships did not have big guns and would be floating targets for subs and aircraft.

Along Wellesley, another reminder of the war had been placed—barrage balloons, tethered to the ground by cables. They formed a spider web to catch planes. The never sleeping sentries had begun to appear in late May in the area north of the Douglas Aircraft plant. On a clear day, squadrons of the balloons could now be seen hovering all the way down the coast to El Segundo. Their presence heightened Trudy's fear that Los Angeles would be attacked.

The crews manning the air monsters had moved in next to the gun placements. Trudy worried the balloons would be accidentally shot down if another aerial battle flashed over the city, the tattered remains crashing on the ground in a spray of gas and flames. Her father reassured her that the bags were inflated with noncombustible helium. She pretended she didn't hear him and walked away. The next day a partially inflated balloon broke loose, rolled down Wesley and tangled its cable in the electrical lines along the train tracks on Exposition Boulevard. Nothing exploded, but a soldier was badly electrocuted.

*　　*　　*　　*　　*

Trudy had found her summer work on a school bulletin board poster listing defense jobs. Labor laws had quickly been amended to allow teens to work adult jobs. For the first time, Trudy realized she was being called on to do something more serious than babysit. Trudy and Nancy went down the list of available jobs. They did not see themselves holding a welding torch, operating a lathe or riveting aircraft fuselages. Nancy saw a notice announcing the need for workers in a shop assembling flashlights for the Navy. The two agreed that was something they could do.

On a Friday afternoon, they rode their bikes to the plant in Santa Monica and filled out applications. They were hired without being asked anything except about their willingness to work evening shifts.

The Monday after the last week of school, wearing old clothes and their hair gathered behind their heads in snood nets, Trudy and Nancy reported for work. They were escorted past the plant's banging and clattering machines to the large backroom where women sat at long tables, laden with parts trays, where they assembled the flashlights. The finish product was slipped into gray rectangular packages which were packed into brown cartons marked with Navy symbols and numbers that were as cryptic as hieroglyphs had once been to Trudy. Like building a wall, sealed containers were stacked on one end of the room to be periodically hauled away.

Because Nancy had delicate little fingers, she was assigned to assemble switches, which another lady then carefully riveted onto the black flashlight tubes using a long-necked machine that fastened the parts with two dull pops. Trudy was set at a table where she screwed in the tiny light bulbs, snapped on the domed glass lenses, temporarily inserted Ray-O-Vac batteries to test the device, dropped them out and re-tightened the end. She wore gray cotton gloves to prevent finger prints smudging the bulbs or the reflector.

There was nothing difficult about the job. The only instruction she received was to not force the parts together. That would damage the threads. If the pieces could not be assembled, she was to put the defective parts in designated compartments on a special tray under the table. The boss lady also expected Trudy to assemble sixty flashlights an hour which seemed easy enough. After less than fifteen minutes, she picked up the rhythm of screwing in the light bulbs, securing the lens, and testing the flashlights. By the end of the first hour she could do the job in her sleep. By lunch break, she had decided this was the most boring thing she had ever done.

"Just remember we are doing this for our boys in the Navy," Nancy counseled her.

Except for a few girls from Santa Monica High, the female

factory workers were older women who had never finished high school. Most worked in the assembly room, but some had begun to operate the equipment in the big machine and paint shops. The word was passed around that more females would be advanced and trained to make the parts, allowing them the opportunity to earn a few cents more an hour.

Trudy didn't like walking by the entrance of the machine shop. The noise hurt her ears and the smell of hot oils assaulted her nose. Just inside the room, next to the Coca Cola vending machine, hung a large calendar with the color image of a barefoot dancing girl with flowing red hair, a skimpy slit skirt, and a lei that barely covered her breasts. The picture was pretty and offensive at the same time.

Trudy soon dreaded going to work. The shop may have been located only a few blocks from the beach, but the assembly room had no ventilation, and by the end of the day, it felt like an oven. The air in the room quickly became soured by too many bodies, and by mid-afternoon Trudy was often drowsy from the heat and tedium.

The lady who oversaw the room had the radio on her desk tuned into a string of soap operas. She had the volume turned up to be heard above the noise from the machine shop. No doubt the foreman concluded that while her girls did their brain dulling tasks, their minds could follow the life of nurse Karen Adams, the romances of Helen Trent, the bright horizon of lawyer Michael West and the other dramatized personalities who always seemed to have new dilemmas or challenges, usually resulting from some problem with a lover. There was never a story of a girl forbidden to go to the prom with a boy because he was a Jew.

Trudy soon could do her task faster than those who assembled the flashlight tubes. During her down-times, she fiddled with the rejected parts and found she could make some work by running her thumbnail in the threading breaking off bumps of paint. Having nothing else to do, she stood up and looked at the lady foreman. No doubt a believer that idle hands were the devil's playground, the woman found other work for her. Trudy thought this a reward for working fast, although she doubted her boss considered the new tasks bonuses. The girl pushed a cart around the plant to gather parts for assembly, swept the floor, and emptied trash cans. She soon became accustomed to the near naked calendar siren whom she frequently walked past and had come to nickname Roxie. She even typed forms in the office—a task she got one day when the owner came into the assembly room and asked if any of the girls knew how to use a typewriter. His clerk went home sick—hung over, one of the girls whispered.

*   *   *   *   *

At home, under the watchful eyes of the high Lama, Trudy put the hieroglyph book and papers in the bottom drawer of her dresser and went to the kitchen to help her mother with dinner.

As she set the table, her father came out of the bathroom all smiles. Trudy had been avoiding him, although some would say her mother had been the villain. Still, the girl found it easier to be around her mother than her father.

Andy plopped his scrawny frame into a chair. His sunburn was peeling off and morphing into a tan. Through their father's connections at Douglas, he got a summer job attaching aileron onto wings of A-20 Havoc light bombers. He and the other boys in his gang worked outside on the edge of the runway. Trudy suspected they engaged in a fair amount of horseplay when the foreman was not around. Still, Andy often mentioned how important the ailerons were to the planes' maneuverability.

Halfway through dinner their father turned to his daughter.

"Would Trudy like to get her driver's license?"

The question caught her off guard. He didn't have sarcasm in his voice. God, he had to be in an especially good mood. Had he bumped his head?

"Of course, I would," Trudy said.

She didn't look at her father to hide the scowl she just couldn't erase. She could feel the muscles around her mouth pulling down the corners of her lips. She should have felt happy and excited that she would finally be able to drive, but her resentment dulled those feelings.

"I'll let you get your license," her father said. "You're doing your part for the war and qualify for a B sticker."

Her mother's car was nonessential for the war effort and had an A sticker that permitted her to purchase four gallons of gasoline once a week. As a defense worker her father's car had the B sticker allowing him to pump twice that amount.

"Does that mean I can drive to work?"

Trudy already knew the answer.

"No, Trudy," her mother said. "But you'll be able to sometimes use the car to go to your friends' and to the show."

"Thanks," Trudy said, trying to express appreciation she did not feel.

"Your mother can take you down to get your license. You must take a written test, and, if you pass that, a driving test. But you got to know the rules of the road first."

"I have the pamphlet," she mumbled.

"Good. Read it. I'll take you around on the weekend when you have a day off. You just can't get in a car and expect to drive. Automobiles are machines. You have to coordinate steering, braking, and shifting gears while watching the road."

"I know," Trudy said, not thrilled with the idea of her father teaching her to drive.

"Trudy," her mother said, "could you get your father's lighter? It's on our dresser."

She silently stood up and walked to their bedroom.

"What's wrong with her?" she heard her father ask.

"It's that time of month," her mother lied.

"And they want women to taxi our planes to Europe."

"Oh, Phil."

Glaring at her reflection in the dresser mirror, Trudy felt like screaming at both her parents. She quickly regained a stiff placid expression. She returned with the lighter, sat down, and resumed eating her dinner.

Later, Trudy felt guilty. She had deliberately been mean at the dinner table. That made her no better than her father. No, that made her worse. He wasn't intentionally being cruel when he didn't back her the night of the junior prom. He just could never stand up to her mother. The girl had needed him to be her champion that night, but her father was not like Gary Cooper or John Wayne. He was like Frank Morgan in *The Wizard of Oz* who made promises he couldn't keep. Like Professor Marvel, he wasn't a bad man. Just a bad wizard.

She avoided looking up at the wall, from where the high Lama looked down, but she could feel him watching her, patiently. She was quite conscious that she had failed his maxim to be kind.

Chapter 25

A Forgotten, Ancient People

In the middle of June, a movie newsreel had shown what the commentator declared were "the first pictures of America's great naval victory in the Pacific, filmed under fire." The footage showed a confusion of smoke, explosive bursts in the sky above the ocean, and seaman watching the action from the ship deck. The voice from the screen declared that American planes and ships struck a "surprise blow" to the Japanese who had planned their maneuver to be a "surprise" attack on Midway Island. The Japanese carrier force was finally caught and four of the floating airfields sunk. Trudy wondered if Uncle Billy's ship had been part of the battle.

Each day brought more news reports about Ally victories, but Trudy suspected the American people were still being given a censored version of the war. By the middle of July, the superior Nazi Afrika Korps had pushed into Egypt and threatened Alexandria and the Suez Canal. *Life* magazine portrayed the German force as a "model small army specializing in high firepower" pitted against the backward British Army that "likes to think of the tank as a very heavy horse," beasts which Rommel destroyed in the hundreds by "fast-firing, fast-moving guns. . . . The Axis was pounding for victory in 1942."

The flashlight factory ran seven days a week. Trudy's days off were staggered and usually not the same as Nancy's. Trudy routinely worked the weekends, which was fine. That way, she didn't have to be around her father.

On the days reprieved from her boring job, she went to the movies and always visited Helga, who said the baby had "dropped." Trudy guessed that meant she could go into labor at any moment. She continued to instruct Trudy about hieroglyphs, answering the girl's questions as effortlessly as if she were giving cooking tips.

One afternoon, a visibly uncomfortable Helga, swaying like an unstable pile of coffee cups, took Trudy in the garage to see Professor

158

Max's work. Normally forbidden to enter this place, Jonathon and Marlene whispered to each other as they followed their mother through the doorway. She turned on the light. Wooden crates were stacked against the opposite wall, and in the middle of the garage, several wooden chests stood in a line. They looked like library map cabinets.

Helga showed Trudy Professor Max's work bench. On the scratched surface were neatly organized brushes, notebooks, pencils, gum erasers, assorted bottles, rags, and a big magnifying glass. Oddly, a figurine of Donald Duck stood next to the desk lamp.

"You brought all of these from Germany?"

"France. They follow us wherever we go."

Probably at great expense, Trudy thought.

"Years ago, during a visit to Egypt, my husband secured a great quantity of ostraca, the potsherds and limestone flacks on which the ancient Egyptians wrote things down. Most of this came from Deir el-Medina, a site of ruins that used to be a workman's village adjacent to the tombs in the Valley of the Kings. It was abandoned during the late New Kingdom. The settlement is one of the few neighborhoods of ordinary citizens whose ruins have not melted away over the centuries."

Helga's tone turned more serious.

"His field inspection of the potsherd and stone flack notes scattered in the village dump suggested he had indeed found an archeological gold mine."

She moved over to a cabinet, reminding the children not to pull out the drawers. She slid one out from the top. Instead of maps, the bin contained fist-size bundles made of thick blankets of cotton-wool tightly packed together. Some had strips of paper under them. Helga carefully pulled out one and unwound the fuzzy material revealing a broken piece of pottery, like a fragment of a cracked garden pot.

"This is a note."

Helga turned on the desk light and held the piece under the warm beam.

"You see these lines? This is hieratic script, the cursive, ordinary Egyptian handwriting."

Helga picked up the magnifying glass and looked at the piece.

159

She then passed the chip and lens to Trudy. The surface had been scratched with faded lines of loops and squiggles, nothing like the writing she had been learning.

"The handwriting is crude," Helga finally said. "The writer was obviously not literate, a tradesman or artesian of some sort or maybe a boy or a girl learning to write."

"I kind of knew that the Egyptians were different from other ancient people," Trudy said, feeling that she had received an affirmation for her passion for these distant folks. Simple girls learning to read.

"These are hard to read. The lines have been eroded over time and the writer could not spell."

What an ordinary failing, Trudy thought. It made the originator of the note more human to her.

"Can you read that?" she asked Helga.

"It takes hours," Helga answered, taking the piece and glass. "The inscription has to be copied on paper using a pencil. There are missing parts of the lines and one must speculate on what the letters are and to fill in what is missing. We use thick paper because we keep erasing lines until the note makes sense. It is much like putting together a puzzle with missing pieces. On this flake, I think the writer wrote 'water of the sky.' That means rain."

Helga rewrapped the shard in its cotton blanket.

"Has Professor Max discovered something important?"

"Many things. Notes expressing problems of workers with construction overseers, sickness, and the troubling conflicts laborers had with their children. If this assumption is correct, literacy among the common Egyptians was far more widespread than originally thought."

*   *   *   *   *

Trudy left the Schneider house oblivious to the ugly reality of war entrenched around her. She realized that the fragmented scribblings of a forgotten, ancient people were just a stone's throw away from her front door. She remembered what Dorothy said in *The Wizard of Oz*. "If I ever go looking for my heart's desire, I'll never go any further than my own backyard." The Schneider garage may not actually have been in her backyard, but she could see the structure from her bedroom window, just past the gun placements and barrage balloon tethers.

Time had forgotten these ancient workers who were probably not even noticed when they lived, people like those living on Wellesley Avenue. The thought that their stories were being brought back to life thrilled her.

In her bedroom, she retrieved the Gardiner book, determined to master the lessons. Helga told her she would begin to teach her to read the hieratic script once she became proficient with formal hieroglyphs. The patient high Lama looked down at her. Allowing her mind to wonder, she thought that someday she might bring back to life someone's forgotten story!

Chapter 26

A Wicked Fairy Tale

ight days after taking Trudy into the garage, Helga went into
labor. Years ago, before she had babies, her mother told her
childbirth was always emotional and intense. Helga had all but
forgotten that warning and not recalled her mother's words until this
third birth. She could not stop thinking of the admonishment.

Helga's going into labor caught Max off guard. When she
telephoned and told him her water broke, he had no way to get home
except by bus. Heaven forbid, Helga thought, he should ask a favor
from someone at the school to drive him home.

"See if there is a neighbor who can drive you to the hospital,"
he said rather sternly. "I will follow."

As soon as she hung up, Helga did something rare. She
disobeyed her husband.

Months before, Max and Helga had discussed taking the bus to
the hospital when the time came, a plan she knew would not work. She
kept this knowledge to herself. Once in labor, her deliveries came
fast—too fast to wait for a bus.

She was surprised that Max had not seen how ridiculous it
would be to put her on a public bus. Nor did he consider the possibility
he would be stranded at the university when the moment came. The
lack of Max's typical pedantic attention to details, when it came to
domestic matters, and his blatant ignorance of childbirth all but assured
that she would have her baby at home. How could he be so
unenlightened, having had two children already born at home? Secretly
she was pleased. The point was she did not want to have her baby in the
hospital where birth was treated like a disease and an unnatural, brutal
experience which God had cursed on Eve and all women.

The more Helga learned about American obstetric care, the
cooler she had become to the idea of going to the local hospital. Her
neighbor Martha Lewis may not remember giving birth because she had

been given gas, but several of the younger German ladies told her about their horrible experience at the maternity ward.

"My arms were tied down and my legs strapped in the air," one woman told her. "At one point, I freed my hand to wipe the sweat off my face and a nurse severely reprimanded me."

"The nurses and doctors are like the Gestapo," another said. "When my baby was ready to come, the delivery room wasn't available. My legs were tied together at the doctor's order and I had to wait hours like this, unattended, before they would let me deliver."

Martha Lewis's doctor treated Helga like a primitive peasant for having her first two babies delivered at home by a midwife. His exam was thorough and clinical, as if she were suffering an abnormality peculiar to females. The reality that she had delivered two babies did not make a difference. Bringing a child into the world did not appear to be a joyful task, only a medical procedure like an appendectomy.

Helga wanted a midwife, but Southern California was too modern to allow such women to practice. She had hoped to find at least a physician who would do the delivery at home, but she soon found that none would. Even the émigré doctors refused. She suspected their reputations would be compromised.

After several weeks, Helga came up with a plan—actually a scheme—to avoid the hospital. She told no one, least of all Max.

She couldn't find a midwife but knew a woman who could deliver the baby. A few empty blocks from Wellesley, lived an old Swiss woman who had assisted a number of mothers in the little town where she and her husband lived before coming to America.

She mentioned her experience in delivering babies when she found out that Helga was pregnant. She said she was always home and could walk over in ten minutes.

Helga never told the lady that she had no intent of going to the hospital and would depend upon her to act the part of midwife.

When the moment came, days earlier than she anticipated, Helga wished she had another plan in place. She called the Swiss woman's house only to be told by her husband that she had taken the bus downtown and would not be home until later than afternoon. Helga

163

then called the Lewis house, but no one was home. Trudy was working. Starting hard labor, she suddenly feared she would have to have the baby alone, like she understood women in primitive places did, dropping them in the fields like cows and horses.

She was frightened and overwhelmed by the increasingly strong contractions as her body began to push the baby out. Sitting on a chair in the living room, she looked at her children who stood in front of her, her own fear reflected in their faces.

"It is all right," she said to reassure them. She forced a smile. "Mommy is going to have the baby now and I'm feeling some pain. Soon you will have a little baby brother or sister."

"I hope it's a girl," Marlene said.

"Mama, can I get you some water?" Jonathon asked.

"Please."

Helga began to silently pray. At this moment, she did not want to be alone. She felt like she was entangled in a wicked fairy tale from her own childhood with evil curses, villainess witches, and tormented princesses, but this was not the Black Forest, an enchantment or a delirious dream she experienced. Her own panic became more an issue than the moments of labor pain. She continued to pray for help, and then, a knock sounded on the front door.

"Oh, God!" Helga cried. She wasn't sure if this was an answer to her prayer or some punishment for her sneakiness.

She told Jonathon to answer the door.

Nelly Mann strolled into the living room. As usual she had dressed impeccably for visiting and wore a pretty hat. Her makeup accented her pretty blue eyes and lush red lips.

"Hello, Helga," she said brightly. Seeing her sprawled in the chair, Nelly's tone changed and she became visibly alarmed. "Oh, my God!"

"I'm having my baby."

"I can see."

"I'm supposed to go to the hospital, but I don't want to."

"Yes, that is not where I would have a baby," Nelly said with disdain. "I would know. I now work at the hospital. Washing dishes."

Helga could not imagine Nelly putting her pretty hands in greasy soap water, but at the moment she didn't care.

"I'm glad you finally found employment but, excuse me, the baby is coming fast."

"Then you have the baby here."

Nelly took off her hat, slipped off her gloves, and put them down with her purse. She looked at the children.

"Little professor, I want you and Marlene to stay here in the living room. I'm taking your mommy into her bedroom so we can bring your little baby sister into the world. Will you obey me?"

"How do you know she will be a sister?" Jonathon asked.

"I just know these things."

Obediently, the children sat down on the sofa.

"I will check with you from time to time, but don't go in the bedroom."

Nelly noticed the oil cloth on the dining room table and removed it. With confident words which Helga could not imagine Nelly uttering, the woman helped her out of the chair and walked her into the bedroom. She asked where the clean towels were kept and if she had a basin.

Chapter 27

The Blue Fairy

As Helga struggled through her labor, Trudy was at home helping her mother with the housework. She had been given the day off from the flashlight factory. She needed a break.

Going outside to get the mail, she noticed Nelly's nice shiny car parked in front of the Schneider house. She wondered if Helga had gone into labor and called Nelly to take her to the hospital. Trudy realized she might need her to watch Jonathon and Marlene.

She walked pass the army encampment. She had grown indifferent to the soldiers' glances and occasional whistling.

Jonathon answered the door.

"I'm going to have a baby sister," Marlene chirped, bouncing around behind her brother.

Trudy asked in German if she could come in the house.

She stepped through the doorway and looked around. Before she could call for Helga, Nelly came out of the master bedroom. In a cerulean dress, Trudy could not help but think of her as the Blue Fairy from *Pinocchio*.

"Oh, good," said Nelly. "Helga is giving birth. Trudy, you can watch the children."

"Here?" Trudy gasped. "She's having the baby here?"

"The baby is coming fast. You take care of the children, please, and I will deliver the baby."

Trudy didn't think people had babies at home anymore—sometimes in cars rushing to the hospital, which always made the newspapers. But not at home.

"If you want to take Helga to the hospital, I will take care of Jonathon and Marlene."

"No, no. She is having the baby here. This is where babies usually come into the world."

Trudy thought it strange that the woman would not rush her to

166

Santa Monica Hospital, but guessed there wasn't time.

"I've done this before. Helga and her baby will be fine."

Nelly went back into the bedroom and Trudy played with the children, who were excited about the baby coming and not scared—at first—but Helga's panting cries soon made Marlene start to tear up. Trudy decided she needed to take the children outside to play.

"Your mother will be fine," Trudy told the children, a little uneasy herself since she had never been this close to a woman giving birth and didn't know quite what to expect. From the little she had heard from her mother and aunt, Trudy learned that the pain was unbearable and modern medicine had made delivery more tolerable. But Helga did not have the benefit of all the new medical innovations.

The children ran around the front yard, playing tag and a silly version of hide-and-seek. When Jonathon and Marlene were chasing each other, and had their backs to her, Trudy looked at the Schneider house, worried for Helga. From what her mother told her about her own birth, the delivery took over a day, which she understood was normal. Trudy worried that she would eventually have to take the children home with her.

Trudy didn't think it had even been an hour when Nelly poked her head out the front door and said with a big smile that the children's baby sister had been born. She called them in the house.

"Your mother is very tired," Nelly told the children before leading them to the bedroom. "You peek in and see your mother and sister, but then you must go back into the living room."

"Yes, Aunt Nelly," Jonathon said somberly.

Trudy followed the children into the bedroom. Helga lay in the bed holding a red faced, squinty infant under her arm. The baby's head rested against her neck. Helga looked spent, but she gave a faint smile when she saw Jonathon and Marlene. Her eyes moved up to Trudy and retained the same smile.

"See. Your mother is happy and well," Nelly said.

"What is my sister's name?" Marlene asked.

"Sophie," Helga whispered.

"Children, you must go now," Nelly told them. "Your mother

needs rest. You will have a whole life together with your sister."

Trudy escorted them back into the living room.

"Thank you, Nelly," Trudy heard Helga say before closing the door.

The delivery was swift and without complication. Nelly must have known her business.

Soon after the children left their mother's bedroom, Professor Max walked in the house. He appeared bewildered by the presence of Trudy and Nelly and the children shouting that mama had the baby in the bedroom.

"You have a pretty baby girl," Nelly told him.

Professor Max walked in the bedroom and stayed there for a long time. Trudy called home. Her mother expressed concern for Helga and asked if an ambulance or the fire department had been called.

"Helga and the baby are fine," Trudy said. Fibbing she said, "the midwife made the delivery, and there were no problems." She didn't think Nelly was a midwife.

"A midwife!" her mother gasped, like Trudy had just told her she had been stealing clothes from a department store.

"I'm going to stay and watch the kids," she said, ignoring her mother's reaction. "I probably won't be home for dinner."

After she hung up, Nelly used the phone.

"Heinrich, Helga Schneider had a baby!" she said and went on to tell him all about the delivery.

Trudy stayed around for the rest of the afternoon and into the evening. She made dinner using ingredients Helga had set out before going into labor. There was some delicious bread with a fruity taste unlike anything that came off the Helms truck. Maybe Bertolt Brecht had a point.

168

Chapter 28

One late August evening, while Trudy, Andy, and her parents sat in the living room listening to Lucky Strike's Your Hit Parade, the show was disrupted by a somber voiced announcer. "We interrupt this program with a news flash," he said. "The Marine Corp commandant, Lieutenant General Thomas Holcomb, announced this evening that Marines have stormed the shores of the Solomon Islands in the South Pacific. This begins the first American land offensive of World War II."

"And the killing at close range," her father muttered. He sat in his chair, eyes closed and a cigarette hanging between the fingers of his extended arm.

Trudy didn't know what he meant at first but realized that ships fire big guns and planes drop munitions from a distance at targets. Men with rifles and bayonets see the faces of the enemy they kill.

The songs resumed. The program ended with Don Cornell singing *I Left My Heart at the Stage Door Canteen*. The final lyrics hung in the air. "A soldier boy without a heart has two strikes on him from the start. And my heart's at the Stage Door Canteen."

How important Nancy's letters must be to Gary. If Trudy had a fellow in the war, she would write him every day, smudge on the reddest lipstick she could find, and imprint each note with a kiss.

"I can dream," she told herself.

Trudy went in her room. Tonight, she would start writing her diary in hieroglyphs, not just an occasional sign here and there like she had been doing for months.

She had already picked cartouche encircled hieroglyphs of certain gods and goddesses to represent the people she knew. *Shu*, the

God of Winds stood for her father, *Isis* the Goddess of motherhood represented her mother, and *Bastet* the gentle and fierce Goddess of cats and children, designated her. She used word symbols to reference other people, being careful to choose references that she would remember like male pygmy to designate her brother.

Writing out hieroglyphs took considerably more time than printing. Most characters consisted of many strokes and demanded great attention to detail. She still had to use an occasional English word.

She first wrote about chatting briefly with Nelly. She created a symbol for her using the glyphs for woman, clothes, and chariot. Trudy thought Nelly was amazing, beautiful, and independent. The only thing that troubled Trudy was the smell of alcohol Nelly always had about her.

Trudy next recorded that school would start in little more than three weeks. She would be a senior.

"What will I be in a year?" she wrote and paused. For a long time, she had intentionally not thought about this, although her mother reminded her that after high school she would have to work a regular job. The implication was clear. She would have employment until she found a guy to marry, started her own family, and kept a house. Uncertain how to address the question, she looked down at the paper, her pen poised above the page. The thought of another possibility came to her, almost like the high Lama whispered the word in her ear. "College." She wrote the word in English and "Why not," not as a question, but as a statement.

Trudy probably could have written more about this but didn't. The three words said enough.

She smiled, remembering Saturday night. She wrote about the neighborhood party. Chuck Lewis had brought home a sound projector, a large shimmering screen and reels of movies from the Walt Disney Studio. After the sun went down, he showed Mickey Mouse cartoons for the soldiers and neighbors.

Chuck had bought several cases of pop, which he put in old metal tubs filled with slick ice shards. Maybe these were things he procured through his work. It had been a hot day and everyone enjoyed

170

sitting on the grass or the chairs on the big back lawn. Even Professor Max, with Jonathon at his side and Marlene sitting on his lap, laughed at Mickey, Goofy, and Donald's funny situations. Trudy never thought that someone so enlightened and scholarly would enjoy silly cartoons.

Trudy vividly remembered how different the yard looked with the gray light bouncing off the screen, backlighting the plants and the people on the grass in front of her. Mixing with the soundtrack were hollow street sounds from Bundy and Pico and faint engine roars from the Douglas plant. At moments, a sweet breeze made a detour through the yard, pleasantly cooling the night with jasmine scented air.

God! She wished she could have found a way to put that magical night in a bottle. She could uncork it whenever she needed to inhale the memory to bump up her mood.

Writing about it, she impulsively created a glyph for Mickey Mouse, drawing three circles, two for ears, and one for the head. She smiled at her invention. She knew she would always recognize what that represented. Hopefully she would remember the event that inspired her making the hieroglyph.

Before going to bed, Trudy decided to write a letter to her Uncle Billy. She didn't know him, and his letter after Pearl Harbor remained fresh and unsettling. Still, she decided he deserved a second chance. He must feel guilt for not being with his buddies during the attack on the Arizona. Taking a breath, she took a piece of good writing paper and began with the salutation, "Dear Uncle Billy."

At one point, she wrote:

I work in a factory that makes flashlights for the Navy. Just think of me when you turn yours on. The flashlight may have passed through my hands. Let the light beam guide you.

That line sounded so dumb she almost tore up the letter, but she continued, mentioning how the whole country was doing its part for the war. She ended with, "Push the Japanese navy to Tokyo Harbor. Love, Trudy."

171

Chapter 29

September

The Saturday before school started, Trudy received a letter from Mary Nakamizo. The return address was a short series of numbers and some place in California called Manzanar.

"I can't begin to tell you how much I miss you and Wellesley," the three pages began. "It seems like it has been a lifetime since we last talked."

Trudy sat down on the front porch's cool concrete, leaned against the post, and continued to read.

> For two months, we lived in a shoe box at the Santa Anita Racetrack. I didn't think our accommodations could get any worse. I was wrong. My family now lives behind barbed wire in a tar-papered barrack, amongst rows of other barracks that were quickly slapped together, isolated in the middle of the dry, windy desert east of Mount Whitney. The dust is as fine as talcum and gets into everything. We all look like we've been patted with a giant powder puff. The soldiers who guard the camp glare at us like we are prisoners. I wouldn't put it past one to shoot a child who wandered too close to the fence. The War Relocation Agency, a civilian group, runs the camp. They refer to us as "evacuees" and the camp as a relocation center. But the place is a concentration camp.
>
> "Trudy, I hope you are not put off by what I'm telling you. I need to blow off steam, and there is no one here I can do that with. Even among the other Sansei (third general American Japanese) I'm criticized. They call me a loud mouth . . .

Trudy could not imagine this. Mary was so soft spoken.

> . . . and have nicknamed me 'Mary Banana.' Yellow on the

outside, white on the inside. My parents are stern with me, which I think you already know. When I'm around the soldiers or a white person I don't know, I bow my head to avoid eye contact. Not out of shame or deference. No. I cannot look up at their faces without glaring.

"My plans about college are up in the air. Berkeley and Stanford are out. I hear that schools in the Midwest and on the East Coast will accept us, but the cost may be too much. . . .

Trudy immediately wrote back. She said that the Nakamizo house was boarded up, safe and sound, and her father continued to watch the place. She did not mention that her father had started a rumor at the army encampment that a Midwest farmer had bought the house from the "Japs."

She wrote about working in the flashlight factory. She also mentioned that she had decided to go to college, although her plans were not as ambitious as Mary's. She encouraged Mary not to give up her dream. As smart and determined as she was, Mary would find a school. "After the war is over and the restriction has been lifted you will be able to transfer to Berkeley or Stanford." How long would that be, Trudy wondered.

*   *   *   *   *

At school, she felt more focused and had a purpose for getting good grades other than for the sole sake of earning A's. But like a graveyard specter reappearing at sunset, the guidance counselor preyed upon her, testing her ambition. This time the lady wanted to put Trudy in business machines and shorthand. Just as she had done the year before, Trudy informed the woman she planned to go to college, actually meaning what she said this time.

"I'm sure you do, honey," the woman said thumbing through some forms on the table that separated the two like a moat. "But you must be practical."

"I am," Trudy said and went on to say that her neighbor, an

173

important professor at UCLA, had encouraged her to go to college. Trudy told the woman she had a special talent with languages. She intentionally did not mention her mastery of Egyptian hieroglyphs. Most adults gave her peculiar looks when she spoke of her ability to decipher and write the ancient text. Even Martha Lewis studied her suspiciously, like Trudy had revealed she could make things levitate.

"You've taken German, no other language. Spanish, French, Latin . . ."

"Well, put me in beginning French."

Instead, she enrolled her in shorthand.

"Remember," the lady said, jotting Trudy's name on the class list, "if you go to college, shorthand will help you take notes."

When Trudy walked in the stenography lab, the first thing she saw was a recruiting poster specifically aimed at the girls. It pictured an austere looking woman in uniform wearing an earmuff headphone. She was poised over a typewriter ready to transcribe a reconnaissance report from a soldier hunkered down in the background, saying into a walkie-talkie, "Calling WAAC . . ."

Before class began, Trudy learned many of the girls were responding to the call. They intended of become WAACs after graduation. These were not "tom boys" but young ladies, several very pretty, who were determined to wear a uniform and do their part to win the war.

"You may be sent overseas!" Trudy cautioned Millie Ward, a girl whose father was now a Marine.

"I want to be sent overseas," Millie replied. She accented her puffy red hair, ruddy complexion and freckles with a yellow blouse that also accentuated her curves. She did not fit the image of a woman who would willingly be bagged in a dull, drab army uniform.

*　　*　　*　　*　　*

After her first day of classes, Trudy experienced strange, conflicting relief and disappointment. Karl was in none. Between the afternoon periods, she saw him walking in the hallway, but she didn't approach him or made an effort to flag him down. She didn't think he had seen her. If he did, he had intentionally walked the other way. She decided the next time she saw him, she would say "hello."

*   *   *   *   *

A month after school started, Trudy's mother received a letter from Uncle Billy. He did not mention receiving Trudy's notes. He did inform her he was being transferred to a Navy oiler, "the dirtiest, foulest, smelliest ship in the Navy." He added that "serving on this bucket is an insult to a seasoned seaman who has served most of his career on battleships." He also wrote that the vessel would frequently be coming into Los Angeles Harbor to load up diesel fuel and aviation gasoline.

*   *   *   *   *

After school, Trudy continued to visit Helga and the Schneider children. Sometimes Nelly came by, walking through the front doorway, fresh and free as a breeze. But her smile and good spirits often seemed forced. Trudy sensed that the woman was having a hard time with no children of her own and no family. Residing in a town where her limited English had to be a handicap and living with a grumpy author who constantly asked her to be his secretary and chauffeur were clearly taking their toll. But their casual conversations in German seemed to relax her. She asked Trudy about her family.

"You only have a brother," she said. "How fortunate. I had so many sisters! The fighting."

When Trudy mentioned she wanted to go to college, Nelly said, "You will make something better of yourself. That is good."

One afternoon, for some reason Trudy mentioned the woman pharaoh Hatshepsut. Maybe she was trying to impress Helga.

Nelly was amazed. "My experience is that women's power is through the bedroom and the domination of their sons."

"Hatshepsut was not only a pharaoh," Trudy continued, "she

175

was one of the great pharaohs. Her temple at Deir el-Bahri is the most beautiful and inspiring structure along the Nile."

Trudy noticed Helga smile, obviously pleased with the girl's growing knowledge of the ancient Egyptians.

Chapter 30

The Letter

Max Schneider sat in the faculty dining hall eating lunch with composer/professor Arnold Schoenberg. The man was gaunt, his eyes tired, and his shoulders stooped. His appearance spoke of bitter discouragement. One of the greatest composers of the twentieth century, he had for five years been a frustrated professor at UCLA. Schneider thought of Schoenberg as a whale beached on the Pacific coast, flopping mightily among spawning California grunions that come out of the sea during full moons. Today, their conversation was superficial and void of the passion that Schoenberg usually expressed about whatever subject they discussed. Both seemed to need a break. Max certainly did. His sleep had been routinely disrupted by Helga getting up in the middle of the night to minister to Sophie.

After lunch, Max went to the mail room where he found a letter from Vichy France, addressed to him in a familiar hand. He ignored the memos and the rest of the correspondents in his box and briskly walked to his office.

In the privacy of his room, he split open the feather light air post envelope and unfolded the delicately thin papers inside. Before reading a word, he heard the voice of the writer and saw the shadow of someone who had touched him years ago—someone he could not forget.

Dear Max

 I write to you because there is no one else left. My family has disappeared, forcibly deported from Germany, probably into a concentration camp in Poland. I have had no word in two years from them, nor do I know of their fate. My family stubbornly remained in Berlin when other Jews were fleeing. I can only assume they were rounded up by the Schutzstaffel in 1940.

I fear the worse. Every Jew who did not run away has been swept up.

I thought I was free of persecution, but that changed when the Nazis invaded Holland. They violated the sanctity of the university and immediately ordered the Jewish faculty to be terminated.

There was no place to hide from the squads of stone-faced Security Police who forced us out of our apartments, crammed us onto trucks, and placed us in the unbelievably crude dormitories of the Vught labor camp. At night, I slept on rough wood floors.

The working conditions were foul, but the knowledge each of us would be deported someday to a death camp made each day's existence nearly tolerable. We could at least say we were still alive.

But the day came when my time ran out. I and hundreds of others were dispatched to the Westerbork transit camp. Some disruption occurred in the rail yard and the train sat on the track for hours. Someone noticed one of the hatches in the roof of our rail car had been broken. Five of us managed to climb out and slip away in the dark. We went to a church, hoping we would be granted sanctuary. The other woman in our group said the young priest here was a good man. What else could we do?

The priest was terrified, like we were lepers. He hesitated for a moment and then told us to go into the rectory. We stayed in the dark basement of the church for days. From there we were taken to a convent, moved one at a time to avoid drawing attention. I am sure if the SS had discovered that we had broken out of the freight car, they would have hunted us down.

You wouldn't think these sisters had the wherewithal for assisting us, but they did. I eventually found myself in southern France. But that was not the end of the ordeal. Soon the French began rounding up Jews. I managed to avoid incarceration and entered the Italian zone—one of the last safe havens in Europe. The French police are forbidden to arrest us here, and so I am safe. Max, I am safe!

178

Mail between unoccupied France and the United States is unreliable. If you are reading this letter, then the trust I put in the Partisan who took this letter to post, has been rewarded.

I am living with a family of Jews who have been here for generations. I assist in their grocery store which means that I dust empty bins. Food is limited.

I kept the letter you wrote to me before leaving for the United States. The concern you expressed for my safety is appreciated. Now stained with sweat, it is a touchstone for me, reminding me that there is integrity yet in the world.

Max, our relationship did not end on the most cordial note. I appreciate your reaching out. Your care and your warning means much to me.

For obvious reasons, I can neither give you a return address nor the name of my contact in Vichy France through whom I have sent this correspondence. If I can, I will write again.

Always,

Rebekah

Max folded the letter, slipped it back in the envelope and held it between his fingers, like a smoker would idly hold a cigarette. Swiveling in his chair, he looked out the window. Below, the large empty campus with its vast lawns and orchards extended to the edge of Westwood Village. Thin palm trees with topknots of fans, and several tall towers whose only function was to display commercial logos, broke the otherwise flat blocks of red tile roofs covering white walled shops, restaurants, and movie theaters. From a distance, except for the narrow modernist steeples, the scene did not look much different from the views in small cities on the French Mediterranean Coast. But there the similarity ended. Max was safe. Meanwhile, Rebekah remained caught in a temporary haven that could be thrown open to the SS if the Italians gave into Hitler's demand to purge all Europe of its Jews.

Chapter 31

Trudy's Decision

In early November, U.S. troops landed along the 1000-mile coast of Morocco and Algeria. 140,000 American soldiers were reported to have waded ashore with tanks, jeeps and artillery, finally moving to engage the Nazi and Italian armies. Like the afternoon whistle blowing full throttle at the steam plant on the corner of Bundy and Olympic, the newspapers and radio stations screamed updated and upbeat stories of the successful American landing. But instead of fighting the Germans, the Yanks were immediately engaged by the Vichy French, who though technically neutral, seemed to side with the Axis. The French were outgunned and soon surrendered.

The Americans pushed east and the British finally pounded Rommel's Afrika Korps off Egyptian sand.

As she rode her bike to school, Trudy noticed blue star service banners in the windows of homes indicating the families who had a son in the service. Trudy was saddened to see two of the blue emblems had been replaced with a gold star banner, meaning that a man had died in action. With the American expansion in the war, there would soon be more gold stars in the windows.

Between classes, Trudy saw Karl and one day several weeks after school started, finally got up the nerve to approach him. She didn't know quite what to say. He froze when he saw her and looked back as if she were asking for a donation.

"Hi, Karl. Long time no see."

"We don't have any classes together," he said rather blandly. For a guy who wanted to be a writer she thought his reply rather trite.

"I've wondered how your writing's been going. If you have had a chance to hear any other playwrights speak, or if your uncle is doing anything—besides driving a cab."

"He's in the Navy. He's younger than my dad."

"I have an uncle who's in the Navy. Wouldn't it be funny if they were on the same ship?"

Karl tried to smile. He responded like he was being questioned by the school principal about a possible infraction. Trudy sensed he feared her brother would jump out of the hedge. Her heart sank. Her expression must have changed because Karl's tone softened.

"You still studying hieroglyphs?"

"My neighbor's teaching me. I now use it to write in my diary. I'm hoping that I'll start learning the cursive version, which is what the ancients used for everyday stuff."

"That's amazing."

The tone of his acknowledgment was enough to make her feel glad she took a chance on speaking to him.

Since they were passing between classes, they didn't have time to say more.

"I just wanted to say 'hi' and see how you're doing," she said, stepping back. "See you around."

"See you," Karl replied and continued his way, glancing around like he was looking out for her brother and his friends. Trudy hoped there would be no trouble. She would kill Andy if he did anything.

*   *   *   *   *

At dinner, Trudy had pushed aside thoughts of Karl and prepared to announce something to her parents. She was a little nervous about her timing, however. Her mother was in a bad mood because Andy had gotten car oil on the towel in the bathroom and effectively ruined it.

"I've been thinking a lot about what I want to do after I graduate from high school," Trudy said, when she sensed her parents were settled in, ready as they would ever be to hear what she had to say.

"Oh, what's that?" her father asked.

"I've decided to go to UCLA."

Her father smiled, apparently accepting the news, but didn't speak and looked to her mother, waiting for her reaction.

"Go to college. What for?" she asked, not in a hostile way, but

181

rather, surprised and seemingly curious.

"Yeah," Andy groused, glancing up from shoveling food in his mouth. "College is just a way to avoid getting a job."

"I want to be a schoolteacher," she replied, and gave her brother a dirty look. Andy rolled his eyes.

Her mother shook her head and didn't say anything, just ate her dinner.

"I've got the grades," Trudy finally said. "I can get in."

"Okay, you got the grades, but how are you going to pay for it?" her mother asked, looking at her critically. "And why do you want to be a teacher? Trudy, they don't make any money. You could do better working at Douglas or the phone company, and you wouldn't have to spend all those years in school."

"I don't want to work in an office. I don't want to be an operator or work in some factory making flashlights or planes for the rest of my life. I want to go to college."

"Trudy, in no time at all you will be married and have kids," her mother said. "Isn't it enough you'll graduate from high school?"

"I want to be a teacher. And who's going to marry me? I'm hardly Snow White."

"You scare boys off. You act too smart."

"I'm not Susan French or Nancy Pierce. And there is nothing wrong being a teacher. They help kids learn, even kids like Andy."

Her brother glared at her. Her father covered his smile by bringing his cigarette up to his mouth.

"I can't understand why you would want to be a teacher," her mother said. "There's nothing in it. If you like kids so much, get married and have your own."

Frustrated, she answered, "It's not the same thing."

"Well, we're not going to chip-in for you to go to college," she said. "You can do what you want, but it won't be on our dime. And you'll still have to pay room and board."

Her mother had already told her that she would have to pay to live at home, once she graduated from high school.

"I'll have to get a job, I know."

Trudy glanced at her father who had put down his fork and continued to suck on his cigarette like it was the only way he could breathe. Their eyes connected for a second before he looked down. She glanced away, fearful she would start to cry. Why couldn't he speak his own mind? She saw his reaction when she first said she wanted to go to college.

Her mother silently and sullenly shook her head and began picking at her food. The fork tines loudly clicked as she stabbed the pale green, wrinkled peas.

"I could become a WAAC instead," Trudy said, annoyed.

"Don't be ridiculous," her mother muttered, avoiding eye contact.

Trudy let the subject drop. There was no sense in trying to change her mother's mind, and there was nothing her mother could say to change hers. With men going off to war and women sacrificing their domestic security by leaving their homes to replenish the ranks of the male depleted work force, there were more important things right now than a spat about college.

Chapter 32

A Growing Mastering of Hieroglyphs

Trudy's mother now allowed Trudy to wear makeup, something she had been doing off and on for months behind her parents' back. She applied cosmetics daily, but the products failed to turn her into a Hollywood beauty. She half-heartedly spread the foundation and blush which hide the reddish blotches but did nothing to conceal the asphalt texture of her skin. And her hair remained as thick, fuzzy, and out of control as ever, flopping down on her forehead like tumble weeds. No soft waves could be coaxed from the tangle.

Women's styles had changed, and girls were applying brighter, redder lipstick that made their mouths fluid pools of rubies. At Susan's encouragement, Trudy occasionally used the color, but she thought her lips looked like a gaudy Christmas decoration.

By the anniversary of the attack on Pearl Harbor, Trudy had become acclimatized to conditions that had not existed before December 7: Meatless Mondays. Masses of women working in ugly defense factories. White-helmeted Civil Defense Corp volunteers stationed throughout the community. Blackouts. War Bond campaigns. Enlistment posters everywhere. On the radio, patriotic commentaries and songs about servicemen and their sweethearts.

Every other movie now concerned the war. Even Sherlock Holmes was portrayed as a modern man uncovering Nazi spies. Stories of brave sailors, soldiers, and Marines appeared daily in the newspapers and magazines.

Blood Drives. Victory gardens. Rationing and shortages. Soldiers and their big guns permanently planted in the fields on Wellesley. Barrage balloons floating over the house. Boys and even some of the girls at school, including Susan, wearing uniforms. The removal of Japanese American citizens from the Pacific coast.

Nothing no longer seemed remarkable.

In early December, Trudy received another letter from Mary

Nakamizo. She wrote about the icy cold, the limited amount of meat in the camp, and the lack of privacy. There were no partitions between the toilets. At least she was more positive about her school.

All the barracks of block 7 have been converted into a high school. The teaching staff are mostly from outside but some, especially the science and math instructors, are ~~inmates~~ evacuees. We are being taught as we would in any other school.

Mary finished her note telling Trudy about her brothers.

My oldest brother, Ronny, remains stationed at Fort Knox. He says he gets flak from some soldiers but not from anyone in his outfit.

Daniel has volunteered to join the army. My parents consider this an honorable act.

Trudy had concerns about her own brother. At the beginning of the war, men had to be twenty-one to be drafted. There was a good chance the fighting would be over when Andy reached that age. Then in October, General Marshall announcement that older soldiers didn't have what it took to endure the strain of warfare. "Modern fighting demands youthful vigor." He endorsed a measure in Congress to drop the draft age to eighteen which the House and Senate quickly passed. Her brother could be drafted in less than a year and a half!

*   *   *   *   *

Two days later, after dinner, when her dad turned on the radio to *Amos and Andy*, Trudy went to her room and closed the door. She took her diary out of the corner of her vanity table drawer and reread what she had written over the last few months. Her writing now consisted mostly of ancient Egyptian. She had to invent a few hieroglyphs for modern objects, but her mastery of the basics had improved since the end of the summer. Helga gave the girl more tips on grammar and format. Trudy felt a burst of satisfaction realizing she could read, weeks later, what she had written.

Last month she had noted:

Mom's reaction was about what I expected when I announced I want to go to UCLA. Dad sat next to her hardly saying anything, although I think he was pleased. Why didn't he say something? He's such a coward!

She had used the modern alphabet to spell out the ancient word for coward, *behau*, instead of using the hieroglyphic script, making the word stand out.

I told them I want to be a schoolteacher which is a big lie. I wish I hadn't lied but this was the only thing I could think of that mom might understand. I really don't know what I want to do. I know what I don't want to do—be a housewife, work in the flashlight factory, or work another factory job or be an office girl.

Trudy had written this without inventing any of her own hieroglyphs. She had to substitute "torch" for "flashlight," but the Egyptians had a glyph for "housewife," "factory," and "office." Because she was using the formal script, it took her more time to write these lines than in English. Hopefully, Helga would soon begin teaching her the cursive hieratic style.

Her motive for going to college still seemed vague and maybe no more practical than her learning hieroglyphs. What could she do with a college degree? Find an educated husband and have his kids? Marrying a doctor or a lawyer would offer a type of security her mother never had. That would be nice. She could live in a house in Brentwood, probably having someone come in to do the heavy housework, allowing her time to read, explore serious subjects, and maybe do volunteer work. The idea was exciting, stirring comfort—and discontent. What nice man would want to marry her? Really. The dream was just a fantasy, a fanciful fairy tale. Whether she went to college or not, she would have no one to support her but herself.

She opened the diary to the next blank page, slipped the lid off her fountain pen, and began a new entry recording the contents of Mary's letter.

1943

Chapter 33

Uncle Billy

Gary had hoped that he would be assigned to the Army's Pictorial Service," Nancy said, one cold and windy afternoon in February. Walking her bike, Trudy escorted her friend to the corner to catch the Santa Monica Blue Bus. Nancy still worked at the flashlight factory. Her family needed the extra money.

"He knows all about cameras and film processing," she added. "Photography is sort of what he was doing at the printing plant."

Trudy thought it would be more dangerous to carry a camera instead of a gun on a battlefield.

"Remember the old saying," Trudy said grasping at anything she could think of to cheer Nancy up. "There's safety in numbers."

"I just don't feel that people around me are lucky."

Last year, her father had been injured in a car accident and that summer her kid brother had been struck down with polio.

"The paper says the Allies are bogged down in Tunisia," Nancy said. "Rain, strong enemy forces, German superior air power—it's all working against them."

"Won't it take weeks for Gary's unit to get to North Africa?" Trudy asked, trying to give Nancy a positive spin on the situation. "By then, the Allies will have things in hand."

"The war won't be over," Nancy said. "He'll just be sent somewhere else."

Trudy didn't have a response to that. She knew that Nancy was right, and that American strategy was to help clear North Africa, cross the Mediterranean and land troops somewhere in southern Europe.

For Trudy, the war had become like a dull pain in her side, something she could normally ignore but other times couldn't escape, especially when she thought of Nancy and Gary, and her uncle. She distracted herself by staying focused on her schoolwork and hieroglyphs, determined to get good grades, to go to UCLA, and to master the ancient writing so that it would become a second language.

*   *   *   *   *

On a Friday, in late March, she decided to reward herself for the hard work she was doing for school and the hours she spent weeding the family Victory Garden. Since the first of the year, she had been dying to see the movie *Casablanca* with Humphrey Bogart and Ingrid Bergman. It was showing in Hollywood. She couldn't wait another two months for the film to come to a local theater.

Her mom hadn't being using her car. It almost had a full tank of gas. She let Trudy drive to Hollywood. After dinner, the girl picked up Susan and Nancy and trekked to the Warner Theater.

The Warner wasn't what Trudy expected for a first-run show. It seemed to have been jammed into a big office building. The marquee had been tacked above the ground floor storefronts. The massive canopy of blinking lights looked like the facade had been haphazardly situated to distinguish the theater entrance from the neighboring haberdashery, women's clothing shop and pharmacy.

Casablanca turned out to be worth the long drive. Trudy fell in love with Humphrey Bogart and cried when Ingrid Bergman flew away.

After the movie, the three girls walked down Hollywood Boulevard, mysterious and enchanting in the night's shadows and growing elfin mist. There were many servicemen on the street, some who whistled at them—well at least at Susan and Nancy. Still, Trudy smiled.

The three were just a few blocks from the Hollywood Canteen on Cahuenga Boulevard. Susan suggested they walk over and mingle with the troops. Nancy reminded her that only screened volunteers could get into the canteen. Trudy was relieved.

An hour later, when Trudy pulled in her driveway, she could see lights on in the living room and kitchen. That was strange. Even before she walked in the house, she heard an unfamiliar voice, deep and raspy. The front door was unlocked. She opened it and saw a big, burly man on the sofa, sitting in front of Andy and holding a bottle of Eastside

192

Beer. A cigarette dangled from the fingers of his other hand. The air in the living room was almost as cold as the early spring night outside, but he had stripped off his shirt, shoes and socks. His chest, belly, and feet were fish white in contrast to his walnut forearms, neck, and face. He stopped talking and with a challenging cock of his head looked at her with a hawking eye. She realized this had to be her Uncle Billy.

"Hi, Uncle Billy. I'm Trudy," she said, countering his silent brassiness with a schoolgirl smile. "Don't you remember me?"

"You were a little kid!" he snorted. "What did you do? Grow up?"

"Yeah, I grew up."

Andy had turned around.

"His boat's in San Pedro for a couple of day."

"The oiler is a ship," Billy corrected. "Not much of one, I grant you, but the bucket is what it is."

"He's got a twenty-four-hour shore leave! He's staying with us tonight."

The boy turned his attention back to his uncle.

"I'm so glad you're safe," she said. "I've been worried about you, with all the battles waging in the Pacific."

"The Japs are getting the crap kicked out of them," he said. "But they're going down fighting. Saw a destroyer hit by a torpedo. The fifteen-hundred tonner didn't sink but lost some men and had to be towed to the shipyard."

"What ship are you on?"

"The Tippecanoe." He looked at Andy. "A disgraceful name for a ship, if you ask me. Obviously, the Navy Department didn't, so they christened oiler AO21 with a moniker that would make anyone think the vessel's a leaky dinghy."

"Did you get my letters?"

"I got one or two," he said, in a tone as indifferent as if he had been asked to pass the butter.

Andy turned to stare at Trudy, silently willing her to get lost.

"I'll let you guys talk," she said. Maybe her brother had been asking the "old salt" about what he could expect if he got drafted into

193

the Navy.

Before she closed the hall door, Uncle Billy resumed his story.

"Where was I? Oh, yeah, they put out this feast of pig and yams. We eat with our fingers, slopping the meal down with grog while bare-breasted native girls wearing grass skirts that hung way down here danced the hula . . ."

Shocked, Trudy shut the door and threw her purse on the bed and quickly walked into the bathroom.

* * * * *

Way past midnight the phone rang waking the house. Trudy heard her parents' door open and her mother pick up.

"Billy, slow down," she said.

Trudy's heart began to race. She jumped up and put on her robe. Maybe her uncle had been in an accident. But that made no sense. He was here. She opened her door.

Without makeup and with her hair in curlers, her mother looked grim and disheveled in the harsh hall light. She grimaced and said, "You got in another fight." Scowling, she listened to Uncle Billy's response, intermittently shaking her head.

Trudy watched, confused.

"It's three o'clock in the morning," her mother finally said. Pause. "Billy, why did you go down there?" Another pause. "So, you left your gear here." She shook her head at the wall. "Do you know what you're asking? There is gas rationing!" Long pause. "Okay, okay. I'll come down." Snapping her finger at Trudy, and making a scribbling motion, she asked, "What's the address?"

Trudy's father, his hair in a tangle and his eyes puffy, barely awake, came out from his bedroom.

"What's wrong?" he asked.

"Billy's backstage at the Follies Theater, hiding from the police. He beat up some pachucos."

The girl took a moment to make the connection. Sailors had been attacking pachucos, Mexicans street gang members, peacocking in their outrageous zoot suits. The Follies was a downtown burlesque house which ran shocking newspaper ads featuring scantily clad women and the tag line "more curves than the Burma Road." Trudy could not imagine her mother entering that place, even to retrieve her brother.

"He was here when I went to bed," her father said, still half asleep.

"Well," her mother muttered. "He left. Get dressed. We're going to pick him up."

"We'll have to take my car," Trudy's father said, walking back into the bedroom.

Chapter 34

Graduation

The morning after her final day of high school classes, Trudy rode her bike to UCLA and secured an application form.

Walking out of the administration building, she held the paper in her hand, looking at the form as if she had a first-class ticket to Europe on the Queen Mary in peace time. She glanced over the lines to be filled out, her heart beating faster, realizing what this piece of paper represented.

Trudy carefully placed the application in her notebook and put the binder in her pack. As she pulled her bike out of the rack, she noticed how pleasant the temperature was and how clear the sky looked. Mounting, she pedaled off the campus and coasted down Hilgard Avenue for a nice ride home.

Two days later, just like the other girls, Trudy put on her best dress for the graduation commencement. Because her class was so big, the school held the ceremony outside. As they had practiced the day before, the graduating class marched out of the boy's gym in their gowns and mortarboards, and in two lines sauntered across the girls' field.

During the ceremony, Trudy mentally checked off items on the agenda outlined on the program. Several tedious speeches were given, all addressing the war, interspersed by the orchestra playing serious pieces of music.

At the end of the ceremony, the students mingled with their parents and guests, the girls hugging their friends and the boys slapping their buddies' backs. Many familiar faces were being seen for the last time. Sadly, their class did not have a yearbook to commemorate their experiences and provide a lasting remembrance. The *Chieftain* was a casualty of the war.

Trudy noticed Karl standing with a big man, whom she took to be his father, and two nicely dressed women whom she assumed were his mother and aunt. She turned, to reduce the chance that Karl would notice her.

Trudy found Susan, then Nancy, and bumped into a few other friends and their families. Her father was soon concerned about the time. He had made reservations for dinner.

Trudy couldn't deny her delight that the family would have dinner at Lawry's in Beverly Hills. They never had patronized such a snazzy restaurant. Famous for its prime rib, Lawry's now substituted turkey cuts for the red meat, which had become extinct even to the elite due to war rationing.

When they walked into the lobby, Trudy was shocked to see Karl and his family standing in front of the hostess's desk. Before she could detour into the ladies' room, she and the boy made eye contact. She felt a sudden quake that caused her to freeze. More out of fear than a genuine spirit of comradery, she walked over to the Blacks, her parents and Andy drifting behind.

"Congratulations, Karl." Looking at his parents and a woman she assumed was the notorious aunt, she said, "My name's Trudy. I've known Karl for years."

"Oh, you're Trudy," said Karl's mother with a sweet smile. She looked over to the girl's mother. "I felt so bad for her. Missing her junior prom because she got sick."

Obviously, Karl had not told his mother the truth. Trudy looked at him, and he smiled. He appeared just as awkward as ever. She could sense Andy standing behind her, probably making no effort to appear cordial.

"It was upsetting," her mother said, in her phony sweet voice, shaking hands with Karl's mother. "It just came on really sudden."

"Karl tells me you plan to go to college. What school?"

"UCLA."

"You probably know that Karl's father teachers there."

The man looked down at Trudy like he was a star and she a movie extra from Central Casting.

"You know Professor Schneider?" Trudy asked. "He's our neighbor."

197

"I know Schneider," the man answered.

As the hostess arrived to show them to their table, Trudy's mother wished the Black family well. Trudy could not believe how easily her mother put on her fake face. Her father smiled and told them how pleased he was to meet them all. Maybe he was. He shook Karl's and his father's hands.

Fortunately, the Mansfields were seated in a corner out of sight of the Blacks. Trudy felt greatly relieved.

When the family returned home, her mother told Trudy to close her eyes and led her into the house. Trudy knew she was being ushered to the dining table. By interpreting her brother's familiar grunts, she figured his impatience involved not wanting to wait any longer for a piece of the cake her mother had baked in her honor.

But when her mother guided her into the chair her father normally occupied at Sunday dinners, Trudy could not smell the expected hint of confectioners' sugar. Perhaps her mother had to retrieve the cake from the kitchen.

On command Trudy opened her eyes and saw in front of her an Underwood typewriter. Totally surprised, she looked up at her parents and told them they could not have given her a more wonderful present. Her reaction seemed to please them. Her father was especially proud.

"With rationing, these are scarce as hens' teeth," he said. "It's not new but you wouldn't know that if I didn't tell you."

The machine actually gleamed. Her father had probably thoroughly cleaned the typewriter.

"You can set up a secretarial service," her mother said, "doing typing for businesses in the area and for soldiers who have something they need to take care of back home."

The comment sucked the joy out of the moment.

"Or doing papers for school," her father added, refreshing the air with oxygen.

Her mother gave him a sideways glance, like he had told a dirty joke, but Trudy smiled.

Chapter 35

The Bundy

Before graduating, Trudy's mother told her in a pleasant enough voice, that being eighteen meant she would have more freedom,—although she was always expected to behave like a lady.

"You'll soon have a job," her mother went on. "When I was two years your junior, I was working and paying my parents to live at their house. It was an obligation that helped me to begin thinking like an adult."

Thinking about finding a husband, no doubt, thought Trudy.

"I plan to get a job," Trudy answered, resentful and determined to not let employment interfere with future schooling.

"Your dad can get you work at Douglas," her mother reminded her.

*   *   *   *   *

With the war, there were jobs galore for women, mostly full time. Trudy found part time work, merely by chance, just a short walk from the house.

The night after her graduation, she had gone to the Bundy Theater to see *One Dangerous Night*, the latest Lone Wolf mystery starring Warren William, who had the eerie presence of a dapper hypnotist. That night, the theater seemed understaffed. A fat man in a wilted tuxedo, whom she had always assumed to be the manager, uncharacteristically sold popcorn and refreshments. On a lark, she asked if they were hiring. Without looking at her, counting change for another patron, he asked, "When can you start?" Later she learned two people had been fired earlier that evening for stealing money from the cash drawer.

During the intermission, she followed the manager into the men's lounge, through a door in the corner marked "private," and up

199

a dim, narrow stairway. He grunted with each step. On the landing, they passed a door, through which, she could hear the clatter of film being pulled through the projector.

In the shadows of the manager's office two windows opened onto the portholes located on each side of the tower above the marque.

"You worked before?" he asked, handing her an information card to fill out. He walked around his desk and, like he was a big sack of cement, dropped into his chair.

"Last summer at the Acme Flashlight Factory."

"They fired you?"

"No. I can go back."

"Why don't you?"

"I don't like working in a factory. And I plan to start college in the fall. UCLA."

"If you work out, I can arrange your hours in the fall so you can go to school and work."

He had to be desperate.

"I live a couple of blocks away. On Wellesley."

"Can you start tomorrow afternoon? Work four to eleven."

"Sure." She had no plans for Saturday night, although her mother had talked about going to the Santa Monica Wilshire and seeing the new Andy Hardy film. She could probably talk her mom into coming to the Bundy instead.

The manager took her to the storage room, next to his office. It was stacked with boxes of candy, rolls of tickets, film cans, and other things inventoried. Across one wall assorted uniforms hung on a rack.

"Find something that fits," he coughed. "Be here by three-thirty and Judy will show you the ropes." He walked out of the room without telling her where she would clock in. Through the wall, she heard his weighted body thumping down the stairs.

Judy turned out to be his pug-nosed daughter who said she was thirteen, but the staff suspected was only eleven. She didn't allow her pre-adolescence size and contour to hinder her when dealing with older people or boys who had smart mouths. Nor did she use her position as "boss's daughter" to win special treatment. Responsible and

200

hardworking, Trudy thought she and Judy were two of a kind.

Judy showed the new hire all the tricks of the candy counter including how to make popcorn and recharge the soda machine when a syrup container ran out. She made it clear that the candy girl was responsible for all that happened in the foyer and had to handle any situation that came up. Only in the worst case was she to signal her father with the buzzer next to the cash drawer—one buzz, patron demanding to speak to the manager, two buzzes, a fight in the theater, and three buzzes, a hold up.

Trudy learned that the theater had difficulty finding help. With so many young men in the services, help was hard to find. On top of that, the Bundy could not compete with the defense plants, which offered young women more money plus the sense that they were doing something to win the war.

The people selling the candy and tickets were a strange bunch, all girls except for one young man, Robert. He rarely smiled. He was 4F, so like Karl probably had asthma or some other medical condition. She never asked.

After work, she smelled like butter and her fingers were sticky with Pepsi Cola syrup. Her father said the uniform made her look older. Her mother said she looked cute. She told neither that wearing the blue and marigold tunic with its matching skirt made her think of herself as special. Being part of the movie experience filled her with a good feeling.

Behind the candy counter, when she idly looked across the foyer and beyond the outdoor lobby and the ticket booth, Trudy realized if she could not see the street through the glass doors, she would not know day for night. Like being deep in a cave, granted, one with thick carpet, streamline moderne curved walls and indirect lighting, daytime and nighttime became confused. That was part of the magic of movies. She had still not outgrown the notion that movie theaters were marvelous illusionists' chambers. For over thirty hours a week, she transformed herself into one of the conjurors' assistants, the functionaries who so awed her as a child.

201

*   *   *   *   *

As a graduation gift, Helga began to teach Trudy hieratic script. She lent the girl one of her German primers. Professor Max soon retrieved for her, from the UCLA library, an old book in English on the subject.

Despite Helga's caution about the commitment it would take to learn this form of writing, Trudy found it to be less difficult to master than formal hieroglyphs. The hieratic symbols were quick lines and curves that abbreviated the strokes of the hieroglyphic characters she already memorized. She found the writing script came rather easily to her. This fed her hope that Professor Max would give her the chance to translate small snippets from his collection. The thought fired her imagination. She envisioned discovering a missive written by a young woman to a friend telling her about . . . her boyfriend being eaten by crocodiles or her cat having kittens? Who could tell what she could uncover.

"What's that scribbling?" Judy asked one afternoon. When things got slow and there was nothing else to do, Trudy took to practicing writing the abbreviated hieroglyphs in a notebook.

Trudy flushed, embarrassed that someone had noticed her practice.

"It's shorthand," she said, thinking at first, she was lying but realizing she was not.

"I've never seen any shorthand like that."

"This is a very old type of shorthand. It's called hieratic script."

"Are you taking notes?"

"Huh?"

"You know. Writing down things that happen or things you notice. Like that man with a funny mole on his nose who just bought Juicy Fruits. I read somewhere that people who write novels and short stories for the *Saturday Evening Post* make notes of stuff like that."

"That's sort of what I'm doing, I guess." Trudy smiled. That was a lie, but a white one.

"Well if you ever use me in your story, make me a heroine who

202

rescues her boyfriend from the electric chair."

*   *   *   *   *

Since there was not much activity in the foyer when the movies ran, one of the two candy counter girls took a flashlight and patrolled the auditorium. The Bundy was a second run theater and didn't have usherettes routinely stationed inside the doors to assist patrons to find seats. Patrolling the evening shows tended to be uneventful. If she really liked the movie, she would stand at the back of the auditorium, watching as much of the film as she could before returning to the candy counter.

*   *   *   *   *

In late July, the newsreel was updated, featuring the first motion pictures of the American invasion of Sicily. It showed scenes of tanks, artillery, jeeps, marching soldiers, and enemy prisoners with their arms raised as they walked past bombed out buildings. Trudy thought of the increasing number of blue stars in the windows and of Nancy's Gary. Was he trekking and fighting his way across the mountain island?

One night in early August, as had become routine, Trudy came home after eleven. As occasionally happened, when she walked past a sentry, she was asked if anything good was showing at the Bundy. The soldiers were now like neighbors.

The house was black. She moved carefully to avoid making any sound. She had been at work since three that afternoon. She knew she needed to eat something. Just thinking of food intensified her hunger. Too tired to put something on the stove, she ate a bowl of Cheerios with a sliced banana.

In her bedroom, after pulling together the blackout curtains, she had already started to undress when she noticed two envelopes leaning against the pillow on her bed. She almost jumped when she saw the top letter's return address: University of California, Los Angeles Campus.

Despite the hour, Trudy found herself suddenly wide awake, her

203

heart pounding and her fingers in a tangle. She picked up the envelope. The thickness suggested that it contained several pages. The correspondence had to be an acceptance letter. Then a demon whispered that the letter had to be a rejection notice. School didn't start until October, and the registration cutoff date was still a month away. Maybe more forms needed to be filled out.

To stop the torment, she ripped open the envelope. She fumbled with the pages and let out a deep breath when she read the cover letter advising that she had been accepted for the fall semester.

She sat on the bed and carefully read all the enclosed materials. They were instructions and hints for registering for her freshman courses.

Being so late, she could tell no one the news. She felt like bouncing around the room. She rushed over to her vanity, pulled open the drawer and snatched her diary to record the news and her reaction. This time in English. She was too excited to use hieroglyphs.

She had almost forgotten the second envelope on her pillow. It was a letter from Mary.

> *No news is good news, I guess. My brothers are in a battalion that is made up of soldiers of Japanese descent, enlistees from Hawaii, along with a few boys from the mainland. They are still in Wisconsin, training. My older brother has been promoted to first sergeant. I guess that's an important rank.*
>
> *No one knows when they will be deployed overseas or if they will ever see combat. One thing is clear. The army doesn't trust them to fight in the Pacific. In reality, if they were sent, they would be loyal, hard fighting American soldiers and would not hesitate to kill "Japs."*
>
> *I got your letter about applying to UCLA. I'm sure you'll get in. Let me know when you are accepted.*
>
> *I graduated from the high school here and am going through the process of enrolling in a college back east. There is an organization, The National Japanese American Student Relocation Council which works out of Philadelphia. They find*

schools, scholarships, grant clearances, and, most daunting, they obtain leaves from the camps. There are many of us here who want to go on to college. The good news is that most of those who were attending UCLA, Berkeley, Stanford, etc. have been permitted to continue their education in Eastern schools. I've been working through a stack of paperwork. . .

Trudy felt better for Mary and felt a kindred connection now that she would be going to college. Being accepted by UCLA changed her sense of who she was. She was now a young woman with a future.

Chapter 36

Hangmen Also Die

By mid-August, Allied forces were moving slowly forward on all fronts like a farmer's tractor carving furrows in a field. The newsreels were dramatic, upbeat and implied that American troops were welcomed as liberators in Sicily. Allied planes were bombing Germany and Italy, day and night, and in Quebec, F.D.R. gave a speech telling the Axis to "surrender now," declaring Hitler "doomed."

The last week of August, Helga asked Trudy if she could babysit that coming Friday evening. She could not. Two days before, Judy excitedly told Trudy that on that night the Bundy would be hosting a sneak preview and important Hollywood people would be attending. Everyone would have to work. Trudy mentioned Nancy. She was working full time at the flashlight factory, learning to use the sheet-metal machines, but still babysat in the evenings.

Trudy had never been to a preview, although studios showed their movies all the time at the smaller neighborhood theaters to get audience reactions before the films' release. She would not be able to watch the film herself. She would be working the candy counter. Still, selling popcorn and Milk Duds to a famous Hollywood star would be thrilling. Maybe Spencer Tracy, Cary Grant or Van Johnson would attend!

The next morning, she told her mother about Friday night. Her mom was excited at the possibility of seeing an important actor or actress and said she would walk to the theater by herself if her husband or son did not want to go with her. Trudy felt important, knowing that her simple job selling candy allowed her to give her mother a special treat.

Around eight o'clock that Friday evening, during the intermission, the early patrons were asked to go in the foyer for a few minutes. Judy, despite her size and girl voice, made the announcement with such authority that the sixty or so people moved out with hardly a mumble. The girl followed them leaving Trudy with her broom and trash can alone in the 900-seat hall. Each time she had been the only person in the empty auditorium, she felt small. Around her were flowing patterns of color and form, in front of her, the great shimmering curtain, and, over her head, a pastel painting of a mythical lady floating on a cloud.

She did not have time to enjoy the experience. She raced down the thirty-one rows, sweeping popcorn and stray pieces of candy and inspecting each seat. Robert came in and moved quickly down the side isles. Judy returned and sectioned off five rows of seats in the center of the theater with velvet rope.

"I have no idea how many people will be here from the studio, but it's better to set aside too many seats than not enough. Trudy, I want you to stand by the door on the right aisle during the show. Bob, stand on the left. If anyone from the studio asks for something—like turning up the sound or focusing the projector—take care of it. When the movie is over, give the customers a survey card as they walk out. There will be booths with pencils set up in the foyer."

"Just like voting for President!" Robert said.

* * * * *

No movie stars came to the screening, but Professor Max and Helga did, the guests of Nelly and her gray mustached husband. He apparently was a friend of the screenwriter. The old writer's eyes penetrated Trudy like an x-ray.

"I had no idea we were coming here," Helga said to Trudy. "So, this is where you work."

Nelly looked stunning. She grabbed Trudy's arm when she saw her and dragged her over to her husband.

"Heinrich," she said to the old man, "this is Trudy Mansfield, my friend who helped me when Helga had her baby. Trudy, this is my husband, the important writer, Heinrich Mann."

Trudy smiled. She noticed the scent of alcohol on Nelly's

breath.

To Trudy's amazement the movie's screenwriter turned out to be Bertolt Brecht. Dressed like a janitor with his bad haircut, cheap suit and funny glasses, he came into the theater and joined the Manns. He chatted with Nelly's husband like they were old conspirators. He must have found someone to make *The Bread King*. Trudy became excited, almost giddy. Did Charlie Chaplin make the movie? Would Sidney Greenstreet play the Bread King? Would Chaplin remember her?

Regular patrons and more people from the studio came into the auditorium. An Asian man entered, dressed in nice cloths. He turned out to be associated with the movie and took his seat with two other men who were engaged in a lively conversation about something which Trudy suspected was related to the film. A rather stern looking man walked down the aisle. He glanced around the room and right through Trudy. As he passed, Trudy noticed he wore a monocle. He approached Brecht and patted him on the shoulder.

"Fritz," the playwright said in German. "I trust you have not disappointed me."

"Motion pictures are not plays. Watch with an open mind."

"When someone tells me to have an open mind, I suspect the person telling me this has closed his."

Trudy heard this clearly.

Patrolling her aisle, Trudy was surprised that no servicemen had come into the theater. On Friday nights, the Bundy often had some of the boys from the neighborhood installations. She was also surprised that her mother had not appeared and wondered what happened.

Her family finally came into the theater. Proud and cocky, Andy walked in escorting their Uncle Billy. His showing up didn't please her, but it was a free country and she had no reason to bar him. Besides, he was a serviceman.

"Your uncle's ship came into San Pedro this morning," her mother said.

Trudy's father gave her a look. Neither had to say anything. Uncle Billy smelled like a still and almost swaggered, walking down the aisle, proud in his white sailor suit, glancing over the seats, no doubt

208

looking for other service men, maybe Marines he could heckle. Trudy had an uneasy feeling when he pulled a paper bag out of his tunic. That was no refreshment procured at the candy counter. He took the seat in front of Professor Max.

Don't make a big deal out of this, she told herself. After all, Andy and her mother sat on each side of the big man. Her father noticed the Schneiders, smiled and chatted for a second before sitting.

The lights finally dimmed. There followed no cartoon or trailers. The curtains opened and the film began with the ominous title, *Hangmen Also Die*, under-toned with equally ominous music.

The hangman of the story was the odious Reinhard Heydrich, who had been assassinated last year in Czechoslovakia. The terrible Nazi was seen only once, in the first scene, smiling menacingly at his Czech lackeys, slinking like a panther and humiliating a decorated general by making him pick up the baton Heydrich dropped deliberately. Speaking only in German under a menacing portrait of Adolf Hitler, "the butcher of Prague's" timbre turned to rage. He screamed his orders that productions of armaments would increase, or many more hostages would be hung. He abruptly marched out of the room, leaving the assembled Czechs in a panic. A few minutes later, word spread that Heydrich had been shot.

Watching the film Trudy was struck with how familiar the Czech characters were. They talked like ordinary Americans, but they were cowed by the ruthless Nazis who killed innocent hostages and tortured suspects. The Czechs suffered rations far worse than the American public was enduring. The movie chilled her.

Halfway through the screening, two men stood up and walked up the aisle close to where she was stationed. In the flickering light from the screen she recognized Brecht and Heinrich Mann. They stopped just a couple of feet from her, turned and stood, smoking. Not knowing Trudy understands German, Brecht muttered in disgust, "That bastard Lang Hollywoodized my story."

"My friend, didn't you realize when you came to this town, you would be expected to behave like a destitute whore?"

"I knew I was taking a gamble. It was Monte Carlo."

"At least you got paid well."

"Look at this! We had an opportunity to show mass resistance to the Nazi occupation, but instead we are watching a pursuit and escape caper. I can't watch this. That aristocrat bastard was prejudice against every good idea I had. All he has done is put together twists to surprise the audience that are flavored like a street vendor's cheap pastry, replete with tawdry sentimental touches, a parade of falsehoods, and little genuine tensions. And these American actors! He has taken license for the box office."

Instead of wandering into the foyer, Brecht and Mann eventually returned to their seats. Trudy didn't know what it meant that she liked the movie the playwright loathed.

When the lights came up, people began to politely applaud. Trudy's uncle stood up, clapped and cheered like a fool. She felt her face flush.

"Billy, sit down," she heard her mother say. She pulled at the elbow of his sleeve.

Billy turned away from his sister and noticed the Asian, who Trudy had learned was the famous James Wong Howe, the movie's cinematographer. "And what is that Jap doing here?"

"He's Chinese," someone called back.

"So what!" Billy snapped. "A heathen has no business being with respectable folk."

Howe's eyes flashed, and he looked like he was about to climb over the seats to engage Billy. The man next to him, snickering, put his hand on the cameraman's shoulder and whispered something. Howe remained poised and ready for one more provocation which did not come. Billy's attention had drifted.

The theater patrons were now either watching the tall husky sailor or deliberately attempting to ignore his presence. Trudy stood like in a nightmare, unable to move, terrified of what would happen next.

Max, standing behind Billy in the next row, motioned for Helga to move out to the end the isle.

"Hail Hitler," Billy snarled, his eyes transformed into glaring gun sights fixed on the professor. Max stopped and stood motionless, like

210

a mole in striking range of a venomous snake.

"I heard you whispering in German," Billy hissed. "What are you? A spy? You've been sneaking around aircraft plants."

Andy laughed nervously.

"I can take your scrawny neck in my hand and snap it like a twig," Billy loudly proclaimed, making a grabbing gesture within inches of the professor's face. "Down with the Third Reich!"

"Billy, let's go!" Trudy's father said, pushing his way between Trudy's mother and uncle. Hardly glancing at him, Billy sent him back with the sweep of his arm. Trudy saw fear in her father's face.

Something in Trudy snapped. She walked down the aisle, squeezed her way past her parents, and went up to Billy. She felt her mother's hand grab her arm.

"Uncle," she said, shrugging off her mother, her voice constricted and her words coming out almost like a whisper, "I work here. I ask you to respect that and to please go home."

In a drunken haze, Billy glared down at her. For a moment he looked like a cobra ready to strike, his mouth twisting as if forming words to spit at her. She felt terror and waited for his big hand to slap her violently, but for some reason she didn't jump back or look away. Instead she remained locked on his brutish eyes.

"Get out of the way," he muttered. "I'll leave."

Trudy backed down the row, her body pushing her mother and father out to the aisle. Andy followed his uncle.

"Come on, little guy," Uncle Billy said to the boy. "Let's find the back door. I'm not leaving with these swells."

Andy looked over to his mother. She frowned and shook her head. Silent, like a leaf falling, he moved to her side.

The people in the auditorium watched the drunken sailor stroll to the exit, sweep away the curtain, and enter the alcove. When the outside door loudly clanked shut, the tension in the theater dropped. People began muttering. Nelly moved down the row behind Helga. Trudy's mother approached the Schneiders, apologizing for her brother whom she said was having a hard time, as one of the few survivors from the Arizona crew. Trudy, hearing this, turned, afraid her eyes would give

211

away her disgust. She moved back to her station and handed out survey cards.

Nelly walked over to Trudy. The woman put her hand on the girl's shoulder and asked, "Trudy, what did you say to that nasty man?"

"I told him to behave or go home," she said, trying to catch her breath, noticing that she was trembling. "I'm embarrassed to say that is my uncle."

"Don't be," Nelly said, sliding her hand down the girl's arm. "My father could make terrible scenes."

Judy entered the auditorium.

"What happened?" she asked.

It took Trudy a second to respond. "We had a drunk patron. He's gone."

"Just what we need," the child usherette squeaked, looking over the reserved seats. The group was moving out. Howe still looked steamed, but his comrades seemed to laugh off the incident.

Trudy's parents and Andy walked up to her. She continued to shake. Almost like the words came out on their own she said to her mother, "I won't go home if my uncle's there!"

"Now, Trudy . . ." her mother began.

The girl began to cry.

"He's crude and violent. He pushed Dad and threatened our neighbors, and I may lose my job."

"He gets this way sometimes. Everything will have blown off by the time we get home."

"Not for me!" Warm tears slide down her cheeks. She continued to hand cards to the patrons walking past, some looking at her with concern and others trying not to notice. "I'm going to stay at Nancy's."

"Do you want the car?" her father asked. "I'll move it on the street."

Her mother glared at him.

"Thanks, Dad," Trudy said, sniffing.

Wiping the tears out of her eyes, Trudy walked down to where Helga and Professor Max still stood like their feet were glued to the floor. She handed cards to the remaining people coming up the aisle.

212

"Phil, there is no reason for Trudy not to come home," she heard her mother snap.

"Well, I don't feel like going home, either. I want Billy out of the house—tonight!"

"Phil, if Billy can't come home and sleep it off he might wander off and get in trouble. I know my brother."

"Pearl Harbor all over again."

"That's rude!"

"But true."

"Respect that he's my brother."

"Fine. You deal with him. I cannot accept that my daughter doesn't feel safe in her own house."

"Phil, don't be ridiculous!"

Trudy thought that Professor Max had spilled Coke on his lap, but then realized he had another type of accident. She almost began to cry again but somehow held her tears in check.

"I'm sorry," Trudy said, looking at Max.

White and somber, he avoided eye contact. Helga, also shaken, was holding his hand. She forced a smile, maybe giving her a nonverbal thank you.

"I don't know what to say," Trudy continued. "I feel so bad for what my uncle did. He's . . . I don't know."

"He's just another bully," Professor Max said in English.

"He's a bully, all right, and has ruined his career in the Navy because of his drinking. If things were up to me, I'd lock him away."

Neither Professor Max nor Helga commented.

"Can I walk back with you? I'm not going home tonight. I'm going to stay at Nancy's."

"Stay with us," Helga said. "It would be more convenient."

"Thank you. That's kind."

*　　*　　*　　*　　*

Later that night, looking out the Schneider's kitchen window, Trudy noticed the yard behind her house was partially illuminated.

213

Curious, she studied the area, partially obscured by the antiaircraft gun. She realized the light was coming from the workshop where her father had, no doubt, retreated. In her mind, she saw him hunched over his drawing table, smoking a cigarette. Trudy wanted to go over and give him a hug.

Chapter 37

Slip of The Tongue

Max Schneider wanted to exit the theater and hide the stain of his fright in the balmy summer darkness outside. He attempted to stand behind Helga, using her body to conceal his wet pants. He could feel the urine turn cool on his leg and the instep of his shoes.

Max had not wanted to go to the movie-house in the first place but went along as a favor to his wife. Helga believed that Nelly, being with her husband, would be on reasonably good behavior, and they would enjoy the night out. Nelly wanted them to witness the screening of a story by Heinrich's longtime friend Brecht. This was something important to her, and after all she had done to help with the baby, it was the least they could do in return, Helga said. The worst he had feared earlier that evening was boredom—that or having to endure watching Nelly make a fool out of herself. He never imagined being shamed in front of an auditorium full of people.

Walking in the dark, the Schneiders were out past curfew for enemy aliens, but, given Helga's acquaintance with many of the soldiers, Max hadn't anticipated any trouble.

Feeling resentful he said, as they walked home in the dark, "I can't believe Roosevelt didn't round us all up and put us away with the Japanese. That's what they would do in Europe."

Once in the house, Max went into his bedroom to get clothes. He changed in the bathroom, where he washed the urine off his body and clean his shoes. By the time he came out, the babysitter was gone, and Helga and Trudy were talking about bullies. He went into the kitchen and poured himself a glass of wine. He was shaken, flooded with emotion which he did not want either his wife or the girl to see.

Back in the living room, Max realized that Trudy and Helga were also wound up. Unlike him, they needed to talk. He listened silently, sipping from his glass. Trudy in her ceremonious usherette's uniform looked out of place in the Schneider living room. He went back to the kitchen for a second glass.

"I could see him pulling wings off flies," Trudy said as he walked back into the front room. "The way he strolled in that gathering of Czech collaborators, so smug and cocky. . ."

He realized they were talking about Reinhard Heydrich. He began to dwell on something he never told Helga, an experience that had impacted decisions he had made for almost ten years.

Max felt the effect of the wine.

"I met Heydrich," Max said to Helga and Trudy, who turned to look at him. "That man on the screen was a mockery. The real Heydrich was pleasant, charming in fact, but as evil as the devil himself."

"You never told me," Helga said.

"Certain things are best not mentioned."

Helga looked at Max who had the uncomfortable sense that she understood the implication of his revelation. Trudy did not seem to pick up the nonverbal exchange between the two.

"You knew Reinhard Heydrich?" the girl asked.

"I had the distinguished honor of being invited to the SS headquarters to discuss with Heydrich and Heinrich Himmler, the head of the SS, a project they had concocted. I would have nothing to do with it."

"I guess that's why you left Germany," Trudy said innocently.

Max did not acknowledge this, but his wife seemed to see significance in his silence.

"I wish you had told me," she said.

"Well, what is done is done," he answered, stiffly. The wine had slightly fuddled his thinking, although he had only two glasses.

Max knew that Helga would not take this up in front of Trudy. The issue would be confronted at a different time. He anticipated this with discomfort.

"That was a noble thing you did," Trudy continued, "leaving Germany before most realized how bad things would get."

"There is nothing noble in running away," Max replied, wishing he had never mentioned Heydrich and could keep his mouth shut. He realized this last comment, uttered without censor, told Helga even more.

"I don't think you ran away, Professor Max. As in a flood, you merely sought higher ground. That's what I think."

Max glanced at Helga whose blank expression did not reveal what she thought. The subject was dropped, but his slip gave Helga enough to see through him. She would not remain quiet after his years of silence and would demand the whole story. They had moved like intellectual vagabonds, eventually settling on the rim of the Pacific Ocean in a place that was all but void of Old-World touches.

The two women continued talking about Nazi oppression in Europe. Max sat quiet, watching and trying to reassure himself that he did not have to tell his wife the whole story.

Chapter 38

Heydrich's Brother

The next morning, Trudy kept trying to excuse herself to go home. Through the window she had watched her mother driving her unpleasant uncle away, but Max kept asking her questions about what Helga was teaching her and about her plans for UCLA. He also gave her advice she did not request. Helga sensed, he dreaded being alone with her. After the young lady finally managed to leave, Max retired to the garage, telling Helga he was not to be disturbed. Before she could protest, he walked out of the house and sealed himself in his workshop.

By two he had not come out. More concerned than incensed, Helga left Jonathon in charge of Marlene. Sophie was already down. She went outside and tapped on the side door of the garage before opening it.

Max sat at his workbench. She walked over to him, but he did not even glance at her. Instead, he concentrated his full attention to the task of carefully brushing baked earth off a large piece of ostraca. The room was dark, except for the illumination from the fixture positioned over his hands and the line of daylight that seeped under the garage door.

"Max," she said.

No answer.

"Max, we need to talk."

"Nothing needs to be said," he mumbled.

"I disagree," she said. "What you said last night. About Heydrich. There is more to the story and it concerns our leaving Germany."

Max put down the brush and potsherd.

"You're smart," he said. "You can deduce the rest."

She wanted to yell at him, but she never had and never would. She would not be her mother, regardless of how much pain she felt. She watched her husband sitting before the dusty surface of the bench, amber grit pushed around his work area by his elbows.

"Haven't I earned your confidence?" she said. "I've traveled with you to this place and done all that I could do to make your life normal." Before she could completely catch herself, she blurted, "I know I'm not Rebekah."

Max looked up at her, the shadowy light causing his face to appear like a stone relief carved in an Egyptian monument. For a moment he did not move.

"Sit over there," he finally said, turning in his chair.

In the shadow, with bird racket piercing the walls, he told her of his ordeal at the headquarters of the Schutzstaffel, the powerful S.S.

*　　*　　*　　*　　*

In 1934, a little over a year after Hitler had been appointed chancellor and the *Machtergreifung*, the Nazis' "seizure of power," Max had received a summons to the SS headquarters by Heinrich Himmler.

In those early months of the Nazi regime, Schneider had kept his opinions to himself. There was now only one side to the news—the Nazi. Posters promoting the new Germany and giant red banners with ugly black swastikas were hung in all public places. Distressing Schneider deeply, intelligent and educated people had fallen for Hitler's crude and ugly message. By nature, he did not like conflict, and he also had a real fear, an aftermath of the 1933 Reichstag fire and the suspension of basic rights. Saying anything critical of the Nazis could bring about unpleasant consequences. Schneider considered himself an honest man, but an honest man in Nazi Germany could be honest all the way to a concentration camp.

Max Schneider, in his mind unnoticed by the Nazis, continued on with his teaching and research at the University of Leipzig. He was not Jewish. He was not a communist, a socialist, nor had he been a member of any political party. His work lay far afield of anything remotely related to Nazi doctrine and their distorted views of history. He stood tall, fair skinned, blond and blue eyed—the Nazis' ideal

German. His new wife, Helga, had the light complexion and sunshine hair of the ideal German woman. He saw no problem for them until the day he realized he had crossed two dangerous men.

There was no immediate retribution, but he knew that he could not continue to refuse working for Heinrich Himmler, the head of the S.S., Hitler's praetorian guard.

Himmler, some said the second most powerful man in Germany, had "invited" Schneider by telegram to discuss a project. According to the S.S. leader's communique this was something of "significant importance to the German people." Schneider had no clue what he had to offer the Nazis. He knew a number of archeologists and other academics were being funded by the Ahnenerbe, an institution Himmler had recently established, to "research" the originals of the Aryan race, but this poppycock had nothing to do with ancient Egypt.

With trepidation and absolute dread, he accepted the invitation knowing he could not refuse.

He took a taxi to Prinz-Albrecht-Strasse 8, the elegant and massive building that housed the S.S. headquarters.

He was ushered into a sparsely furnished room where he met Himmler and Reinhard Heydrich, chief of the Nazi Party's intelligence service. Their immaculate black uniforms decorated with the insignia of the S.S. made Schneider's gray suit appear drab. They greeted him with the Hitler salute which he knew he had to return.

What first struck Schneider was how unassuming and benign Himmler appeared and how charming the dangerous Heydrich was. A remarkably ordinary looking man, Himmler had the face of a store clerk and Heydrich the gentle eyes of a good father. After expressing some pleasantries, Himmler said, "I must say Professor, you and Herr Heydrich could be brothers, fine specimens of the Aryan race that you are."

Schneider didn't know what to say and glanced at the head of the Nazi intelligence services who did not seem offended and even smiled pleasantly at the professor.

Himmler came to the point which revealed that he was anything but soft or benevolent.

220

"The Führer wishes us to provide historical proof of the inferiority and inherit deceitfulness of the Jewish people, a tribe of slaves who were the base laborers of ancient Egypt."

"There are some experts," Heydrich added, "who say the Jews fell in league with sorcerers who desired the Egyptians no good and used evil magic to set up their nation, Israel. One needs only read the Jewish Bible, their own accounts of events, to appreciate their corruptness and wickedness. The Jew is a devil in human form."

"Your name," Himmler continued, "was given to us by several of your peers as a leading German authority of ancient Egypt with special knowledge."

Schneider began to feel his pulse race. He suspected he had been setup by someone who wanted to punish him for his relationship with Rebekah Wolff.

"I'm afraid you have been misinformed," he said, his mouth suddenly dry, "and my credentials overstated. The focus of my work are ancient languages . . ."

"Which makes you ideal for uncovering archeological proof of the origins of the Jews."

"I know nothing of this," Schneider said honestly. "My research has never revealed anything about the presence of the Hebrew tribe in Egypt or of Egypt's relationship with Israel." The only person he knew who did was Rebekah.

Himmler and Heydrich studied Schneider. Max didn't think of himself a coward. For a long time, he had imagined himself a man not easily intimidated. In truth, his life had never been put in any real danger—until this meeting. The only threat he had ever dealt with before was poisonous snakes and scorpions in Egypt.

"No matter," Heydrich finally said, brushing aside the professor's point like it was only a speck of lint on his black sleeve. "You have the knowledge and the expertise to do this research."

"Excuse me, Herr Heydrich," Schneider replied. He took a breath and forced himself to continue. "I will not deceive you. My taking on this task would be like a dentist performing an appendectomy."

221

Himmler silently smiled. A chubby faced man of modest stature, his eyes were penetrating and unsmiling. Schneider was sure the Reich leader knew that he was overstating his case.

"You understate your potential," Himmler replied. "Think of this! You are being given the opportunity to produce something that will be studied by the Führer himself, a work that will be published and I can say with total conviction, read widely by the German people."

"What can I say?"

"That you will do this."

"I am overwhelmed, but . . ."

"But?"

"I know my limits," Schneider said meekly, sweating by now.

Heydrich shook his head like a professor who had been given the wrong answer. Himmler glared at Schneider, the Schutzstaffel leader's smile becoming even more menacing and unfriendly.

"I can recommend men who would be better qualified," Schneider said. He felt himself a coward and an academic traitor, although he knew many anti-Semitic professors who would jump at the chance to concoct some thesis lightly seasoned with documented historical tidbits.

"We want you," Heydrich said, ignoring Schneider's offer of the names of those more *qualified*. "After you have had time to consider this offer, you will accept." The lack of malice in his voice made the statement even more frightening.

The twenty minutes Schneider sat in the room with Himmler and Heydrich seemed to be a time that would never end. When Himmler finally excused himself, Schneider was drained. Heydrich escorted Max out. He smiled at Max as he gave him the Hitler salute in parting, but his grin was unsettling, as if he was privy to a private joke. And then, to Schneider's annoyance, the chief of the Nazi Party's intelligence patted him on his back like Max was a little child.

Max exited the main lobby in a panic. It wasn't until he was on the street and a cool breeze blew down the street that he realized he had wet himself. On the train ride back to Leipzig he sat numb, ashamed, and desperately considering what he must do. To disguise his "accident" he poured a glass of red wine on his lap. Self-conscious, he thought he smelled like a derelict drunk.

Within months Schneider and Helga were safely in France, his reputation as a researcher and scholar being the ticket that got them out of Germany.

*   *   *   *   *

"Helga, I know these years have been difficult for you. Maybe I should have told you about the meeting with Himmler and Heydrich." He paused. "I was ashamed. I experienced the same . . . mishap I did at the theater. And to deal with the dilemma I found myself in, I took the coward's way out."

Helga reached out and touched him on his arm.

"Max, Trudy deeply admires you for what you did. I do too and I could have before, had I known. I would not have been happy about leaving the Fatherland, but I would have gone not only willingly, as I did, but with an understanding and respect for your integrity. You did not behave the coward."

Chapter 39

The Co-Ed

Trudy's first day as a student at UCLA started at nine a.m. on Wednesday, October sixth, when she sat with an adviser. He asked her what she had chosen as her major. She said she was thinking of becoming a teacher. The adviser's bored, unexpressive face suggested he had heard this answer more times than he wanted to count.

"Remember," the man droned, "every student entering a curriculum leading to the certificate of completion for the kindergarten primary teaching credential must show ability to play on the piano music suitable for use with young children. . ."

This sounded like a recital of something from the school catalog. He went on to say she would have to take a piano test. Well, she didn't really want to teach little kids, so not playing the piano wouldn't be a problem.

"German," she said, deciding she might as well declare this as her major, knowing the Schneiders would be a resource.

"German?" he asked.

"I want to major in Germanic language."

"German? Education? Which is it?" Impatient, he held the pen over the paper, ready to strike the sheet and put down the choice, once and once only.

"German. That will be my major."

He filled out a form and told her what classes she needed to take her first semester. He frowned when she told him that she had a part-time job.

"It is wise if you use your savings to make this first term one of freedom to give full time to your academic work . . ."

All her savings, maybe seventy-five dollars from working since graduation, making thirty cents an hour, would not cover her books and other fees for the freshman year. She'd still have to work to keep up with this and other expenses, like lunches, clothing, bus fare, room and board and the little make up she wore.

". . . University work demands the best that a student can give to it. You must adjust to your new surroundings, establish sound habits of study, and maintain a good scholastic standing. You are building a foundation for the rest of your university course . . ."

*   *   *   *   *

Trudy had to take time off work the following Saturday to register for her classes. Mr. Sands, her boss, frowned when she told him she'd be at school in the morning and wouldn't be able to start work until two.

The registration process took longer than she anticipated. Putting her classes together was like working a crossword puzzle.

Because most eighteen-year-old boys were being drafted, the majority of male students enrolling were sailors and Marines. The Navy's V-12 program sent them to college to earn a bachelor's degree that would qualify them to become commissioned officers. The sailors dressed in their blue "crackerjack" suits with their black neckerchiefs draped neatly over their chests. Their sailor hats were set on their heads, each with a distinctive twist. The Marines wore their green service uniforms with khaki colored shirt and tie and a green cap. They all carried what looked like standard issued notebooks.

She rode her bike home, changed into her uniform, and went to work, three hours late. Susie, who worked the candy counter, glared when she raced into the foyer. A movie was running, so only a couple of kids were buying snacks. She took a detour upstairs to the office where she clocked in, ran down the stairs, and walked briskly back to the counter.

"It's about time," Susie muttered. "I have to take a break. I have my monthly visitor."

Trudy finished getting a little girl her popcorn, and for the first time that day was able to relax. She stood behind the counter looking across the foyer and the outdoor lobby to the street peeking back from behind the ticket booth. The ordinary world, sunny and warm for the middle of October, contrasted with the maroon, gold, and baby blue of the foyer walls, patterned carpet, and her stiff uniform.

*   *   *   *   *

That evening, as Trudy finished the dishes, the telephone rang. Her mother picked up. She wondered if her boss was calling, asking her to work an extra day.

"It's Nancy," her mother said, coming in the kitchen. "She sounds upset."

Trudy's stomach turned over. She instantly feared her friend had bad news about Gary.

When she put the receiver to her ear, she could hear Nancy panting on the other end.

"Nancy, what's wrong?"

"I got a letter . . ." she began and started to sob. "From Gary!"

"What's happened?"

"He . . . he . . . he's in a hospital."

"How badly was he . . . How badly was he wounded?"

"His legs were shot off!"

Chapter 40

Shambhala

When her classes started at UCLA, Trudy's life became a series of sprints from one location to another. At school, she bumped her way through crowds of students, as they exchanged lecture halls. On the days she worked, she would bicycle home, jump into her usherette outfit, and walk briskly to the theater. On days she didn't work, she could take the bus home. Even then, to get to the bus-stop on time, she had to swiftly navigate through shoppers leisurely strolling on the sidewalks of Westwood Village.

In most the classes, the professors did not make an appearance. They assigned the task of lecturing to serious looking young men and a couple of women. Teaching assistants. They sometimes used words she did not know. She had to look them up in her dictionary after class. If nothing else, she was expanding her vocabulary.

All the reading and homework didn't seem to stop many, maybe most, of the students from participating in the activities promoting camaraderie and school spirit. She knew football was big at UCLA but was still amazed at the size of the pep rally the first week of school. The sailors and Marines in the officer program were eligible to play on the team, which to Trudy seemed patriotic.

During the first days of school, Trudy was troubled by the news about Gary. She worried that he would be a different man.

The evening when Nancy called, Trudy drove over to support her friend. Nancy had been so distressed Trudy could not understand half of what she said on the phone.

When she walked in the Pierce living room, Trudy began to feel tense. The somber mood of the house was overwhelming. Nancy's brother sat by the radio, sullen, with his crutches at his feet and his history book opened in his lap, one foot twisted unnaturally inward, the lasting effect of polio he had contracted. Mrs. Pierce was at the hospital visiting her mother who had been diagnosed with cancer and was not expected to make it. Nancy's kid sister sat at the dining room table

227

surrounded by an invisible wall of sandbags, obviously constructed to keep a distance from her family.

Trudy already knew about the misfortunes that had happened to Nancy's family. Now the bad news about Gary.

Nancy took Trudy into her bedroom. Her bedspread and pillow were twisted and rippled like a topographical map of the valleys and ridges of some wild and torturous country. She handed Trudy Gary's letter.

Dear Nancy

Don't be shocked by the handwriting and the correct spelling. I'm lying in bed and a nurse is writing for me. If I wasn't so doped up with morphine or whatever they're giving me, I'd be writing myself.

I got bad news, Kitten. I've been shot up really bad and the doctors had to cut off my legs. Just below the knees. You don't have to know all the details about the battle which I can't remember all that clearly anyhow. There was a lot of fighting up close to the Germans, who pushed us back from our forward position. We were lucky not to be captured. We were pulling back when we got hit. The medics managed somehow to get us out of there on jeeps fitted with racks for the stretchers.

You wrote that you gave blood. I thought of you when they started giving me plasma. I imagined that somehow this came from you, a real gift of life. That thought kept me going.

I'm in a hospital in southern Sicily, on a ward with other guys who lost limbs. The rumor floating around is we're going to be shipped back to the States. By the time you get this letter, I may be on a boat.

I guess I am lucky. Some of the guys got bad infections and a few didn't make it. The doctors say I'm out of danger and that my wounds are healing. They feed us good and want us to drink a lot of milk which comes in fifty pound bags and tastes like diluted sawdust.

I'll write again soon. Keep me and the other boys in your

prayers.
   Love always,
    Gary

Trudy noticed the letter's date, August 22, 1943. Almost two months had passed.

* * * * *

The Sunday before her classes began, Trudy visited Susan, who had taken a job working at Eddie "Rochester" Anderson's Pacific Parachute Company. Susan thought it would be a different experience, working for Rochester, the colored man who played Jack Benny's valet on radio. Trudy had never known that a Negro could own a factory. Her friend swore her to secrecy. Her parents and everyone else only knew she worked at a small defense plant in L.A. She always cashed her paychecks and destroyed the paystubs before coming home. Her precautions were obvious. A nice white girl would never work for a Negro.

Trudy was shocked to see that her friend's beautiful complexion had been spoiled with acne which she could not disguise with all her makeup tricks.

"I see you're losing your pimples," Susan commented, aware of Trudy's reaction. "I'm getting them. I guess they're being rationed."

"What's causing your skin to break out? I mean, you're too old to start getting pimples."

"Nerves, I guess."

Her face also looked a little puffy, maybe because of the change in her diet due to rationing. But even with the changes in her appearance, she remained the most beautiful person Trudy knew. The pimples did not trash her face.

While Nancy's concerns were understandably more disturbing, Susan also had worries. Her longtime boyfriend, Robby Thompson, had missed passing the military's officer's qualifying exam by three point and had been drafted in the Navy that August.

229

"Anything new?" Trudy asked.

"Robby and I are getting married," she said with an embarrassed smile.

"What!"

Susan nodded, and looked at Trudy like she was waiting for her approval.

My God, Trudy thought. They were so young. Maybe it wasn't that Susan and Robby were so young, but that Trudy and her friends were now older. With the war, couples were getting married sooner rather than later.

"That's exciting news. When do you plan to do this?"

"The middle of November. After he completes boot camp, he will have a three-day pass before he has to ship out for the next phase of his training. He has been selected to be in air ordinance which has something to do with putting bullets and bombs on planes. I guess he'll eventually be on an aircraft carrier."

"You must already be making plans."

"The ceremony will be simple. The wedding will be here. The minister will stand in front of the fireplace and have us take our vows. I'll wear my best dress. With the war, it doesn't seem patriotic to have a fancy wedding. We'll have to borrow ration coupons to purchase the ingredients for the wedding cake."

"I'll snatch some from my mom."

"Thank you."

*   *   *   *   *

After one week of classes, Trudy already found herself behind in her reading. There was not enough time during the day and in the evenings to do her schoolwork. She stayed up as late as she could but found herself nodding off by midnight. More asleep than awake, her eyes tracked the words on the page, but she retained nothing. In the morning, she began drinking coffee to wake up, forcing down a cup or two, although she disliked the bitter taste. Thank God coffee rationing had ended that summer.

The long breaks between classes proved a blessing. While other students lounged on the Esplanada in front of Royce Hall or joined a pep rally, she went to the library and sat down where, two years before, she had studied hieroglyphs.

*   *   *   *   *

Wednesday, during the third week of classes, she took the bus to school and that afternoon hurried down Westwood Boulevard to catch her ride, racing more than usual around the strollers. The last class of the day, public speaking, had gone over. The instructor, Mr. Murray, didn't seem to have a problem keeping the students past the normal end of class.

That afternoon, each student had to introduce himself, telling the class something special about them. Trudy mentioned she could read Egyptian hieroglyphs. No one seemed impressed.

At the bus stop she noticed Professor Max standing at the curb. She slowed her stride. She had not seen him since the morning after the incident at the Bundy. She approached him with trepidation. She feared that his opinion of her had been damaged by her uncle's cruel behavior.

"Guten Tag, Professor Max," she said cautiously.

He turned to her and raised an eyebrow. She had read in stories of a character doing this but had never notice before an actual person making this gesture.

"Trudy, you're taking the bus today," he said in English and added in German, "I thought you rode your bicycle to school."

"My bike has a flat tire," she replied, continuing the conversation in his native language. "The rubber's old and I don't know if it can be patched. I'll have to sell my first born to get a new inner tube."

"I used to ride my bike when I was student. Most do in Europe. The exercise stimulates the brain."

"I think about the lectures," Trudy said. "I'm taking German literature."

Schneider asked the name of her professor and what she had

231

been assigned to read. He didn't appear impressed with either.

"Do you still have time to practice your hieroglyphs?" He looked at her as if genuinely interested.

"I write in my journal using hieroglyphs." Journal sounded more impressive than diary. "I've begun to use hieratic script. It goes so much faster."

"You've learned that unusually fast. My wife has been tutoring you for only a few months. How do you express words that the Egyptians had no name for?"

"I mix in a little English or invent my own." She hesitated. "I use the glyphs for gold, ocean, and man to stand for you."

"Golden-Man-From-Over-The-Sea. I assume that is reference to my blonde hair, not my gold teeth."

"I didn't even know you had gold teeth."

He appeared amused but then became more serious.

"You have a talent. You've learned a language which has been dead for almost two thousand years."

"I'm still learning."

"Trudy, you're too modest." He paused for a second, seeming to reflect on what he wanted to say next. "A woman I knew in graduate school had a similar gift. She mastered several ancient languages of the Near East. You might meet her someday. There is a possibility she will be coming here to teach."

The chance to meet someone else versed in ancient expressions of communication pleased and frightened her. Would she be more critical of her efforts than the Schneiders? Would she look down on her as merely a college freshman?

A newsboy walked past the bus stop hawking the afternoon edition of the Los Angeles Times. The professor gave the boy a nickel and tucked a paper under his arm.

Their bus chugged up to the curb. Those waiting began to form a line.

Trudy noticed a girl from her English class. She stood a few feet away, apparently waiting for another bus. She watched Trudy and Professor Max chat. Trudy wondered if the fascination was their talking in German or the fact that a fellow freshman was informally chatting with a professor.

As the bus pulled away, Trudy felt pride, hoping the other student was amazed with her for both reasons.

Looking at Professor Max, she wondered if he was in a better mood because a friend from his university days might come to UCLA.

Schneider snapped open the newspaper and began to read the front page. Trudy glanced at the page which had a big photo of a German ball bearing plant that had been destroyed by U.S. Flying Fortresses. The other stories concerned "Nips" losing air cover in the Solomon Islands and the Red army advancing on the Dnieper River. Then she caught the headline at the bottom of the page: "Shangri-La Affirmed as New Carrier Name."

"That doesn't seem right," she said.

"What's that?"

"Oh. I'm sorry. That story about the Navy naming a war ship *Shangri-La*. Shangri-La is a hidden refuge from war in the Himalayas. According to the story, residents there live in peace and strive to be kind. Naming the carrier the Midway would be more appropriate."

The man glanced at the article and nodded his head.

"Shangri-La, Shangri-La," he muttered, glancing away from the paper and thumbing through the massive mental storage files in his head. "Oh, yes. No doubt a variation of Shambhala."

"Shambhala?" Trudy asked. She had never heard the name.

"To the Hindus, the Himalayas were the great divide between their lands and the home of the gods and a mighty race of enlightened and virtuous supermen. It was known as Shambhala. This legend fascinated many Europeans in the last century, an interest which has continued in Germany. Like with so many folk sagas, the Nazis have taken Shambhala and incorporated the fable into their mythology of the superior Aryan race. They declare the Germanic people can trace their origins to the lost Tibetan kingdom of Shambhala."

"But that's not my Shangri-La, is it?"

"No, but likely inspired by the same folklore, but given a decidedly different cast."

233

*　　*　　*　　*　　*

When Trudy walked in her bedroom, she found a letter on the
bed from Mary.

> *I was amused with your letter describing your first week*
> *of school. You're going to be a busy, busy girl.*
> *The students who graduated high school here have to deal*
> *with the problem that the big, prestigious Eastern universities are*
> *off limits. The schools open to us are small liberal art schools,*
> *none with pre-med programs.*
> *I am not so determined to go to college that I will major*
> *in classical French literature. There are nursing programs, but I'm*
> *not interested in being a RN. I will wait until I find a college on*
> *the military's expanding approved list that will prepare me for*
> *medical school.*
> *All of the schools are in places that are very cold in the*
> *winter. Compared to West L.A., Manzanar is cold, but it*
> *doesn't snow that much and while it gets below freezing sometimes,*
> *never below zero.*
> *I miss the balmy climate, the afternoon breeze coming off*
> *the ocean, and the city lights. I have to admit that I'm a big city*
> *girl.*

Trudy felt bad for Mary, but knew she was a fighter. She'd be in
college next fall, and would eventually become a physician. Mary's
dream was strong.

Mary also wrote about her brothers.

> *Ronny and Daniel have been shipped oversea and are*
> *either in Africa or Italy. They are infantrymen in the 100th*
> *Battalion. I worry for their safety. I can imagine their squad being*
> *place on the point of most danger.*

Trudy could understand Mary's concern. To many, the Japanese

234

Americans were still the enemy and "sacrificing" them to draw out or blunt German fire would to them be an appropriate fate.

Chapter 41

Rebekah Wolff

Max Schneider was indeed in a better mood, and Trudy's assumption was partially correct. Max eagerly hoped his friend would come to UCLA to resume her academic career, but that was insignificant to just knowing she was no longer in harm's way. Early in October, Helga had passed on the news of Rebecca's safety.

That day, Nelly came by to visit. She remained the outcast in the German émigré community and had become even more shunned by the Manns. Helga had heard that Heinrich's sister-in-law, Katie, had told others that Thomas had begun making it a point to be "away" when Nelly accompanied her husband to the house.

Since Sophie's birth, Helga felt gratitude and sisterly affection for Nelly however annoying she might be from time to time. If Nelly was Catholic, Helga would have asked her to be Sophie's godmother.

Nelly was excited about a story in an émigré newspaper. It concerned Heinrich's struggle to find a publisher.

The visit was brief. After Nelly left, Helga, bored with housework, sat down while the girls napped and read the newspaper which Nelly had left behind. She skimmed the article about Heinrich and hunted for more interesting stories. What drew her attention was the account of how four Jews living in France, managed to slip through the grip of the S.S. and traveled on foot down the Italian boot to freedom in Allied control Naples. One of the women was identified as Rebekah Wolff, "a noted authority on the Egyptian influence in ancient Palestine and Syria."

Helga crumpled the newspaper when she saw the name. Taking a breath, she pulled open the paper and finished the article, her heart beating.

Somehow Rebekah and the others had managed to stay one step ahead of the S.S., who were hunting Jews throughout Europe like a pack of dogs chasing a nest of rabbits across an open field. For years, the four had found refuge in Italian occupied France. But then in September, when Italy's Grand Council of Fascism suddenly arrested the pompous Mussolini and all but changed sides in the conflict, the S.S. immediately swept into the Italian zone to round up all of the Jews in the area. The four escapees crossed the Alps into Italy, evading the Germans who had now taken control of the norther part of the country. Somehow they managed to cross enemy lines to freedom in Naples. It was a daring escape, but Helga was not surprised that Rebekah had managed her deliverance. She had the spirit of an athlete and did not believe in the impossible.

Helga told herself not to think bad thoughts about Rebekah. She had known Wolff when studying at the university and Rebekah was a third-year doctoral student. The woman from Berlin was one of the nicest people she knew at the university.

In her second year, Helga's newly acquired talent with hieroglyphs qualified her to become a research assistant. It was through this position that she met Rebekah and Max.

Helga looked young for her age, and most of the graduate students called her *Das Kleine Mädchen*—The Little Girl. But Rebekah never did, and always addressed her by her name. At one point, she encouraged Helga to pursue her dream to earn a doctorate in Egyptology.

In those early days, one could not think of Rebekah without associating her with Max. For hours, the beautiful, gifted, and buoyant raven haired Rebekah and the handsome, blonde Max worked together, almost snuggling, inspecting potsherds and fragments of papyrus. On their free time, they went for long bicycle rides in the hilly country around Leipzig. They were inseparable.

Many of the students and faculty looked in disgust at the two. Rebekah was the daughter of a Berlin rabbi, one of the few of her ethnicity to attend the university, and one of the first woman to be admitted to the Egyptology doctoral program.

Before they earned their doctorates, something happened. Upon returning from field trips in the Near East, they were no longer gliding in harmony. They remained cordial to each other, and Helga could see

Max had not lost his passion for Rebekah, but she was distant. Helga could see the pain in his eyes when he looked at the woman. He did not pout or make scenes, but his behavior toward Rebekah was much more formal.

Helga did not give this much thought at the time.

Upon earing her Ph.D., Rebekah went on to teach at Utrecht University in the Netherlands. Max remained at Leipzig. The romance between the two fellow graduate students had been of no significance to Helga—until she became involved with Max. Although his relationship with Rebekah was over, Helga began to think of her as "the other woman," Max's first love, and a threat to their developing bond. Physically, she was gone, but the memory of how Max doted upon the woman and Helga's jealousy of Rebekah's beauty, charm, and intellect remained like trunks of rotting clothes in an attic.

Helga put the paper down and went in the kitchen. She wanted to stop thinking about Rebekah Wolff, but the fight in her head would not go away. She was disturbed that she had such a strong, distressed reaction to Rebekah's amazing journey to freedom. The woman had never done anything to her. Instead of being troubled, she should feel joy for this good news. Helga felt unsettling guilt for sinning through her thoughts.

She scoured a pan she had left soaking in the sink the night before. She had to do something to disengage herself from her evil thinking. Like preparing for the sacrament of penance, she began to feel contrite and accept the need to reconcile herself with God—and Rebekah. She decided that her penance would be to give Max the news of the woman's personal exodus from Hitler's horrible bondage.

*   *   *   *   *

"I learned something today that you will want to know," she told him that evening after the children were in bed. Her words seemed mechanical, like they were being played from a record.

"What is that?"

"Rebekah Wolff is alive, a refugee in Naples, Italy."

238

Max did not speak for a moment.

"How did you find this out?" he finally asked.

"It was reported in the German language newspaper."

She passed over the tabloid which she had folded around the story. He took the thick bundle of print and silently read the account without any visible show of emotion.

"I know I cannot compete," Helga said, shocked at the way the words just came out of her mouth.

"What do you mean?" he asked, looking up. He appeared confused.

She had opened the door to the attic.

"Max, I know you and Rebekah were . . . in love. That you loved her deeply. And for all I know, you still do. But the obstacles thrown up were too much for the two . . ."

"Actually, that is not true," he cut in.

Helga waited for him to say more.

"We had conflicting ambitions," he finally said.

Helga did not understand.

"Rebekah's life, her first love was her work. Her dream was to one day establish a school of ancient studies in Palestine."

"She made a great sacrifice to follow that dream. She also had you make a sacrifice, I assume unwillingly."

Max looked at her. She felt, for the second time in two months, his discomfort at being exposed.

"Let me show you something," he finally said, standing up.

He went outside apparently to the garage and five minutes later returned with his large magnifying glass and a saucer size piece of ostraca.

"I want you to read this."

Confused, she took the potsherd and the hand lens. The handwriting was clear and written with care. This was not a note scribbled off in hast. The author had deliberately and carefully recorded the message, so the reader would not struggle to decipher the words.

"The surface had been caked in mud, unusual for a piece from the site but not remarkable. I had spent hours carefully cleaning off the caked-on dirt."

Helga held the broken piece of pottery up to the light. She read the message inscribed without difficulty.

I must tell you again my heart is happy with love for you, mixed throughout my body like salt dipped in water. Your love strengthens me, and I am full of power. You see this and still you hold back. You remind me that my heart had once been for Norfret and rebuked me, declaring that she will always be first in my heart. But she is gone, taken from this life, and I have grieved. She is now only a memory, like of a distant bountiful harvest one remembers fondly. She was your dear friend and you also grieved her passing to dwell in the land of Osiris. Since her death, we have enjoyed two good seasons of the flood. During the two calendar cycles, you have become the center of my life, my joy, and to you I have come to give my love fully. If Norfret's ghost were ever to appear, I would not give up that love. There is no power that can shake me. What more can I say or do to convince you that you have become first of all things to me?

Helga put down the glass and looked at her husband.

"I wish I could express myself like that," Max said.

"I think the ancients were more comfortable with their tenderness than men are today," she said brushing her eyes with the back of her hand.

*   *   *   *   *

Two weeks later, Max received a letter from Rebekah. The envelope had been processed through British military mail.

Dear Max

This is the first time I've been able to write to you in over a year and am grateful that you are there to share the tale of my deliverance. . .

240

She described her journey on foot through Italy. She encountered leery peasants, endured hunger, and had to dodge the German squads that were spreading out, like a water leak, through the country north of Naples. To achieve final safety, she risked being shot by both the Germans and American forces as she crossed between enemy lines.

The refugee camp in Naples is run by the British. Our "refuge" is fenced with barbed wire, but we are free to move about the compound, even if we cannot leave. They feed us well and have given us clothing and good medical care. Most of the refugees are Jews from northern Italy. Jews in Italy under Mussolini were relatively safe until his overthrow and the S.S. flooded the Italian boot.

I am in good health, but like so many refugees, I remain in political limbo, an undesirable alien who may have escaped from hell, but now lives in purgatory with no permission likely granting passage to heaven. Palestine is the obvious relocation, but the British have clamped down on immigration. I sense I'm being watch closely by the British who probably suspect I'm a Nationalist Zionist.

You need to know I have a daughter. She is barely nine. She is a beautiful girl and all I have. We have managed to stay together when so many have been separated. She needs more than the normal amount of attention. She is mentally slow. Most of the other children ignore her. Some have teased her and even a few have been cruel. You would think that children who have shared with her the abuse of the S.S. would be like comrades, but the experience has not softened those who are by their nature bullies. I keep a close eye on her.

Max had never imagined that Rebekah would marry and have children. It took a moment for this to settle in with the picture he carried in his mind of the young, single academic he had known in the

241

late twenties.

He knew better than to assume that a person with such a bright mind would only have children who had special gifts. Still, the news of her daughter troubled him. How she managed to keep her despite the S.S.'s practice for culling out and disposing of the weak had to be a story in itself.

Every night motion pictures are shown, mostly American. I think we see the same films that the soldiers watch. Many comedies and westerns. I did not find Chaplin's The Great Dictator funny. Hitler is not a joke.

Max gave the letter to Helga.

"Would you object if I encouraged Rebekah to come to Los Angeles?" he asked.

Helga hesitated, and then glumly shook her head.

"Can she do that?"

"Rebekah needs an opportunity to regain her status, a base from which she can pursue her work. That can be here."

Max soon learned that Rebekah would need more than a sponsor to get permission to enter the United States.

"The climate in this country remains hostile to refugees," Schoenberg had told him, "which in many American minds means Jews. She has to be a person of international reputation in her field whose presence in America would enhance the nation, intellectually, politically, or scientifically."

She also had to have employment.

Max spoke with the chairman of his department, who wanted UCLA to move out of its second-tier rating in the field of Oriental Studies. He envisioned UCLA as a school with an international reputation at the same level as the University of Chicago.

"Despite spending the last three years underground in the south of France," he told the chair, "Rebekah Wolff remains the world's leading authority on Egyptian influence in Palestine and Syria. Her coming here would complement our department faculty."

The man nodded his head, but remained silent. Max could almost see the wheels turning in his head.

Chapter 42

Cold Water

D ays after Nancy received Gary's letter, five more appeared in the Pierce mailbox. The last written had been posted seven days before, on the afternoon of his admission to a military hospital in Texas. It was composed in his own hand. The voyage home, he wrote, had been uneventful except he and many of the boys got seasick.

> *The pain is under control and is gradually going away. What I cannot get over is the feeling I still have in my toes. The doctors and nurses tell me this sometimes happens, but talking to the other boys in the ward, I found that most have these feelings. We call them our ghost legs and arms . . .*

Nancy and Trudy's scheduled conflicted. The only time they could talk was late at night, whispering on the telephone. Fortunately, the cord was just long enough to allow Trudy to pull the handset into her room. She sat on the floor beside the closed door and spoke in a low voice, fearing that at any moment her mother would come out of her parent's room and tell her to hang up and go to bed. In the warm dim light of her table lamp, the high Lama watched her from the wall.

Nancy read each note, sometimes pausing with a swell of emotion when she came to a line that troubled her.

One night Nancy confided she felt so bad, she felt like jumping off a cliff. "When I think of the future, all I can see is a dark bottomless pit."

Trudy thought of saying something from *Lost Horizon*, "You shouldn't be looking at the bottom of the mountain. Why don't you try looking at the top sometimes?" Instead she said, "Gary is going to need you to be there for him. You have to be brave." Her words sounded wooden. She didn't think they helped Nancy.

Trudy saw Helga less and less after she started school. She missed their chats and the occasional advice. Having gone to college herself, Helga knew better what Trudy was experiencing than her mother who now thought of UCLA as a place where her daughter could meet a man who would go on to become a lawyer, doctor, or some other high paid professional. Trudy found her mother's hints and occasional blatant suggestion of this contrivance increasingly annoying, but she knew better than tell her to drop the subject.

*   *   *   *   *

Working at the Bundy and being a full-time college student was hard and exhausting. Trudy wondered how she would make it through her first semester. Her mother kept telling her to take it easy, but Trudy knew she couldn't do that if she wanted to keep up. She continued writing in her journal, mostly in hieroglyphs, given her increased mastery of the language, but kept the entries brief.

One night, just before Trudy was scheduled to clock out, Nelly Mann came into the theater. She looked tired, and weary, like movement itself had become a burden. Trudy wondered what the woman was doing out so late. She also could not help but think of Nancy when she watched her walk across the foyer. Would her friend someday become a gray shadow of herself, completely spent and disheartened?

Nelly smiled when she saw Trudy behind the candy case.

"I would hope my daughter would be as tall and as responsible as you. Always working. Always studying to better herself."

Trudy didn't know what to say and smiled. Nelly purchased a Hershey bar with almonds.

"Pretty Trudy," Nelly said, leaning on the glass counter, her purse dangling off her wrist, like a useless appendage.

"I'm not pretty," Trudy replied. She had grown impatient with false compliments. "And I've got pimples and can't do anything with my hair."

"Pimples?"

Trudy pointed to the red tents on his cheeks.

"*Pickel*, I had them when I was young. Just like you. But, see? They're all gone. Yours will go away. You have attractive hazel eyes and your hair is thick. So thick and rich. I could show you how to wear it."

Was it the drink speaking, or did Nelly mean what she said? And could she do something with the tangled rat's nest?

"If you could," Trudy said, meekly, hoping that Nelly was her Fairy God Mother.

Nelly smiled.

"My place is too small. I will meet you at Helga's. Do you have a heavy comb?"

Trudy shook her head no.

Then buy one. The biggest you can fine. And bring a towel. I have hair shears. You know not to brush your hair, wet or dry, yes?"

Trudy shook her head again. She did it all the time.

"When you dry your hair, first use your fingers and then the heavy comb with course teeth. Never the fine teeth. And always, always wash your hair in cold water."

Why had no one told her these things before? Did Nelly really know what she was talking about?

Nelly drifted into the auditorium. Like a spent Roman candle, Trudy's hope dissipated with a puff. She realized they had not set a date or a time to meet at the Schneider's house.

*   *   *   *   *

Trudy had to push herself out the door two mornings later with more effort than usual. Even the three cups of coffee she gulped down did little more than make her edgy. She had been up late the night before babysitting the Lewis kids for Martha, who had to rush off on some family emergency downtown. She could at least study psychology and German literature after the children went to bed. Chuck was working at the Disney Studio on military training films and would not be home until very late—if at all. Martha told her he sometimes slept in his office on the floor.

After a few weeks attending UCLA, Trudy noticed that she had begun to feel like a college student, not a high school girl lost on the large campus. She didn't have the time nor the interest to join the pep rallies and icebreaker events that seemed to be occurring daily, but she had gotten into the rhythm of each day's class schedule and had begun to adjust to the large lecture halls.

Trudy had come to know a few of the people who sat around her, mostly young women, with whom she shared notes after the lecture and chatted before class begun. She didn't tell anyone that she worked behind the candy case at the Bundy Theater.

There were many Navy cadets and Marines in her classes, but they tended to ignore her, choosing instead to flirt with the pretty girls. She couldn't deny she felt jealous.

*   *   *   *   *

That evening, after listening to *Amos 'n Andy* with her parents, Trudy retired to her room with the new issue of *Life* magazine. She needed a break. She skimmed the war articles with their grim, gray images of battles in Europe and the Pacific. She glanced at the full-page ads for companies who, before the war, made cars, tires, and similar consumer goods. These ads now called attention to the tanks, aircraft, and war machine parts that they were building to fight the Axis. Even the Curtis Candy Company touted that its Baby Ruth and Butterfinger bars, now scarce in stores and at the Bundy, were going to the boys in the service.

She read a curious article about Los Angeles by Roger Butterfield, who described the city to be the "damnedest place." Sunshine, autos, Amee McPherson, Forest Lawn. The pictures and story did not give an impression of the Los Angeles she knew.

Flipping the page, she saw pictures of soldiers who had lost their legs and arms and were being fitted with *prosthetics*, artificial limbs that allowed the servicemen to regain mobility or some use of their arms and legs. This marvelous care was being provided at McCloskey General Hospital in Temple, Texas. She assumed this was the facility where Gary Pico was being treated.

Turning another page, she almost jumped, seeing his picture. As a nurse stood beside him, he practiced walking on artificial legs. The caption identified him as Cpl. Gary Picco, obviously, a misspelling. He wore shorts revealing the metal and leather frame that supported him on his new plastic legs and spring-loaded civilian shoes. Otherwise, the devices would be totally hidden by civilian trousers, shown on the next page, as he or another amputee strolled with a normal gate. The head of the walker had been cropped off.

Trudy jumped up and ran to the phone. The laughter of some radio show echoed in the hall as she dialed Nancy.

"Nancy, have you seen this week's *Life?*" she asked, almost breathless with excitement.

"No." Trudy picked up from the drone and weary tone in Nancy's voice that she was either tired or in one of her funks—or both.

"There is a picture of Gary walking!"

"Say that again."

"There is a story in *Life* about boys who lost limbs and how the army medical corps is fixing them up with mechanical legs or arms. There are pictures of Gary strolling like he's walking across the street."

"Oh, my God! In the new issue of *Life?*"

"I can bring ours by tomorrow on my way to school," she volunteered. She realized she hadn't asked her parents if they were done with the magazine. She might have to purchase a second copy.

"Oh, Trudy! Gary wrote that he was getting something that would allow him to walk. I figured they were just wooden legs."

248

Chapter 43

The Dreamer

December came quickly, but the days had not feel festive. On Christmas Eve, Trudy had to go to class and then work at the theater which was now opened all night. While her family drank eggnog, she sold popcorn to the few who came out to see Betty Grable and Cesar Romero in *Coney Island* and Humphrey Bogart in the *Maltese Falcon*. Robert would not relieve her until midnight.

Tired and feeling clumsy Christmas Day, Trudy got up after her mother prepared breakfast. At least, they weren't going to have Christmas dinner at home, although she felt no thrill about spending the day at her aunt's, way out in South Pasadena.

Christmas was on a Saturday, and she had to work Sunday, but Monday was her day off, and she would not have to return to school until Wednesday. She was looking forward to the break.

*   *   *   *   *

Monday afternoon, bored with homework, Trudy decided to walk over to the Schneiders.

The army had finally removed the anti-aircraft guns and search lights, leaving behind a few men to tend the barrage balloons, an assignment which had to be as boring as watching the hour hand on a clock move.

"How is school life?" Helga asked.

"Demanding," Trudy admitted. "I don't get much sleep. With my job and all the homework and reading, I barely have time to practice hieratic script."

"My husband says you're using it to record entries in your journal."

Trudy nodded, flattered that Professor Max would share this with Helga.

249

"You learned hieroglyphs when you were in college." Trudy said. "How did you become interested?"

The kettle in the kitchen began to wheeze and quickly became shrill. Helga had already set out the tea cups, spoons, and bowl of sugar on the dining room table. Trudy followed her into the kitchen.

"Oh, the story is not impressive at all," she said, pouring water into a pretty blue china tea pot. She looked up at Trudy. "I was fifteen. My family traveled to Berlin that year. We visited the cultural landmarks including the Ägyptisches Museum. On display was the bust of Nefertiti and many other wonderful objects. People normally don't realize that Germany has a fine collection of Egyptian treasures. My parents and sister thought the objects pretty, but I was totally captivated. I wanted to stay longer, but Papa said we had already spent enough time. After returning home, I went to the library and began to read about the ancient people of the Nile."

The two sat down in the dining area, and Helga carefully poured the tea, holding a napkin under the spout. She did not use tea bags, and bits of tea leaf floated out and into the cups. Trudy spooned a little sugar into her cup and stirred.

"Have you been to Egypt?"

She took a sip of the tea, and it burnt her tongue. She put the cup down. Helga sipped hers, giving no indication that the hot liquid was scorching her mouth.

"With my husband." Helga smiled. "We honeymooned there and traveled up the Nile by steamer. The valley is magical. During the nights on the river, in the moonlight, one feels lost in time."

Trudy glanced out the window. There, between the bushes silhouetting the panes, was her whole world, walled in by the long row of distant mountains that dwarfed the Hollywood Hills. The afternoon light brightened the snow on Mount Baldy and its shoulder domes, giving the range an orange glow.

"I've never even been on the other side of those mountains," she said, suddenly feeling self-conscious and provincial, although people around the world thought of Los Angeles as a green and golden magical place, where the locals lived in perpetual sunshine.

"You've never been on a train?"

"Just the streetcar."

"You've always lived here."

"I was born at Hollywood Presbyterian Hospital. As far back as I can remember, I have lived on the Westside. This is the world I know." She motioned to the window. "On days like this, I see those mountains capped in white, but you know something? I've never been up there or to the snow. On clear days, I can see Catalina Island from the beach, but I've never been there either. I've never been to San Diego or Santa Barbara or even L.A. Harbor. What have I done? I've been to my uncle's citrus groves way out in Claremont and picked lemons. I've been up to Griffith Park Observatory and looked at Saturn's rings through the big telescope. I've seen the backside of movie sets behind the fences surrounding studio backlots. I've walked along Hollywood Boulevard at night." She smiled. "I once had a conversation with Charlie Chaplin."

"What did you talk about?"

Trudy hesitated, feeling something painful and sweet. She fought the tears forming in her eyes.

"He told me people think too much and feel too little. He told me to be a dreamer and listen to my heart."

Trudy forced a smile. She glanced away from Helga and reached for the tea cup and took a sip, not burning her tongue this time. After a moment, she looked back at Helga.

"It is easy to dream when you're young," Trudy said.

"Yes, it is."

"I hope to get good enough at deciphering hieratic script that you and Professor Max will allow me to translate some of the notes in his collection. I'm patient, you know."

"Let that be part of your dream."

1944

Chapter 44

Transitions

With determination, Trudy completed the fall semester, surprising herself by earning all A's. In the spring, she repeated this feat. At Professor's Max's suggestion, she took French, which seemed to come rather easy, although the language and voice were quite different from English and German. At one point, the teacher told her she spoke French like a German.

Her German class required a mountain of reading, but her mastery of the language was superior to most of the other students. The course was merely time consuming, not difficult. Fortunately, she could do much of her reading standing on aching feet behind the candy counter, sometimes smudging butter on the pages of her textbooks. She intentionally volunteered to take shifts on slow evenings, working to midnight. The Bundy being an all-night theater, some of the workers from Douglas would come before their graveyard shift began or after finishing their night shift. She suspected some came in from the assembly line just to sleep. The country was now building planes at a rate that no one would have imagined possible before the Pearl Harbor attack.

In early June, the Allied army breached Hitler's European Fortress and pushed into Northern France. D-Day! Hundreds of thousands of Americans, British, and Canadian soldiers crossed the cold beaches of Normandy and could not be stopped by machine guns or Rommel's heavy armor and tanks. Trudy felt exceptionally proud and patriotic, and for the third time gave blood.

After school ended and her summer break began, she felt a need to do more to support the war. Like many people in Los Angeles, she took a second job, although she was averse to working again in a factory. Susan, who recently had a premature baby, had put the bug in Trudy's ear to apply at Rochester's Pacific Parachute Company. The job would at least be offbeat. And scandalous! When she wrote in her diary that she took the job, she wondered if she was rebelling against her mother for the prom incident.

Pacific Parachute employed a mixture of Caucasian, Mexican, and colored girls. The plant superintendent was a Negro man. The situation was totally unheard of and would not have been permitted if the war was not going on.

Trudy folded and trimmed silk with the left-handed scissors the company had in its tool crib. At first, she was frightened. She had never been in a place where the white people were outnumbered by people of dark skin. She had never been anywhere where more than a couple of dark faces were in the crowd. But like at the flashlight factory, the employees did their job and got along.

She never told Nancy or her mother about her coworkers or that she was working for a colored man—regardless of how famous and popular he was on radio. Her foreman, a Negro lady, spoke like she came from the deep south, but she knew her stuff and was more responsive to the girls under her than Trudy's foreman had been at the flashlight factory.

Trudy soon discovered that her father knew about Pacific Parachute and it's mixed race workforce. She thought she was in trouble, but he looked at her like he was seeing something for the first time, not in a disapproving way. He smiled and nodded his head. She never realized her father had such a liberal attitude.

"Don't tell your mother a whole lot about your second job," he said lighting a cigarette. "You know how she is."

Trudy understood. Her mother, like every other mother—and most fathers, would have a screaming fit and demand she quit. Basically, all her mom knew was she worked at a defense plant handling "industrial" silk.

Trudy and her father called the company "PPC." Sometimes he dropped her off on his way to work. "PPC" was certainly hers, Susan's and her father's shared secret about which she could tell no one.

One day in late June a newspaper photographer came into the factory to take pictures. Trudy turned her back when the cameraman shot photos of Eddie Anderson and his partner walking through her section. She didn't want her mother, Susan's mother or anyone else seeing her picture in the newspaper.

*　　*　　*　　*　　*

Trudy often missed dinner and had to whip up something after she got home from the parachute company before going to the Bundy. Sometimes she just ate popcorn or Hershey chocolate bars. The snacks didn't fill her, and throughout the summer she was just as tired as she was when in school. The summer off from UCLA would not give her a chance to recharge her batteries. She rarely wrote more than a line or two in her journal. Her dream of becoming a hieroglyph research assistant seemed dimmer and dimmer.

One night a tipsy Nelly Mann came into the theater. Even when her expression was visibly twisted by alcohol and her blonde hair was slightly unfurling, she remained a beautiful older woman.

"Hello, Trudy," she said coming up to the candy counter, leaning on the glass case for support.

"Good evening, Nelly. Is your husband with you?"

Trudy realized asking was not nice. Obviously, Nelly came alone. She always came alone.

"Heinrich is home with his books, pondering some deep subject. It was best I left him to his work." Her eyes glided over the rows of candy as if she were trying to focus. "Are the movies any good?"

"I haven't had time to see either, but I understand *The Falcon Takes Over* is the best in the series. It's showing right now."

Noticing the German literature book that Trudy read when there were no customers, Nelly leaned over and said, "I wrote a book once. About my life. Heinrich read what I had accomplished and burned the manuscript. He then used my childhood of poverty and hardship in his story *Ein ernstes Leben.*" Nelly leaned back. "The book sold well." She looked tired, even beaten. Trudy smelled the alcohol on her breath and gave her a package of mints, putting her own nickel in the cash drawer.

*   *   *   *   *

Early in the spring, Andy had resumed his job assembling wings at Douglas for the A-20 Havoc light bomber. Still in school, he and his friends rode their bikes to the plant after their last class. Like a lot of boys, the school advanced him half a grade, graduating Andy six months early. Two days after the graduation ceremony, he began working full time at the aircraft plant.

He and the family knew that the job was temporary. He had turned eighteen before graduation. At any moment, he would be called up for military service. With the expanded fighting in Europe and the Pacific, the military's manpower needs continued. The boys slipping into the draft pool when they turned eighteen were almost all being put in uniform within weeks of their birthdays.

Trudy's mother seemed to age ten years the day the envelope from the Selective Service was delivered, addressed to Andy. Trudy got home before her brother and knew something was wrong as soon as she stepped in the house. She thought of Nancy and guessed her mother had just learned that Uncle Billy had been a casualty. Her father sat in the cushioned chair next to the fireplace, sucking somberly on his cigarette and looking into space—not a reaction she would expect if the family got bad news about Billy. Looking up at Trudy, he forced a smile.

"A letter for Andy just came from the draft board," he said. This was expected but the news still hit her in the gut like a rock.

When her brother came home from Douglas, he was in a chipper mood. Their parents and Trudy looked at him like he had been sentenced to the gallows.

"Something wrong?"

"You got your letter from the Selective Service."

"Well, it's not like I didn't expect one," he said. "Where is it?" His mother handed him the envelope. He ripped it open.

"'From the President of the United States,'" he read, after shaking open the notice. "'Greeting! You are hereby ordered to report for induction on July 26.' There are instructions where I'm to report and what to bring. Why are you looking at me like that? You knew this was coming."

Their mother turned around and walked into the kitchen, sobbing.

"You're going to war, son," their father said.

"So are all the boys," Andy said like it was no big deal. "I'll be all right."

Andy had been in ROTC for most of the war. Besides having the boys march in formation, the program had been preparing them for this moment. The families had not been schooled for sending their sons and brothers off to war.

*   *   *   *   *

The day he had to report, their father stayed home from work. With their mother and Trudy in the backseat, he drove Andy to the Selective Service office, south of the Westwood Village, where he picked up the bus to the induction center. Other boys were being dropped off by their parents and sometimes their girlfriends. Little knots of people stood outside the Selective Service office, saying their goodbyes, trying to appear like everything was normal. Andy lit up a cigarette and smoked openly in front of his parents. His taking up the habit was certainly no surprise. Their father gave him a fresh pack of Camels. When the bus came, the young men lined up and boarded. They opened the windows and waved to their families and girlfriends as the former school bus groaned, belched black smoke, and pulled away from the curb. The last Trudy saw of Andy, he was looking over to one of the other boys, maybe a friend, smiling and pulling his head back into the bus.

*   *   *   *   *

Trudy returned to school, a sophomore. By working two jobs, she had managed to save more money than the year before. Back at UCLA, she continued to work at the Bundy to afford to pay her mother rent and buy books and school supplies. She began to ride the bus more

259

often, not feeling as cautious about saving every nickel. And often she would ride home with Professor Max.

"The war in Europe is not going to last longer than a few more months," Professor Max predicted one afternoon. "Maybe half a year. The Red Army is near Prussia and moving into Hungary. Some of the German generals have been in open revolt. Paris and Rome have been liberated. The British and Americans are moving to the Rhine."

When she walked into the house, her mother had the radio on and was dusting the living room furniture. She put down the rag and looked at Trudy with an *I've got something good to tell you* expression.

"A letter came today from your Uncle Billy. He's safe and got himself transferred off the oiler. He's now on a heavy cruiser, the Indianapolis. He says the ship is chasing what's left of the Jap navy around the South Pacific."

Trudy, annoyed that her mother would tell her this, obviously communicated her displeasure with her silent reaction. Her mother frowned.

"Trudy," she snapped. "Get over what happened last year. Your uncle is defending us. Respect that."

"Yes, mom," she said and stood like a soldier told to stay at attention, waiting for her mother to tell her "at ease."

"That's all I wanted to tell you," her mother groused and resumed flicking the dust rag over the corner chiffonier.

In her room, the high Lama's serene expression conveyed forgiveness and reminded her not to be rude.

$$*\qquad*\qquad*\qquad*\qquad*$$

With the Navy's V12 program, Trudy was accustomed to seeing most of the male students in uniform. Still, she was surprised a few weeks after Andy was drafted to see one fellow in army khaki with sergeant strips walking across the court in front of Royce Hall. He looked familiar and then she realized the soldier was Karl Black.

"Karl, is that you?" she asked, running up to him.

Karl stopped and watched her approach.

"Karl, don't you remember me? It's Trudy. From high school."

"Trudy! You said you were going to UCLA."

"Well, here I am. I'm a sophomore."

Smiling, he nodded.

She glanced at his shirt and the insignia on his arms.

"Look at all those strips. You're a staff sergeant."

"How 'bout that. And I never spent a day in ROTC."

"You told me the military wouldn't want you."

"Well, last year they started drafting any guy under twenty who had two arms and two feet. Because of my asthma, I don't quality to go overseas, so they've assigned me to Fort Roach."

"Where's that?"

"The Hal Roach Studios in Culver City. We make morale and training films. How to brush your teeth, the dangers of venereal disease. Subjects like that."

"Do you write . . . scripts?"

"No. I'm in charge of a crew who builds sets. So. How are you?"

"I'm doing well. School's been good. I'm . . . working at a theater and I'm still learning hieroglyphs."

"Are you engaged, or do you have a boyfriend?"

"No. How about you? You got a special person?"

"I have a girlfriend. Met her at Roach. She cuts film. An assistant editor."

Trudy felt her heart drop. She forced a smile.

"I got to go," he said. "I'm doing something for my dad."

"It's good to see you, Karl. Take care of yourself."

*   *   *   *   *

In October, Mary had finally left the camp to go to Haverford College in Pennsylvania. Although a small liberal arts school, the institute gave a Bachelor of Science degree in biology. She was not the first "Nikkei"—those of Japanese descent—to be enrolled in the school. The students and faculty had become accustomed to seeing their faces on campus. The people in the town accepted their presence.

> *The place is green and beautiful and nothing like what we know in California. Many of the trees are maples whose leaves, right now, have turned gold. In the evening, there is a sharp chill in the air.*
>
> *In the dorm, there is one other person of Japanese descent, a strange girl from Seattle, Washington. She is neither shy nor quiet and in some ways like your brother.*
>
> *I've never seen so many towheads! They are friendly and curious. Most don't understand what happened to us in California and about the concentration camps. They know we had to move from the coast, but few realize that it was at the point of a bayonet.*

Mary would no longer see letters from her brothers who wrote to their mother and father. She continued to post notes to them weekly, sharing tidbits about her new adventure. She hoped they would occasionally send her a letter.

Mary noted they had seen combat in southern Italy, being part of the "Purple Heart Battalion." Neither brother had been wounded in the terrible, dragged out battle for Monte Cassino, but they had been in combat and seen many of their comrades killed and seriously wounded. "My brother and their comrades are a proud bunch and consider it their honor to die for their country. I just pray that they don't have to."

262

Chapter 45

Reunions

O n Halloween eve, Trudy received a phone call from Nancy. Squealing, she told Trudy that Gary had returned home.
He had not written upon his discharge from the military hospital, nor had he telegraphed his travel plans. He arrived at Union Station with no one to greet him. He took city buses to get to his old neighborhood and carried his big duffle bag, the size of a fat, ten-year-old child, three blocks to his house. Not having a key, he had to ring the doorbell once he got home. His mother almost fainted when she answered the door.

"He doesn't walk with a cane or limp," Nancy said. "Just like in the picture in *Life* he sort of walks like he did before the war. He can't run. That's all."

Apparently, Gary had been home two days before calling Nancy. Trudy thought this strange.

"I didn't go to work today. I wanted to be with him. It's been a long time since he's been home, and there is so much for him to get used to. The war's changed everything."

And changed Gary, Trudy thought.

"You wouldn't think he had been gone that long." Nancy said. "He looks the same, a little thinner and quieter. He doesn't want to talk about Sicily and the war. I understand most of the boys don't talk about their service. They just want to move on."

The next evening was Halloween. Nancy and Gary came to the Bundy to see the sneak preview and maybe stay for *Address Unknown*. Although a Tuesday night, the theater was busy. Trudy stood behind the counter, engrossed in serving popcorn, pouring soft drinks, dispensing candy, and counting change. This night there was no special seating for studio bigwigs. She figured they wanted to sit with the crowd to judge the audience's reaction. She had no idea what movie would be previewed.

Looking up, Trudy saw Nancy and Gary enter the foyer. Nancy, her arm wrapped around Gary's, her body leaning into his, was smiling, even before she made eye contact with Trudy. The young man, tall with sandy hair and rather pale, wearing a khaki uniform with twin corporal chevrons on his sleeves, seemed unsure of himself. He looked around the room at the people milling about.

"You remember my friend, Trudy," Nancy said, looking up at her boyfriend as they approached the candy counter. Trudy smiled at them as she took someone's quarter and gave them back a dime and a nickel.

"Hello," he said.

"Gary, welcome home," Trudy said trying not to ignore her customer who smelled like he hadn't bathed in weeks. They stood for a moment watching Trudy do her job and then wandered into the auditorium.

Many people anticipated that the sneak preview would be a horror flick, and it was. Universal's *House of Frankenstein*. As the film ran, Trudy helped Judy, who had grown six inches since Trudy starting working at the Bundy and had acquired a softer, more womanly voice. They set up wooden booths for the audience to fill out their preview ballots.

Nancy had invited Trudy to join her and Gary at an all-night coffee shop after the show. Trudy hesitated. She had to be up early the next morning and felt she would be a distraction, even a nuisance, to the reunited couple. But Nancy insisted Gary didn't have a problem with her joining them.

Trudy felt a little strange walking into the coffee shop in her Pepsi stained uniform. They were seated at a booth.

"How did you like the preview?" she asked.

"It was scary," Nancy said pulling her shoulders up and severing.

Gary smiled, seemingly amused by Nancy, and shook his head.

"It was okay, I guess."

"Weren't you scared?" Nancy asked, looking up at him. "I mean, it was creepy with all those monsters."

He silently shook his head.

"It takes more than Frankenstein's monster, a vampire or a werewolf to scare me now."

"I guess it would," Trudy said. The terror he had experienced on the battlefield and his ordeal in the hospital were beyond her ability to imagine.

The sudden somberness in Nancy's expression indicated that she understood him too.

"No. You wouldn't be frightened by the boogie man. You've faced an enemy with tanks, guns and bayonets."

"I don't feel too bad," he said. He sipped his water. "I mean, there were guys I saw whose faces were burned off, those who were paralyzed from the neck down and others whose heads were blown apart and patched back together with big parts missing."

Gary said this without rancor. Nonetheless, he appeared lost for a moment in his own thoughts, looking at the sweat on the water glass. He blinked, breaking his gaze and turned to Nancy, who had become somber and quiet.

"But I'm here. I'm thinking of taking up tap dancing."

"Gary!" Nancy grabbed his hand and looked up at him. "Don't make jokes like that."

"I'm not joking," he said softly. He was smiling but avoided looking at her eyes.

*   *   *   *   *

The next day, as Trudy, sleep-deprived and late for school, rode her bike off to Westwood, Rebekah Wolff came to the UCLA campus where she was welcomed by the Dean of the School of Arts and Letters, the Chairman of the Department of Oriental Studies, and Max Schneider. As the four walked across the quad to Royce Hall, the Dean proudly pointed out the university's broad open fields beyond the Janss steps and, on the horizon, the gray glint of the Pacific Ocean visible between the trees. The sky was unusually clear.

Being part of the party that greeted Rebekah allowed Max to

265

overcome his uneasiness about seeing her. She seemed amused by his presence and shook his hand along with the others, giving his a squeeze he doubted she gave the others.

Max was pleased the other men were impressed and charmed with their new colleague. Speaking flawless English, she gave a summary of her work and what research she would like to resume. Though she was thin, her eyes sunken and hair dull, she had a warm, disarming smile and moved with the lanky stride of an athlete. After the meeting in the dean's office, the four colleagues had lunch in the faculty dining room. Following the meal, Rebekah asked to see Schneider alone.

He took her to his office. She sat down in the nondescript wood side chair in front of his desk. He pulled his around to be seated in front of her.

This was the first time the two had been alone in more than thirteen years. He suddenly felt awkward and his thoughts were disjointed, not due to old animosities, just an uncomfortableness, a stiffness of not knowing what to say, what to ask. They had never had a chance to become at ease with each other as former lovers. And there had been a lot of history that occurred in those thirteen years. Part of the history was tattooed on her arm and reflected in her prematurely aged face and thin body.

She did not attempt to hide the ugly numbers.

He was troubled to see how old and spent she appeared. In his mind, she had remained in her twenties. He also felt disquieted that someone he had once loved had been branded and brutalized by his—their—own countrymen, consumed and driven by a passion of hatred and a nonsense ideology.

She reached out and touched him on the cheek. There were almost tears in her eyes.

"How did you do this?" she asked.

"Do what?"

"Max. There are few Jewish refugees being granted visas to come to the United States. Even those who have family here are struggling with red tape. I know you're behind this."

"I pulled strings. That's the American expression for what I

266

did."

"You have become a master puppeteer, then."

Seven months ago, he and the department chairman met with the Dean of the College of Letters and Science and Bruce Kingsley, one of the three members of the Interim Administrative Committee controlling academic affairs. Schneider feared Kingsley's temporary position would promote indecisiveness.

"She's expressed an interest in coming to California?" the dean had asked at the meeting.

"She won't be petitioning to return to Germany," Schneider replied.

"Dr. Wolff notified Schneider that she is in Naples, Italy," the department chairman said. "At this moment other schools, I'm sure, are unaware of her status, but that will change soon."

"You say she is an important scholar."

"These are letters," the chairman said opening a folder, "from various oriental archeologists who know her work. You may wish to examine them."

Max could not believe how cool he maintained himself at that meeting. Academic politics had never been his strength. And Rebekah's refugee status turned out to work in her favor. Kingsley had strong views about the refugee situation and considered appalling the government's unwillingness to allow more into the country. He probably would have instructed the school to offer her a position if she had been just a graduate student.

Within five weeks, Max had gathered together the documents needed from the school for her to be admitted into the United States. Next, he contacted Rebekah, encouraging her to accept the school's offer and apply for a visa.

That first letter he wrote was the hardest. Normally, he scribbled out words quickly and decisively, but he found himself struggling for the appropriate words to reconnect and inform her of the offer she would receive from the university.

"How do I begin?" he wrote. "Your letter allowed me to exhale, knowing that you are safe. . ."

These words failed to adequately express his anger for all she had endured—the brutality, the work camp, her dangerous journey through France, her torturous trek down the Italian boot, and now her being stranded in a tide pool controlled by the imperialist British.

I must conclude, with all that has happened in the world, your options are limited. Materially, I fear you have lost everything, but your reputation and your mental gifts remain. These cannot be stolen.

Max recounted what he remembered of her work in Egypt and in Palestine. He avoided mentioning their personal issues. He described his new life at UCLA, and Los Angeles' strong émigré community. He then got to the point.

The University of California Los Angeles is interested in you joining the faculty. The university's department of history and archeology is growing and has the potential to be a great institution. The school can make arrangements to allow you into the United States. Consider this a stepping stone for your eventually establishing a position in Palestine.

Two months later he received her response. She thanks him for reaching out and the school's invitation to join the faculty.

I have submitted, as required, six copies of Form BC to the United States Department of State's Visa Division. The University of California has been identified as my financial guarantor and you have been designated my moral sponsor. I made the presumption you would agree to this. There is no one else.

Months later Max learned that the State Department had sent a note to the University stating, "The Department questions the plausibility of Wolff's importance to your institute." The Dean told

Schneider that Kingsley blew up and contacted the new Undersecretary of the State Department, Edward Stettinius, and obtained the phone number of the letter's originator. Kingsley placed a direct telephone call to this man, not giving a damn about the cost. The administrator castigated the letter's condescending tone, challenged the official's authority to second guess the school's academic needs, and demanded to know when Wolff would be granted permission to leave the refugee camp in Italy to come to California.

"I've heard Kingsley when he's angry. That State Department weasel must have peed in his pants."

Schneider was not amused by the comment.

The Dean also mentioned that it had been to her benefit that her family had vanished. A State Department ruling issued in 1941 made it all but impossible for any refugee with close family in Europe to be granted a Visa.

"The S.S. could not have devised a crueler exception," Schneider said.

Later, Max learned that Rebekah had almost been moved to a refugee camp in New York, the only one in the United States where a few Jews and others stranded in the south of Italy were given temporarily shelter. This option turned out to be a ploy by someone in the State Department to keep her from coming to UCLA. Those who accepted to be housed in the camp were only guests and at the end of the war would be returned to their homeland. No exceptions. Fortunately, Rebekah read the fine print and declined the offer.

Max had no intent of telling her the obstacles the University had to overcome, blatantly tinged with anti-Semitism, to make it possible for her to come to California. How different was the American attitude toward Jews from the German which had allowed such terrible consequences?

*   *   *   *   *

There was a moment of stiff silence.

Rebekah smiled. For the first time, she looked around his office,

269

a room with books and stacks of papers, a window overlooking Westwood. Not much different from any professor's office in any part of the world. Only the furniture and fixtures were a different style.

"I hope," she said, "I have it in me to live up to the honor you've done. You have moved a mountain for me to be here. I hope that I may earn the esteem and honor to justify your kindness."

"Tell me about your daughter," he said to change the subject. "What is her name?"

Rebekah stared and seemed a little unsettled by his question. "Betje."

"That's a Dutch name. You met your husband in Holland?"

"I never married."

"Oh," Max said flustered and suddenly feeling his face blush. "It's not what you think."

The weary look had returned. Her shoulders slumped down.

"What I tell you must not be said to anyone else. In the Vught labor camp I took her on and identified her as my daughter. She needed protection. Betje was one of several children that had been from a special Jewish school for the mentally deranged. Despite the bureaucratic efficiency of the S.S., somehow her papers were loss.

"She is a pretty girl. I suspect she was singled out by one of the camp officers who took a fancy to her. I think he eventually became bored and dumped her into our cell."

"You became her adoptive mother."

"Someone had to."

Schneider couldn't imagine how she managed. A young child would be an extra burden.

"Does the State Department know this?"

"No one knows! Don't you understand? I identified her as my daughter. The authorities have not questioned this. How could they disprove my declaration? It isn't like the German government is cooperating with the Americans. The poor girl hardly speaks, even though she can understand Dutch and follow simple instructions."

"What does she call you?"

"Grietje."

"Grietje?"

Rebekah shrugged.

Max sensed she did not want to continue with the subject of her "daughter" and wondered what subject he might bring up.

"You must be staying in the apartments across the street," he said.

"I assume that is where the new faculty is housed upon their arrival," Rebekah said with a question in her voice.

"That's where they put us when we came here."

"Us?"

"I'm married. I have three children. You might remember my wife. Helga Traugott."

"Oh, Miss Traugott! The little girl. She was so pretty, so nice, reliable, easy to work with. Intelligent. I feel good for you."

Max debated what he should say next. Weeks before he had struggled with himself whether or not he should show Helga the letters between him and Rebekah. He concluded it would be wrong to hide them. His wife may continue to infer whatever she would about their past relationship, but the turn of events made holding back the correspondence seem petty.

"Helga discovered you were in Naples," he finally said. "She read an account of your escape from the SS."

Max saw the impish, inquisitive look he remembered from their university days.

"Are you telling me that I am here because of Miss Traugott?"

Someone gently knocked on his door. Max looked at his watch.

"I'm afraid this is my office hour." He had one troubling student who kept coming by and bothering him.

Opening the door, he was relieved to see Trudy.

"Oh, I'm sorry," she said in German. "I didn't know you were with someone. I only wanted to return this. I found a used copy."

She held out the text of hieratic script that he had all but forgotten he had lent her.

"That's not a problem," Schneider said, taking the monograph. "Come in. I want to introduce you to someone."

271

Trudy stepped into the room.

"Let me introduce you to Professor Rebekah Wolff. Some time ago, I think I told you about her. She is the old colleague who has joined us. Professor, this is my neighbor, Miss Trudy Mansfield, a second-year student who learned to read and write hieroglyphs before she enrolled in the university and uses hieratic script to write in her journal. My wife is her teacher, but she has learned much on her own."

"I'm pleased to meet you, professor," Trudy said in her smooth fluent German.

"You read Egyptian hieroglyphs and use hieratic script. That is truly impressive."

"Thank you."

Max invited Trudy to take his seat. He backed up and sat down on the edge of the desk.

Trudy put her book bag on the floor. She looked up at Rebekah. He noticed that something appeared to bother his neighbor.

"I hope you have a good experience at UCLA," she said obviously ignoring whatever had distracted her.

"If the other students are as talented as you obviously are, I think I will be happy here."

"Thank you." Trudy appeared to blush.

"I'm amazed with your conversational German," Rebekah said. "Your family must speak the language."

"Hardly! I don't think my brother even speaks English. He's in the army now. Professor Max's wife has been conversing with me for years."

"She is a good teacher. This doesn't surprise me."

"You know her?"

"Years ago, at the University of Leipzig. She was extraordinarily helpful when I was a graduate student."

The room became leaden with an uncomfortable silence. Trudy seemed uneasy. Was it the mention of Helga? Or did something show that Trudy noticed concerning their past?

"You know, I should be going," the young woman said moving in the chair like she was about to stand up. "You have important things

272

to talk about."

"No, please stay," Wolff said. "It's been a long time since I've conversed with a student."

"Oh?"

"I was a professor at the University of Utrecht in the Netherlands. The Germans invaded, and I was placed in a forced labor camp. I escaped and hid in southern France."

"I figured you had been in a concentration camp," Trudy said somberly.

"It's that obvious?"

"The tattoo is."

Wolff glanced at the ugly blue numbers crudely lanced in her flesh.

"How did you get away?" the girl asked.

Rebekah recounted her story. Trudy studied Wolff like she was someone who had returned from the land of the dead. In a sense, she had.

Rebekah's eyes appeared to become darker and more sunken as she spoke. She had seen firsthand the devil's work.

"Professor Wolff, I'm so glad you are here," the girl said. "I really wish it was under different circumstances. You've been through so much. I feel honored to meet you and talk to you like this."

Rebekah studied the girl's face. Stoic, she shook her head. Max knew her well enough to suspect she did not want to be an object of another's awe or pity.

"I am one of the lucky few. I am alive, and I am here, and we are having this conversation only because of luck."

Chapter 46

The Lone Palm

Aweek before Christmas, Trudy saw in the newspaper that Thomas Mann's sister-in-law had killed herself. The page six headline jumped out at her.

With dread, she read the story which confirmed that it was Nelly who had committed suicide. The article reported that the wife of Heinrich Mann "was worried because she was scheduled to appear in court the next day to be sentenced on a charge of reckless driving. . . Mann could think of no motive for Mrs. Mann's act."

Troubled, Trudy could not stop thinking about Nelly. She reflected on the last time she saw her at the Bundy. She recalled how tired and old Nelly looked. She also remembered her comment about wanting a daughter—a daughter who she imagined would be like Trudy.

Trudy stopped at the Schneider house before going home.

"Have you hear about Nelly?" she asked

"I received a call before I saw the story in the morning paper."

"I'm sorry. She was your friend."

Helga silently nodded.

"I've never known anyone who has taken their life," Trudy said. "I will always remember the day Sophie was born and what she did for you. I never would have thought that someday . . ." She did not know how to finish that thought and looked at Helga.

"It's not the first time she tried to kill herself," Helga said. "You wouldn't know that, of course. Nelly had a hard life and most of the Germans in Los Angeles avoided her. She drank."

"She was always so nice to me. Do you know what's going to happen? I mean, will there be a funeral?"

"I have not heard."

"If there is, please let me know. I want to go."

Helga looked at Trudy like she was examining something on her face. She nodded her head.

"If there is, I will tell you."

*   *   *   *   *

That evening, as she studied, Trudy remembered that Nelly had once told her she wrote a story that her husband read, burned, and then used as the basis for one of his books. She closed her text and pulled out her journal. She found the note she wrote about Nelly visiting the Bundy. Trudy had even recorded the name of Heinrich Mann's book, *Ein ernstes Leben*. The next day she went to the UCLA library. The work was not listed in the catalog. She thumbed through the English translations of his literary creations finding only one story that recounted the life of a woman born in poverty who eventually became a bar maid. *Hill of Lies*, probably the English title for *Ein ernstes Leben—A Serious Life*. Trudy thought the English version had a more appropriate title. Nelly's husband had stolen her story and passed the tale off as his own. Trudy checked out the volume.

Later, Helga told Trudy that a grave-side service would be the next day. Nelly would be entombed at the cemetery in Santa Monica. Trudy would have to skip two classes, but knew a student whose notes she could copy. Helga was not going. She did not explain why, and Trudy did not ask.

That evening at the Bundy, Trudy began to read the *Hill of Lies*. Disgusted with the lurid events the young protagonist Marie Lehning faced, she nearly put the book in her bag several times but forced herself to continue reading. If indeed the story was inspired by Nelly's earlier years, the narrative revealed how different Nelly's life had been from her own and the unbelievable difficulties she had endured as a girl and young woman.

As an adult, the main character, Marie, moved to Berlin where she at first became a seamstress and later a bar maid. Trudy was troubled to discover that Marie eventually had a child who was taken away by the father's sister. Marie tried to get the baby back, but a bar maid had no standing to demand justice. Trudy wondered if Nelly had a baby who she had been forced to give up. If so, the infant, she

275

realized, would now be about her own age. If this were true, Nelly's laudation and her wish that her daughter be like Trudy, had a deeper meaning.

Trudy looked up from the book. The last time she had seen Nelly was when she stood on the other side of the candy counter with the blackness of night behind her.

*   *   *   *   *

Trudy had never been in a graveyard. She had ridden her bike by the Woodlawn Cemetery on Pico where Nelly was to be buried, but she had never been on the grounds. The place was spooky with the headstones visible through the heavy clumps of dusty ivy hanging down the chain link fence.

For years, thousands had been dying in the war, but here in this somber place, a small group came together to bury one misplaced woman. Trudy recognized the strange Bertolt Brecht who stood by the pale, somber Heinrich Mann. She also recognized Thomas Mann whose picture she had seen in the newspaper. She realized that except for her all the mourners were the family and friends of Nelly's husband. They circled around the coffin, after which an older woman introduced the people to each other. They were important German writers and their wives, authors whose works she had been reading in school. When she came to Trudy, she asked her in English how she knew Nelly. It surprised her that the lady assumed she was an American. Trudy, hesitated, not sure whether to reply in English or German and self-conscious of being an outsider. She decided to answer in her native tongue, since that was the language spoken to her. "She was my friend. She encouraged me to do well in college." The others looked at her like she had come to the wrong service.

The Germans gathered around the coffin. A large flower wreath adorned the sealed lid. The fronds of the tall, lone palm that grew a few feet away chattered in the wind as if making snickering comments about those below. Heinrich Mann cried quietly. The service, if it could be called that, was informal. There was no minister. Trudy was the only

276

person there who actually came to remember Nelly.

The Lord's Prayer was mumbled by the funeral director. After this, no one took up his invitation to say a few words in remembrance. Listening to the clicking fronds mocking their silence, Trudy felt trapped among strangers. She had an urge to say something but, looking around at the great intellectuals and their wives, realized she was a nobody—like Nelly had been to them, the disrespected "bar girl" from Homburg. Nelly had flitted like a moth on the edge of the flame of the German literary elite. Her life story had been stolen. Now she was being placed in the ground under the annoying palm tree, in the sandy earth just a few blocks from the Pacific Ocean, where she would soon be forgotten, far from the cold Baltic where she had grown up in poverty.

After the service, Heinrich Mann and Brecht stood off to the side and exchanged a few quiet words. Those who stood around Trudy spoke in German and probably thought she did not understand their language. She heard whispered comments, supportive of Heinrich but contemptuous of Nelly. "The most remarkable thing about Nelly was Heinrich's extraordinary love for her." "She took tablets so she'd be taken to the hospital rather than jail." "She should have stayed in Germany with people of her own kind." "Heinrich does not have a cent because Nelly spent all his money."

Trudy began to cry, sniffed and wiped her eyes with her fists. Self-conscious, she glanced up and noticed Thomas Mann looking at her. His expression was stern and unfriendly.

Heinrich Mann and Brecht moved toward the gathering. The old man somberly nodded and remained painfully silent as his compatriots said kind things. Trudy stepped back as the two men moved closer to her, now somber and in control of her emotions. When Nelly's widowed husband made eye contact, she froze. He stepped up to her.

"I'm sorry for your loss," she forced herself to say. She could not help but noticed the age difference that had existed between him and Nelly. He was an old man.

"You are Helga Schneider's neighbor who helped Nelly deliver the baby."

"Yes." Trudy answered, without correcting him about the details, surprised that he recognized her. "Frau Schneider could not find a babysitter but asked me to give you her condolence." That may have been a lie, but at least was probably true in spirit.

The old man nodded, looking bleakly at the ground.

"I can tell you she valued Frau Schneider friendship," he mumbled, "and your acquaintance."

Trudy had to catch herself before she started crying again. She noticed the strange Brecht watching her closely, like he was reading her thoughts. He appeared amused, which made her feel exposed.

Heinrich Mann avoided further eye contact.

"Thank you," she said. "I will pass your words onto Frau Schneider."

The two men walked on. Trudy felt like she had been holding her breath and reminded herself to breathe. She could not believe she had just exchanged words with the German literary icon while the great Bertolt Brecht observed, no doubt analyzing her. She wished Karl Black were around to tell him about today. Even more, she wished he had accompanied her to the funeral. He would have been thrilled to be so close to his idol and found significance and meaning in the gathering. His presence would also have been reassuring, even though he now had a girlfriend.

Chapter 47

Brothers

By the end of 1944, the Allies were clearly winning the war. People around Trudy shared the confident view that victory was in sight. Before Christmas, the Germans launched a major counter offensive along a sixty-mile front penetrating Belgium and Luxemburg. This "dent" reminded people that the war was not over and could drag on, but the eventual outcome remained inevitable. The victory would come at great costs and sacrifice. The Mansfields now had a blue star on their window, a star that Trudy and her parents feared could turn gold.

Trudy was especially touched by a film she saw early in December. *The Canterville Ghost* was a story about a weak-kneed American soldier stationed with his company in an English castle. His ancestor is the cowardly ghost who haunts its halls. Both find their courage by the end of the movie.

*　　*　　*　　*　　*

The Wednesday after Christmas, the family received a letter from Andy. He didn't write often, probably because putting words on paper was a chore, given his poor spelling. He reported that he and the others at the army training base were upbeat. Patton's First Army was smashing the Germans. Some in his squad believed that by the time they got to Europe, the fighting would be over.

Andy had been sent to Fort Knox to become a tank mechanic. He reported that he had been assigned to train for tending a new tank, the M26 Pershing. "I can't tell you anything tecnical [his spelling], but I can tell you I'm learning good stuff about engines, braeks [his spelling again], and other stuff I will sure use after the war at a job working on cars or trucks."

Trudy's father shook his head, frustrated with the boy's continued dream of becoming a mechanic.

"Well, at least he will probably be safe," he said. "He's not in the infantry or driving a tank."

Two days before New Year's, Trudy came home from the Bundy and found on her bed a letter from Mary. The week before, a big front-page headline revealed that the Army had lifted the "ban on Japs," allowing them to return to their homes on the coast. Some objected, accusing the government of "coddling" the enemy.

She opened the envelope with excited anticipation. Maybe Mary had heard from her parents of their plans to come back to Wellesley

Dear Trudy,

The worst thing I feared that could happen in the war has. One of my brothers was killed. Ronny. The news of that had hardly settled in when I learned that my other brother, Daniel, lost his arm.

My parents received a telegram about Ronny and immediately cabled me. I learned about Daniel a few days later. His commanding officer had sent my parents a letter and said that they should hear from him soon. He will live. That's all I know.

It has been a struggle to go to class. The other students and the teachers have been understanding. I'm not the first student to lose a brother in the war, and people are not shocked, but saddened. I know two other students who have lost brothers and a girl her father.

I understand that my brothers' regiment has had many casualties. Some of the men have been wounded more than once but returned to their unit after they healed. Ronny had a wound from a grenade I never knew about, but he was back in the war within a few days. He won a purple heart. As I write that, it sounds like he got a prize for being wounded. He didn't win anything. He gave blood and he gave his life for this country.

Their regiment is nicknamed the Purple Heart Battalion, I guess, because so many of them have been wounded in battle. Their motto is "Go for Broke," which I understand is Hawaiian slang. They put everything on the line to prove that they are patriotic Americans. It angers me that people still see them as

yellow aliens who shouldn't be allowed their citizen rights or have
the opportunity to better their lives in this country.

I haven't heard any more about Daniel. I guess he will
be brought back to the States. He can no longer fight.

Trudy saw the light coming from the workshop and took the letter to show her father. He sat in a fog of cigarette smoke. Around the board crumpled sheets of paper with notes and figures were spread out. He leaned over his drawing table using his drafting straight edge, compass, and temples to create some pattern that didn't look like anything to Trudy.

"Dad, I thought you'd want to see this," she said stretching her arm around him and laying Mary's letter next to his pack of cigarettes.

Her father put down his pencil and picked up the sheets.

"Oh, damn," he said. He turned in the chair and read the correspondent. Folding the letter, he looked up at Trudy.

"The Nakamizo family has had more than their share of grief in this war," he said.

"Dad, this has been a hard war," Trudy said, feeling empty of any other thought.

"Do you have any letter writing paper? I want to send off our condolences to Harry and Silvia."

*   *   *   *   *

After the first of the year, Trudy noticed that two service banners, one with a gold star and the other blue, had been hung on the wood covering the front window of the Nakamizo house. Her mother hadn't noticed.

"Maybe their church hung them," she guessed.

That evening Trudy mentioned the banners to her father.

"I hung them," he said in a matter of fact tone. He may have just said that he had brought in the mail.

Trudy thought that courageous. There were still a few soldiers in the neighborhood tending the barrage balloons, reminders of a scarier

281

time in the war. They no longer feared the Japanese would launch an aerial attack.

"A couple of soldiers happened to walk by and asked me what I was doing," her father went on. "I mentioned what had happened to the boys of the Nakamizo family. They told me they had read in the Army's *Yank Magazine* a story about the 442 in Italy. That's the regiment they were probably in. Almost all the men have Purple Hearts. The two turned to the window, stood at attention, and saluted the banners."

Trudy saw a kindness in her dad's eyes that was usually disguised with a smirk. For a moment, he seemed to have removed the mask that she realized he wore to hide his tenderness and vulnerabilities.

"That was decent of you to hang those banners," she said and glanced away, not wanting to embarrass him.

She went to her room where the high Lama looked down at her. His serene smile remained reassuring after all the years of war. The wise man seemed pleased that she had forgiven her father and that she could see that in his own ways he showed courage.

1945

Chapter 48

Krefeld

Each day Helga read the *Los Angeles Times* with growing relief that the war would soon be over, but she still had concern for her family who lived west of the Rhine River in Krefeld. The small city would soon be caught in the battle between the advancing Allied armies and Hitler's stubbornly resisting divisions. Her heart sank when on January twelfth she saw a story reporting that "RAF rips rail yards at Krefeld."

Helga had heard no news from her family since the U.S. entered the war. They lived on the outskirts of the city, a safe distance from the bombing, but it disturbed her nonetheless to read of the air-raid, in which "a great portion" of the city had been bombed by the British and heavily damaged. One part of her brain reminded her that the industrial areas were far from her family—another part feared that some bomb had gone astray and landed on their house.

Each day, Helga read the paper looking for more news about Krefeld. The front page gave daily accounts of the American, British, and Canadian forces pushing against the German line. By the end of February, they gained such momentum that their armies were moving into the Ruhr region, her childhood homeland.

On March 2, the *Times* reported U.S. tanks had slashed into Krefeld and the next day confirmed that Krefeld fell with "astonishing speed." For the next few days, the paper mentioned the city and gave an account of how the citizens of Krefeld "were going about their usual business with U.S. troops busy rounding up German soldiers."

Helga felt some relief, but her concern would not completely dissipate until she actually got word that her parents, siblings, their children, and her old friends were safe. When would postal service resume? Krefeld was in American hands, but that meant nothing. It would probably be months before civilian letters could be exchanged.

*   *   *   *   *

"Will we return home after the war?" she asked Max that evening. He sat across from her in his chair, the light from the living room floor lamp illuminating the papers in his lap like an island in the dimness.

"How can we?" he replied.

"You are an important Egyptologist. Leipzig will want you back."

"No. Many in the school eagerly became Nazis and benefitted from Hitler's fascination with ancient Egypt. To them I am a traitor."

Helga could hear the cold night air whip the outside of their house. She could almost feel the damp fog moving in from the gray Pacific, engulfing their residence.

With a glum turn of his mouth, he looked at the letters on the table at his side and picked up the two pieces, one a gas bill and one an invitation to an émigré event they would not attend.

"What's this?" he asked, slipping out the invitation and ignoring the issue.

"An invitation to Salka Viertel's to honor Bruno Frank."

"Hmm." He pushed the paper back into the envelope.

"Can't we find some way to return?" she asked, feeling her hope weakening like the dim, dancing flame of a sacramental candle's spent stub.

"Germany is a shamble. Who knows what will remain and what the Fatherland will be like when this is over. There will be a political vacuum once the Nazis are out of power. Helga, the country will not be the Germany we knew eleven years ago." He looked back up at her like he was bearing news of a deceased loved one. "This is our life now. Aren't there worse things?"

*   *   *   *   *

Helga fell into mourning. For years she had maintained the belief that all would be the same as before when the cruel fascists were

286

gone. But the Nazis had not only brought physical ruin to Germany. They had stained the German people's soul. She thought of the University of Munich's underground protest group, the White Rose—three idealistic young people, who spread flyers against Hitler's evil on the campus. Students, no older than Trudy, they had stood up for old German values and were guillotined by the Nazis.

Watering the roses in the front of her house, she felt the presence of the mountains off in the east, the range that Trudy had told her formed the border of her world. For five years those peaks had also been the wall that defined Helga's life. She wondered when she would again move out of this balmy region of casual, informal living where Max and a few other Germans stood out with their Old World formality. She had to admit that in ways she had become acclimatized in dress and manner. She had become accustomed to being addressed by her first name and spoke English with most people now, even Jonathon and sometimes with Marlene, who had started kindergarten. Only with Max and Trudy did she regularly speak German and with Sophie, who was speaking a strange mixture of the two languages.

* * * * *

A few days later, Max surprised her by announcing that he had bought Nelly's car. Heinrich Mann wanted to dispose of the vehicle and remembered the Schneiders were in need.

"It is time that you learn to drive," Max said. "In this city bus and streetcar services are limited and with the children older, it is harder to manage errands."

His driving apparently had never been entertained. She also suspected he wanted her to drive to affirm they had fully integrated into Los Angeles life.

The car smelled of Nelly—a combination of cigarette smoke, alcohol and some sweet cologne. Trudy mentioned that her mother always put baking soda in the refrigerator to exercise foul odors. The next day, Helga bought two large boxes of the powder at the market. Before using them, she thoroughly cleaned the fabric and vacuumed the sheets of rubber flooring.

The car's ashtray overflowed with black and gray tobacco dust and squashed cigarette butts with Nelly's red lip prints. Helga found a whiskey bottle, half-full, under the seat. Pushed down between the front bench and seat back she discovered a wadded note. She started to throw the paper in the trash, but, curious, she uncrumpled the sheet. The paper had the Schneider street address.

Trudy had her father come over and look at the car. He first started the engine, drove the car around the block, and opening the hood, looked around the engine and checked the oil.

"The wheels need to be aligned," he said. "You can tell by the way the tires are wearing and how it wants to pull to the right. You say the car was sitting here overnight in the driveway? There is no oil drips which means the seals are good. The brakes are good, the engine's okay but get the oil changed."

The next afternoon after school, Trudy started teaching Helga to drive.

The woman had little experience with machines. The first time she tried to release the clutch petal to engage the engine, the car lurched violently, and the motor stopped. The jerk threw Trudy forward in the passenger seat, but she laughed, saying the same thing happened when she started to learn. She went on to say it took a little time to get the rhythm right, balancing between the clutch and gas pedals, like trying a new dance step. She told Helga to keep practicing shifting it into gear and braking. The next day, they were driving around the streets in the neighborhood. As Helga turned onto Wellesley, Trudy told her how important it was to navigate around the potholes in the street, craters that could ruin the tires.

* * * * *

After she secured her license, the first place Helga drove with Max and the children was to Westwood. At a restaurant they met Rebekah Wolff and her daughter, Betje, for an early dinner.

Helga knew she would eventually have to see Rebekah. She kept reminding herself that Wolff had always been polite and encouraging, and she had to think of her that way. She still worried that Max had old feelings, but her concerns changed into guilt when they walked into the restaurant. Although her smile remained sunny and she had her quick, intelligent bearing, the strain of the concentration camp and years of evading the *SS* had recast Rebekah's face into a deeply lined and mottled effigy of her former self. Her daughter, a girl about Jonathon's age, stood beside her mother in a pretty dress. She had the face of an angel, beautiful hair but a deadness in her eyes and a lassitude that sucked the joy from anyone who looked at her. Helga made herself smile and shook the woman's hand and said *hallo* to the girl. She felt she was looking at a pair who somehow managed to escape from the nether world.

Max stood to the side like a bridge between his family and Wolff and her daughter. They made small talk about Los Angeles until the host came forward and escorted them to a table.

Squirming Sophia was placed in a wooden booster seat at Helga's right. Jonathon and Marlene chose to sit to their mother's left and away from Betje. Neither child was rude, but Helga could sense they were uncomfortable. Rebekah Wolff's daughter had an unsettling presence. Even Sophia was unusually quiet and watched Betje somberly.

The adults talked about Rebekah's first semester teaching at UCLA. Coming to this country with none of her papers and books, she had spent a great deal of time in the library reading and gathering materials to prepare her lectures. She mentioned the capable girl Max had introduced who spoke beautiful German and read hieroglyphs.

"I believe you have been training her," Wolff said.

"That would be Trudy Mansfield," Helga acknowledged.

"She reminds me of you when you were at the university."

Helga would not deny the similarity, despite their different backgrounds. Her own father had gone to the university and her mother read the classics, while academics were not part of Trudy's upbringing.

"Did you go on for your doctorate?" Rebekah asked Helga, a question that she feared would come up.

"I earned a *Magister* before I married Max, but, no, I never

289

pursued the doctorate. I have continued as his research assistant."

Helga sensed Rebekah's disappointment. Her unspoken reaction awoke her own disgruntlement.

She glanced to Betje, who watched Marlene and Jonathon but made no effort to engage them. Helga noticed the ugly tattoo on the girl's arm peeking out from her sleeve, a mark that would be a lifelong reminder of the horrors she had experienced. Helga's mood dampened. Betje was such a pretty girl, with fair and delicate features, but anyone could see she was not normal. What a burden for Rebekah to be a widow who had lost her entire family and now endeavored to reestablish herself professionally while making a new life for herself and her troubled daughter in this strange place.

"When we arrived in this city," Helga said to fight the malaise, "I was profoundly struck with the difference between Los Angeles and what we knew in Europe. It's not just the obvious—the food, the clothing, transportation, street signs and signals, but the customs, the shocking way, for example, people here will ask personal questions. I am available to talk and help you adjust. I only have Sophie with me during half the day. I would watch your daughter, if you ever have an engagement."

Rebekah smiled.

"You are kind to offer."

"You were always good to me at the university. It's the least I can offer."

Chapter 49

Betje

Trudy felt like an inconsequential mouse walking across the patterned terra cotta floor, under the arched wooden ceiling beams of the UCLA Library foyer, and then down the Moorish tiled stairway. Her destination, on the ground floor, was a secluded corner amongst the stacks where there were tables and chairs.

She had spent half an hour upstairs in the airy reading room skimming the library's copy of that morning's *Los Angeles Times*. The paper confidently reported that Hitler's armies were in shattered disarray, Berlin ablaze "in its final agonies," and the U.S. and Red armies about to linkup for the final sweep of the Nazi Reich. At least the war in Europe would soon be over.

To study and to occasionally write in her journal she preferred the privacy in the vast book stacks of the ground floor to the open space with its tall arched windows. Besides, the sky was gray steel gloom. She found the windowless area behind the bookshelves cozy, if a little dim and cool, but the tables had reading lamps. She could hide behind their amber glow.

Less than two weeks before, the awful news broke that President Roosevelt had died suddenly of a cerebral hemorrhage—the war so close to being won and the man who had lead them through their darkest days gone. Americans would not hear the triumphant words he would have delivered over the radio, in his familiar sturdy voice. She cried when word flashed of Roosevelt's death.

In the stacks, librarians toiled away, shelving all the books that were constantly being pulled.

For the remainder of the afternoon Trudy did not have classes but hesitated going home. She would have to help her mother do chores or weed the victory garden—if it wasn't raining. Susan would be at the Selective Service office, now a volunteer worker, and Nancy at the flashlight factory, so she had no one to visit.

Thinking of Nancy, she remembered how her friend feared that Gary didn't want her around anymore. Nancy's mother told her she should forget about him.

"He doesn't call. He doesn't really want to talk when I call. When I see him, he won't look me in the eye or say anything about anything except what you might chat about with someone on a bus. It's like he wants to break off our engagement but doesn't know how to tell me."

Trudy remembered Gary when the two came to the theater on Halloween. He didn't seem that different from a lot of guys who had a problem, just keeping stuff to himself and maybe hinting at what bothered him.

"He's a broken man," Nancy said. "The war has changed him. But I don't care. He's still Gary."

Trudy didn't know what to say. She knew nothing about these things. Maybe Susan would have an idea and almost said so to Nancy but didn't.

"You've got to talk to him," Trudy advised instead, feeling impatient with Nancy, and going with her gut that Nancy had to stop pussy footing around if she wanted to get through to Gary. "Go over to his place. Don't call ahead. Just go over and tell him that he's acting like he doesn't want you around anymore. Ask him if he wants to get rid of you. Ask him to tell you the truth."

The line went dead for a moment.

"I guess you're right," Nancy finally said.

Trudy now worried that her suggestion would only make things worse.

Trudy drifted over to the table behind the rows of bookcases where many of the volumes about Egyptology were shelved.

Noticing again the fragrance of books, in her mind the smell of knowledge, she sat down on a hard wooden chair. She found the smell fortifying and reassuring.

She pulled out her German reader, but she soon became bored with her studies. She got up and walked over to the bookcase and looked at the spines of the volumes on ancient Egypt hoping that something might catch her eye, maybe something she had not noticed before. She pulled out a book written by the legendary James Breasted, a study of the woman pharaoh, Hatshepsut. Trudy sat down and for an hour read snippets about her long and successful reign of "the first great woman in history."

In Hatshepsut's splendid temple, her fame still lives and the masonry around her Karnak obelisk has fallen down, displaying her name and records and exposing the gigantic shaft to proclaim to the modern world the greatness of Hatshepsut.

Trudy set the book aside to check out. She would have something to read at bedtime to stimulate her dreams.

Inspired, Trudy began writing in her journal, her mastery of hieratic script allowing her to write as freely as if she were putting down her thoughts in English.

She wrote that she felt guilty for not being home to help her mother, who, no doubt, had a lot to do and wouldn't have any time to get out of the house. It would be nice for her mother to go window shopping and maybe have tea with one of her friends—if she had friends.

Since there were no windows where she sat, she had no idea if it had begun to rain. Thank God, she thought, she had taken the bus instead of riding her bike. She dreaded getting soaked.

She closed the journal, slipped it in her knapsack and picked up the Breasted book to check out. Standing up she put on her jacket, slung the strap of the bag over her shoulder and started to leave. Walking around the table she saw Professor Wolff walking in her direction through the stacks.

Visibly tired, the woman was accompanied by a dull-faced blond girl of about nine. She chatted softly to her young companion and didn't noticed Trudy. She carried an old leather briefcase. Trudy doubted the professor had brought the attaché from Europe.

As they approached each other, Dr. Wolff realized Trudy was coming toward her. She stopped and smiled.

293

"Hello," she said in German. "Trudy, yes?" She motioned to the girl "This is my daughter Betje. Say 'hello' to Trudy, Betje."

The girl had been walking with her head down and did not look up. Trudy could see Betje was nothing like her mother. Her fair complexion and features were salt to her mother's pepper. Trudy also realized, even in the dim light, the child was pretty despite her sullen expression. Trudy had an unsettling thought. Like her mother, Betje was a refugee from concentration camps. What had that experience done to someone so young?

"Betje," Trudy said. "It is good to make your acquaintance."

The girl did not respond.

Professor Wolff brushed her daughter's hair with her hand. She spoke to the child, but not in German, maybe Dutch. Strange.

"I'm sorry, Trudy," said the professor. "Betje is a child who has had problems all her life. Even before the war. My pretty girl was born with a mental impediment. Her ordeal in the camps was bad. I could not always protect her, and she's . . . ."

"I take no offense," Trudy said too quickly. She did not want to think what had been done to her. Trudy had read of how Nazis brutalized the women and even girls who caught their fancy. Was this what Dr. Wolff meant? She didn't want to ask but couldn't stop thinking about the possibility.

"You were leaving," the professor said. "I don't want to keep you. It would also be better to talk later."

Trudy knew she meant without Betje present. She nodded her head and said she would come by during Professor Wolff's office hours. She looked at Betje who avoided eye contact.

"Maybe sometime I can meet you and Betje. And Betje, we can have some ice cream!"

The girl did not respond.

Walking away, Trudy felt she had been stained by Betje's torment.

*   *   *   *   *

Trudy sat curled up in a seat toward the back of the public bus, indifferently glancing out the smudged glass. She managed to have the seat to herself, although the vehicle was full of passengers, and some people were standing. Outside, the streets and neighborhoods she knew so well looked dull and almost colorless. At least it had not yet begun to rain.

Professor Wolff's daughter troubled her. What had she experienced to make her so empty? Given what they had been through—being arrested, housed in brutal concentration camps, escaping, and running across half of Europe, seeing and experiencing God only knew what horrors—she could not be expected to be normal. She may have been born mentally retarded or something, but her ordeal had to have been too much.

The bus slowed, its brakes squealing as it approached Bundy, where Trudy had to catch another bus. She stood up and picked up her book bag. In another twenty minutes, she would be home.

Chapter 50

Legacy

On May seventh, the newspapers proclaimed V-E Day in the boldest and largest type Trudy had ever seen on a newspaper front page. Hitler was dead. He took his own life. The Nazis surrendered unconditionally, and "five years, eight months, and six days of bloodshed and destruction" in Europe were over. There was hardly anything else people talked about that day aside from their hopes for a Japanese surrender.

There was still bloody fighting going on in the western Pacific, and this had Susan in a jumpy mood. Her Robby had been drafted into the Navy and was now on an aircraft carrier, the USS Saratoga. His ship was part of the Fast Carrier Task Force and engaged the enemy in the combat area where Japanese kamikaze planes had sunk an American destroyer and smashed into other war ships causing considerable death and destruction.

For the Mansfields the end of the combat in Europe provided personal comfort. Andy had been sent to Europe, and from his last letter, written in early March and just received, they learned that his tank maintenance crew had crossed the Rhine soon after the army established a bridgehead on its eastern bank. Of course, his mother still fretted, fearful that he had been injured. Until a letter came posted after the end of the fighting, she would not be confident that her boy was okay.

On the same day of Germany's surrender, Trudy's father helped Harry Nakamizo pull the wood boards off the windows of the returning family's house and replace the broken glass. They rehang the gold and blue stars on the living room window glass. Sylvia stood in the weeds where there had once been a lawn, silently watching the two men open her house. With Helga's camera Trudy record the moment. She wanted a picture for Mary.

The barrage balloons and their ground crews had been removed earlier in the year. Nakamizo's fields lay feral, covered with tall grass and bright blooming wild mustard. Former gun placements still circled with sandbags pitted the ground. The latrine holes had been filled, but debris and trash were everywhere.

Mary had written Trudy that both her brothers were decorated for their valor. Daniel was awarded the Distinguished Service Cross and Ronny, posthumously, the Congressional Medal of Honor.

> *Ronny's citation read, "Mortally wounded he charged up a barren slope, single-handedly destroying a machine gun nest." He is buried in France.*
>
> *I feel proud, angry and pained. The country has acknowledged my brothers' sacrifices and bravery. Ronny was given the highest military decoration, which only a few men have earned. His name and the description of his heroism will eventually reside in some dusty archive. Nothing will be said of his facing racism and standing up to it by being a brave soldier who died for his country.*
>
> *I was moved when the school newspaper picked up the story of my brothers' deeds and described what our family has endured since Pearl Harbor. "We are a better society than to have allowed this injustice," the editor wrote.*

Trudy walked over to the Schneiders house. With the shots of the Nakamizos' homecoming, she finished the roll of film and wanted to return the camera to Helga. The end of the war in Europe meant Trudy no longer had to keep the expensive Leica.

Helga was in a somber mood. Trudy had thought the end of the fighting in Europe would bring relief.

"Is there something wrong?" Trudy asked in German.

"Have you seen the last issue of *Life?*"

Trudy didn't think the Schneiders read the American news photo magazine.

"I haven't had a chance."

"It will turn your stomach. I've known for years of the concentration camps and the likelihood of foul conditions, but . . . " Helga grimly shook her head. ". . . I failed to comprehend the magnitude of the crimes and how German people were seduced. So many saw only what they wanted to see."

"What do you mean?"

Helga walked to the dining area and picked up a letter from the table and pulled out one page.

"I received this from my sister before the attack on Pearl Harbor stopped mail between Germany and America. Just read this part."

She handed the page to Trudy.

> *You will remember Traudl Humps, a friend of our young sister. The girls had met in the BDM*. Traudl had gone to Commercial College and has for almost a year been employed as one of Hitler's secretaries.*
>
> *Traudl says the Führer is in private a nice man who does not drink and often eats with his staff. He is very fatherly which the poor girl needs, given that her father divorced her mother years ago.*
>
> *Traudl says that Hitler does not talk much about the war and talks little about politics. He did say to her that we fight for an ideal and not for Jewish capitalism, which is what spurs on our enemies. In the end, good is always victorious.*
>
> *Helga, the Führer has been our savior! He has led us from troubled times and has made the German people proud again! Good will be victorious!*
>
> *May you someday soon return to the New Germany!*

"My sister is not simple or uneducated, but she turned a blind eye to what was happening to the Fatherland. If nothing else, how could

---

*Alliance of German Girls

she have forgotten the brutal removal of the Jewish neighbors, including Dr. Eisner, who saved our mother's life. How could she have forgotten about the forced sterilizations?"

"Forced sterilization?" Trudy had no idea what she referred to.

"The Nazis decreed that those who were defective would be sterilized to prevent them from contaminating the German race. Our neighbor, Angela Haug's daughter, Miezl, was picked up in 1934 by the authorities after a panel of Nazi judges and physicians ruled she be sterilized because her deafness may have been hereditary. My family should have been incensed by this act perpetrated by the new Nazi authorities. This was an affront to their Catholic faith and basic decency, but . . ."

"People don't want to believe the worst about their country," Trudy said in an attempt to calm Helga, "or their leaders."

Helga shook her head.

*   *   *   *   *

After the visit, Trudy saw the ghastly photos in *Life* magazine of the liberated concentration camps which revealed the years of untold death and misery. One picture locked itself in her mind—a young man forcing his head and arms under a door as he futilely attempted to escape the flames set by the Nazis to destroy evidence of their atrocities. She couldn't stop thinking of the man caught in that unbelievably narrow crawl space.

Unexpectedly, a thin sunbeam dimly lit the darkened place she had drifted into.

"You were right to tell me to speak up with Gary," Nancy told Trudy, calling from a telephone booth a block from the flashlight factory. "At first he did not want to talk and even said that maybe it wouldn't be a bad idea if I stayed away. I asked him if he really wanted to get rid of me. He was silent for a moment and admitted that he didn't think I know what it would be like living with him. I told him I could

299

try, and we'd soon know if it wouldn't work out. He didn't say anything for a minute, and I started to think that it was over between us. Then he said there was something I had to see. He took me to his bedroom and took off the artificial legs and showed me the ugly scares of the leg stubs. He said that when the prosthetics were off, he could only crawl like a baby. I wanted to look away, but I didn't and told him it made no difference. I think he wanted to cry, but he's a guy, so I cried for both of us and hugged him so tight. He told me that he loves me."

Nancy ended the call by thanking Trudy.

"I don't think I would have talked to him like that if you didn't encourage me."

After the conversation, Trudy decided advice was easy to give. The task was deciding which to follow. Nancy realized what she needed to do.

Chapter 51

Honorable Men

In late June, Trudy's parents finally received a letter from Andy. In his wobbly scribble, he wrote that his unit of mechanics with unfired rifles slung over their shoulder had followed behind the advance units of the Seventh Army. A day after the war in Europe ended, he sat down at a table in a German beer garden and, sipping the "local suds" composed his letter.

He reported that he and his unit had settled in a town in southern Germany, the name of which he did not know how to spell. While most of the locals were somber but civil, there were some people who acted like they were genuinely glad the Americans were there.

He mentioned that his squad passed by a concentration camp. "The place is piled high with death. Sickening. The inmates are from Russia and Poland, starved nearly to death. Many of them are women. It's rumored that old Blood and Guts Patton threw up when he walked through a camp."

*   *   *   *   *

By the middle of summer, the country's euphoria for the victory over Hitler's Germany had subsided. Americans had come to the somber realization that the war in the Pacific had not diminished and continued in a bloody fury. The Japanese island of Okinawa had finally been captured but only after weeks of fighting and thousands of American dead. Most were convinced that the conflict would probably bleed on well into the next year and possibly beyond.

In August, without any expectation, news of something unbelievable and disturbing flashed across the country. Washington announced that the "most terrible destructive force ever harnessed by man," a weapon so terrible that one munition equaled the loads of twenty thousand superfortress bombers, had been unleashed, destroying a major Japanese city. The Japanese were totally defenseless against this atomic bomb. Hope rose that the Japanese would finally have the sense to surrender.

On August 15, a week after the announcement of the dropping of the first atomic bomb, the newspaper headline read "Peace! Victory! Japs Accept Allied Terms."

This should have been a source of unconditional joy in the Mansfield house. The war in the Pacific was finally over.

The announcement would have been a wonderful relief if the newspaper had not also reported on the front page, that Uncle Billy's ship, the Indianapolis, had been sunk by a Japanese submarine on July 30 with most of its crew killed.

Trudy's mother crumpled on the sofa when she read the article. Trudy thought at first her mother was overwhelmed with relief for Billy and Andy—until she picked up the newspaper and saw the story about the Indianapolis. She sat down and put her arm around her mother.

"Wouldn't the family have gotten a telegram if he's dead?" she finally asked.

Her mother shook her head.

"He's dead," she sobbed. "I feel it in my gut."

"The Navy would have notified the family even if he's missing."

"I think Billy has somebody in San Diego listed as next of kin."

Trudy did not ask who or why, not wanting to know more about her uncle. She felt terrible for her mother. At least Uncle Billy died a hero, if he were dead. She guessed that was something good she could say about him.

Over the next few days, the whole neighborhood and local merchants had been told about her mother's brother. Even the sailors who survived the sinking and days in the shark infested water went through hell. The loss of the Indianapolis was being called the worse disaster in U.S. Navy history.

302

One afternoon in the middle of September, Trudy's mother left
the house to do clothes shopping in Santa Monica. Trudy didn't work
that day but stayed home to practice reading hieroglyphs, a leisure
activity she had little time to pursue. She sat on the living room sofa
with a book that Helga had lent and read texts carved on old
monuments.

She heard the postman drop the mail in the box on the front
porch and got up. She almost jumped when she saw a letter addressed
to her mother, the postmark August 20 and written in her Uncle Billy's
hand.

"Oh, my God," she gasped. "He survived the sinking!"

Trudy ran into the house and placed the envelope on the dining
room table. Fumbling around the house, she tried to stay busy to
distract herself until her mother came home. She was too excited to
continue reading hieroglyphs. She may not like her uncle, but she felt
for her mother. She would be overjoyed to learn that Billy was still alive.
As much as Trudy disliked him, she would never want him dead.

It seemed to take her mom forever to return home. She had
probably decided to window shop. Trudy finally heard the car roll down
the driveway and pull in the garage.

Her mother walked in the house carrying two small bags. Trudy
ran into the living room and pointed to the envelope on the table.

"Mom! A letter came from Uncle Billy. He's alive."

Her mother dropped the packages and her purse on the chair
and without taking off her hat or gloves took the envelope and ripped
it open. Silently reading the letter, her eyes became hard. Before coming
to the last page, she crumpled the papers and threw the papers down on
the table. She didn't look at Trudy. Taking off her hat, she walked into
her bedroom and slammed the door. Trudy picked up the letter,
flattened the paper and read the note.

303

Hi Sis,

Well the war is over and we can all feel safe. We blew the Japs sky high with those atomic bombs that I just learned the Indianapolis carried from San Francisco to Tinian. We had no idea that we had this special top secret cargo on board.

You've likely read that the Indianapolis was sunk by a Jap submarine on July 30 and have been worrying your heart out about me. Most of the crew went down with the ship or were eaten by sharks. I just learned this too. That's right. I was not onboard. I've been in Guam and most of that time in the brig falsely charged with desertion. It was all a misunderstanding, but the SP, who picked me up on the beach, were not all that friendly or willing to listen to me. I simply lost track of things, and I failed to report back on time from shore leave. It was an unauthorized absence, to use correct Navy jargon, unintended, and an embarrassment that me, a seasoned sailor, missed my ship.

You don't have to know all the details, but I was commiserating with a lady friend on the island who went through hell with the Jap occupancy. She had some fine rum which she had hidden from the Japs and one thing lead to another.

I've been busted down to the lowest pay grade, have spent a month in confinement, and forfeited most of a month's pay. It could have been a lot worse. The baby face officer in charge of my case wanted me court marshaled. But I've had a good record in the service, always did my job, whatever my assignment, and had never been absent from my post.

I'm waiting to be reassigned. In the meantime, they have me working in the mess.

No telling when I will be in town again. The war is finally over, but there is still a lot of mopping up. With the Jap surrender the Navy will be carrying men and equipment to their islands. I may be assigned to work in a Jap port. . . .

Trudy put down the letter. She now had another reason for disliking her uncle.

*   *   *   *   *

As the afternoon progressed, Trudy found herself becoming increasingly irritated and bitter. She kept her gaze down to avoid seeing the image of the high Lama watching her whenever she went into her room. She finally walked over to the Nakamizo house. Mary was home on a break from school.

Inside, the Nakamizo house was simple and clean. The Mansfield house was clean too, but this was a different kind of cleanliness, carried in the air as a soft sweet and peppery scent. If Trudy didn't know, she would have had no idea the place had been boarded up for years.

For almost three and a half years the two young women had not seen each other, and both had changed. Mary's hair was longer, and she now wore makeup. Here clothes were also a different style from what the young ladies wore in Southern California, probably Pennsylvanian in fashion. And she now smoked.

"I think of you," Trudy said as the two sat in the living room, "and of Nancy and of all the others whose brothers, husbands, boyfriends, and sons gave so much to win the war. Most just boys, good guys who put their lives on hold when called to do their duty. And then there's my uncle. He became a career sailor because he couldn't stay out of trouble in civilian life. Twice in the war he's right there in the center of the bull's eye, and both times he gets drunk and staggers away right before the targets are hit. Mary, I don't understand. Why has he gotten out of the war unscathed when others who didn't deserve to die or lose an arm or their legs paid such a great price? How come anytime Billy does something bad, like he did at the Bundy, there are no repercussions?"

Mary reflected on the question for a moment, tapping ash into

305

the bowl on the table.

"I don't know, Trudy. Is there an answer anyone can give?"

"I guess not."

Outside, Trudy heard the piercing conversation of the blackbirds. What were they debating? What could be so important that they had to carry on in such boisterous chatter? The answer to her question?

"I don't like saying this," Mary finally said, "but Ronny's death was honorable. And so was David's losing his arm. I guess your uncle denied himself a similar honor. He will always be an unhonored man."

"Like he cares."

"Others do, so he will have to live with that. Not you."

Trudy considered Mary's point, aware that his family would always be ashamed of him. She guessed that his reputation for not being with his shipmates at the most critical moments would follow him in the Navy as long he stayed in the service. He would always have that albatross hanging from his neck.

Chapter 52

Study Hard and Do Well

Trudy returned to school an upperclassman, drifting around the campus with the casual confidence of a student well-grounded in academia. Her classes were now mostly related to her German major. She guessed she would someday be teaching the language in a high school. She remembered that some of her teachers, especially Miss Ramsey, had a passion for instruction and made an effort to make their subjects academic licorice for their students. Maybe Trudy could create the same enthusiastic relish in her own students.

A week into the semester she was already questioning her major.

In *German Literature From 1885 to the Present*, a small class with only fifteen students, the first work assigned was Thomas Mann's *Joseph der Ernährer* According to the teacher, Mann portrayed Pharaoh Akhenaten as a liberator of the Egyptians who enlisted the talented Joseph to lift the people of the Nile out of the brutal, superstitious polytheism of their ancestors.

As she listened, Trudy remembered the monument texts she read that summer about Hatshepsut, the great woman pharaoh. Her reign ended more than a hundred years before Akenaten's began, and she ruled her people justly. In fact, the Egyptians seem to value fairness above almost all else.

Her thought must have been written on her brow. The instructor looked at her inquisitively.

"Is there an issue?"

"Well," Trudy squirmed in her chair, "he certainly doesn't know his hieroglyphs if he is depicting the pharaohs and the people of the Nile before Akhenaten as brutal. I'm sorry. I spent the summer reading proclamations of nobles from the century before." Her teacher looked confused by what she said. "I read Egyptian hieroglyphs." She hated saying that. The statement made her sound like she was bragging.

307

"You appear to be in the wrong department," the professor said with a snicker.

"I also speak fluent German, and I have had conversations with Thomas Mann's brother, Heinrich Mann."

"Ah, a celebrity."

Trudy felt herself shrink in her chair.

"No. I knew his wife." Trudy realized that she was way out of line and meekly said, "Sorry."

"Very well. We are concerned here with Thomas Mann and the themes he so neatly wove together in the four parts of this powerful history. . ."

"Stay focused," Trudy told herself. She didn't know why she spoke like that. She should not have mentioned either her mastery of hieroglyphs or Heinrich Mann.

*　　*　　*　　*　　*

The next morning, Trudy's mother sat in the kitchen, still in her robe and her hair disheveled. She had woken up with a terrible headache.

"Do you have to go to school today?" her mother asked, no doubt hoping Trudy could stay home and do the laundry and whatever other chores she had scheduled for the day.

"I have a quiz," Trudy fibbed.

If she told her mother that it was not good to miss a class, she probably would have been told that skipping one class wouldn't make any difference.

As it was, her mother said, "One quiz is not going to make a difference in your grade.".

"It's not good to miss a quiz," her father said, sitting next to Trudy's mother, his face behind the newspaper.

"All that work," her mother grumbled.

"That's college," her father replied. "It's just like a job."

Trudy stood up and asked her mother if she wanted anything. Eyes closed, she merely shook her head. Her expression suggested just doing that took effort. Trudy wondered why she didn't go back to bed. She sat slumping like a broken sack of salt.

Turning her attention to the stove, Trudy fried herself two eggs and toasted a slice of bread. As the skillet hissed, she threw together a tuna sandwich which she packed along with an apple for school. She couldn't afford to buy lunch at the cafeteria.

Aware of the time, she transferred the eggs and toast to a plate and quickly ate her breakfast and between bites sucked in hot coffee.

Trudy's father folded the newspaper and stood up. He glanced down at her mother. "Honey, why don't you go back to bed."

Her mother nodded but made no effort to move. Trudy's father stood at the table for moment and then walked out of the kitchen.

"You going to be okay, Mom?" Trudy asked.

"I'll be okay," her mother answered, eyes still closed, speaking as if each word pressed on her brain.

"Why don't you go back to bed like Dad said? When I get home this afternoon, I'll do whatever chores you need done."

"I might have you go grocery shopping."

Trudy heard her father close the front door.

"I'll go to the market when I get back from school."

*　　　*　　　*　　　*　　　*

During her break after German Literature, Trudy went into the library to retreat to her hiding place on the ground floor. There she found Professor Wolff sitting at the table where four years earlier Trudy had read about Egypt and hieroglyphs.

Trudy noticed the woman was pale, her eyes vacant and dull before she looked up and saw Trudy. Like switching masks, she smiled, her eyes crinkling before Trudy could say hello. Her color remained ashen.

309

"Hello, Trudy" Professor Wolff said in a whisper. They were in the library, after all.

"I'm sorry. I didn't mean to disturb you," Trudy replied in German.

"You do not disturb me. I'm just catching up on things."

Trudy noticed Professor Wolff had stacks of index cards arranged in several neat piles.

"What are you teaching?"

"Two senior courses of Oriental studies."

"Maybe someday I will be your student."

"What is your major?"

"German."

The professor raised her eyebrow.

"You speak flawless German, but I would have thought you would be studying history or anthropology."

"Why do you say that?"

Rebekah Wolff smirked, like a wise teacher who thought the answer obvious to a question posed by a student.

"You have a passion for ancient Egypt. You study with Helga Schneider and converse with Professor Schneider. You read different forms of hieroglyphic script. You're bright, hard working. I had assumed that you planned to go on and earn a doctorate in Egyptology."

"Until I met you, I didn't even know a woman could be an Egyptologist."

"Well . . ." The professor paused and picked up an index card. "Now you know."

Trudy felt her face flush, like she had opened a hot oven and saw inside a lavish dish ready to be lifted out.

She silently watched the woman write something on the card. This little conversation seemed to exhaust Professor Wolff. Trudy didn't know what to say.

"You have a lot to do," Trudy finally said, "and I have a great deal of reading."

"Continue to study hard and do well," the professor said glancing up from her cache of scholastic atoms.

Trudy backed away and strolled down the isle of books on ancient Egypt. She looked at the titles, many which she had slipped out at some point. Like the carved relief of a pharaoh amongst his children, Allen Gardiner's *Egyptian Grammar* occupied its place on the top shelf. For a moment, she stood under the heavy gray green primer, her mind racing with a new exciting thought. Turning, she briskly walked on, running her fingertips over a row of book spines.

2009

Epilogue

All But Lost And Forgotten

Sitting on the corner of her bed, propped against the wall and surrounded by her grandmother's diaries, Kat skimmed more of the notes, occasionally reading the details of certain entries that caught her attention. On her lap lay the Christmas message from Helga Schneider and the printout of the Google garbled translation.

> *The postcards and notes from Egypt brought back memories of the journey max and I took the Nile on our honeymoon. Thank You. The postcards reminded me of a conversation we had a long time ago-I believe you had just started college. I said, our expedition to Egypt. I was watching you, looking out the window behind me. You revealed that in fact, been never on the other side of the San Gabriel Mountains and never been more than a few miles from your home. You were embarrassed. I knew even then you would one day the world will travel.*

By the time Kat stopped for the night, she was still not finished looking through all the composition books written in English. When she had time, she would start all over again and carefully read the entries from beginning to end. At least those in English. The one's in hieroglyphs would probably remain unread forever. It didn't have to be that way. Her grandmother tried to interest her in the Egyptian writing when she was younger, but Kat was more interested video games and soccer. Maybe she could still learn. She would have some time during the summer—if she pulled her nose away from her tablet.

She picked up the instrument and opened her Word document *Hermione 2009* which could only be accessed by using the password

315

"Fawkes!" Her grandmother's photo of the old man watched her from where it sat on her dresser.

She typed the date and sat for a moment with her fingertips resting on the virtual keys. She then began to type.

> *I should have been studying. Instead I spent the evening reading Grand Mom's diaries. She wrote so much when she was a girl!*

Kat frowned. She highlighted and cut the words. Leaning her head back against the wall, her forefinger pressed against her lips, she asked herself what she had learned today. What had she *really* learned reading her Grand Mom's diary? She considered the question for a moment, and then had a somber thought. She leaned forward and replaced her fingers on the virtual keyboard.

> *I learned something today. Time is a cold-hearted, callus pickpocket. Yes, a selfish thief who each year snatches stories of people lives till there is nothing left.*
>
> *My grandmother told me stories about her early life, but I discovered there was SO MUCH she didn't tell me. My own children, if I ever have any, will know even less and theirs probably nothing at all, except for the vague inscriptions on the back of old family photos. I knew her as an old woman. Even hearing her tell stories, I never really imagined or had a picture in my mind that she had once been a girl my age. I remember Grand Mom telling me about the day the Japanese bombed Pearl Harbor, but I never realized that she believed women would only be silent observers of the war, watching their brothers and maybe their fathers go off to fight. What a different world.*
>
> *Brittany was wrong about Grand Mom and Charlie Chaplin. Completely wrong. He sat next to her at a lecture and they started to talk. Grand Mom didn't recognize him! She felt*

she had said something stupid. He put his arm around her and reassured her, telling my grandmother to stop thinking and start listening to her heart. His words stuck. That I can say.

Until today, I never had a clue that she thought she was ugly when she was my age. She was a stunning, beautiful woman. I never knew she couldn't go to her prom because the boy who would be taking her was Jewish. I never knew she hated her father for months after that for not standing up to her mother who had refused to let her go. But she was also proud of her father for standing up for the Japanese neighbors who were forced into concentration camps after Pearl Harbor.

I never knew there had been an air raid over Los Angeles during World War II or that big guns were stationed in the lots next to their house. I never knew she worked in a parachute factory during the war. I never knew my great grand uncle was a petty officer on the battleship Arizona on December 7. I'm not sure if he was killed or survived. A number of the pages she wrote the weeks following the attack are unreadable because they got wet at some point. Either way, he is a family hero and I'm proud.

Those are things I could read because she wrote with a clear hand and in English. Then she got all excited about Egypt and hieroglyphs. The first word she learned stood for woman. I will remember that mark. She began to teach herself their language and began writing the rest of her diaries in those old letters. And from that point the story of her life becomes hidden with just a note here and there in English, like the day she got the acceptance letter from UCLA. She wanted to dance around the room.

There are hardly any pictures of her as a kid or as a teenager. The photos of Grand Mom and her childhood friends, Helga, Susan, Mary, Nancy, were all taken when they were older. There is just that one shot of her in the parachute factory.

317

I guess that's how I will always think of her as a young woman,
with her back to the camera. That's so sad.

Kat leaned back and read what she entered. She saved the
document and exited Word. Half hidden in a shadow, the kind mystic
looked back at her from across the room. She gathered together the
diaries and slipped them under the bed. She extended her legs into the
bed covers and turned out the light, her head filled with fragments of
her grandmother's distant life and her mind immersed in that far away
time.

References and Historical Notes

While this is a work of fiction, the realities of being Trudy and the events that happened around her are historically accurate (unless otherwise noted here). So are the events described that occurred before and during World War II.

This story would not have been written in the 1940s. At that time, the United States was a very different place with attitudes and expectations that would seem strange today. Assumptions about gender, minorities, and goals are not the same. In that regard this is a work written with a twenty-first century view of these subjects.

Chapter 1
Metropolitan Tahiti

Wellesley Avenue in spring, 1941, was a desolate place of contradictions in the City of Los Angeles—an urban land which was also full of contradictions. Streets, curbs, and sidewalks were laid down in the 1920s, and the land was subdivided into city lots. A few houses were built by the early 1940s but most of the parcels remained empty and were farmed by Japanese Americans.

German immigration to America before World War II and the presence of German intellectuals in Los Angeles are documented in several publications including Jean-Michel Palmier's *Weimar in Exile: The Antifascist Emigration in Europe and America*, Cornelius Schnauber's *German-speaking Artists In Hollywood*, Kevin Starr's *The Dream Endures: California Enters the 1940s*, and Otto Friedrich's *City of Nets*.

Max Schneider and his family are fictitious and not based on any actual persons. Professor Schneider's experiences , however, were not unlike many German academicians who settled in the United States. His wife's isolation was not only typical of these German wives but was the typical experience of women whose families moved to the underdeveloped westside of Los Angeles in the late 1930s and early 1940s. In this regard, I recall memories of many things my mother told

321

me about that time after my parents and brother moved in 1940, to a house one block east of Wellesley. Family photographs and photographs from the Los Angeles City Public Library's collection are revealing of the region's appearance where cabbage and lima beans were big crops. (To get a sense of Los Angeles being distinct and isolated see *The WPA Guide To The City of Angeles* published in 1941.)

Harry Nakamizo is named in honor of the president of the Shimpo Industrial Company of Kyoto, Japan, I Nakamizo. In the 1960s and 1970s I had the rewarding experience of managing the American importation of his company's potter's wheels and met with him several times. In 1968, I even took him to Disneyland.

Chapter 2
Shangri-La

Lost Horizon was a 1937 Frank Capra film that captures the way many Americans thought about the world as a vast globe with many mysterious, exotic places unlike anything found in the United States. It is important to note that before World War II, the typical American did not travel out of the country. Their ideas about the rest of the world came from movies, newsreels and the gray photographs in magazines like *Life*.

The Dawn of Civilization was one volume of the twenty-four series *Wonder Books* sold at the Safeway market in the late 1930s. Many working-class families purchased the set, providing a less expensive alternative to the *Encyclopædia Britannica*. These multi-volume publications provided fingertip access to human knowledge or, more accurately, what Americans in the middle of the twentieth century considered full human knowledge which was based on a presumption that Western civilization was the cradle of science, art, and enlightenment.

Chapter 3
"Ich Bin In Der Schule Lernen"

Trudy's observation that Mary Nakamizo was "pretty in an exotic, oriental kind of way, like Charlie Chan's daughter reflects the stereotypes of the middle twentieth century and the influence of 20th Century Fox's Charlie Chan movies. The series propagated common naive views that Americans had of Asians (whom they referred to as "Orientals").

Chapter 4

The *Great Dictator* and *Double Date* did show at the Tivoli Theater in the spring, 1941. Throughout this work, film listings are accurate. Movie chains and independent theaters published their programs in the *Los Angeles Times*.

Walt Disney had for years attempted to procure the film rights to P. L. Travers' *Mary Poppins*, a book that his daughters loved.

Wörterbuch der ägyptischen Sprache is a classic multi-volume dictionary of the Egyptian Language by Adolf Erman.

The Egyptian symbol for woman used here is from E.A. Wallis Budge's *An Egyptian Hieroglyphic Dictionary*, Vol I.

Chapter 5
A Girl with A Brain

The quotes from *Time Magazine* come from the April 28, 1941 (Vol 37, Num 17) issue.

Chapter 6
Nelly

It was actually Thomas Mann's son who compared Nelly Mann

to an infectious disease (see Evelyn Juers *House of Exile: The Lives and Times of Heinrich Mann and Nelly Kroeger-Mann*). The dinner honoring Heinrich and Thomas Mann, at which Nelly made a scene, is described in Salka Viertel's *The Kindness of Strangers*.

Nelly's comments about her husband's struggles to find a publisher are quoted from Hamilton's *The Brothers Mann*.

Chapter 9
Sunday

Tensions between the United States and Japan had been increasing for months.

"Glamour Girls Are Suckers," supposedly written by the actress Carole Landis but no doubt penned by a studio publicist, was a typical article found in the movie fan magazines in the middle of the Twentieth Century. This particular article appeared in the December 1941 issue of *Photoplay*.

The issue of *Life* magazine, with General Douglas MacArthur on the cover, was dated December 8, 1941 but actually published a week earlier.

The live broadcast of the concert of the New York Philharmonic Orchestra was interrupted briefly by John Daly, announcing the Japanese attack of Pearl Harbor. In Los Angeles, KNX broadcasted the concert beginning at noon. The later news announcements concerning the attack come from recordings of the CBS news coverage.

Chapter 10
The Day After the Date Which Will Live in Infamy

The December 8, 1941, headlines and radio news broadcasts are all historically accurate and drawn from that day's issues of the *Los Angeles Examiner* and the *Los Angeles Times*.

Reference to Bob Tanaka, one of the school's three yell leaders, and Helen Matsui, a member of Tri-Y, the girl's service club, come from the 1942 yearbook, the *Chieftain*. Many of the school's students were of Japanese descent. The mood on campus and tensions between the Japanese Americans and other students is based on my brother's recollections of the days after Pearl Harbor.

There was no Miss Ramsey at University High. She was inspired by the school's social studies instructor, Arthur C. Ramey, who taught at the school in the early 1940s. The other teachers mentioned are fictitious.

Chapter 12
Knox's Admission

Germany declared war on the United States on December 10, 1941. Two days later the U.S. Congress declared war on Germany and Italy.

The article reporting the Japanese Broadcast appeared in the December 13, 1941, issue of the *Los Angeles Times*, not the *Los Angeles Examiner*. On December 16, Knox revealed the extent of destruction and death, including the sinking of the Arizona.

In the middle part of the last century, the *Examiner* was commonly read by family's like the Mansfields, so it is identified as the newspaper to which they subscribed. Because archival copies of the *Los Angeles Examiner* have not been possible for me to retrieve, the articles attributed to the *Examiner*, with the exception of the December 8, 1941, edition, actually are from the *L.A. Times*.

Chapter 13
Blackouts

Trudy has a good memory. Her recount of the final scene in Charlie Chaplin's 1936 *Modern Times* is accurate. The "Tramp's" relationship with "The Gamin" is indeed an expression of what psychologist Robert Sternberg refers to as "Companionate Love."

The account of the blackout is based on my brother's memory including being challenged by the sentries when he and his friends

325

attempted to walk home one night from the movies.

Chapter 14
Enemy Aliens

The Internment of Germans in France at the start of World War II is described by Dregna Deacor in her paper, From Potential Friends to Potential Enemies: The Internment of 'Hostile Foreigners' in France at the Beginning of the Second World War (*Journal of Contemporary History*, 2000, vol 35(3), 361-368).

Chapter 17
Air Raid!

Much of this account is based on my brother's memory of the "Battle of Los Angeles." According to him, the guns along Wellesley were not fired. The anti-aircraft guns that lit the sky that night were shooting further south around Mines Field, which is now Los Angeles International Airport. My brother remembers the wild speculation next day at University High School. The "America - We Are Ready" sign that Trudy sees was actually put up in Little Tokyo after the attack on Pearl Harbor.

Chapter 18
The Bread King

General De Witt's proclamation and classification of aliens and Japanese Americans comes from a story published March 4, 1942 in the *Los Angeles Times*.

The comments made by Brecht are from *Bertolt Brecht: Journals 1934-1955*. Reference to Fritz Kortner's view of Los Angeles's climate were recorded on November 18, 1941. Brecht's comment about the Bread-King and Americans still being nomads was written on October 4, 1941. While some of his remarks are based on entries written years later after the date of this fictitious public engagement, they are the type of ideas that Brecht could have had at the time.

"We think too much and feel too little," is a line from Charlie Chaplin's speech in *The Great Dictator.*

Chapter 19
The Book Of The Dead

The story "Palm Springs Hotel Taken Over by Army" was published in the *Los Angeles Times* on April 13, 1942.

The *Book of the Dead* is not the ancient name for the Egyptian text, a section of which Trudy notices in the Schneider living room. That name was given to the work by Karl Richard Lepsius The version that Trudy and Helga read comes from E.A. Wallis Budge's *The Egyptian Book of the Dead: The Papyrus of Ani*, originally published in 1895.

Chapter 20
The Junior Prom

The inspiration for Gary's letters bedecked with cartoons was inspired by the notes my brother, Allan, sent home from boot camp in late 1944. The line about the Winchester rifle is a direct quote from one of those letters.

Chapter 21
A Cameo Broach

Doolittle's raid of Tokyo occurred on April 18, 1942, but the public did not learn about this officially until early May. The *Los Angeles Times* reported the attack on Monday, May 11, 1942.

Chapter 23
The Ghost Audience

University High had an exceptional theater. My cousin Jimmy, who was eleven years my senior, was a member of the school's stage crew in the late 1940s and early 1950s. He was also a professional stage magician, performing under the name "Aubrey."

Chapter 24
Hieroglyphs and Summer Jobs

The 1942 yearbook, the *Chieftain*, was prepared for printing before the students of Japanese descent were relocated.

The incident in which a barrage balloon broke loose and tangled in power lines actually happened in Long Beach. No one was injured. This incident was reported in the *Los Angeles Times* on June 6, 1942.

During the war, teenagers, who by law had not been permitted to work in factories, and women were called upon to replace the men who joined the services. See Richard Lingeman's *Don't You Know There's A War On?*

Chapter 25
A Forgotten, Ancient People

The news footage of the Battle of Midway was a segment of the Universal Newsreel released to theaters on July 15, 1942.

The editorial of the fighting in North Africa is from the July 20, 1942 issue of *Life* magazine.

Chapter 26
A Wicked Fairy Tale

The delivery accounts that Helga were told are based on stories published in 1957 in the *Lady's Home Journal* as reprinted in Richard and Dorothy Wertzs *Lying In: A History of Childbirth in America*.

Chapter 27
The Blue Fairy

To the best of my knowledge, midwives did not routinely deliver babies in urban France in the middle of the twentieth century. Women delivered their babies in hospitals like in the United States.

Chapter 28

Trudy's thought that, if she had a boyfriend in the service, she would find the reddest lipstick and seal each letter she wrote with a kiss was inspired by a "Speaking of Pictures" feature, "These Lips send Kisses to U.S. Fighting Men," published in the July 20, 1942 issue of *Life* magazine (vol 13 No 3).

The assumption that Chuck Lewis would be working overtime at the Walt Disney Studios on films for the military reflects the reality that during World War II the studio had become an important vendor for the services. See Bob Thomas's *Walt Disney: An American Original*.

Chapter 29
September

For a vivid account of the Japanese American relocation to Manzanar, see *Born Free and Equal*.

"Women's power is through the bedroom and the domination of their sons" is a quote found in Nigel Hamilton's *The Brothers Mann*.

Chapter 30
The Letter

In spring of 1940, Italy attacked the south of France as German forces drove toward Paris. The truce that ended the war between France and the Axis, conceded a small area in the South of France to Italian control. The Italians disregarded Hitler's demand that Jews be purged from their country and the territories they controlled—in contrast to Vichy France whose leaders complied. Until the fall of Mussolini, the Jews in the Italian enclave in the southeast corner of France were spared being rounded up and transported to concentration camps.

Chapter 31
Trudy's Decision
It was almost a year since Germany declared war on the United States that American land forces actually engaged Hitler's troops.

Chapter 32
A Growing Mastering of Hieroglyphs
George Marshall's call for the drafting of 18-year-olds was reported on October 15, 1942 in a front page story of the *Los Angeles Times*.

Trudy's uncertainty about what she could do with a college degree reflects the prevailing attitude of the time about educating women. An example of this can be found in the 14 Edition of the *Encyclopædia Britannica*, under the listing Women, Education of.

Chapter 33
Uncle Billy
As best as I can determine, the Tippecanoe did not come into Los Angeles Harbor to load it tanks at this time in the war. In the Pacific, the ship went to San Francisco and Seattle to get oil which it transported to Alaska.

Chapter 34
Graduation
The process of applying for college was different in 1943. Applications were submitted in late spring and early summer for the fall semester which started in October. Instructions for applying were found in the General Catalogue of the University of California for the fall and spring terms 1942-1943.

It is hard to imagine the sacrifices the average American made during World War II. Many common things were rationed and impossible to find. Other items, like new typewriters and bicycles, were simply not available for nonmilitary use.

In 1943, American automobile manufacturers committed their total production for the military. There were no civilian cars built that year.

Lawry's, an upscale restaurant in Beverly Hills, noted for its prime rib, changed its menu and offered turkey instead. In the middle of the last century, turkey was something few people ate except on Thanksgiving and Christmas days, so it would be considered a rare treat.

Chapter 35
The Bundy

When I was a child, I would walk or ride my bike to the Bundy to see the Saturday matinees. My family often would go in the evening to see the double bill features. It was a convenient neighborhood, "second run" theater. I remember the murals of a beautiful woman, possibly a fairy, painted on each side of the curtained screen.

The original plans for the Bundy are at UCLA and detail the layout of the second-floor offices. The appearance of the auditorium is all based on my memory since the plans do not detail the design.

The struggle of Japanese Americans desiring to go to college during the war years is recounted in Allan W. Austin's *From Concentration Camp to Campus: Japanese American Students and World War II*.

Chapter 36
Hangmen Also Die

The Fritz Lang motion picture was actually released in spring 1943. It is doubtful that Bertolt Brecht attended the preview, if there was one, and certainly would not have invited his friend Heinrich Mann. Brecht had different ideas about how to structure the story and became angry at Lang. His comments to Mann come from his journal entry dated October 16, 1942. (*Bertolt Brecht: Journals 1934 - 1955*).

Chapter 37
Slip of the Tongue

Curfew for enemy aliens was put in force on March 27, 1942 by General DeWitt, commanding general of the Western Defense Command. Japanese, German and Italian nationals were ordered to remain in their homes from 8:00 PM to 6:00 AM. See "Enemy Curfew Order Planned" published in the March 24, 1042, issue of the *Los Angeles Times*.

Reinhard Heydrich was one of the most evil Nazi leaders. He was feared, even by other top Nazis. See Jochen Von Lang's *Top Nazi: SS General Karl Wolff, The Man Between Hitler and Himmler* and Peter Padfield's *Himmler: A Full-Scale Biography of One of Hitler's Most Ruthless Executioners*.

Chapter 38
Heydrich's Brother

Heinrich Himmler's use of academics to support Nazi ideology has been documents in Christopher Hale's *Himmler's Crusade: The Nazi Expedition to Find the Origins of the Aryan Race*, although his interest in the Jews of Egypt is my own invention. For example, in 1940 Himmler established The Institute for Research and Study of Heredity to do "research on the area, spirit, and heritage of the Indo-German race." "The Jew is a devil in human form," is translated from the March 1940 edition of *Der Sturmer*, a weekly Nazi newspaper, reprinted in *Nazi Conspiracy and Aggression, Supplement A*. See also Heather Princle's *The Master Plan: Himmler's Scholars and the Holocaust*.

The Ahnenerbe was actually established a year later than noted in this chapter.

Chapter 39
Co-Ed

The counselor's words regarding the ability to play the piano and a freshman needing to commit full time to his or her first term are direct quotes from UCLA's 1942-1943 *General Catalogue.*

Chapter 40
Shambhala

Susan's working at Pacific Parachute Company was inspired by a story in the June 15, 1942 edition of *Life* magazine (vol 12 No 24) that included an account of Eddie Rochester Anderson's parachute plant which was actually located in San Diego but for the purpose of the story moved to Los Angeles.

The newspaper stories, including one about a new aircraft carrier being named the Shangri-La, were actually published in the *New York Times* on August 17, 1943. I took poetic license to place the stories in the *Los Angeles Times* and to have them appears months later from the date they actually were published.

For information concerning the Nazi fascination with Shambhala, see Christopher Hale's *Himmler's Crusade: The Nazi Expedition to Find the Origins of the Aryan Race.*

Chapter 41
Rebekah Wolff

Rebekah Wolff's journey from the Italian zone in France to Naples was inspired by Susan Zuccotti's book *Holocaust Odysseys: The Jews of Saint-Martin-Vesubie and Their Flight Through France and Italy* (2007).

The ancient note Max shares with Helga was styled after New Kingdom love songs published in *The Literature of Ancient Egypt* (1972), edited by William Kelly Simpson. Some of the phrases (example, *love for you, mixed throughout my body like salt dipped in water*) were drawn from these songs.

The American attitude to the Jewish refugees in the 1940s, that Schoenberg refers to, has been well documented. See Arthur Morse's *While Six Million Died: A Chronicle of American Apathy* and Henry Feingold's *The Politics of Rescue: The Roosevelt Administration and the Holocaust, 1938 - 1945,* and Saul S. Friedman's *No Haven For the Oppressed:*

United States Policy Toward Jewish Refugees, 1938-1945.
In reality, UCLA did not have a Department of Oriental Studies in the early 1940s.

Chapter 42
Cold Water

Trudy quotes a line from the 1937 movie, *Lost Horizon.*
"Los Angeles is the Damnedest Place" was published in the November 22, 1943, issue of *Life* magazine. The story about prosthetics actually appeared two months later in the January 31, 1944, (vol 16, no 5) issue.

Chapter 43
Dreams

Many of the Fox theaters in the Los Angeles area were opened all night during the war, including the Bundy.
Like many people her age, Trudy never traveled. For her to visit her aunt and uncle in Claremont, some forty miles away, would be an adventure. The geography of Los Angeles being what it is, the distant mountains and Channel Islands would be visible markers of the borders of her world.

Chapter 44
Transitions

Nelly's statement that her husband burned her manuscript and used her story is based on an account of the incidents described in Evelyn Juers' *House of Exile: The Lives and Times of Heinrich Mann and Nelly Kroeger Mann.*

Chapter 45
Reunions

The Bundy theater had a sneak preview on Halloween, 1944. I could not determine what movie that was. Since the *House of Frankenstein* was released in December that year, I chose it, since it seemed like an appropriate date to preview a horror film.

The procedures established by the State Department made it next to impossible for a Jewish refugee to secure a Visa. What Rebekah Wolff had to do and the requirements she had to meet, reflect the process in the first half of the 1940s. Other obstacles, which in her case I did not expose her to, were the local consul objecting to a Visa issued by the Primary Committee (kicking it back to Washington) and an intimidating review by the Interdepartmental Visa Review Committee if the Primary Committee rejected the application. The procedure and the statement regarding the 1941 rule (which is a direct quote from the regulation) come from Arthur Morse's *While Six Million Died : A Chronicle of American Apathy.*

I took a little liberty with Wolff having been tattooed. Only prisoners in Auschwitz were tattooed. Different serial numbers were used to identify Jews, Poles, and other prisoners.

Chapter 46
The Lone Palm

The newspaper account of Nelly Mann's suicide was printed in the *Los Angeles Times* on December 18, 1944.

Nelly's funeral is based mostly on Evelyn Juers *House of Exile: The Lives and Times of Heinrich Mann and Nelly Kroeger-Mann* and Salka Viertel's *The Kindness of Strangers.* The negative comments about Nelly come from this source and were made by Thomas Mann, Marta Feuchtwanger, and Klaus Mann.

Chapter 47
Brothers

On December 17, 1944, The U.S. Army lifted the ban on Japanese Americans living on the west coast and permitted them to return to their homes. While California Governor Warren encouraged people to support the decision, many Congressmen, local officials and the *Los Angeles Times* objected to the move. The next day, the United States Supreme court ruled that "loyal" Japanese Americans could not be detained in the camps. At the same time, the court ruled that the Army had the authority to move Japanese Americans in 1942 on the grounds of "military necessity."

The stories of Mary's brothers are very typical, given the valor of the Japanese American soldiers and the high rate of battle related casualties. (See Bill Hosokawa's *Nisei : The Quiet Americans.*)

Chapter 48
Krefeld

The story of the potholes on Wellesley is based on what my brother told me about the crumbling asphalt on Amherst, the next street over, during the war. He recounted how people damaged their tires or axils by inadvertently driving into the pits.

The *Magister* degree that Helga reports that she received is considered to be equal to a Master's degree, given in the United States. Helga would have been an exceptionally educated woman (in both the U.S. and Europe) in the 1940s.

Chapter 49
Betje

The accounts of the war and statement of Berlin "blazed in its final agonies" are from page 1 of the April 23, 1945, issue of the *Los Angeles Times.*

James H. Breasted was an Egyptologist and prolific writer of the early half of the twentieth century, but he never wrote a book devoted only to Queen Hatshepsut. The quotes are actually from James Breasted's 1905 work, *A History of the Ancient Egyptians.*

Chapter 50
Legacy

The announcement of the V-E day comes from the *Los Angeles*

Times headline on May 7, 1945.

Several Japanese Americans received the Congressional Medal of Honor, the highest U.S. military decoration. A number of these were given posthumously during the Clinton administration. Mary's comment that her brother's name and deed would reside, forgotten in a "dusty archive" is borrowed from a statement on the U.S. Army's Medal of Honor web page.

Traudl, mentioned in the letter Helga's sister wrote, is based on the accounts of Traudl (Humps) Junge, Hitler's secretary during the last years of the war (*Until the Final Hour: Hitler's Last Secretary*).

The enforcement of sterilization in Nazi Germany is described in Fritz Redligh's *Hitler: Diagnosis of a Destructive Prophet* and George Victor's *Hitler: The Pathology of Evil.*

Nancy's confronting Gary was inspired by the scene in *The Best Years of Our Lives* in which Wilma demands that her fiancée, Homer, tell her the reason he is avoiding her. Homer had lost both hands in the war, and finally tells her what it is like at night when he removes his hooks. *The Best Years of Our Lives* is one of the finest movies ever made about the psychological impact of war.

Chapter 51
Honorable Men

The news about the Atomic bomb was published on August 7. The headline for the end of the war with Japan and the story about the USS Indianapolis ran on Wednesday, August 15, 1945, in the *Los Angeles Times.*

Chapter 52
Study Hard and Do Well

German Literature From 1885 to the Present was a course offered at UCLA in the mid-1940s. Thomas Mann's *Joseph der Ernährer* (Joseph the Provider) was published in 1943 in Stockholm and an English

337

translation the following year in New York by A.A.Knopf. Whether or not this work would have been included in the course's assigned reading is debatable. It is certainly questionable that it would be reviewed so early in the semester, but as a professor myself, I can say that instructors usually have the freedom to organize the subjects of their courses anyway they choose.

Colette Cungo

About the Author

B. R. Johnson is a clinical psychologist and an adjunct professor at California State Polytechnic University, Pomona, teaching in the Psychology Department. He grew up on the Westside of Los Angeles where most of the story takes place. Dr. Johnson was born in 1943, and the L. A. he knew in his early years was not that different from Trudy's. While he was too young to actually remember the war years, his mother and older brother told many stories about their experiences, accounts which have been incorporated into the narrative, have inspired scenes, and have added textural details.